Shadowed Scars

A Fragments of Love Novel - Book 2

Series: Fragments of Love

Book 1: The Gathered Fragments of Us

Book 2: Shadowed Scars

Published by: Mireille Martinelli

First Edition: January 2026

ISBN (Paperback): 979-8-9941723-0-8

Content Warning

Please Read

THIS BOOK IS A love story—and like all love stories worth telling, it doesn't shy away from the hard parts.

Shadowed Scars contains depictions of domestic violence, including physical abuse, emotional manipulation, and stalking. There are scenes that may be difficult to read, moments that might stir something you weren't expecting.

I wrote this story with care, but I also wrote it with honesty and, at many points—tears. Maliyah's journey isn't sanitized. Her scars—the visible ones and the ones she carries inside—are part of who she is and part of how she heals.

If these themes are difficult for you right now, it's okay to set this book aside. It will wait for you should you decide to pick it back up again. Your wellbeing matters more than any story. If you choose to continue, know this: there is light at the end. This is a romance, and I believe in happy endings—earned ones, hard-won ones, the kind that mean something because of everything it took to get there.

And if anything in these pages resonates a little too deeply, you'll find a full list of resources at the back of this book. Real help. Real people. Ready when you are.

Take care of yourself.

—Mireille

SHADOWED SCARS

A Novel

Mireille Martinelli

Thank you to everyone in my life who supported me in the creation of this book.

Thank you to my Wattpad community without whom I would never have had the courage to do this—and keep doing it.

Thank you most importantly to the inspiration for Maliyah. You are not forgotten and you never will be.

Prologue:

As is all past

MALIYAH

I caught myself scanning the parking lot again.

The old instincts had returned since moving back to Boston. I'd reverting back to checking over my shoulder, noting exits, even watching for men who moved with that certain predatory ease I remembered too well. Living in Florida for as long as I had, should have been enough distance. Enough time for Bryce Callahan to forget I existed.

But standing outside Harbor House Road's main building that afternoon, about to sign paperwork that would make me the new director of their Ever House shelter, something in my gut whispered otherwise.

I ignored it. I should have known better than to believe in fresh starts.

Inside Carmen Rodriguez's office, I sat perched on the worn leather chair, convincing myself the past was exactly that. Past. That moving back to Boston wouldn't matter because Bryce had surely moved on, built a life that had nothing to do with mine.

That day, I didn't know how wrong I was. I didn't know I'd moved back into his world. That he was still here, living his life too close to where I was rebuilding mine.

And one chance encounter would be enough to bring it all back.

My sister's family had rallied around each other with such fierce protection after nearly losing Macy. Watching them piece themselves back together had solidified something for me—I wanted my kids to grow up surrounded by people who loved them, by family who would show up no matter what storm came next. So, I moved back to Boston to give my kids that family.

"Mama, can I go to the playground now?" My four-year-old, Zoe, tugged at my sleeve, having exhausted the entertainment value of watching me stare at paperwork.

I smoothed Zoe's dark curls away from her forehead, catching a whiff of her strawberry shampoo. "In a few minutes, baby." I kissed the top of her head and returned my attention to Carmen and the paperwork she was reviewing with me.

Carmen's smile softened as she looked at Zoe, then gestured toward a large interior window. Beyond the glass, colorful foam mats covered the floor where two children were building a tower of blocks while a staff member sat cross-legged nearby with an infant. A climbing structure with rounded edges stood in the corner. "The staff can see every corner from their station," Carmen said, her voice dropping slightly. "And you can watch her from right here while we finish up."

Relenting, I watched Zoe run off, before turning back to Carmen, who said, "I know it was a big decision, but honestly, Maliyah, you're exactly what this place needs. Harbor House Road will be lucky to have you and I can finally retire, knowing this place is in good hands."

The organization was larger than my facility in Florida. The on-site child-care served kids from infancy through age five, with partnerships for older children at a nearby school.

Carmen slid a glossy brochure across the desk. "There's an elementary school three blocks away. Principal Winters keeps a counselor specifically trained in trauma response on staff." She tapped a sticky note marking the tuition page. "Lucas's tuition is waived as an employee benefit and he could come here after school for our programs."

Switching Lucas to this school would mean another transition for him, but the quality of education and its proximity were too good to pass up.

A tug at my elbow pulled my attention away from the paperwork. Zoe stood there, her small fingers clutching a gray stuffed elephant with over-sized floppy ears, its trunk curved upward as if smiling. Her eyes sparkled with triumph, a smudge of pink glitter decorating her left cheek.

"A charitable foundation keeps us stocked with toys for the kids who come through here." Carmen nodded to the elephant. "That's Lani, short for Laniyah." She held her hand out to Zoe. "Can I see that for just a minute? I promise to give it back."

Zoe tentatively handed it over. Carmen showed me the back where there was the tiniest of pockets, barely perceptible if you didn't know it was there. She pressed different spots until she found what she was looking for, then guided my hand to the same area. I felt a small disc through the stuffing. If she hadn't shown me, I'd have missed it entirely.

"They're equipped with trackers that parents can sync to their phones for extra security," Carmen quietly explained. When she handed the elephant back to Zoe, she showed her the retractable strap on the back so she could wear it like a crossbody. "Less likely to lose it this way."

I nodded to Zoe, and she ran back to the play area, clutching Lani tight.

I tried to take it all in. The care this organization had for its people—staff included. Zoe safe here with me. Lucas thriving at a school three blocks away. A salary almost twice what I made in Florida. This job was perfect.

I handed the completed forms to Carmen, my heart fluttering as I straightened my posture. "I'm excited to get started."

Carmen's eyes crinkled at the corners as she leaned forward. "There we go!" She glanced at her watch. "It's already past one. Why don't you and Zoe enjoy what's left of this sunshine, and we'll see you bright and early tomorrow morning? Eight-thirty?"

"Are you sure?"

"Absolutely." She stood and walked around her desk. "Maliyah, there's a lot of work to be done here, so take the time and enjoy it while you can. You can't imagine how glad I am to have found someone I know will give this role as much as I have."

As Zoe and I left the office, I was brimming with anticipation.

Heading toward the car, I pictured a future. One where Zoe's hand was in mine as we crossed the three blocks to Lucas's new school, his backpack bouncing against his shoulders. I imagined Friday evenings at the Museum of Science, Sunday brunches at Felicity's where the kids would build forts with their cousin.

The sun warmed my face as we walked.

Not once did my mind stray to the darkness. Not once did I consider the things that would come back to haunt me.

Chapter 1:

Finding Ground

MALIYAH

I crossed the main lobby of Harbor House Road toward my office, still pinching myself that this was real. Even so, I caught myself eyeing the entrance every few minutes, scanning faces. It was a vigilance I thought I'd moved past after living in Florida for so long. But being back in Boston had reawakened old instincts—and old habits can be hard to break.

Getting started had gone smoother than I'd expected—Carmen had been incredibly helpful with the handover before she retired, and my replacement in Florida had only had a few questions after I'd turned the reins over. Everything was falling into place perfectly.

Lucas was still adjusting to his new school after we switched last week, but he was doing okay and he liked his teachers. Zoe loved the on-site childcare—so did I, for that matter. For the first time in years, everything felt like it was exactly where it should be.

The conference room was already half-full when I arrived for our weekly staff meeting. Delilah sat at the head of the table with her laptop open, fingers flying across the keyboard. Keisha had claimed the seat nearest the coffee pot, cradling a mug that read "Relax, I'm a social worker. I've seen worse." Martin sat opposite Keisha and was thumbing quickly across his phone, while Diana sat looking like she needed a nap.

I breezed into the room with a smile that felt stretched across my face, the third cup of morning coffee still warming my palm. "Morning, everyone!" My voice rang out a notch too bright against the Monday faces around the table. I slid into my chair, smoothing my skirt under me, and glanced at my watch. "Let's keep this quick—I can see Diana's already eyeing the door."

Delilah pulled up the monthly report on the projector. "Intake numbers are up twelve percent from last month. We're at capacity for residential beds, with a waitlist of seven."

"Childcare enrollment is steady," Diana added. "We had two new kids start this week."

Keisha tapped her pen against her notepad. "Counseling sessions are booked solid through the end of the month. I was thinking we could do some groups for those who don't need the same level of individual care. Maybe offer evening hours."

"Good problem to have. Why don't you put some ideas to paper and we can see what might work," I said. "Martin, anything on your end?"

"Security audit's complete. Made some recommendations for the residential site—better lighting in the parking area, need to fix a broken camera. We'll be ready for the building safety assessment next month."

I tapped out everyone's comments on my screen. My fingers hovered over the keyboard as I lifted my gaze to scan the tired Monday faces around the conference table. "Anyone else?"

Silence. Diana shuffled her folders. Keisha took another sip of coffee.

"Alright then. Good work, everyone. Let's—"

"Oh!" Delilah's face lit up. "Before we go, I have to show you what my grandson did yesterday." She pulled out her phone, scrolling through photos. "He took his first steps on camera! Waddled right to me!"

"Oh Lord, I'm guessing Crystal isn't ready for him to be running around already," Diana said, leaning in.

"Nope! But I am! I'm over the moon to start running around with him." Delilah beamed.

Keisha laughed. "That's adorable. Meanwhile, I texted my son to take out the trash yesterday and got back 'k' with a thumbs-up emoji. Found the same trash still sitting there when I got home. He was real surprised when I swiped his headphones off and distracted him from his video game. His avatar ran right into the grenade he'd thrown. Boom! Dead avatar equaled time to take the trash out!"

"Teenagers." Martin shook his head. "My daughter used to hang on my every word. Now I'm apparently the most boring person on the planet. Asked if she wanted to go to the Red Sox game with me last weekend—you know what she said? After the longest stare of my life, she finally says, 'That sounds like a you thing, Dad.'"

"A you thing?" Diana pressed her hand to her chest. "That hurts."

"Tell me about it."

"I miss when she was little," Diana said, her voice softening. "Remember when she used to come here after school? She'd run around the lobby pretending to be the receptionist, answering the fake phone."

Martin's expression shifted, something tender replacing his usual stoic demeanor. "Yeah. She was here for daycare until she was five. Those were the days."

"They grow up so fast," Delilah said quietly.

The room quieted, and Diana elbowed Martin, making a joke about him having to worry over prom and boys. Delilah smiled at her phone screen one more time before tucking it away, while Keisha caught my eye and gave me a slight nod, as if to say, "You're one of us now." I felt my shoulders relax for the first time that morning.

I thought about Lucas and Zoe. How Lucas was already losing his baby face, how Zoe was starting to read simple words. How quickly they were becoming themselves—independent, opinionated, growing.

"They really do," I agreed, then cleared my throat. "Alright, for real this time—let's get the day moving."

I was picking up intake files from the front desk when I heard a familiar voice behind me.

"Maliyah?"

I turned to see Detective Reed Morrison approaching, his expression shifting from professional to something warmer when he saw me. He was escorting a young woman who looked to be in her early twenties, her left eye bearing the telltale yellowing of a healing bruise.

"Detective Morrison." My voice came out higher than I intended, and I found myself tucking a strand of hair behind my ear. I'd wondered if I would run into him again with my new job. He'd been the cop assigned to help my sister with Macy, and I might have hoped to run into him again when I moved here. That hope coming true sent a little thrill through my body. "What brings you in today?" Stupid question, Maliyah. A blush crept up my cheeks as I looked back at the young woman with him.

He glanced at the woman beside him, then back to me. "Just helping someone get connected with resources." His voice was gentle, the way it got when he was in protector mode.

I nodded, understanding immediately. I'd been in this business long enough to recognize the signs—the way the young woman held herself, the careful distance she maintained from Reed despite his obvious attempts to be non-threatening.

"Nadine," Reed said to his companion, "this is Maliyah Davenport. She's the director here." He looked back at me. "Actually, Maliyah might be exactly who you want to talk to."

I stepped forward, offering what I hoped was a reassuring smile. "Hi there. I'm Maliyah. Would you like to sit down and talk for a few minutes?"

The relief that crossed her face was immediate. Sometimes, women just needed to see another woman to know they weren't alone.

"Reed, thank you for bringing her in," I said. "We'll take good care of her."

"I know you will." His eyes held mine for a moment longer than necessary, and I felt that flutter again. "I'll, uh, maybe I'll call you later? You know, like to check in?"

I blushed—again. "I'd like that." Professional director of a trauma shelter, reduced to a teenager with a crush in thirty seconds flat.

After Reed left and I'd gotten Nadine settled with one of the intake counselors, I realized Lucas would be in soon. My first two weeks as director had been a whirlwind, but moments like this—helping women find safety and resources—reminded me exactly why I'd made the right choice coming here. As we walked to the car, I couldn't help but smile. Everything about my new life felt right—the job, being here in Boston, even these unexpected moments with Reed that left my heart racing.

"Mama, can we get ice cream?" Zoe asked as she popped into my office once things had quieted down after introducing Nadine to one of our counselors.

I tapped my watch and shook my head. "First, we need to boil water at home, tesoro." I brushed a stray curl from her forehead, tucking it behind her ear.

"Can we make the twirly kind?" Zoe twisted her finger in the air, mimicking the spiral of fusilli.

"Si, signorina." I winked, remembering her homework sheet covered in food vocabulary. "And you can be my little chef and tell me the names of everything in Italiano." One day Italian vocab, the next flower names. Keeping up with the kids' curriculum was exhausting for me as a single mom, but I did my best—and made it fun where I could.

Zoe clapped her hands, her silver bracelet jingling against her wrist. The front door banged open, followed by a stampede of sneakers squeaking across the lobby floor. "Mom! They have a real science lab with actual microscopes!" Lucas' voice rose above the chaos of all the shouts and laughter, breathless with excitement. His backpack hung off one shoulder, papers spilling from the unzipped top.

Diana appeared in my doorway, her cardigan buttoned wrong and hair windblown. "Made it back in one piece," she said, glancing at her watch. "Though I think Mrs. Abernathy's spelling test might be a tough one to prep for tomorrow."

I laughed and rolled my eyes. "Great!" Yup, mom-life.

I went about getting the kids settled so I could finish my day out.

Even as I chopped vegetables that night, part of me kept glancing at my phone. The kids had their routine, I had my dream job—and maybe, just maybe, something else was beginning too.

Chapter 2:

Creative Differences

MALIYAH

I was elbow-deep in Lucas's science project about the solar system midway through the week—poster board and markers littering the kitchen table. My kitchen table looked like a craft store had thrown up all over it and the idea of cleanup exhausted me. Zoe was "helping" by adding purple glitter to what was supposed to be Mars, her tongue poking out in concentration. Lucas didn't complain even once.

Lucas frowned at his drawing, then tapped his yellow crayon against the half-finished planet. "Mom, I think Saturn looks weird. It needs more rings." His homework sheet was spread beside him, covered in his careful six-year-old handwriting listing facts about each planet.

"Saturn has plenty of rings, buddy. Maybe focus on—" My phone buzzed against the counter, and I glanced over to see an unknown 617 number—Boston. "Hold that thought."

I tried to wipe glitter off my fingers with a paper towel, and failed. Giving up, I answered. "Hello?"

"Maliyah? It's Reed. Reed Morrison."

"Hi." The word came out breathier than I'd intended. My hand flew to my collarbone—Good Lord, Maliyah, dramatic much?—but I kept walking. I lowered my voice, stepping around one of Zoe's dolls—a doll that was somehow also covered in glitter—as was my shirt now. Dammit.

"How did Nadine's intake go?" he asked. I curled into the corner of the sofa, his voice warming me from the inside out.

"Good. She's staying at Ever House tonight. I'm glad you brought her in."

The line went quiet for a beat too long, and I pressed the phone closer to my ear, holding my breath. His exhale came through first, then his voice, lower than before. "Listen, I umm—I know you're probably swamped, but I was wondering if maybe, you know, if you might—ahem, want to grab coffee sometime. No pressure, just... I'd like to see you when you're not in the middle of something, of course."

I found myself curling deeper into the corner of the couch, one leg tucked underneath me, fingers twisting a loose thread on my sweatpants that had glitter stuck to it too—note to self, no more glitter... ever. "Yeah. Okay, I'd like that," I said, glancing toward the kitchen where a half-finished planetary system tilted precariously on our table. "Most days I'm just trying to remember if I'd made sure that everyone was dressed before we went out in the world."

"Even better." His voice was warm, and I could picture him grinning. The mental image made my cheeks flush. "So, coffee? Tomorrow maybe? I know a place that makes excellent lattes and terrible small talk."

"Mom!" Zoe's voice carried from the kitchen, high-pitched with indignation. "Lucas is hogging the red marker!"

"I am not!" Lucas shot back. "You already used it for the entire sun! And the sun is supposed to be yellow anyway!"

"But I like red better!"

"Just a second," I called back, dropping my head into my hand, I spoke into the phone. "Sorry. Art project crisis. Apparently there are strong creative differences about what color the planets and sun should be."

Reed chuckled, a sound that made warmth spread through my chest. "Sounds serious. Rain check on the coffee then?"

"No, I'd like that. Coffee, I mean. Not now, of course. Tomorrow works." I paused, glancing toward the kitchen where I could hear Lucas explaining why the sun can't be red to his sister, using the patient tone meant for situations when he thought someone wasn't understanding something important. "Just so you know, my life is pretty much controlled chaos most of the time. Two kids, new job, trying to figure out life in a new city again. It's a lot."

"I like chaos. Keeps things interesting." There was something in his voice that made me think he meant it. "Besides, after spending most of my days dealing with paperwork and bureaucracy, a little chaos sounds fun."

We spent a few more minutes working out the details—a café called The Grind not too far from the shelter, at ten the next morning. Something casual, low-pressure. At least that's what I told myself as we talked. I felt like I recognized the name, but I couldn't quite place it.

"I should probably go referee the art situation before they decide to redecorate my kitchen walls," I said, though I found myself reluctant to hang up.

"Probably wise. I'll see you tomorrow, Maliyah."

The way he said my name made my pulse quicken. "See you tomorrow."

After I hung up, I stayed in my living room for a moment, phone still in hand, trying to figure out why my heart was beating so fast. It was just coffee. People had coffee all the time. Colleagues, friends, people who'd worked together on helping someone find safety.

But even as I told myself that, I knew it wasn't entirely true.

"Mom!" Lucas appeared in the doorway, poster board in hand, his hair sticking up at odd angles from where he'd been leaning over his work. "Is Jupiter supposed to have a red spot or a red stripe?"

"Spot, honey." I followed him back to the kitchen, where Zoe had somehow managed to get glitter not just in her hair but also on her cheek and the front of her shirt. "Okay, let's finish this masterpiece before we turn the entire apartment into a craft store."

For the next hour, I helped Lucas perfect his project while simultaneously trying to contain Zoe's artistic enthusiasm. She'd moved on from Mars and was now adding what she called "sparkle dust" to Saturn's rings. My God. What monster invented glitter?

"Why is Earth so boring?" Zoe asked, holding up the blue and green planet Lucas had carefully colored to match the globe picture he'd brought up on his tablet.

"Earth isn't boring," Lucas said seriously. "Earth has oceans and mountains and people and dogs. That's way more interesting than Mars."

"We should get a dog—a big fluffy one that's soft! And look," she thrust the planet forward, her eyes wide with pride, purple glitter cascading onto her sneakers, "isn't it great that Mars is purple and sparkly now? Real Mars is boring, but mine has magic dust storms!"

I laughed as Zoe sprinkled one final handful of purple glitter onto Mars, but pretended not to hear the dog comment. I imagined the 5 AM walks in Boston winter slush, the vet bills, the inevitable "Mom, I'm too tired to take Fluffy out" excuses. "Time to wrap this up, astronauts," I said, guiding little hands to drop markers into containers and brushing craft debris into the trash. Later, as I tucked blankets under chins and kissed foreheads, my fingers lingered on my phone. I scrolled through my contacts, pausing at the number I'd saved under "Reed Morrison," then checked my reflection in the darkened bathroom mirror, wondering when I'd last done anything with a man?

Actually, I knew the answer to that question, and it wasn't a pleasant memory. Jacob had been charming too, at first. He'd made me laugh, made me feel special, made me believe that maybe I could have something good for once.

And then he'd left when things got complicated. I came home from work one day to find the closet half-empty, hangers askew like he couldn't wait to get out of there. On the kitchen counter sat a folded piece of notebook paper with "Maliyah" scrawled across it. His handwriting slanted right, each letter pressed so hard into the paper that I could feel the indentations when I flipped it over. "I'm suffocating," he'd written. "I don't want to be a father, I'm releasing all rights to the kids." As if our children were some sort of object he could simply transfer to another name. Fuck him and the horse he rode in on.

Six months later, I sat in a courtroom clutching that same wrinkled paper while he avoided my eyes, his lawyer whispering frantically in his ear. The judge wasn't impressed—neither was I.

I shook my head, forcing away those thoughts. I'd pick my kids over that asshole any day. Reed wasn't Jacob. This wasn't even a date—just coffee between colleagues.

But as I peeked in on Zoe and Lucas in their beds, I couldn't quite convince myself that's all it was.

Chapter 3:

From Chaos to the Quiet

MALIYAH

Morning came too quickly yet not quickly enough. I'd changed a dozen times before ending up back in the first damned outfit. Clothes now littered my room, creating a graveyard of fabric that would later require me to hang up or wash again. I had a tendency to just wash it if I didn't want to grab it off the floor. I know—ridiculous.

The sweater was a cloud-soft knit that clung to my body like a second skin, its deep sapphire blue bringing out amber flecks in my hazel eyes. The V-neck dipped just low enough to hint at tiniest bit of cleavage, and the sleeves fell perfectly at my wrists to ward off the cold. But was a it too much for coffee? The way it traced every curve I'd earned through motherhood... I didn't want him to think I was trying too hard.

I caught myself in the mirror—*Fuck, is that glitter? How many showers does it take to get rid of this shit?*

Bet Reed is already dressed and waiting, probably spent all of five minutes getting ready. Guys have it so much easier—just run fingers through that thick dark hair until it's artfully tousled, throw on a worn-soft T-shirt that somehow still looks expensive, pull on those perfectly faded jeans that fit in all the right places, and walk out the door without a second glance in the mirror. No makeup, no outfit changes, no agonizing over whether your sweater makes you look desperate or if your jeans make your ass look too big or too flat.

"You look pretty, Mama," Zoe announced from the doorway, still in her pajamas with her hair sticking up in about twelve different directions. "Are you going somewhere special?"

"Just meeting a friend, sweetie." I knelt down to smooth her curls, breathing in the scent of her strawberry shampoo from last night's bath.

Lucas padded into the room on sock-clad feet, his backpack already slung over one shoulder, hair still damp from his morning shower. He leaned against the doorframe, fidgeting with the zipper of his navy blue hoodie as he asked, "Can you pick me up early today? Tommy said his mom might take us to the science museum if we finish our projects. He's got that new dinosaur exhibit with the moving T-Rex."

"We'll see. Depends on how my day goes." I helped him adjust his backpack straps and kissed the top of his head. "Be good for Mrs. Patterson, okay?"

"I'm always good."

He wasn't wrong. Lucas had always been the easy kid—thoughtful, responsible, almost too mature for his age sometimes. Zoe was my wild child, all energy and emotions and creative chaos. They balanced each other out, most of the time.

Within the hour, I was sitting in my car outside The Grind, checking my makeup in the rearview mirror and wondering if I should cancel. I really don't need to get my hopes up, so maybe it's better to call it a day before anything even starts.

The café looked welcoming enough—a little trendy for the neighborhood, but with gentrification, I'm really not all that surprised.

I wiped my hands against my jeans for the third time, feeling the rough material rub against my skin. I'd rub them raw before the date was even underway.

I'd been on exactly three dates since Jacob left. Three awkward dinners with men who seemed nice enough on paper. One guy ran for the hills the moment he realized I had kids—young kids at that. Another was a little too interested in playing instant daddy. Neither option had been appealing. The third wasn't even memorable enough to recall why I wasn't interested.

My phone buzzed.

Reed: *Running five minutes late. Don't leave.*

Me: *Just parked. I'll grab us a spot.*

Well, in for a penny...

When Reed walked through the café door a few minutes later, my fingers tightened around my empty mug. The espresso-thick air caught in my throat as he scanned the room, his gaze landing on mine. He moved between tables with an easy confidence, jeans fitting just right, the sleeves of his gray henley pushed up to reveal forearms tanned and corded with muscle.

A flush crept up my neck. When he smiled, the blue of his eyes deepened like water in sunlight, and my heartbeat skipped, stumbled, raced ahead. I crossed and uncrossed my legs under the table. The second he smiled, I knew I was in trouble.

"Sorry," he said, sliding into the chair across from me at the small table I'd claimed by the window. "Last-minute call from the captain."

"Everything okay?"

"Meh—Nothing to write home about." He asked me for my order over the background of the hum of machines and blended voices. Mocha latte, of course—if you can't have sugar in your coffee, then what's the point of coffee?!

Minutes later, he returned, blueberry scones and a spinach and feta pie in hand.

Reed sat back in his chair and grinned. "So, how'd the solar system turn out? Did you have a masterpiece on your hands?"

I laughed, my coffee nearly sloshing over the rim. "Oh God, I was pretty proud of Lucas and how easily he allowed Zoe to 'help.' Mars—" I shook my head, "—Zoe decided the real Mars was 'boring' so she painted it purple with glitter that's still embedded in my kitchen table, and on the floor, and I found some in my hair this morning." I pulled out my phone, swiped to the photo, and turned it toward him. "Lucas the morning rolling his eyes at her antics while she chattered on about how everyone will remember which one was Mars! The teacher's going to need sunglasses to grade it."

"Smart kid. Both of them, I'm guessing."

"Too smart sometimes." I wrapped my hands around my coffee mug, grateful for something to do with my nervous energy. "Lucas reads at a fourth-grade level, and Zoe can argue her way out of anything. I'm going to secretly move them into my sister's house once they're teenagers and pretend like I had nothing to do with it."

He guffawed at that, but became more serious when he said, "They're lucky to have you. Not every kid gets a mom who drives from Florida up the coast to make sure they're near family."

"You remembered that?" Heat crept up my cheeks.

He tapped his temple, "Details are important."

"Of course, Detective. Nothing gets past you, does it?" I took a sip of my latte, trying to calm my nerves. "So, how long have you been with Boston PD?"

"Ten years. Started not too long after college." He took a sip of his coffee—black, no sugar—unfathomable. "What about you? Always wanted to work in social services?"

The question made something tighten in my chest, the way it always did when people asked about my career path. Most people assumed it was a calling, something I'd planned since childhood. The truth was messier than that.

"Not always, no. I sort of fell into it." I took a sip of my latte, buying time. My fingers tightened around the mug. "I had my own... experience." The words stuck in my throat like ground coffee. "Ended up in Florida after needing to—" I swallowed hard, glancing at his badge clipped to his belt. "After getting away. The shelter there helped me when I had nowhere else to go." I forced a smile that felt brittle on my face. "Started volunteering, then working part-time. Went back to school. Got my degree." I shrugged, as if the years of nightmares and looking over my shoulder were nothing. "The rest is history, I guess."

Not trying to share my entire life story in one fell swoop, so I just left it there.

Reed must have noticed my hesitation because he didn't push. Instead, he leaned back in his chair and grinned. "Well, whatever it was, you seemed to have landed exactly where you're supposed to be. With people who trust you and need you."

"I'm honored to be there for them." I met his eyes. "Sometimes all someone needs is to know they're not alone."

Something shifted in his expression then, became more serious. "Yeah. I get that."

We talked for what felt like hours—about work, about Boston, about our likes and dislikes, some of our pasts, some of our hopes. We talked about everything except the thing that was humming between us—almost too scared to put a name to it. Reed had me in stitches with stories like the drunk guy who called 911 to report his own shadow following him, and the time he had to help an elderly woman who'd accidentally super-glued her dentures to her nightstand. But I couldn't shake the feeling he was keeping something at a distance. He was friendly, but he was also... careful.

When he walked me to my car, I slowed my steps, fumbling with my keys until they almost slipped from my fingers. His hand caught mine as we both reached for them, warm against the chill in the air.

At my car, he faced me while he rocked back on his heels—once, then twice, hands disappearing into his pockets as his shoulders hunched forward slightly. "I had a good time," he said, his confidence momentarily replaced by something that reminded me of a shy kid asking his crush to the dance.

My "Me too" came out barely audible, my lips barely moving, as if speaking at full volume might shatter this thing hovering between us.

"Maybe we could do it again sometime."

I nodded, just not trusting my voice. Reed Morrison was dangerous to my carefully ordered life, and we both knew it.

But as I drove to work, I was already hoping he'd call again soon. And that scared me almost as much as it excited me.

Chapter 4:

Into the Quiet

REED

I sat in silence, the hum of the refrigerator and the clatter of the ice maker filling the room, as I stared at my phone. What the hell was I doing?

Coffee had been good. Too good. I couldn't stop replaying it—the way Maliyah had smiled when I'd walked in, how her whole face had lit up talking about her kids. The playful tone when she'd teased me about being a detective. How natural it had felt, like we'd been doing this for years instead of an hour over lattes and pastries.

My apartment felt too quiet suddenly. For some reason tonight seemed worse than usual. I grabbed a beer from the fridge and settled on the couch, flipping through channels without really seeing anything, finally settling on an old Patriots game.

The smart thing would be to keep this professional. Maliyah had kids—two of them—and from what I'd gathered from the background I'd quietly run when investigating the issues around her brother-in-law's ex-wife, she'd had enough shit happen in her life that she didn't need a bachelor like me coming in and messing things up any further.

Because that's me. I'm not looking to settle down. I had enough of commitment after shit broke down with Sara and she hightailed it all of eight months ago.

"You're great at the fun parts, Reed," she'd said while packing her books into boxes. "But the moment things get real, the moment I need you to actually be present for something difficult, you check out. I can't build a life with someone who isn't interested in building something lasting with me."

She hadn't been wrong. When her father had her heart attack, I didn't handle it well. I'd found excuses to work late instead of hanging out at the parents house with her after he was released home. When she'd started talking about moving in together, I'd agreed mainly because it felt like I had to. But then, she started throwing hints around about getting engaged. Nope. I'd started picking fights about stupid things and disappearing. Doing everything I could to avoid her instead of dealing with the issues head on.

My phone buzzed. John's name lit up the screen.

I considered not answering. But John was persistent, and ignoring him would only make him more curious.

"Yeah?"

"So." John's voice came through way too cheerful. "Guy! Where have you been? Something's up. Spill."

"Nothing to spill."

"Morrison. I've known you for almost our entire lives. You're a terrible liar."

I took a long pull from my beer. "I got coffee with someone. No big deal."

"Coffee." John's tone said he wasn't buying it. "No shit? With who?"

"Just someone I met through work."

"Through work." A pause. "Wait. Is this that chick you talked about when we were in the field? The one from the shelter who had that sister—was her name Felicity? You know, the one who had all that shit go down with the husband's ex! Is that who you're talking about?"

Shit. John was too good at this.

"Maybe."

John let out a low whistle. "Maliyah, right? Reed, man, she's—"

"I know what she is." I cut him off. "Which is why this was just coffee. Just keeping things friendly."

"Right. Friendly. That's why you're sitting alone in your apartment tonight definitely drinking beer and overthinking."

"I'm not overthinking."

"You're absolutely overthinking." I could hear the grin in his voice. "So how'd it go? This 'friendly' coffee?"

I found myself talking despite my better judgment. Told him about the café, about how easy the conversation had been, how she'd talked about her kids with this mix of exhaustion and pride that made my chest ache.

"She sounds great," John said when I finished.

"She is."

"So what's the problem?"

"There's no problem."

"Reed." John's voice shifted, became more serious. "We've been partners for a decade, and best friends for more years that I can count before even that. I watched what happened with Sara. I watched you sabotage that entire relationship because you got scared."

"I didn't—"

"You did. And you know you did." He paused. "Look, I'm not trying to give you shit. I'm trying to make sure you don't do the same thing again."

I stared at the ceiling, the beer going warm in my hand. "What if I can't help it?"

"What do you mean?"

"What if this is just who I am? The guy who can't handle anything real?"

"So, you're scared."

"No!" I took another drink, dropping my head back and sighing. "Yeah."

"So what are you going to do about it?"

That was the question, wasn't it? I thought about the way she'd looked at me across the table this morning, the careful hope in her eyes when I'd said I wanted to see her again.

"I don't know."

"Well, here's what I know," John said. "You're going to call her again. Probably tomorrow. Because despite all your commitment issues and self-sabotaging bullshit, you actually like this woman. And it's at least good that you admit it terrifies you."

He wasn't wrong.

"The question is," John continued, "how do you stop yourself from running this time? And instead try something different?"

After we hung up, I sat in the dark living room, an old Patriots game playing on mute, beer long since gone flat.

John's words circled in my head. Are you going to run like you always do?

I thought about Sara. How she'd looked at me when she left. She was resigned. Like she'd known for a long time that it was coming.

I thought about Maliyah this morning, the way her fingers had drummed on the table when she was nervous. How she'd opened up just enough to let me see the edges of her past. How she'd smiled when I'd said I wanted to see her again, even though I could see the caution in her eyes.

She'd been hurt before. I could see it in the careful way she held herself, the way she'd mentioned "getting away" and needing the shelter. Someone had made her feel unsafe, and she'd rebuilt her entire life from that.

And here I was, a guy with a proven track record of bailing when things got real, thinking about asking her out again.

The smart thing would be to keep my distance. To keep things professional. To not risk hurting someone who'd already been through enough.

But sitting there in my too-quiet apartment, I realized something: I didn't want to do the smart thing. I didn't want to keep my distance.

I wanted to see her again. Wanted to hear more about her kids, learn what made her laugh, know what she read before bed. Wanted to see if this thing between us could be something.

And that scared me more than anything.

Because John was right—I was absolutely going to call her again. I was sure of it at this point.

A few days went by before I realized I still hadn't called Maliyah. I'd been called into an armed robbery that same night. While we'd made our arrests, John and I rolled right into another case and then another. Today, I was knee-deep in the most mundane shit the job had to offer. A storage unit burglary out in Dot—some kid broke into his uncle's unit looking for vintage baseball cards to sell, found nothing but Christmas decorations and old tax returns. The uncle wanted to press charges. The kid was seventeen and crying in the interview room.

John and I spent two hours on paperwork on a case that would probably die with the Magistrate.

"This is what we went to the academy for," John muttered, signing his name for the third time on the same form. "To referee family drama over dusty boxes of ornaments."

"Hey, I'll take that ceramic Santa over the shit storm we saw in the last few days," I deadpanned.

"I'll take the shit storm, man. The kid literally called it 'creepy grandpa Santa' in his statement. Do you see this shit?" His shoulders shook as he tossed the statement back on the desk, the paper landing with a soft slap against the worn surface. The corners of his eyes crinkled, and he ran a hand across his stubbled jaw, still chuckling under his breath.

My shoulders shook as I let out a snort, the tension in my neck finally releasing. "Fuck man, a Santa with teeth and eyes that follow you just aint right.

We wrapped up around four, both of us grateful to escape the fluorescent lights of the station. John grabbed his jacket from the back of his chair, then stopped, studying me with that look he got when he was about to stick his nose where it didn't belong.

"So," he said. "You call her yet?"

"Who?"

"Don't start with that shit again." He crossed his arms. "Maliyah. Your coffee date. The one you've been moping about for three days."

"I haven't been moping."

"You literally sighed four times the other day while checking your watch. Four times, Reed. I counted."

"I was tired, man."

"Bullshit." John leaned against the desk. "You gonna call her or just keep sighing your way through the next three days too?"

I grabbed my own jacket, avoiding his eyes. "I don't know, John. Maybe coffee was enough. Maybe I should just leave it there."

"Why would you do that?"

"Because it's complicated. She's got kids, a whole life. I'm not—" I stopped, shook my head. "I'm not that guy."

"What guy?"

"The family guy. The committed relationship guy. You know this about me."

John was quiet for a moment. Then: "You know what I think?"

"That you should mind your own business and let me live my life?"

"I think you're already in this whether you admit it or not. And the longer you wait, the weirder it gets." He grabbed his keys. "Call her. Or don't. But stop torturing yourself either way."

He headed for the door, then paused. "Come on, man. Sarah said she wants to grab a drink. Let's go meet her, yeah?"

"Yeah, fine. Whatever."

"Good. I'm desperate to spend more time with you while you're brooding. Makes for good entertainment."

"Asshole."

But I was still following him out the door. I could go for a drink.

Chapter 5:

Uncharted Territory

REED

It was a weekday night, so the bar was pretty quiet. John had claimed our usual booth in the back while I grabbed a few beers. I slid in across from him, already feeling tension seep from my bones. I'd gone into the station for a bit to close out some paperwork on a case we'd wrapped up yesterday. The case had been straightforward—surveillance footage, cooperative witnesses, suspect who confessed within twenty minutes. Sometimes the job was actually easy.

"So?" John said, not even waiting for me to order. "Let's get into it."

"What?"

"Come on. Get outta here with that shit." He flagged down the waitress, ordered two beers without asking. "Get ready before Sarah gets here. She's been grilling me about her, and since I haven't had anything to share, you should be prepared."

I took a long pull from my drink, buying time. "Fine. But it's still really all up in the air, so don't get any damn ideas, yeah? The coffee date was good, well—It was really great, actually. We lost track of time just talking. Nothing too heavy, but we got past all the useless small talk pretty quick. You know, the kind of conversation where you actually learn something about the person—likes, dislikes, you know what I mean."

"Like what?"

"Man, I don't know—like what we like to do, and what it's like working in our worlds. She told me a bit about her past up here before Florida. Shit, she even told me about the kids' deadbeat dad. Real asshole. I maybe shared a little about Sara, but not a lot. Definitely not ready for that deep shit."

John's eyebrows shot up in question. "Okaaaaaaaaay."

"Whatever, man." I turned the bottle in slow circles on the table. "We're casual. Not fucking getting married tomorrow."

John snorted, his beer pausing halfway to his lips. "Okay. That makes sense. You're leaving room so you can run screaming like a kid escaping Godzilla—arms flailing, eyes wide with panic, probably knocking over a few innocent bystanders on your way out of town. I get that strategy. Classic Reed Morrison escape plan."

"Fuck you. You're such an idiot." I smiled despite myself. "That's not it—I guess."

"Then what is it?"

I stared at my beer, watching condensation slide down the bottle. "I really like her, John. Like, more than I've liked anyone in a long time. And that scares the shit out of me."

"Because of the commitment thing."

"Because of everything. The kids, the possibility of getting serious—fuck, can we stop talking like a bunch of chicks? Getting deep in my feels over a beer really wasn't my plan tonight."

The booth cushion compressed with a soft hiss as Sarah appeared, dropping her purse on my side of the booth in the way she had for years now—since my side was almost always empty. She tucked her hair behind one ear and slid into the booth beside John, her ring catching the dim bar light as she cupped his jaw with both hands. Their kiss lasted just long enough to make me glance at my beer. When I looked up, she'd already pivoted toward me, leaning forward with her elbows on the table, chin propped on her hands like a kid waiting for a bedtime story.

Sarah's eyes lit up with mischief, her smile widening until I could see the slight gap between her front teeth. She leaned halfway across the sticky table, close enough that I caught a whiff of her perfume. "Hey, Reed," she said, drawing out my name with that sing-song quality she always used when she thought she had me cornered. "Tell me about the new girlfriend! When do I get to meet her? And don't you dare hold back on the juicy details."

"Nope! Not this shit, man. She's not my girlfriend. And I'm not talking about it yet. I don't know what it is, so you can just cool your jets. I promise—If I decide to run away to Tahiti with her, you'll be the last to know."

Sarah reached across and punched my shoulder. "You're such an ass," she said, but her laugh softened it. "I've watched you pull this same crap for as long as we've been friends. You know what I want? Double dates where I'm not stuck listening to you two talk about the Sox or the Pats all night." She rolled her eyes dramatically, but beneath the performance, I caught something genuine—a flash of hope in her expression. She'd been trying to see me settled for years now. I looked down at my beer, avoiding her gaze. The truth was, I wasn't sure I'd ever be ready for what she wanted for me.

"Double dates require an actual relationship," I pointed out. "We've had coffee. Once."

"And?" Sarah stole John's beer, took a sip, made a face. "How was it?"

"Good."

"That's all I get? Good?" She looked at John. "Did he pull this with you, too?"

"Don't put me in the middle of your nefarious plans, babe. I'm not telling." All this as he nodded his head. *Fucker.*

"Fine! It was really good," I amended. "We talked—long enough that she went into work late. She's smart, funny, doesn't take my shit. I like her."

"And you're terrified," Sarah said, reading me like she always did.

"Maybe—not admitting to anything."

"Because of the kids."

"I don't know, Sarah." I drained half my beer. "Okay, yeah. I'm not exactly known for my stellar track record with commitment—you know why."

Sarah's expression softened. "Reed, you can't let the past define you forever. You haven't found the right one, Sara included. That doesn't mean the she isn't out there. And you can't keep letting your past and your fear stop you from being happy."

Eye rolls and silence was all I had for her at this point.

"Reed, you have to get past your shit."

I pushed my beer away and ran a hand over my face, feeling three days' stubble scrape against my palm. "Okay, Dr. Phil's star team, thanks for all the insights." The overhead lights caught in the amber liquid as I twisted the bottle between my fingers. "I'm done talking about this shit. You know the things I've seen—what I've dealt with." My voice dropped, the words coming out rougher than I intended. I leaned back against the cracked vinyl booth, the material cool against my neck. "Drop it. Let's talk about the Sox instead. You see who they just picked up?"

Sarah raised her glass in mock triumph. "Look at that—the great Reed Morrison, opening up about his feelings for a full five minutes before he called it quits." The tension around our booth dissolved as we all chuckled, my shoulders finally dropping from where they'd been creeping toward my ears.

My phone buzzed. SPAM lit up the screen.

My heart sank a little as I stared at the SPAM notification, thumb hovering over the screen for a moment too long before I set the phone face-down on the table.

"Have you called her?" Sarah asked, leaning into John.

I sigh. I haven't. And that's part of the problem. Had it been too long? Did all the distractions of life take away my chance?

"No. We had a few cases that popped up and things got away from me."

"So call her."

"I will."

"At least shoot her a text, man."

"Yeah, alright. I'll reach out. I'm off tomorrow, so I'll give her a call. See if she wants to grab a bite this weekend."

"Good. Yeah. Do that. I need that couple life!"

I clapped my hands once, loud enough to make the couple at the next table glance over. "Okay—moving on!" We spent the rest of the night shooting the shit about nothing that mattered—work, sports, Sarah's latest battle with this guy at work trying to one up her. My beer went warm in my hand as I laughed and just enjoyed time with my life-long friends. The knot in my chest loosened with each round, and by midnight, Maliyah's name had disappeared from our conversation, but not from the back of my mind, where her smile kept flickering like a light I couldn't quite switch off.

I grabbed an uber home, the driver's old Camry smelling faintly of pine air freshener and old fast food. The leather seat squeaked beneath me as I shifted, pulling out my phone for the dozenth time. My thumb hovered over her contact—Maliyah Barrett. Each time I almost pressed call, I'd lock the screen again, looking back outside—watching Boston's streetlights slide across the black glass like shooting stars failing to grant my wish for courage.

I won't be that guy who calls a single mom at midnight. I may be an asshole, but even I have limits. But tomorrow. Tomorrow, I would call her.

Chapter 6:
Family Package

MALIYAH

"Higher, Mama! Higher!" Zoe called from the swing, her legs pumping furiously as she tried to match the rhythm I was pushing her—hard enough that I was even out of breath. The afternoon sun felt warm on my shoulders as it beat down on the playground near Moakley Park. Seagulls wheeled overhead, their cries competing with the squeak of swing chains and high-pitched chatter of kids.

"Any higher and you'll launch into orbit," I said, giving her another gentle push. "And then how would I get my favorite little girl back?"

Zoe giggled, her curls flying behind her as she swung forward. "I'm your only little girl, Mama! I wanna go to space and see my purple Mars!"

Lucas looked over as he came down the slide for the umpteenth time. Just before rounding to climb up again, he said, "You can't breathe on Mars, Zoe. You'd need a space suit and an oxygen tank and—"

"I know that!" Zoe shot back. "I'm not stupid!"

"I didn't say you were stupid. I was just saying—"

"Kids," I said, stepping between their bickering before they could work themselves up over something neither of them actually cared about. "Lucas, how's the slide treating you? Zoe, you want to try the slide too? Or maybe the monkey bars?"

The playground was expectedly busy for a weekend afternoon. Families scattered across the grass, kids climbing on equipment while parents huddled in clusters or hunched over glowing screens. A toddler in a red shirt tottered dangerously close to the edge of the platform while his father's thumbs flew across his phone, his eyes never lifting to check his son's wobbling balance. I caught myself holding my breath until he steadied himself, then exhaled slowly as I gave Zoe another push. Between Zoe's fearless climbing and Lucas's tendency to wander off when something caught his interest, I was always in motion and always at attention.

"Mom, can I go on the big slide?" Lucas pointed to the towering metal structure that spiraled three stories high, its surface gleaming dangerously in the afternoon sun. A group of lanky pre-teens whooped as they thundered down its curved descent.

"The one that's practically scraping the clouds? The one where I'd need binoculars to see you at the top? Absolutely not."

"But Tommy went on it last time and he's only seven and I'm *almost* seven!" Lucas's lower lip jutted out, his sneakered foot scuffing circles in the wood chips.

"Tommy also broke his arm falling off his bike last month and ended up in a cast." I squeezed his shoulder gently. "I don't want you playing daredevil today, Lucas. Your bones are exactly where they belong."

Lucas sighed dramatically but trudged back to the smaller slide. I continued pushing Zoe, who was now making airplane noises.

The sound of footsteps on the jogging path caught my attention—someone running at a steady pace along the waterfront trail that bordered the playground. I glanced over and nearly dropped my hands from Zoe's swing.

Reed Morrison, in running shorts and a gray t-shirt that was damp with sweat, was slowing to a stop near the playground fence. He was breathing hard, earbuds in, clearly having been in the middle of a serious run. Looking my way up, finally catching his eyes, I saw that he'd caught me staring—as evidenced by his cocky smirk and eyebrow raise. Asshole. He'd called a couple days ago—after radio silence. *Don't look at me with those sexy eyes. Jerk.*

"Mama, why'd you stop pushing?" Zoe complained as her swing began to slow.

"Just a second, sweetie." I gave her another push, watching as Reed pulled out his earbuds and walked over to the fence.

"Hey," he called out, still catching his breath. "Fancy meeting you here."

"Small city," I said, trying to keep my voice casual—going for detached—even though my pulse had picked up. "Had a long week? Looks like you're getting your exercise in."

"Something like that. Sorry I checked out for a bit. Picked up a couple heavy cases that pulled my attention. Called the other day though. Was hoping to catch up." He wiped sweat from his forehead with the hem of his shirt, giving me a brief glimpse of abs that made my mouth go dry—*Dear God*. "Beautiful day for the park."

Yeah. Beautiful day.

"Mama, who's that?" Zoe called over loudly enough for the entire playground to hear.

"Why don't you come over instead of yelling. This is Detective Morrison, honey." I said as she got closer. "You remember him? He helped out when everything happened around Macy."

"Oh! Hi, Detective!" Zoe ran over like she was ready to apply for Reed's assistant job—yeah, I get the appeal. "Do you have to work today? Do you have your gun with you? Can I see your badge?" Zoe's enthusiasm made me wince inside. After he'd vanished so quickly after our coffee date, I couldn't tell if the warning bells in my head were legitimate caution or just my bruised pride talking.

"Detective Morrison, you remember my kids, Zoe and Lucas?"

Reed seemed uncertain though, not quite ready to approach and clearly picking up on my hesitation. So, I decided for him. "Come on, come over and say hi properly." I called out to Lucas as I went to catch up with my daughter.

Lucas wandered over from his slide, and I felt that familiar mom-tension of trying to manage two kids while having an adult conversation. Reed's eyes darted between my children as I gestured toward them with an open palm. "Reed, you remember my kids, Lucas and Zoe?" Lucas stood with his shoulders slightly hunched, studying Reed—deciding if he should say something or not. Beside him, Zoe bounced on her toes, her braids swinging, eyes wide with the unfiltered curiosity of a four-year-old meeting someone who carried a real gun for work.

"Hi, guys," Reed said, stepping closer but still maintaining some distance. "How's everything going?"

"Good!" Zoe bounced on her toes repeating her very important, life-altering questions—at least for a four year old. "Do you still have your gun? Can I see your badge this time?"

"Zoe," I said automatically. "We talked about this. If someone doesn't answer you, it's not polite to push."

Reed laughed. "No big deal. Asking the essential questions, I see. Sorry, no gun today—just running gear."

"How fast can you run?" Lucas asked, breaking out of his shell a bit. He studied Reed with that serious expression he got when he was trying to figure something out, and waited for his answer.

"Pretty fast. About seven minutes for a mile on a good day."

"That's really fast," Lucas said, impressed despite himself.

"You're all sweaty," Zoe observed with her typical four-year-old bluntness.

"That happens when you run five miles," Reed said, lifting the hem of his shirt to wipe his face again, honestly—it's even better up close. Maybe I *could* forgive him for getting caught up in work—it's not like we're in a relationship. It was just coffee.

Damn. My mouth went dry, and I found myself staring at a spot just over his left shoulder, like I was checking cloud patterns while his abs gleamed just out of focus for me. I counted silently to three before I trusted myself to speak.

I noticed him glancing around the playground—at the other families, the noise, the general chaos of weekend family life. A younger kid nearby was having a full-on meltdown about who-knows-what, his wails echoing across from more than thirty feet away. Another kid was demanding ice cream from his frazzled-looking father—a father who was clearly losing patience and ready to call it a day. Nothing says "sexy single mom package deal" like being surrounded by small humans with no filter and infinite energy.

"Five miles?" Lucas's eyes widened until I could see white all around. "That's really far. Are you married? Does she like to run too?"

Reed's mouth opened and closed like a fish gasping for water. A flush crept up his neck, turning the tips of his ears crimson against his dark hair. I felt heat bloom across my own cheeks, my tongue suddenly cemented to the roof of my mouth—I wanted to find a rock and crawl under it. The playground sounds seemed to fade into a distant hum.

"Um—not married," he finally managed, his voice cracking slightly. He shifted his weight from one foot to the other, leaving small impressions in the soft ground beneath his feet. "Five miles *is* far," he added, latching onto the safer topic like a lifeline. "Do you like to run?"

Lucas shrugged one small shoulder, his Batman t-shirt rippling with the movement. "Sometimes. I like bikes better though."

"Bikes are cool too." Reed's fingers tapped nervously against his thigh as he took a half-step backward. His eyes darted to his sleek black fitness watch, thumb brushing over its face, then back to me. "I should probably get going. Still have a couple more miles to finish up."

"Of course," I said, trying not to let disappointment creep into my voice. Damn this felt awkward. "Don't let us keep you."

"It was good seeing you all again. I Um—listen, I know it didn't—" he paused, looking between me and the kids. Instead of picking back up, he pulled his earbuds back out from his pocket.

"Will you come back to the park?" Zoe asked with the directness that made me want to disappear into the wood chips.

"Um... probably not today," Reed said, fumbling with his earbuds, dropping one, then picking it up with a nervous laugh. He brushed it off, glanced at the kids, then at me, then away. "Okay maybe if I—ahem—try calling you again?" His question was to me, obviously, but it was like he couldn't look me in the eyes. Nervous? *What the hell.*

"Yeah. It's okay."

His lips curved upward, just enough to crinkle the corners of his eyes without showing teeth. Then he jogged backward a few steps, turned, then stopped abruptly as if he'd hit an invisible wall. Hands resting on his hips, his shoulders rose and fell with a deep breath before he continued running, his pace uneven. Twenty yards down the path, he looked back, his face a battlefield where want fought against fear, like a man who'd either missed his train or was about to be hit by it.

"Is he your friend? Because he seemed kinda weird." Lucas asked, cutting right to it.

"Well, sort of," I said quickly. "He's just someone I know from work."

"Oh. Okay. I guess that makes sense then," Lucas responded.

Yup. Just what I was thinking. I sighed and said, "Come on, let's go back to playing. Who wants to try the monkey bars?"

Both kids took off running, temporarily distracted. But as I followed them across the playground, I couldn't help glancing back toward the jogging path where Reed had already disappeared around the bend.

The way he'd looked when faced with the reality of my life—not just me, but me with two energetic kids getting all up in his space—had been telling. I tucked away the knot of confusion in my chest like something I'd have to come back to later. Like all things in life, hindsight is 20/20. Something I thought of as I traced the scar on my collarbone. A subtle reminder of how I'd know that better than anyone.

Chapter 7:

A Chance?

MALIYAH

The call came the day after the playground encounter. Zoe perched on the edge of the bathroom counter, legs swinging, while I battled the mass of curls that had knotted overnight. The comb snagged on another tangle, and she winced. My fingers worked methodically, patiently separating each springy coil. So different from Lucas's almost straight strands. His hair portrayed no hint of his father's tight, thick-textured curls. I'd spent countless nights watching online tutorials, learning to twist and braid and seal in moisture. Yet this morning, her hair seemed to have a mind of its own.

"Ow, Mama! You're pulling too tight!" Zoe squirmed on the bathroom counter, her legs kicking against the cabinet doors.

"Sorry, baby. Almost done." I loosened my grip on the hair tie, trying to find the sweet spot between secure and comfortable. "There. You look beautiful."

Zoe twisted to examine herself in the mirror, moving her head back and forth while patting her new pigtails with approval. "Can I have the sparkly clips too?"

"Just one on each side. We're saving the others for special occasions."

As soon as I clipped it in, my phone buzzed on the counter, and I glanced at the screen. Reed Morrison. My stomach did that stupid flutter thing it always seemed to do when I saw his name.

"Alright, sweetie, go and play. Mama will clean all this up."

I helped Zoe down from the counter and stepped into the hallway before answering. "Hello?"

"Hey, Maliyah. It's Reed."

"Hi." I tried to keep my voice neutral, even though I was still feeling weird about how awkward things had been at the park.

"Listen, I wanted to call and see how you were. And—Um—to apologize too. You know, for not calling and then... for making things kind of weird. At the playground." He paused and cleared his throat. I could hear what sounded like traffic in the background. "I feel like I acted like a complete idiot."

"You didn't—"

"I did. And I wanted to explain." Another pause. "Would you maybe want to grab dinner? Tonight? Or maybe tomorrow? I know it's short notice, but I figured if I waited much longer I'd chicken out."

I found a small smile peeking on my face—despite my reservations. "You were going to chicken out of calling me?"

"Absolutely. I'm not exactly known for my smooth moves when it comes to... something like this."

"Something like this?"

"Yeah—like whatever this is we're doing. Or—I mean, what I'd *like* to be doing. that is to say—dating, I guess? I'm out of practice."

I leaned against the wall, watching Zoe through the open bathroom door as she carefully applied lip balm like it was the most important task in the world. "Dinner sounds nice. But Reed, before we make plans, I need to know—are you okay with the fact that I have kids? Because the other day was weird and, you know—after coffee, when I didn't hear from you. I think I just assumed maybe my life may be a bit more than you'd want to handle right now. If it is, that's fine, but I need to know now rather than a month in."

"That's actually what I wanted to talk to you about." His voice got quieter, like he was moving away from wherever the traffic noise was coming from. "It's not that I'm not okay with it. It's just... complicated for me. I think I just want to be careful, you know?"

"Careful how?"

"Kids get attached, right? They start thinking about possibilities that might not be real. I didn't want Lucas and Zoe to get the wrong idea about what we were doing if we're just... you know—figuring things out."

I considered this. It wasn't the worst reasoning I'd ever heard from a man when it came to dating someone with children. In fact, it was kind of thoughtful, even if his execution had been awkward. It'd felt more like he was scared of them rather than wanting to protect them.

I was skeptical, so I asked, "So you were trying to protect them?"

"Trying to protect everyone, I guess. Including myself." He let out a breath. "Look, I'm not going to lie to you. The idea of getting in deep where there's instant family terrifies me. I've never been good at commitment, and I don't want to screw up something good because I'm afraid of something serious."

At least he was honest. I had to give him points for that. "So what exactly are you suggesting?"

"Maybe we keep things between us for now? Get to know each other without involving the kids until we figure out if this is going somewhere. I know that probably sounds selfish—"

"It doesn't sound selfish. It sounds realistic." I watched Zoe wander into her bedroom, heard her start singing some song from a Disney movie. "I actually appreciate you being upfront about it. Most guys either run for the hills or try to be super-dad on the second date. Both options suck."

"So... dinner? Somewhere kid-free where we can actually talk?"

I found myself nodding even though he couldn't see me. "Yeah. Dinner sounds good. I'm sure my sister would be happy to watch the kids tonight and they've been asking for their cousin Macy. I'll check with her and text you. But Reed?"

"Yeah?"

"I need you to understand that my kids aren't going away. They're always going to be part of the equation. So if you decide you can't handle that, please don't drag this out."

"I understand. And Maliyah? I don't want to hurt you. Any of you. I'm just trying to be honest about where I am right now."

"I appreciate that. More than you know."

We made plans for seven o'clock at a small Italian place downtown. After I hung up, I stood in the hallway for a moment, trying to figure out how I felt about the conversation.

"Mama!" Zoe called from her room. "I can't find my backpack!"

"Coming, baby!"

As I helped Zoe locate her backpack under a pile of stuffed animals, my mind replayed Reed's words. I paused, holding her tiny purple water bottle, my thumb absently tracing the unicorn sticker that was starting to peel at one corner. The careful way he'd said "kids get attached" had surprised me—so far the couple of men I've been out with either pretended my children didn't exist or tried too hard with exaggerated high-fives and forced enthusiasm. I zipped Zoe's lunch into the front pocket and exhaled slowly. Still, something in his careful phrasing made my shoulders tense, like when someone starts a sentence with "No offense, but..." before saying exactly what will offend you. I sighed, I was overthinking it, I knew that.

"Mama." He adjusted his backpack straps. "Are worried about something? You have that look."

"What look?"

"The look you get when you're thinking about something but don't want to tell us what it is."

Sometimes my six-year-old was too perceptive for his own good. "Not worried about anything, but I might go out with a friend for dinner tonight. You and Zoe would stay with Aunt Felicity."

"Who's the friend? Is it the detective?"

I should have known he'd remember. "What if it were? Would that be okay with you?"

Lucas shrugged. "I guess. As long as he's not going to be our new dad or something. I don't need a dad."

The matter-of-fact way he said it made my chest tight. "Nobody's going to be your new dad unless you want them to be, okay? And even then, it's not something we need to worry about today."

"Good. Because I think we're fun without anyone else."

Zoe bounded into the kitchen at that moment, backpack bouncing against her back. "I'm ready! Can we have pancakes for breakfast?"

"We're having cereal today, baby. We're running late."

"But I don't like cereal!"

"You liked it yesterday."

"Yesterday was yesterday. Today I want pancakes."

I poured cereal into two bowls, added milk, and set them on the table. "Today we're having cereal. Tomorrow we can talk about pancakes."

"No, mama! I don't want it!"

"Zoe, we need to get moving. It's cereal or a plain hardboiled egg with an apple." I took out the baggie of eggs I prep for the week which I know she hates.

Zoe sighed dramatically but climbed into her chair. "Fine. But I'm going to tell Aunt Felicity that you're hiding away all the fun food."

"I'm sure you will."

As the kids ate breakfast, I found myself watching them and thinking about Reed's words. He was right that kids got attached quickly. Lucas had already been through the disappointment of his father leaving. Zoe didn't even remember Jacob, but that didn't mean she wouldn't notice if another man disappeared from our lives, though.

Keeping things separate for now is what I would have done anyways. After dropping Lucas at school, I called my sister and confirmed she'd watch the kids. Macy would be over the moon, she said. I let Reed know and I spent the rest of the day at work trying not to think about dinner. Three client meetings, a staff check-in, and a phone conference with our insurance provider about coverage for new trauma therapy programs. I was slammed, so eventually I forgot about anything that had to do with Reed and all the unanswered questions.

As the end of my day approached, I caught myself staring at the same spreadsheet for twenty minutes without processing a single number. My cursor hovered over the "save" button three times before I finally shut down my computer and grabbed my purse.

Back home, I got the kids settled with dinner and went to get ready. Standing before my closet, I moved hangers aside with increasing force, then starting the search all over again. Nothing looked right. I texted Felicity a selfie of me in a sad, baggy, black dress and three question marks.

Thirty minutes later, my doorbell rang. Felicity burst in with a duffle bag slung over her shoulder, Macy trailing behind with a tote stuffed with markers and construction paper.

"Extra half hour of bedtime," I whispered as Felicity unzipped the bag. "Non-negotiable terms. My kids better not be up when I get home—favorite aunt status or not!"

I sorted through the ridiculous number of options Felicity brought and settled on the perfect one. The deep blue wrap dress hugged my hips in a way that made me pause before the mirror. I smoothed the fabric over the curves that three decades, two pregnancies, and countless late-night ice cream sessions had sculpted. Felicity whistled low, circling me with narrowed eyes. "Turn," she commanded, twirling her finger. "Again. Slower." She looked me over, "Damn, you look hot."

"Yeah, I do!" And I did. I looked hot. Reed Morrison, eat your heart out.

Felicity asked, "Are you nervous?"

"A little. It's been a little while since I've been on an actual date—like with dinner in a restaurant where they deliver food to your table instead of you getting it at the counter."

"You'll be fine. Just remember to ask him questions about himself. Men love talking about themselves."

"That's cynical, even for you."

"Not cynical. Practical. Trust me on this one."

I kissed the kids goodbye, promising to be home before they went to bed, and went down to my car. I'd asked to meet him there rather than have him pick me up, so I climbed into my car and started off toward downtown to meet.

I gripped the steering wheel tighter, my fingertips tingling against the worn leather as I caught myself checking my lipstick in the rearview mirror at every red light. The car felt suddenly too warm despite the evening chill, and I cracked the window, letting the cool air brush against my flushed cheeks. It was going to be a good night. I felt it in my bones.

Chapter 8:

Be Careful

MALIYAH

The restaurant was small and intimate, with dim lighting and exposed brick walls. The kind of place that was clearly designed for conversation.

Reed was already there when I arrived, sitting at a corner table and looking like he'd put some thought into his outfit too. Dark jeans, a button-down shirt, blazer. He stood up when he saw me, and I felt that familiar flutter in my stomach.

His eyes caught mine as he rose from his seat, the corner of his mouth lifting in that half-smile that makes my stomach flip. "Hi," he said, his voice low as he pulled out my chair with a gentle scrape against the hardwood floor. His gaze traveled over my wrap dress, lingering on where it tied at the sides. "You look beautiful tonight, Maliyah."

"Thank you." I settled into my seat, trying to calm my nerves. "This place is nice. Very... intimate."

His eyes widened, and he shifted, one hand reaching up to tug at his collar. "Too intimate?" The confidence he'd shown moments ago disappeared in an instant. "I can ask for a different table if you want. There's one by the window, or maybe near the bar area?" He gestured vaguely toward the front of the restaurant.

"No, this is perfect." And it was. Private enough to talk, but not so secluded that I felt trapped if things got awkward.

The waitress came over with menus and took our drink orders. I asked for a glass of wine, figuring I needed something to help me relax.

"So," Reed said after the waitress left. "I feel I owe you an explanation."

"You already explained on the phone."

"Not really. I gave you the diplomatic version." He leaned back in his chair, studying me. "The truth is, seeing you with your kids scared the hell out of me. Not because there's anything wrong with them—I'm sure they're great kids. But because it made everything feel so... real."

"Real how?"

"Real like this isn't just coffee and casual conversation. Real like if we keep doing this, I'm going to have to figure out if I'm ready to be part of something bigger than just the two of us."

The waitress arrived with the wine and, impressed with her timing, smiled at her—waiting before we continued our conversation.

Alone again, I took a sip of the wine, allowing the full-bodied flavor to linger before saying, "And you're not sure if you are."

"I'm not sure of anything. Which is why I thought maybe we could take this slow. Figure out if we even like each other enough to worry about the bigger questions."

"That's fair." I set down my wine glass. "But I need you to understand something. I'm not looking for someone to rescue me or solve my problems. I've been doing fine on my own for a long time now. If we decide to do this, it's because we want to. It's not because I need you to fix my life."

"Good. Because I'm definitely not the guy to call for fixing anything. I can barely keep my own life together most days."

The honesty was refreshing.

"So what are you looking for?" I asked. "In general, I mean. Not necessarily with me, but in your life."

Reed considered the question while looking around the restaurant. "Honestly? I don't know. For most of my adult life, I've just been focused on work and keeping things simple. No complications, no long-term commitments. But lately, that's been feeling kind of... empty."

"What changed?"

"I'm not sure. My ex and I ended when I couldn't see us making it in the long term, but honestly I took the cowardly way out. I avoided our issues instead of addressing the elephant in the room. I don't want that to happen with us, so I guess I'm going with clear communication. And I'm scared as fuck." He looked at his hands, opening and closing them like his nerves were vibrating down to his fingers.

When he looked up again, he voice was clear—without any sort of uncertainty. "I like you, Maliyah. I like you more than I've liked anyone in as long as I can remember. And that says something for me. So, this is me being real."

"Okay," I said, processing his admission. "Well, I certainly don't have anything figured out. I'm making it up as I go along, just like everyone else."

The waitress returned to take our dinner orders, interrupting the moment but giving me some time to process. When she left, I found myself studying his face, trying to read what he wasn't saying.

"Can I ask you something?" I said finally.

"Sure."

"What are you most afraid of? About this, I mean."

Reed was quiet for a long moment, turning his water glass in slow circles on the table. "Screwing it up. Getting involved and then realizing I'm not cut out for it. Hurting you and the kids because I thought I was ready for something I wasn't."

"And what would screwing it up look like?"

"I don't know." He ran his hand down his face, landing on his neck and rounding the back. "Getting scared and pulling away when things get serious. Not being there when you need me to be. Letting Lucas and Zoe get attached and then disappointing them."

I appreciated his honesty, even if it wasn't exactly reassuring. "Those are all valid concerns. But Reed, nobody knows if they're ready for anything until they try. And yeah, there's a chance you might decide this isn't for you. There's also a chance I might decide you're not for me."

"Have you thought about that? What would make you walk away?"

"Well, if I got to a point where I was comfortable with you getting closer to the kids, but then it seemed like you were just tolerating my kids instead of accepting them as part of who I am. If you tried to make me feel like I had to choose between you and them. If you weren't honest with me about how you were feeling. Those are just a few things, but some pretty heavy ones, I think."

Reed nodded. "Fair enough. What about the good stuff? What would make you want to stick around?"

I smiled. "If you made me laugh. If you were kind to me, and ultimately to my kids if you did meet them properly. If you showed up when you said you would and did what you said you'd do. If you made me feel like myself instead of trying to turn me into someone else."

"Those don't sound like very high standards."

"You'd be surprised how many men can't meet them."

We placed our order, talking while we waited. Bu the time our food arrived, we'd fallen into easy conversation, spending the next hour talking about everything except the heavy stuff. Work, books, movies, travel. Normal getting-to-know-you conversation that reminded me why I'd been attracted to Reed in the first place. He was funny and smart and easy to talk to.

When the check came, he insisted on paying despite my protests. "This is a date, Maliyah," he said, pulling out his wallet. "I pay."

I scoffed, but let it slide—this time.

Reed smiled, and for the first time all evening, he looked completely relaxed. "I want to take you out again. Will you let me?"

"I felt my cheeks warm and knew they'd turned pink. "I'd like that."

When we left and headed out to our cars, I found myself feeling good about how things went and what we'd shared. Reed's honesty was actually more reassuring than not. At least I knew what I was dealing with.

"Thank you for tonight," I said when we reached my car.

"Thank you for agreeing to come out with me, and for giving me a chance. I'm still figuring out how to navigate this. But I want to figure it out. With you."

He leaned in and kissed me softly, his lips warm against mine in the cool night air. His hand came up to rest at the curve of my jaw, steady and sure. That nervous flutter I'd been feeling all night transformed into something deeper—a slow-burning heat that spread from my chest down to my fingertips, making me want to pull him closer and forget all the reasons I should be careful.

Damn. That was one solid flipping kiss.

When I got home, Felicity was on the couch reading while the kids slept in their rooms.

"How did it go?" she asked, looking up from her book.

"Good. Really good." I kicked off my boots and sank into the chair across from her. "I think I might actually like this guy."

"Even with all his baggage about commitment?"

"Maybe because of it. At least he's honest about what he can and can't handle right now."

Felicity closed her e-reader and studied my face. "Just promise me you'll be careful. I know you're tough, but I don't want to see you get hurt because you're hoping he'll change."

"I know. And I promise."

As Felicity gathered her things and headed home, I found myself with a little nervousness in my stomach. For the first time in a long time, I didn't feel like I was settling. I felt like I was taking a chance on something that might actually be worth the risk.

Chapter 9:

Getting to know them

REED

Three months. That's how long Maliyah and I had been doing this dating dance, and I was finally starting to feel like I had my footing. We'd managed countless dates—actual sit-down dinners, movies, even a couple of comedy shows downtown where I knew I could make my girl laugh so hard that she might snort wine through her nose. I'd never found snorting attractive before, but on her it was perfect.

The careful boundaries we'd set up had worked. We'd kept things as just us. Last week, when I'd canceled our dinner plans after a double homicide in Roxbury, she'd DoorDashed coffee and dinner to the precinct later that night for John and me. When I'd popped by her office the following day with breakfast and an apology, the smile she gave me was worth the lack of sleep that came with getting up early after a long night. Just last night, as I'd rambled about something even I can't remember, she'd leaned forward, chin resting on her palm, and asked me every question she could think of—showing she actually cared.

We'd been out with John and Sarah. Had a couple double-dates with Felicity and Caden. We were settling in and it was fucking good. Better than good.

It was more than the dating though. She had this... steadiness about her. Like she knew exactly who she was and what she wanted, and she never felt like she needed to apologize for any of it. It was something I'd never experienced before. She was the definition of what they call an independent woman, and it was sexy as hell. It scared the shit out of me—but I couldn't get enough of her. Which is why I'd suggested the farmer's market.

"I think I'm ready," I'd told her last week over dinner at that Thai place she loved. "To meet them properly, I mean. Not just random encounters and not just *as friends*." And then nerves got the better of me and I hurried on, "If you're okay with it. If you're ready for that too."

She'd looked at me for a long moment, fork halfway to her mouth. "Are you sure? Because once we cross that line, there's no going back. They'll start asking questions, making assumptions."

"I know. And I think... I think I want them to."

The words had surprised me as much as her. But sitting there, I loved every minute of watching her face light up when she talked about Lucas's assignment he'd waited until the last minute to do, and her story about Zoe's attempt to teach their neighbor's cat to fetch—successful attempt, I might add. I'd realized something right then, I wanted to be part of that world. Not just standing on the outside edge, looking in.

So here I was, walking through the SoWa Open Market on a sunny Saturday morning, coffee and a bag of pastries in hand from the vendor thirty feet behind me. I was looking for a woman with two kids and trying not to feel like I was about to take the biggest test of my life.

I spotted them before they saw me. Maliyah was crouched down next to Zoe, who appeared to be trying to decide what to buy among a table filled with plants... just plants—that's a new one for me. Lucas stood a few feet away, looking bored out of his mind and I can't say I'd blame him. The girls looked like they were staring at a table filled with weeds. But even as they stood—all of them doing something different in the vendor's tent, they still looked so much like a complete unit that for a second I almost turned around. But then, I realized I wanted to be in that unit.

And in the blink of an eye, Maliyah had looked up and seen me. The instant her face broke into a smile, my chest started to do weird things and I couldn't imagine ever wanting to be anywhere else.

"Reed!" Zoe spotted me and immediately abandoned the patch of—is that grass? In less than five seconds, she was standing right in front of me poised to fire off all the questions I knew she had building already in her head. "Are you here to buy stuff too? I'm trying to pick something. Do you have a cat? There's a cat at our neighbor's house. I'm teaching it stuff. Have you heard of catnip? It's a plant. They have catnip. Do you think the cat would like it? the lady said—"

"Okay, okay." Maliyah came over and saved me from the longest conversation I'd ever had where I didn't need to actually participate. She bent down leaning close to Zoe, "why don't you let Reed actually answer one of your questions, yeah?"

"Oh, yeah." The great thing about kids is that they really don't care. You get honesty regardless of what you want. "Sorry! Have you ever heard of catnip?"

Guess she picked one! "I haven't. What is it?"

"It's so cool!" She grabbed my hand and dragged me over to the booth. Where she'd been staring at a patch of grass. "Look! Here it is!"

Sure enough, that patch of grass was actually catnip. Huh. So weird. Luckily, I didn't need to know anything about it since Zoe was all too happy to teach me everything there was to know. How a four year old knew this much about catnip was beyond me though.

"Very cool." I looked to Maliyah and held up the pastries. "Okay if I offer some pastries to the kids?" I asked quietly to try and keep out of the kids' hearing in case she didn't want them to have the sweets. "I brought coffee for you and me but I got enough pastries for everyone." I held up the bag. "Chocolate croissants, some kind of berry thing the lady at the bakery's stand said was awesome, and a couple assorted donuts."

"Can I have the chocolate one?" Zoe asked, already reaching for the bag—so much for trying to be quiet. I failed to account for sonic hearing when it came to Zoe and her sweets.

"If your mom says it's okay."

Maliyah laughed, "valiant effort, but she'd be able to hear you offer donuts even if you were across the market."

Lucas stepped up, bouncing on his toes a bit, "What'd you bring? I want a donut, but it depends on which kinds you brought."

I looked at Maliyah for approval. At her nod I turned back to the kids but then I did a double-take. I looked back at her and saw how beautiful she looked today—relaxed in a way that made you think of carefree candid photos. Jeans and a light sweater, her hair pulled back in a ponytail with light wisps escaping and curling around her face. She had a natural confidence that came from being exactly where she belonged—she was stunning.

"You didn't have to bring food," she said, not realizing I was mesmerized by her.

Coming back to the present, I cleared my throat. "Wanted to. Besides, I figured if I was going to crash your family time, I should at least come bearing gifts."

"You're not crashing anything. We invited you, remember?"

Lucas looked up at me with that serious expression I was getting used to. "Are you going to follow us around all day?"

"Lucas," Maliyah said quietly.

"It's okay," I told her, then crouched down to Lucas's eye level. "I'm going to hang out with you guys for a while, if that's cool with you. But if you want me to leave at any point, just say so, okay?"

Lucas studied my face for a moment, then nodded. "Okay. Can I have a donut now?"

"Absolutely." I handed the whole bag to them and let them duke out who got which sweet.

For the next hour, I followed the three of them through the market, and it was... nice. Better than nice. Lucas warmed up once he realized I was genuinely interested in things he found interesting like the tent with handmade puzzles and the guy who made miniature furniture.

Zoe decided she was my tour guide—an interesting accomplishment for a four year old who was there for the first time, but even I had to admit it was adorable. She was so sure of herself as she dragged me from stall to stall and explaining the importance of homemade things and how she wanted to be a vendor someday.

"This lady makes soaps that smell like food," she announced, pulling me toward a display of colorful bars. "But you can't eat them." She looked at me solemnly, making sure I was paying attention, and said, "I asked."

"Good to know," I said seriously. "What's your favorite smell?"

"Lemon cake. But Mama says it makes her hungry so we can't buy it."

Maliyah appeared at my elbow, shaking her head. "We're not getting the soap, Zoe."

"Smart kid. Knows how to work a crowd. Have you seen how many free samples she's pulled off?"

"Don't encourage her."

But her eyes were crinkling at the corners, and I found myself thinking that this was exactly what I'd been missing without knowing it. The easy chaos of family life.

We were looking at some kind of special honey display when my phone buzzed. I glanced at the caller ID and felt my stomach sink.

"I have to take this," I told Maliyah as I flashed my phone at her. "Work."

She nodded, already turning her attention back to the kids as I stepped a few feet away.

"Morrison."

"Reed. We've pulled a case in Dorchester—armed robbery, suspects fled on foot, and we're setting up a perimeter. How fast can you get here?"

I checked my watch. It was barely noon, and I'd been planning to spend the whole afternoon with them. "Give me twenty."

"Make it fifteen if you can."

I hung up and walked back to where Maliyah was negotiating with Zoe about the variety of soaps—*wait until they get to the vendor with the lotions.*

"I have to go," I said quietly. "Work emergency."

Maliyah looked up, and I saw understanding flash across her face. No disappointment, no guilt trip—just acceptance. Another thing I was learning to love about her. *Love. Fuck.*

"Everything okay?"

"Armed robbery. They need all hands."

"Go. We'll be fine."

"I know you will. I just... I was having a good time."

She smiled. "So were we. Rain check?"

"Definitely."

I said goodbye to the kids, promising to come by and see their purchases sometime before the end of the weekend. As I walked back toward my car, I found myself already thinking about seeing them again.

This could work. We could work. For the first time since I'd met Maliyah, I felt completely sure about that.

I had no idea how wrong I was about to be.

Chapter 10:

Maybe we'll run into each other again

MALIYAH

As Reed disappeared into the crowd, I found my eyes drawn to his retreating back. There was a definite feeling of warmth in my chest as I considered how well the last few hours had gone—much better than I'd dared to even hope. Reed had done so well with the kids—he hadn't tried too hard and didn't talk down to them. At some point, Lucas had actually smiled at him, which was saying something. We wandered around for a bit, but honestly my heart wasn't in it anymore.

"Is Detective Reed back yet?" Zoe asked, looking around like he might be hiding behind one of the market tents.

"No baby, he had to go to work, remember?"

"Yeah, but I kinda hoped he'd be back soon."

"Oh, sweetheart. He won't be back today, but he said he'd come over this weekend, right?"

"Yeah, okay!" And just like that, her mind was off to the races on a completely different topic—the difference in all the apples she saw and how we were planning to go apple picking this Fall. And pumpkin picking. And berry picking this summer. And don't forget Christmas trees. Oh, and baby animal week. I swear my kid has an unnatural fascination with farms and the outdoors. This is *not* me. I was happy to be indoors where there was an extreme lack of bugs and creatures. But I promised to do these things since the kids love them.

"Come on," I said, steering them toward the far end of the market. "Let's go grab the catnip you wanted and then head home."

We were walking past a booth selling handmade pottery when I heard someone call my name. Not Maliyah—the full version, the way my mother used to say it when I was in trouble.

"Maliyah?"

I turned around slowly, as my blood went cold. Bryce Callahan. There he was. Fear gripped me as I saw the man ten feet away. He looked almost exactly the same as he had more than a decade ago—salt and pepper at the temples now, more evil in his eyes. Same dark hair, same sharp cheekbones, same smile that once quickened my pulse with anticipation before it learned to race with dread. Next to him stood a petite blonde woman with kind eyes and a careful, guarded smile.

"I thought that was you," Bryce said, taking a step closer. "You look good. Maybe a little filled out, but still good."

I instinctively moved so that I was between him and the kids, my hand finding Zoe's shoulder. The casual cruelty in that comment—the way he could make an insult sound like a compliment—hadn't changed. My body had changed, yes. Two pregnancies, a decade of living. But standing here now, I was grateful for every pound, every stretch mark, every sign that I'd survived him and built a life anyway.

I said his name aloud. "Bryce." A technique I'd learned—identify the threat, make it real.

"Are these your kids?" His eyes flicked to Lucas and Zoe, and I felt something protective and violent rise up in my chest. "They're beautiful."

"Thank you." My voice sounded steady, which was a miracle considering my heart was pounding so hard I was sure even he could hear it.

The blonde woman stayed by his side, quiet, with a small smile on her face. Of course, he hadn't introduced her. So, when I looked to her she finally spoke. "I'm Diane, Bryce's wife."

I looked her over. No visible bruises or injuries, but I knew better than most that the damage wasn't always visible. "It's nice to meet you, Diane."

There was an awkward pause where nobody seemed to know what to say.

My chest felt tight, like someone had wrapped bands around my ribs and was slowly tightening them. The familiar metallic taste of fear coated my tongue, and I had to consciously control my breathing—in through my nose, out through my mouth.

I studied Diane more carefully while Bryce just stared at me. Her posture was slightly turned toward him, deferential. The way she kept her hands clasped in front of her, the careful smile that never quite reached her eyes—I recognized the signs. She was performing, the way I used to perform when Bryce would introduce me to his colleagues or friends. Pleasant, agreeable, invisible unless he needed me to speak.

For a split second, I considered pulling her aside. Telling her to run. But I'd learned that lesson the hard way—women don't leave until they're ready. And warning her would only put a target on my back. Bryce would know I'd said something. He always knew.

My peripheral vision catalogued everything without making it obvious—the pottery booth to my left with several people browsing, the family examining handmade bowls twenty feet away. Surrounded by people. Safe for now. I clocked the main exit, then the side passage between the food trucks. When we left, I'd use that one. He wouldn't see which direction we went.

Bryce was studying me with an intensity that made my skin crawl, and I was trying trying to figure out the best way to get out of this place without him knowing which direction we went or being able to follow me.

"So you're living in Boston now?" Bryce asked. "I thought you'd moved away."

Silence. I owed him nothing.

"Did you come back for work?"

"Hmmm?" I felt a non-answer was best at this point.

Another pause. Diane was looking between us. While she looked like she wanted to say something, she clearly knew silence was better for her—at least Bryce would surely think so.

Zoe tugged on my sweater, and I looked down to see her holding up a small wooden toy from one of the nearby stalls. "Mama, can we get this for Detective Reed? It's a police car."

"Maybe later, sweetie."

When I looked back up, Bryce was watching Zoe with an expression I couldn't read. "Detective Reed?"

"Yes, *Detective Reed*." I said firmly, with just enough enunciation to make a point. "We should get going. The kids are getting tired."

"Of course." Bryce smiled, but there was something cold in his eyes. "It was good to see you, Maliyah. Really good. Maybe we'll run into each other again."

"Probably not."

"I have a feeling we will." His response wasn't so much a thought, but a declaration.

I ignored it. Ignored him. Instead, I took Zoe's hand and put my other hand on Lucas's back, steering them away from Bryce and Diane as quickly as I could without running. My hands were shaking as I patted my purse and felt the comfort of my Sig P365 that I kept with me at all times for safety.

After I broke free of Bryce, the first thing I did was get licensed and trained. After my kids came, I couldn't take the chance of ever being caught unarmed again—not with my history, and not with this job. So I made sure both my kids went through age-appropriate gun-safety instruction the moment each of them turned four. Not because I wanted them anywhere near guns—God knows I didn't—but because ignorance was more dangerous than knowledge. I'm not a huge gun fan, but I'll be damned if I ever walk through the world unprotected from the devil again.

As I walked, I kept glancing to the side so I could catch them in my periphery—making sure I wasn't too obvious that I could see him. I refused to let him think he scared me. *Fuck him and the hellhound he rode in on.* He kept an eye on me until we disappeared into the crowd.

"Mama, who was that man?" Lucas asked as we walked toward the car.

"Someone I knew a long time ago."

"He seemed weird."

I buckled them into their car seats before responding carefully. "You know how sometimes you meet people who just don't feel right? Like when something in your belly tells you to stay away from someone?"

Both kids nodded.

"Well, that man is someone I'd rather you didn't talk to if you see him again. If he ever approaches you, you walk the other way. You come find me right away, okay?"

"Okay," Lucas said. "Is he a stranger-danger person?"

"Something like that. You don't need to be scared, just be smart. Always trust your feelings about people. And remember our password."

Both responded in unison, "Supercalafragilisticexpialadocious!"

"Good. And if someone says they don't know that word, or give you a different word, what do you do?"

"Run away and find you or go find the police," Lucas said immediately.

Zoe nodded seriously. "Because it's our secret word and you'll tell them the password if they are supposed to know."

"That's right."

For the drive home, I tried to remind myself that Boston was a big city, but even I knew that it wasn't that big. It made sense that I might run into people from my past, but I'd definitely gotten too lax, and I should have known better.

Walking through our apartment front door, I couldn't shake the feeling that this wasn't over. The way Bryce had looked at me, the way he'd asked about where I was living now, the way his eyes had lingered on the kids...

I'd spent ten years building a life where I felt safe. And in the space of a five-minute conversation, that safety felt like it was starting to crack. I thought about calling Reed, but he was dealing with work and had enough on his hands. I thought about calling Felicity, but she would just freak out—I didn't really need to feel her anxiety right now. I had enough of my own.

That night, I went through routines I hadn't used in years. After the kids were asleep, I moved through the apartment methodically. Double-checked the deadbolt, tested the chain lock, made sure the sliding door to our tiny balcony was locked and the security bar was in place. I pulled the curtains tight across every window, not just drawn but overlapping, eliminating any gaps.

I dragged a dining room chair to the front door and wedged it under the door handle as an added precaution. On the TV, I pulled up the feed from the cameras I'd installed all around the apartment facing the windows and doors. Even the ones in the kids' rooms which faced outward toward the street. Every camera I'd installed connected to my screen. I would sleep with my phone attached to my hand and all the cameras on my TV.

My jerk of a landlord wouldn't allow a permanent alarm system to be installed, so, I'd had battery operated cameras placed strategically throughout the apartment—I've learned difficult lessons from my past and from the women I've supported over the years. Even all these measures somehow felt inadequate now.

I sat with all the lights off, the glow from the TV screen the only thing lighting the room. Hearing each creak of the floorboards above made my pulse spike. Every car door slam outside sent adrenaline shooting through my veins. I kept my pepper spray within reach and my gun stowed safely in its case nearby.

The encounter played on repeat in my mind. How long had he been watching us before he approached? Had he followed us to the market, or was it really just a coincidence?

My phone remained silent in my hand. Again, I thought about calling Reed, but what would I say? That I ran into my abusive ex-boyfriend who had said hello and scared me? Reed was dealing with real shit. My paranoia could wait.

But deep down, I knew this wasn't paranoia. Bryce didn't do coincidences. And if a coincidence did happen, he didn't let them slide without taking advantage. My phone buzzed. Reed's name lit up the screen.

Reed: *Case wrapped up. I know we planned on tomorrow, but I miss you. Can I come by tonight? After the kids are asleep? I want to talk to you about something important.*

I stared at the message, my thumb hovering over the keyboard. I should tell him. I should tell him about Bryce, about the cameras, about the chair wedged under my door. But what would I say? That I ran into my ex and he said hello? That he scared me just by existing?

Reed was finally ready to open up, to be vulnerable. I could hear it in the way he'd texted. And I was sitting here in the dark with pepper spray in my lap.

I typed back: *I miss you too. Come over. I'll put the coffee on.*

I hit send before I could change my mind.

Chapter 11:

Old Wounds

REED

"So let me get this straight—you spent the morning at the farmer's market with Maliyah and her kids, and you're actually smiling about it?" John raised an eyebrow as he leaned back in the booth at Murphy's, nursing his second beer. While the lighting was dim, I could still see the amused smirk he wasn't even trying to hide.

I shrugged, taking a pull from my bottle. The beer was cold and familiar, helping wash away the adrenaline from the day. "It was good. Really good, actually."

"Right. Not like you haven't had the most important person in your life tell you that would be the case." John grinned. "That's me, by the way. In case you needed a reminder—which I'm sure you don't."

I laughed, a short bark that echoed off the wooden panels of our booth. "Got that, genius." I shook my head, watching him grin back at me with that same cocky smirk he'd had since we were ten. Ass.

"Sarah's going to lose her mind when I tell her. She's been waiting for you to get your shit together."

The robbery case had wrapped up with disappointing speed just an hour ago—two suspects now cooling their heels in lockup. A pair of neighborhood knuckleheads with more attitude than sense had strolled into the corner liquor store on Dorchester Avenue—faces fully visible to the security cameras. How they didn't realize the owner had been their Little League coach when they were younger was beyond me. John had suggested

Murphy's and cold beers to wash away the anticlimactic outcome, muttering something about our youth getting dumber as the years go by.

I, however, thought maybe teenagers weren't getting dumber—maybe we were just forgetting what it was like to be young and reckless. The memory of John lobbing cherry bombs across our high school cafeteria flashed through my mind, his teenage face just as exposed as those of the current idiots in question. I bit my tongue instead of mentioning it, but couldn't help the small smile that tugged at my lips.

I'd agreed to drinks partly because I needed to unwind and partly because I wanted to talk through what had happened this morning. Not that I'd admit that to him.

"The kids are good kids," I said. "Smart. Funny. You know, it's not like we haven't hung out with them in the past few months. It's just that this time was different, yeah? More official." I snickered, "Zoe's a force of nature—made me laugh the entire time. And Lucas warmed up in a good way."

John studied my face over his beer. "You really like them."

"Yeah. I do."

"All three of them."

I took another drink instead of answering, but John had known me since we were kids growing up in the same neighborhood. He could read the silence.

"Shit, Reed. You're falling for her. For all of them."

"I don't know what I'm doing, man." The admission came out before I could stop it. "Three months ago, I was convinced I couldn't handle this. Now I'm buying pastries and actually caring about catnip."

"Catnip?"

I smiled despite myself. "Had to be there."

"Were you actually interested or just faking it for the kids?"

I sat back, traced a finger through the condensation on my beer glass. Zoe's face flashed through my mind—the way she'd lit up showing me each thing she came across. Her negotiation skills with the vendors, so earnest and excited every step of the way. "That's the problem. I wasn't faking anything."

John signaled the waitress for another round. The Saturday night crowd at Murphy's was the usual mix of off-duty cops, firefighters, and neighborhood regulars. The kind of place where you could drink in peace.

"So what's the issue?" John asked. "You guys have been dating for a few months now. Sarah loves her—won't shut up about her, actually. The kids are great. You're happy. What's got you twisted up?"

I stared at the label on my beer bottle, peeling off one corner with my thumbnail. The paper came away in small, stubborn pieces. "It's so real, John. It's not just dating anymore. Those kids are starting to count on me. Lucas asked when I'm coming back. That means something."

"And that scares you."

"Yeah. It does." I blew out a breath. "You know why."

John's expression shifted, became more serious. "I know, man."

I nodded, and suddenly I was nine years old again, sitting on the front steps of our house in Southie. The neighborhood was quiet except for the distant wail of sirens—a sound that would make my stomach drop for the rest of my life. Mom's friend Mrs. O'Brien had her arm around my shoulders, and I kept asking when Dad was coming home. She wouldn't answer, just kept patting my back and crying.

I remember standing outside Mom's bedroom door that night, knocking so softly my knuckles barely made a sound. The hallway was dark except for the blue glow of the nightlight in the bathroom. I knocked again, called her name, pressed my ear against the wood. Nothing. Just the sound of my own breathing in the silence of our house.

I thought of the times I'd sit at our kitchen table doing homework—mom staring at nothing. Her coffee always in front of her in a mug, though she rarely actually drank it.

She'd make the same coffee he loved every day for the rest of her life. Black, two sugars. I can still hear the spoon clinking against the ceramic mug—clink, clink, stir, silence. She never drank it. Just made it. Set it on the table where he used to sit. Let it go cold. I'd learned eventually not to even ask her what was wrong any more. The answer was always the same hollow silence.

"I was eight when we lost him," I said quietly, pulling myself back to the present. "Lucas turns seven soon, so really I was only a year older than he is now."

John was quiet, letting me continue.

"And I keep thinking—what happens if I don't come home one day? What happens if I become that father figure to them and then leave them the way my dad left me?" I finally looked up at him. "I watched my mom fade away for years, John. She never came back from losing him. Just lived life a shell of herself, leaving me to figure shit out on my own. That's what love cost her."

I became a cop because my dad was a good cop—the kind whose funeral drew a line of dress blues that stretched for blocks down Broadway. He died protecting and serving, and every morning when I pin this badge on, I feel the weight of what it means and what it stands for. But this job... someday Maliyah might open her door to find my captain standing there with his hat in his hands. The thought of those kids maybe having to pick out a suit or dress to wear to a church full of bagpipes and folded flags—it's—" The words got caught in my throat. I couldn't even say them.

"Reed—"

"I know what you're going to say. That I can't live my life based on what-ifs. That lots of cops retire with their pensions and move to Florida. But you didn't watch your mom fade away because the man she loved got killed on the job. You didn't grow up knowing that love can destroy you."

John leaned forward, elbows on the table. "You're right. I didn't go through what you did. But Reed—your dad knew the risks better than anyone. He'd seen cops die. He'd been to those funerals. And he still chose your mom. Still chose to have you. Not because he didn't understand the danger, but because he thought you were worth the risk. Don't you think Maliyah deserves to make that same choice?"

"Easy to say when you're not the one who might fuck up a kid's life."

"First—do you think I don't want kids some day?" I winced, rubbing my hand across my jaw. "You're right. That was unfair."

"Second—You think Maliyah doesn't know the risks? She's dating a cop, man. She's not stupid. She knows what that means." John's voice softened. "And maybe she's strong enough to handle it. Maybe she'd rather have whatever time she gets with you than spend her life wondering what could have been."

I hadn't thought about it that way.

"And the kids?" I asked quietly.

"Kids are resilient. Way more than we give them credit for. We see it every day in our work. They survive shit that would break most adults." He paused. "But you know what really fucks kids up? Adults who are there but not really there. Adults who hold back because they're scared. You want to protect them? Then stop deciding for them what they can handle and just show up. All the way."

The waitress brought our next round. I was grateful for the interruption, needed a moment to let his words sink in.

"Sara used to say I lived like I was afraid of my own life," I said finally. "Like I was so scared of something bad happening that I wouldn't let anything good happen either."

"Was she right?"

"Probably." I picked at the new bottle's label. "But sitting here now, think-ing about this morning... about Maliyah and those kids... Maybe I don't want to live that way anymore."

"So what are you going to do about it?"

That was the question. I thought about Zoe's hand in mine as she dragged me around the market. Lucas's tentative smile when I'd shown genuine interest in his thoughts. Maliyah's face when she looked at me—like I was someone worth believing in.

And then I thought about leaving the market early for work, and how wrong it had felt to walk away from them.

"I don't know," I admitted. "Part of me wants to go all in. Part of me still wants to run."

"Which part's winning?"

I stared at my beer. "Changes every minute."

John was quiet for a while, watching the Sox game on the TV above the bar. Finally, he said, "You know what I think your problem is?"

"I'm sure you're going to tell me."

"You're trying to make this decision for them. Maliyah, the kids—you're deciding they can't handle the risks of loving a cop. But that's not your call to make, man. That's theirs."

"What if I'm not enough? What if I can't be what they need?"

"What if you are?" John looked me dead in the eye. "What if you stop what-iffing yourself out of the best thing that's ever happened to you and just try? You're different with her, you know? Better. Lighter."

"Is it crazy that I want to see her tonight? That I miss her? Which is fucking ridiculous since I saw her this morning." I dropped my head, rubbing the back of my neck where tension had been building. My phone sat on the table. I brought up her contact photo—Maliyah laughing at the harbor, hair blowing across her face—staring up at me. My thumb hovered over the message bubble, I want to text her. To tell her how I feel.

John laughed. "That's not ridiculous. That's what happens when you're in love, you idiot."

The words hung in the air between us. In love. I waited for the panic, for the instinct to backpedal, to laugh it off, to say John was being dramatic. But it didn't come. Instead, there was just... certainty. Warm and terrifying and completely inevitable.

"Yeah," I said quietly. "I think I am. And I think I need to tell her about my dad," I said quietly. "About why I've been so scared. She deserves to know what she's signing up for."

"She does. And Reed? I think you'll find she's a lot stronger than you're giving her credit for."

I picked up my phone and started typing.

Me: *Case wrapped up. I miss you. Can I come by tonight?*

I stared at it. Too casual. I deleted it and tried again.

Me: *I know we planned on tomorrow, but I need to see you. Can I come over after the kids are asleep?*

Still not right. One more time.

Me: *Case wrapped up. I know we planned on tomorrow, but I miss you. Can I come by tonight? After the kids are asleep? I want to talk to you about something important.*

I hit send before I could overthink it.

A minute ticked by. Then another.

Then her response came through.

Maliyah: *I miss you too. Come over. I'll put the coffee on.*

I left money on the table and said goodbye to John. Outside, the air was crisp and clear, the kind of night that made Boston feel like home.

For the first time in years, I felt like I was walking toward something instead of running away from it.

Chapter 12:

Walls down?

MALIYAH

The glow from the TV cast flickering shadows across the living room as I sat in the dark, watching the camera feeds. Front door. Balcony. Windows. Nothing moved except the occasional car passing by, headlights sweeping across the screens before disappearing into the night.

When I'd gone through the evening routine with the kids—dinner, baths, bedtime stories—my mind held onto its memory of Bryce's smile. That cold, calculating smile that said he knew exactly how much he'd rattled me.

I have a feeling we will.

No we will not see each other again. I'll do all I can to prevent it.

My phone buzzed. Reed's name lit up the screen.

Reed: On my way. Be there in ten.

I stared at the message. I should tell him. I should tell him about Bryce, about why I'm sitting here in the dark with cameras on and a chair wedged under the door. But he'd said he wanted to talk about something important. Something about him, not me.

I typed back: Okay. See you soon.

The apartment felt too quiet. Every creak of the floorboards above made my shoulders tense. Every car door slam sent my pulse spiking. I kept my pepper spray in my pocket, within reach. My Sig was secured in my holster with me all night now.

When the buzzer rang at nine fifty-two, I jumped.

"Hello?" My voice came out steadier than I felt.

"Hey, it's me."

I buzzed him up, then looked at the chair still wedged under the door handle. Shit. I yanked it away and shoved it back toward the dining table just as his footsteps hit the landing.

When I opened the door, Reed looked conflicted and mussed. His hair was messier than usual, like he'd been running his hands through it repeatedly, and there was something vulnerable in his expression I hadn't seen before.

"Hi," I said, stepping aside to let him in.

"Hi." He leaned in and kissed me—slow and lingering, his hand coming up to cup my jaw. When he pulled back, his thumb brushed across my cheekbone as his eyes searched mine. Then he followed me into the living room, and I watched his eyes sweep the space—taking in the details the way cops do. His gaze landed on the TV, still showing the camera feeds. Then back to me. His eyes traveled down, pausing at my waistband where the holster was visible under my sweater.

He didn't move further into the room. Just stood there, taking it all in.

"Maliyah." His voice was quiet, careful. "Why are you wearing your gun in your apartment?"

I opened my mouth, closed it again. The carefully rehearsed explanations evaporated.

"And what's up with the cameras," he continued, gesturing to the TV. "You're monitoring every entrance."

"I have coffee," I said, moving toward the kitchen. "Let me just—"

"Maliyah." His hand caught my wrist, gentle but firm. "Talk to me. What happened?"

The concern in his voice, the way he was looking at me—like I was something precious that might break—undid something in my chest. I'd been holding it together all evening, going through the motions with the kids, sitting here alone in the dark telling myself I was fine. I was handling it.

But I wasn't fine.

"I saw someone today," I said, the words coming out rushed. "At the farmer's market. After you left."

Reed went completely still. "Who?"

"Bryce." Just saying his name out loud made my hands start shaking. "My ex. He was there with his wife. He saw the kids, Reed. He was trying to get me to share things about what I'm doing now."

I watched Reed's expression shift—concern bleeding into something harder, more controlled. His jaw clenched, and when he spoke, his voice had that careful cop tone. "Did he threaten you?"

"Not directly. But he said—" I had to take a breath. "He said he had a feeling we'd run into each other again. It wasn't a question, Reed. It felt like he was making me a promise."

"Okay." Reed's hand slid from my wrist to my hand, his fingers lacing through mine. "Okay. Come sit down. Tell me everything."

He guided me to the couch, and I realized my legs were shaking too. How long had I been standing here wound so tight?

"Start from the beginning," Reed said, angling toward me on the couch. "What did he say? What did he do?"

So I told him. The whole encounter—how creepy he was, the comment about my body, the way he'd looked at Lucas and Zoe. Diane standing there silent and deferential. The veiled questions about my life. The way he'd watched us leave.

Reed listened without interrupting, but I could see the fury building behind his careful expression. His body was eerily still, though.

"When I got home," I finished, "I did what I used to do for the first few years after I left him. Cameras on, chair under the door, armed." I looked down at our joined hands. "Old habits."

"I want to ask you something. You don't have to tell me if you're not ready, but I think it would help."

"Okay. Go for it."

Reed leaned forward, his voice gentle. "Can you tell me anything about what happened between you two? I'm trying to understand why seeing him scared you this much."

I took a shaky breath, trying to find words that wouldn't completely fall apart saying. "He... he had some issues. I had to learn to be careful with everything as to not set him off with a misunderstanding." I looked down at our joined hands. "Eventually I just left. Took off and moved to Florida without a word. Started over completely."

"Okay. How long ago was this?"

"A long time." I swallowed hard at that. "Long enough that I didn't think it would ever be an issue again. But... do you think I could leave it there for tonight? I'm not sure I have it in me to go any deeper right now."

Reed squeezed my hand, then lifted it to his lips. The brush of his mouth against my skin sent warmth spreading through me—safe. I felt safe. His gaze held mine—unwavering, certain—as if he could see straight through to all the broken pieces I'd been trying to hide."There's no pressure," he said, voice dropping to that low register that seemed to vibrate in my chest. "You tell me the rest when you're ready. I'm not going anywhere."

"Okay," I whispered.

"Tell me something. How long were you sitting here alone before I got here?"

"Since the kids went to bed. Around eight."

"That's almost two hours, Maliyah." His voice cracked slightly on my name. "You've been sitting here scared for two hours and you weren't going to tell me."

"You said you wanted to talk about something important. About you. I didn't want to—"

"No." He cut me off, he reached forward, hands gently framing my face, making me look at him. "No. This IS important. *You* are important. This bastard shows up and scares you—you call me."

"I was going to tell you. I just—" My voice broke. "I don't know."

"Maliyah." Reed's thumb brushed across my cheekbone, catching a tear I hadn't realized had fallen. "Your shit is my shit now. That's what this is. That's what I came here to tell you tonight."

"What?"

"That I'm all in. That I want this—want you, want Lucas and Zoe, want Saturday mornings and weeknight dinners and all of it." He leaned his forehead against mine. "And that means when something scares you, you tell me."

I closed my eyes, letting myself lean into him for just a moment. Then I pulled back.

"I need you to understand something," I said. "I appreciate that you want to protect me. I do. But I can't have you going into cop mode and trying to control this."

His expression shifted—not quite defensive, but close. "What is that supposed to mean?"

"It means you're already thinking about running his name. Checking for warrants, complaints, anything you can use. Maybe bringing him in for questioning."

Reed didn't deny it.

"And I need you to not do that. Not yet."

"Maliyah—"

"I'm serious, Reed. This is exactly the kind of thing that escalates situations like this. If you go after him officially, he'll know I told you. He'll know I'm scared. And men like Bryce don't respond well to shows of force. They escalate."

Reed stood up, running both hands through his hair. "So what? I'm supposed to do nothing? Just let him walk around knowing you're local now, knowing what your kids look like?"

"He already knows those things. Running his name doesn't change that. It just tells him I'm scared enough to involve the cops."

"You ARE scared enough. You're wearing your gun in your apartment, Maliyah."

"Because I'm being smart and prepared. Not because I'm panicking and making bad decisions." I stood up to face him. "Reed, I know how these situations play out. This is what I deal with every day."

"You get I'm a cop, right? I deal with this shit every day too."

I stared at him. Trying to communicate to him how he was missing the point.

Finally, he caved. "Then tell me what you want me to do."

"I want you to trust my judgment on this. I want you to support me, not take over."

He looked at me for a long moment, and I could see him fighting against every instinct he had. "I don't know if I can do that."

The honesty was like a punch to the gut. At least he wasn't lying to me.

"Then we have a problem," I said quietly. "Because I won't be in a relationship where someone makes decisions about my safety without me. I've been there. I won't go back."

"That's not fair. Bryce controlled you. I'm trying to protect you. Those aren't the same thing."

"Reed, if you're making decisions about how to handle this without listening to what I need, then you're putting pressure on me. Pressure I don't need right now. You do see where I'm coming from, right?"

Reed stared at me, and I watched the realization hit. His shoulders dropped slightly.

"Fuck," he said quietly. "You're right. I'm—shit. That's not what I want."

"I know it's not. But Reed, your need to protect me doesn't override my need to control my own life. It can't."

He nodded slowly, then moved back to the couch and sat down heavily. "Okay. So tell me. What do you need from me?"

I sat down beside him, close enough that our knees touched. "Right now? I need you to not run his name. Not yet."

"Maliyah—"

"Let me finish. If he contacts me again—any contact at all, whether it's him showing up somewhere he shouldn't be, calling, texting, anything—then yes. Then we use every resource you have. Then you run his name, check everything, do whatever cop stuff you need to do. But that has to be my call. Not yours."

"What if I run it and find out he has a pattern? What if there are other women who've filed complaints? What if his wife has called the cops on him?"

"Then we'll know that when and if I decide it's time to run it."

Reed was quiet, processing. I could see him working through the logic, the cop part of his brain reluctantly agreeing with the victim advocate part.

"I hate this," he said finally.

"I know."

"I want to find him and make sure he never comes near you again."

"I know that too."

"But you're asking me to trust that you know how to handle this."

"I'm asking you to trust that I know MY abuser. That I've been on this side of it and I know what helps and what makes it worse." I took his hand. "I'm not saying you don't get a say. I'm saying I need final say on my own safety."

Reed looked down at our joined hands, his thumb brushing across my knuckles. "Okay," he said quietly. "We do it your way. For now. But if he escalates—"

"If he escalates, we reassess. Together. As a team."

"As a team," he repeated, like he was testing out the words. Then he looked up at me. "I'm not good at this."

"At what?"

"At not controlling things. At trusting someone else to handle a threat." He let out a breath. "My whole job is about taking control of bad situations. And now you're asking me to sit back and wait."

"I'm not asking you to sit back. I'm asking you to stand beside me. There's a difference."

Something shifted in his expression. "Yeah. Okay. I can try to do that."

We sat there for a moment in silence, both of us trying to figure out how to navigate this.

"I'm glad you texted tonight. I'm glad I got to see you." I said finally.

Reed's expression changed—became more vulnerable, less controlled. "Yeah. I'd wanted to tell you something, but after this, it feels—"

"No. Tell me. Please. I want to know."

He studied my face for a moment, then nodded. "Okay. But first—are you okay? Really?"

I considered lying. Considered saying I was fine. But we were trying to do this differently.

"No," I said honestly. "I'm scared. And I'm angry that I'm scared. And I hate that he still has this power over me after all this time."

"He doesn't have power over you. You took precautions. You armed yourself. You made a plan. That's not him having power. That's you taking it back."

The words landed like a weight being lifted from my chest. "What did you want to tell me?" I asked, suddenly desperate for whatever he had to say—anything to pull me out of the swirling vortex of my own thoughts, even if just for a few minutes.

"Okay. Yeah." Reed's jaw tightened. He looked down, then back up at me. "I want to tell you about my dad. Need to tell you some of it—might help explain some shit about me."

Chapter 13:

It Goes Both Ways

REED

"I was eight when we lost him," I said, the words coming out rougher than I'd intended. "Lucas turns seven soon. So I was only a year older than he is now."

I watched understanding dawn in Maliyah's eyes. She got it—the age parallel, why seeing that kid made my chest tight, why the thought of becoming something permanent in his life scared the shit out of me.

"I'm listening," she said softly.

I took a breath, trying to figure out where to start. It had been years since I'd talked about this—really talked about it. Not the vague version I gave people who asked about my dad being a cop. The real story. The one that still woke me up sometimes.

"My dad was a good cop. You know, his funeral drew dress blues for blocks—that's how many people came out to show their respects." I stared at our intertwined fingers before letting go, dragging my palm roughly across my face like I was trying to wipe away memories better left in the past. "He responded to a domestic violence call in Southie. Pretty routine—wife finally called it in after years of taking it. My dad was first on scene."

The memory played out in my head like it always did—grainy, like old footage. I hadn't even been there, but I'd reconstructed it a thousand times from what I'd been told and what I'd eventually read in the official report after becoming a cop.

"The guy shot him the second he opened the door. Before my father could even identify himself. His partner took the shooter down, but it didn't matter. He'd already killed my father. What was done, was done."

Maliyah reached for my knee, her palm settling there like an anchor. The heat from her hand burned through my jeans, steadying me against the tide of memories.

"I was nine when they knocked on our door. Mrs. O'Brien—our neighbor—she's the one who held me while they told us. Not my mom. Mom—she just..." I had to stop, clear my throat. "She just stood there. Didn't cry, didn't scream. Just stood there like someone had unplugged her."

I could still see it—the way my mom had looked right through the officers at our door. The way Mrs. O'Brien had pulled me against her side, her hand trembling on my shoulder. The way everything had gone quiet except for the sound of my own breathing.

"After that, it was like she disappeared even though she was still there. Weirdest thing—every morning she'd get up and make his coffee—black, two sugars. She'd put it in front of where he'd sat and just let it sit there getting cold. For years. Did it all the way up until the day she died."

"Reed—" Maliyah started, but I needed to finish this.

"Didn't take long for me to learn how to take care of myself. I learned to make my own meals, get myself to school, all of it. She was just... gone. I think I realized years later that I lost both my parents on that day—just took another twenty years for her to catch up to him."

I finally looked up at Maliyah. Her eyes were shining with unshed tears, but she was holding it together for me. Letting me get through this.

"Every time I pin my badge on," I said, my voice rough, "I know there's a chance I don't come home. Most days the risk is small. But sometimes it gets real. And I can't stop thinking about what it would do to Lucas and Zoe—to you—if we got as close as we could. If we became real—like permanent. And then I just... disappeared. The way my dad disappeared from my life."

"Is that why there's always been a bit of distance?" Maliyah asked gently. "Something holding you back?"

"Yeah." I ran a hand through my hair, frustrated with myself. "I kept thinking if I didn't get too close, if I kept things casual, nobody would get hurt when I inevitably screwed it up. Or worse—if something happened to me on the job."

"Reed—"

"But I want this, Maliyah." The words came out in a rush. "I want you. I want Saturday mornings with you and the kids. I want to be there when Lucas turns seven, eight, and beyond. I want to teach Zoe whatever random thing she decides is important that week. I want all of it, even though it terrifies me."

"What changed?" Her voice was barely above a whisper.

"You did. This did. We did." I gestured between us, trying to find the right words. "You've become so much to me. I know it's only been a few months or so since we've started seeing each other, but—"

"And to do this—with not just me, but with my kids too..." She pulled back slightly to look at me fully. "You need to be all in, Reed. Not just when it's easy. Not just when you're not scared. All the way in."

"I know." I took both her hands in mine, needing her to understand. "I can't promise I won't get scared sometimes. But I can promise I'll do everything I can to talk to you instead of pulling away." I paused, knowing this next part was important. "And I will respect your boundaries with this Bryce thing—to a point. Can we agree to both give a little on that one? I'll respect your boundaries. You give by realizing I can't just turn the cop side of me off."

She searched my face for what felt like forever. I held my breath, waiting for her to tell me it wasn't enough, that I was asking too much, that she deserved someone who wasn't carrying around all this baggage from a nine-year-old boy who'd watched his mother fade away.

"Okay," she said finally. "Yeah. I can agree to that. As long as we stay a team."

"Team," I echoed, and then I couldn't wait anymore. I leaned in and kissed her—not gentle this time, but deep and certain. Making a promise with my mouth that my words couldn't quite capture. That I was done running. Done keeping one foot out the door. Done letting fear of what might happen keep me from what was right in front of me.

When we pulled apart, we were both breathing hard.

"I don't want to go," I said, hesitant. I knew with everything that had happened with Bryce, I shouldn't leave her alone. But I also didn't want to overstep, didn't want to assume. "You know, with everything going on."

"Yeah—neither do I. You could stay," she said. "On the couch. I'd really rather the kids and I not be alone tonight."

Relief flooded through me so fast it left me dizzy. I hadn't realized how much I'd been bracing for her to say no, to tell me she needed space, that I'd dumped too much on her tonight.

"Yeah. The couch works for me." I pulled her against my chest, needing to feel her solid and safe in my arms. Her cheek pressed against my shirt, right over my heart, and I wondered if she could feel how hard it was beating.

We sat like that for a long time, talking about everything and nothing. About my dad's funeral—the bagpipes and folded flag. About her years in Florida. About the kids and what they'd been like as babies. Sometimes the words came easy, sometimes we just sat in comfortable silence, her head on my shoulder, my arm around her waist.

Time melted away. I wasn't sure when we'd stopped talking, just that at some point I realized she was describing a memory and I was holding her closer, and it felt like the most natural thing in the world.

By the time Maliyah finally got up to grab me a blanket and pillow, it was past two. My back was going to hate me for sleeping on this couch, but I didn't care. I wasn't leaving her alone tonight. Not after everything she'd told me about Bryce. Not with the way her hands had been shaking when we'd gotten home.

She checked on the kids one more time while I turned the camera feeds back on. Old cop habit—I pulled them up on my phone too, made sure I could see every angle. If that asshole came anywhere near this building, I'd know.

Maliyah came back and leaned down to kiss my cheek. The simple gesture hit me harder than it should have—sweet and domestic and so far from the emotional distance I'd been keeping for years.

She started toward her bedroom, then paused. "Reed?"

"Yeah?"

"Thank you. For more than I can even explain."

"Babe, that goes both ways."

I watched her disappear into her room, heard the soft click of her door closing. Then I settled back against the couch, phone in hand, camera feeds on the screen.

Something in my chest loosened, like a knot I'd been carrying for years had finally come undone. I'd never shared what I did here tonight before with a woman I'd dated—but Maliyah was different. I'd just cracked myself open for her, and somehow I was still breathing. Scared shitless, but breathing easier than I had in years.

My phone buzzed—John, texting at two in the morning like the asshole he was.

John: So? How'd it go?

I smiled despite myself.

Me: Good. Really good.

John: You tell her?

Me: Yeah.

John: And?

Me: I'm sleeping on her couch. Long story. Tell you tomorrow.

John: Sleeping on her couch is not the victory I was hoping for, man.

Me: Fuck off. It's exactly where I need to be.

John: {Middle Finger emoji} Night, fucker.

I set my phone down and closed my eyes, but I wasn't sleeping. Not yet. I was listening for any sound that didn't belong. Watching for any shadow that moved wrong on the camera feeds. Standing guard the way my father had stood guard for people he didn't even know.

The difference was, I knew exactly who I was protecting. And this time, I wasn't going to let anything happen to them.

Chapter 14:

Standing Guard

REED

Boston winter meant darkness in the early morning hours and well before dawn, I heard the soft pad of small feet on hardwood. I'd been awake for the past hour—hell, I'd barely slept at all—but I'd at least closed my eyes and tried to rest between listening for every creak and checking the cameras intermittently. Maliyah's breathing had finally evened out around three. I'd been listening and, in reality I never stopped.

A small figure appeared in the doorway, backlit by the nightlight in the hall. Zoe stopped when she saw me, her head tilting to one side like a confused puppy.

"Why are you on our couch?" she whispered, her voice still thick with sleep.

I sat up, keeping my voice low. "Your mom had trouble sleeping last night, so I came over to help. I didn't want to wake anyone, so I slept out here."

"Oh." She padded closer, her bare feet making soft sounds on the floor. She was wearing pajamas covered in unicorns, and her hair stuck up at odd angles. "Is Mama sick?"

"No, sweetheart. She's just tired. Sometimes grown-ups have trouble sleeping when there's lots of stuff going on."

"Like when I can't sleep because I'm excited for Santa or the tooth fairy?"

"Sort of like that, yeah."

She launched herself onto the couch with a flying leap. "Oof!" The air rushed from my lungs as her tiny palms smacked against my midsection, her weight surprisingly solid for someone who couldn't weigh more than forty pounds. I instinctively curled forward, catching her before she could bounce off.

She bounced on the cushions, voice rising with excitement. I pressed a finger to my lips and whispered, "Shh, let's not wake your mom and brother, okay?"She nodded solemnly, eyes wide, then leaned in close. Her whisper came out loud enough to wake the neighbors. "You know what would be really good right now? Pancakes."

I glanced toward Maliyah's bedroom door, which was still firmly closed. She'd been so wound up last night, so scared despite trying to hide it. If I could give her even a couple more hours of uninterrupted sleep, I would.

"I think we can make that work. But you'll have to help me. I don't know where everything is."

Zoe's face lit up and I felt the couch move as she bounced. "I'm a really good helper!"

We made our way to the kitchen, Zoe pointing out where the pans were kept, where the eggs lived in the fridge, and the exact spot where Maliyah kept the "special" spatula that was apparently the only acceptable utensil for flipping the perfect pancake.

"We're not allowed to use the stove," Zoe informed me seriously as I pulled out the carton of eggs. "Only grown-ups can do that part."

"That's a very good rule."

"And for the eggs—because you can't have pancakes without eggs—you have to crack them into the bowl first, not in the pan. That way there are no shells since mama says shells are 'a nightmare to swish out.'" She said the last part in what was clearly an imitation of Maliyah's voice.

I pressed my lips together to keep from laughing. Fish out, swish out—close enough. I nodded solemnly and met her expert gaze. "That's excellent advice. Thank you for the tip."

Lucas shuffled into the kitchen about ten minutes later, his hair sticking up on one side and his eyes still half-closed. He stopped short when he saw me at the stove, then glanced around like he was trying to figure out if he was still dreaming.

"Morning," I said, keeping my voice quiet.

"Why are you here?" Not hostile, just genuinely confused.

"Your mom couldn't sleep last night, so I came over to help out. Figured I'd let her rest this morning and make you guys some breakfast."

Lucas processed this, then nodded and climbed up onto one of the bar stools. "She does that sometimes. The not sleeping thing."

"Yeah?"

"Usually when she's worried about something." He picked at a small tear in his pajama sleeve. "Is she okay?"

The kid was too perceptive for six—almost seven. "She's fine. Just had a lot on her mind. But that's what I'm here for. To help."

Zoe bounced over to her brother. "Reed's making pancakes!"

"I can see that, dummy."

"Lucas," I said gently. "I don't think your mom would like it if she heard you call people names, what do you think?"

He had the grace to look sheepish. "She wouldn't. Sorry, Zoe."

She stuck her tongue out at him, and I decided to let that one slide.

By the time I had eggs, pancakes, and some cut-up fruit arranged on plates, it was almost seven-thirty. The kids had walked me through every step of their morning routine—how Lucas liked his eggs "not runny," how Zoe needed her pancakes to be shaped inside cookie cutters, how they were supposed to brush their teeth right after eating, and approximately forty other details that seemed crucial to a solid morning routine.

I found myself checking Maliyah's door every few minutes, listening for any sound that she was awake. Part of me wanted her to sleep as long as possible. Another part of me wanted to see her face, to make sure she was really okay.

"Should we wake her up?" Zoe asked around a mouthful of eggs.

"Let her sleep a little longer," I said. "She could use a little extra rest."

Lucas studied me over his orange juice. "Are you going to stay here from now on?"

The question caught me off guard. "What do you mean?"

"Like, since you're Mom's boyfriend? That's really why slept over, right? I'm six and three quarters, I see things."

I set down my coffee mug carefully. This felt like important territory, and I didn't want to screw it up or laugh at how serious and fucking adorable this kid was. "Your mom and I are... we care about each other a lot. And I want to be around more, if that's okay with you guys."

"Do you love her?" Zoe asked, her eyes wide and curious.

"Zoe!" Lucas looked mortified. "You can't just ask that!"

My throat felt tight, but I looked her in the eyes and said, "You know, I think I should talk to her about that first. What do you think?"

"Yeah. That's a good idea."

"So, I know you guys must have some really big questions, and I don't have all the answers yet. But I can tell you that I care about your mom very much, and I care about both of you too."

Lucas looked at me for a long moment, then nodded slowly. "Okay. That's good, for now—I guess."

Zoe leaned forward, her eyes wide with excitement. "Do you want to be a daddy someday?" The question hit me like a bucket of ice water. My mind went blank as I stared at her hopeful little face, and I felt a trickle of sweat run down my back.

"Zoe!" Lucas groaned. "Stop asking so many questions!"

"I'm just wondering!"

I laughed despite myself. "It's okay. I don't mind." I looked at both of them. "How about I just say this—I think you two are really cool and I like spending time with you. Is that good? At least for now?"

Zoe beamed at me, and even Lucas looked pleased, though he tried to hide it behind another sip of orange juice.

Around eight-thirty, I heard movement from Maliyah's room. The kids heard it too and immediately started whispering excitedly.

"Should we surprise her?"

"We should stay quiet so she doesn't know Reed made breakfast and we already ate it!"

"That's not a surprise, she's gonna see when she comes out, dummy."

"Lucas!" I warned again.

He sighed. "Sorry. But she will see you."

"Fair point, but no name calling, yeah?"

A few minutes later, Maliyah's bedroom door opened. She emerged looking rumpled and disoriented, her hair loose around her shoulders and her eyes still heavy with sleep. She was wearing the same oversized Red Sox t-shirt from last night and sleep shorts that showed off her legs in a way that made me forget how to form coherent thoughts for a moment.

She stopped short when she saw the three of us at the kitchen table, her eyes moving from the kids to me to the empty plates.

"What time is it?" Her voice was rough with sleep.

"After eight," I said. "You needed the rest."

"You..." She looked around, taking in the clean kitchen, the kids already dressed—wait, when had they gotten dressed? I'd helped Lucas find clean clothes about twenty minutes ago while Zoe had insisted she could dress herself—hadn't even noticed that they'd done it all themselves. "You made breakfast?"

"Reed cooks really good!" Zoe announced.

"He let me have two pieces of bacon," Lucas added.

Maliyah's eyes found mine, and I saw something shift in her expression. Something soft and vulnerable that made my chest ache.

"I figured you could use the extra sleep," I said. "The kids walked me through everything. I'm pretty sure I got most of it right."

She moved into the kitchen, and I stood to pour her a cup of coffee. When I went to hand it to her, she stepped into me and wrapped her arms around my midsection. I put the coffee down on the counter behind her, my hand brushing against the warm ceramic. Her forehead pressed against my chest, and I felt her exhale against my shirt.

My arms found their place around her—one wrapping lightly around her head with my hand buried in her hair, the other around shoulders holding her tightly against me. The kids' chatter faded to background noise as we stood there, neither of us speaking, her fingers gripping the back of my shirt.

She stepped back and leaned her forehead on my chest for a moment before she looked up at me and whispered, "Thank you." Reaching for her mug, she stayed close enough to me that I could still feel her warmth radiating between us. She cradled the mug between both palms, inhaled the steam rising from the surface, and closed her eyes as she took that first essential sip.

"No thanks are needed. I wanted to." I glanced at the kids, who were watching us with unabashed interest.

"Reed didn't know about the special spatula," Zoe informed her mother. "But I showed him."

"Of course you did, baby." Maliyah's voice was thick with emotion, and I saw her blink rapidly a few times.

"Why don't you two go brush your teeth?" I suggested to the kids. "I think I heard something about the library later?"

"The library!" Zoe jumped up, nearly knocking over her orange juice in her excitement. "Can Reed come with us?"

Lucas looked hopeful too, though he tried to play it cool. "Yeah, that would be okay, I guess."

"We'll see," Maliyah said. "Go brush your teeth first. Both of you."

Once the kids had thundered off to the bathroom, Maliyah sagged against the counter. I moved closer, close enough to see the faint purple shadows under her eyes.

"Hey," I said softly. "You okay?"

"I slept," she said, like she couldn't quite believe it. "I actually slept."

"I know. I checked on you a few times."

"Did you stay up all night?"

"Most of it. Couldn't really sleep anyway." I reached out and tucked a strand of hair behind her ear. "Figured if one of us was going to be awake, it might as well be me."

"Thank you," she whispered. "For being here. For letting me rest. For taking care of my kids."

"Wouldn't be anywhere else," I said.

"Maaaaama! Lucas is hogging the sink!"

Maliyah laughed, the sound slightly watery but genuine. "Welcome to my life."

"I like your life," I said honestly.

"Even the chaos?"

"Especially the chaos."

She kissed me again, quick and light, then went to referee the bathroom situation. I finished putting a plate together for Maliyah, feeling oddly domestic and not hating it even a little bit.

When she came back with both kids in tow—teeth brushed, faces washed, and only mildly bickering—she looked more like herself. Still tired, but steadier.

"So," she said. "Library?"

"If you're up for it."

I watched her consider, saw the moment she squared her shoulders and made a decision. "Yeah. I'm not letting yesterday keep us locked inside. We go to the library on the weekends. That's what we do."

I slid the plate across the counter toward her—pancakes that were supposed to look like dinosaurs, fluffy scrambled eggs, and two strips of bacon. "Eat first, then let's go," I said, watching her eyes widen at the sight. "Can't face the library on an empty stomach."

Lucas pumped his fist. "Yes! Reed can help carry the books!"

"That's literally the only reason we're bringing him," Maliyah said with a straight face, and I laughed.

"Hey! I can offer other services too. Like... I don't know, reaching high shelves?"

"Ooh, that's useful," she teased. "Okay, you can come."

As the kids ran off to gather their library books, Maliyah caught my hand. "Seriously though. Thank you. For everything."

"Maliyah, You don't have to keep thanking me."

"I know. But I'm going to anyway." She squeezed my fingers. "Last night was... I was really scared, Reed. And you didn't try to take over. You just... stayed."

"I'm not going anywhere," I said. "Even when you're scared. Especially then."

She nodded, blinking hard. "Okay. Good. Because I think we're going to need that."

Zoe came racing back into the room, arms full of books. "Ready!"

Lucas followed at a more sedate pace, his own stack of books tucked under one arm. "I'm ready too."

"Then let's go," Maliyah said, and the smile she gave me was full of hope and promise and just a little bit of fear that she was trying to be brave about.

I grabbed my jacket and followed them toward the door, watching Maliyah double-check the locks and pocket her phone. She was still on guard, still watching for threats. But she was trying to live her life anyway.

And I was going to be right there beside her while she did.

Chapter 15:

Shadows

MALIYAH

The library had been perfect. Reed carried the bag with both kids' collections of books while Lucas peppered him with questions about whether detectives have ever actually used magnifying glasses and Zoe insisted on showing him every single butterfly in her picture book. Twice. He'd handled it all with such patience, shifting to the outside of the sidewalk when we crossed streets—a protective gesture so natural he probably didn't realize he was doing it.

I'd found myself stealing glances at him throughout the afternoon. The way he met Lucas's eyes when they spoke, treating my son's conversation with genuine consideration. The patience with Zoe's endless "but why" questions. Was I allowed to want this? To imagine someone sharing not just the joy of my children, but the exhausting, beautiful weight of them?

"Mama, can we read one of our new books when we get home?" Zoe asked, skipping beside me.

"After lunch, baby."

"Okie dokey."

We were half a block from my building when I saw him.

A tall figure in a dark sweatshirt standing near the coffee shop on the corner, partially hidden behind the outdoor menu board. Same build. Same way of holding his shoulders—weight on one leg, hands in pockets, head tilted slightly like he was watching something.

Watching us.

My breath caught. My steps faltered.

"Maliyah?" Reed's voice came from beside me. "What's wrong?"

I blinked, forcing myself to focus on the spot. The figure stepped back, melting into the shadow between the coffee shop and the dry cleaner next door. There one second. Gone the next.

"I—" My heart was hammering so hard I could barely hear my own voice. "I thought I saw someone."

Reed followed my gaze instantly, his body language shifting. Alert. Assessing. "Who? Him?"

"It's nothing." But my hands were shaking as I fumbled for my keys. "I'm being paranoid."

Reed leaned closer, his voice dropping to a murmur only I could hear. "Maliyah." His eyes darted briefly to the kids then back to me. "Someone you know?" The careful phrasing and the slight tilt of his head told me he understood—this wasn't a conversation for little ears

He could see I couldn't answer—not with the kids right beside us.

Showing his understanding, Reed said, "Let's get inside."

The kids, oblivious to the tension, chattered about their books as we climbed the stairs to my apartment. Reed stayed behind us, and I noticed him checking that the entry door closed securely before following. Positioning himself between my family and the street below.

Once we were inside with the door locked, Reed helped the kids spread their library books across the living room floor while I tried to shake off the lingering unease.

Maybe I was being paranoid. Maybe it had just been someone who looked similar from a distance. But the way my chest had seized up, the instant recognition followed by the disappearing act—it felt too familiar.

"Okay guys," I said, forcing normalcy into my voice. "How about you look through your books while Reed and I make some lunch?"

"Can we have grilled cheese?" Zoe asked, already absorbed in a book about penguins.

"Sure thing."

In the kitchen, Reed immediately moved closer, his voice quiet. "Talk to me. Did you catch sight of him?"

I busied myself getting bread and cheese from the refrigerator, needing something to do with my hands. "I don't know. I thought him for a brief moment, but it could all just be my anxiety." I paused, setting the ingredients on the counter.

Reed went very still. "Where? Was it when we rounded the corner? Or on the same street here? Exactly where did you think you saw him?"

"Near the coffee shop on the corner—half a block down. Right off of Broadway. But, Reed, it was just a flash. What if I'm just being paranoid?"

"Two sightings in two days isn't paranoia, sweetheart," Reed said as he brushed the hair back from my face. "That's a pattern."

I turned the stove on low, hands still shaking slightly. "I feel like I need to tell you everything. About Bryce. About what happened back then."

"Okay." Reed's voice was careful, gentle. "I'm listening."

"We dated for pretty much all of college. He was charming, kind, fun, smart. My parents loved him. Even Felicity liked him at first."

The butter started to sizzle in the pan.

"It started small. He had a temper about certain things—if I spent too much time studying, if I had a male professor, if I couldn't make it to dinner with his parents or go away for the weekend with his family." I forced myself to keep talking, my voice cracking as the memories flooded in. "Early on it was just words. Yelling. Guilt trips."

Reed was completely silent behind me. I was still doing everything I could to avoid looking into his eyes.

"The first time he got physical—I was so surprised that I don't think I even realized what was happening. We'd been arguing about a study group I'd been to where there were other men. He'd grabbed my arm, twisting the skin until it burned. Then, before I knew it, his hand was on my face, thumb and fingers pressing into my cheeks so hard that my teeth cut the inside of my mouth."

I rubbed my arm absently, my fingers tracing the underside of my forearm. "For days afterward, I tugged my sleeves down whenever they rode up. I became a pro at makeup—building thin layers over the marks until they disappeared."

I turned to look at him, eye to eye. "It wasn't long before he felt empowered and a bruise became a break, indentations from fingers became swelling from a fist."

"By my senior year, I'd learned to read his moods." Dropping my head a bit and breaking eye contact, I continued, "I was out to lunch with a girlfriend. Her boyfriend saw us and pulled up a chair—along with his roommate." I could see it so clearly—the restaurant, the moment I'd looked up and seen Bryce through the window, watching. "He was waiting for me when I got home that night."

I had to stop. Had to take a breath. I turned back to look at the stove where the grilled cheese sandwiches were browning.

"When it was over..." My voice cracked. "Stitches on the inside of my lip. More along my hairline. Had a ruptured eardrum on my left side that required surgery." I reached up to touch my earlobe. The room tilted slightly, just as it had that night when my head cracked against the plaster and for hours the world went silent on my left side—for weeks I felt like I was under water.

Reed came up behind me. His fingers found the hem of my shirt, gathering the fabric with a gentleness that made my breath catch. The warmth of him pressed against my back, solid and steady as a wall between me and the rest of the world. My shoulders, which had been rigid with tension, softened under his touch. When his forehead came to rest in the curve where my neck met my shoulder, I didn't flinch away. Instead, I leaned back, just slightly, into the shelter of him.

"What happened then?" His voice was barely above a whisper—if his lips hadn't been so close to my ear, I never would have heard him. "How did you get away?"

"Felicity." I straightened, still feeling his warmth but creating just enough space between us. "When I could finally see straight, I didn't even think to call 911. I called my sister." A bitter laugh escaped me. "She found me on the bathroom floor. Got me to the ER. After the surgery and overnight stay, this nurse connected me with Passageway. They became everything—shelter, counseling, a roadmap when I couldn't see past the next hour."

My legs felt suddenly hollow. I eased away from his warmth, pulled the food off the stove, and found the nearest bar stool, letting my weight collapse onto it before my knees could give way.

"I had an old roommate in Florida—Grace. Bryce never met her, didn't know about her—she'd left after a month at BU, but we'd kept in touch. Felicity loaned me money to get there. I was only twenty-two." I looked down at my hands. "We never told our parents about what he did. They both passed not long after in a car accident. You know, I was too afraid to come back, so I didn't go to their funeral. Felicity came down soon after and we celebrated their lives together, spreading their ashes."

"Jesus," Reed breathed.

My shoulders relaxed, and I felt the familiar warmth spread through my chest that always came when I talked about the work that had saved me. "Passageway connected me with an organization in Florida that supports domestic violence victims. I started volunteering because it was the only place I felt safe." I waved a hand, encompassing years of work, therapy, rebuilding. "Eventually it became my life's work. And then—here we are. Back in Boston. Less than six months back, and I run into him."

Reed busied himself with plating the food for the kids. "Stay. I'll be right back." He grabbed a couple waters from the fridge. From my perch on the counter stool, I listened as Reed's voice drifted in from the family room, followed by the familiar sounds of plates being set down and Reed telling them to put the books up so they don't get dirty.

It wasn't long before I heard him approach and felt his warmth at my side. He leaned into the counter next to me. Not looking at me—just side by side as we sat there. The sounds of the kids chattering filling the silence.

He dropped his head. "I'm so fucking sorry."

"I should have told you sooner. It's been almost fifteen years, Reed. I thought he wouldn't care anymore, though, and that it was better left as a memory."

"Men like Bryce don't stop caring about control." Reed's voice was gentle but firm. "Will you let me help you? Really help. I won't take over or make decisions for you. But this is a much bigger deal than I realized—those kinds of injuries." He let out a breath. "Maliyah, that's not the kind of guy who just stops."

I looked at this man asking permission instead of assuming, respecting my boundaries even when every instinct probably told him to do more.

"Yes," I whispered. "Okay. You're right."

He stood and pulled me up with him, wrapping his arms around me. My cheek pressed against his shirt, and I felt the first tear slide down. Then another. Each one carrying away a piece of the weight I'd been holding alone.

After a few minutes, I pulled back. Reed's expression had shifted—analytical, processing.

"You have documentation from back then? Hospital records, police reports?"

"Yes. Photos too."

He looked relieved. "That's good. I'd like to make some calls. See what I can find out about him—what he's doing now, if there have been any complaints." He paused, pulling out his phone. "And we can change your routines for a while. I can drive you places when I'm available. What do you think about having Felicity help out too?"

"Let's see how things go. I don't want to freak her out if it's nothing." I could tell he didn't love that, but he didn't push—didn't force it.

"Maliyah, I think we should file a report. Document everything."

My stomach tightened and the old familiar fears skated through me, whispering to hide away instead. But I looked at Reed. I saw his determination. I saw that he was really here with me. And that he would walk with me on this. "Okay.

"But Reed, I need you to understand—I spent years learning to take care of myself and my kids. It's not that I don't want your help—I do. I just need to feel like I have a choice in how that help looks."

"I won't take over. We'll do things just like we did here—talking it out and coming to a plan together."

I nodded, my shoulders relaxing. Something in his eyes—steady, unwavering—told me more than his words could.

Reed wrapped his arm around me, pulling out his phone with his other hand. "Maliyah?"

"Yeah?"

"Whatever this is with Bryce, whatever happens—I'm right here."

He pulled me close, and I let myself lean into him. The sound of my children's voices drifted in from the other room—ordinary, everyday chatter that suddenly felt extraordinary. My body knew what my mind was just catching up to: with Reed, I wasn't just letting Reed help me. I was letting him in.

"Mama!" Zoe's voice called from the living room. "Lucas says his truck can eat all my butterflies but I don't think that's true! Is it true?"

Reed laughed against my hair. "Duty calls."

"Damn," I muttered. "There goes our moment."

But as I went to referee the debate, I realized something else. This chaos, this life I'd built—I wasn't facing it alone anymore.

And for the first time in as long as I could remember, that didn't feel terrifying.

It felt like hope.

Chapter 16:

Lines Drawn

MALIYAH

The restaurant was everything Reed had promised—quiet, intimate, the kind of place where conversations stayed private and the wine list was longer than the menu. It wasn't crazy formal, but it was just the right amount of "date-night-sexy." We'd been going strong for three weeks now, ever since I'd told him about Bryce. He'd taken me out to several places, the kids sometimes too. But the ambiance here—this was my favorite.

"You're quiet tonight," Reed said, reaching across the table to brush his fingers against mine. "Everything okay?"

I smiled, turning my hand to catch his. "Just thinking about how nice this is. Quite the difference from last night's dinner where Lucas and Zoe's squabble ended in spaghetti all over my blouse."

"I thought it was a really sexy look," he said, his eyes bright and the corner of his mouth twitched upward as he took a sip of wine.

The server appeared with our appetizer—some kind of flatbread that looked too pretty to eat. Reed had ordered it, knowing I'd been eyeing it but hadn't wanted to order too much food—he knew I would pick at it even if I protested.

"How are they doing with staying at Felicity's tonight?" he asked, putting a piece of flatbread on my plate then on his.

"I'm sure they're fine. They've been begging for a sleepover, missing being with them all the time. I have it on good authority that a movie night with too much sugar should be underway right about now.

"It's good that they are so close to each other. Plus, they get a bunch of attention and all the junk food they want? Seems like a childhood dream." Reed took a sip of his wine, then set the glass down carefully. "It also gives us nights like this."

"Nights where we can actually finish conversations?"

"Nights where I can focus on you without little voices making exaggerated 'mwah-mwah' sounds from around the corner." He smiled, eyes crinkling at the memory of yesterday—how my lips had barely brushed his while I stirred pasta sauce when Zoe and Lucas had burst into the kitchen, Lucas covering his eyes with splayed fingers while still peeking through, Zoe dramatically jumping up and down singing "Mom and Reed k-i-s-s-i-n-g..." clearly that song has not gone extinct from when I was a kid. They'd squealed in delighted unison, before dissolving into giggles and running back to the den.

Reed's expression grew serious. "Speaking of focusing on you—I did some checking on Bryce." What he'd found hadn't been reassuring—Bryce worked for his family's consulting firm, had upgraded his home to an overly-expensive condo in Back Bay, and had exactly zero arrests or documented complaints. A clean record that could mean he was reformed or simply better at not getting caught.

"Have you heard anything more about—" I started to ask, then stopped. We'd agreed not to let Bryce dominate our conversations, not to give him power over the good things we were building. We both failed miserably at this, though.

"Nothing new," Reed said, understanding immediately. "But I've got a friend keeping an eye out. If he shows up anywhere he shouldn't, we'll know."

I nodded, grateful for the reassurance even as part of me wondered if we were being paranoid. It had been over a week since I'd last thought I'd seen him at the grocery store. I couldn't tell if I was going paranoid-crazy or if he was just good at making me feel that way. In the last few weeks I'd sworn I'd seen him on four separate occasions.

"Good evening."

The voice came from behind me, smooth and familiar in a way that made every muscle in my body tense. I knew without turning around, but I looked anyway.

Bryce stood beside our table, one hand resting on the back of an empty chair, looking exactly like he belonged there. He wore an expensive suit that probably cost more than my monthly rent, his dark hair perfectly styled, that same confident smile that had once made my heart race and later made my blood run cold.

Beside him stood Diane, her blonde hair pulled back in a neat bun, wearing a simple black dress that looked tailor-made to fit her. Her eyes darted between Reed and me, then quickly down and away.

"Maliyah," Bryce said, his voice warm like we were old friends meeting by chance. "What a pleasant surprise."

Reed's hand tightened around his wine glass. I could feel tension radiating from him, could see the way his shoulders had shifted into a more alert position.

"Bryce." I kept my voice steady, though my heart was hammering. "This is my boyfriend, Detective Reed Morrison. Reed, this is Bryce Callahan and his wife Diane."

Reed rose to his feet, towering over Bryce. The smaller man extended his hand in greeting, but Reed's arms remained at his sides, hands curled into loose fists. The air between them crackled with tension as Reed's jaw tightened, his eyes never leaving Bryce's face. After several uncomfortable seconds, Bryce's outstretched hand faltered, then slowly withdrew. His practiced smile dimmed as the power dynamic shifted visibly away from him.

"I know who you are and that you are ancient history." Reed said. It wasn't a question.

Bryce's slimy smile sliding back into place. "I'm glad to hear Maliyah still thinks about our times together. I certainly remember them fondly. In fact, I was just telling Diane how nice it was to run into Maliyah recently. Such a small world, Boston."

"Getting smaller all the time," Reed replied, his voice deceptively casual.

An uncomfortable silence stretched between us. Diane shifted from foot to foot, her purse clutched tightly in both hands. I noticed a faint yellow bruise on her wrist, mostly hidden by her sleeve but visible when she moved.

"Well," Bryce said finally, "we should let you get back to your dinner. Enjoy your evening."

He started to turn away, then paused as if something had just occurred to him. "Oh, Maliyah, I meant to ask—how are your children adjusting to the move? Such a big change for little ones."

The question hit like ice water. He was reminding me that he knew about Lucas and Zoe, that he'd seen them, that he remembered.

Reed moved with such sudden authority that Bryce instinctively retreated. Something in Reed's stance changed—shoulders squared, chin lifted slightly—as years of on the job experience transformed the space between them into his territory.

"I think you should move along now," Reed said, his voice low and controlled. "Before this conversation becomes less pleasant."

Bryce raised his hands in a gesture of innocence. "Just making conversation with an old friend."

"Maliyah is not your friend—old or otherwise." Reed stepped closer, close enough that Bryce had to tilt his head back slightly to maintain eye contact. "And her children are none of your concern. In fact, I'd prefer if you didn't think about them at all."

"Reed," I said quietly, not wanting this to escalate but I still felt grateful for his protection.

"Is there a problem here?" Bryce asked, his tone carefully reasonable, but I caught the flash of anger in his eyes. He wasn't used to being challenged, especially not by someone he didn't consider his equal.

"Not yet," Reed replied. "But there will be if you keep showing up where Maliyah and her family are. Funny coincidences have a way of becoming patterns, and patterns get noticed."

Diane tugged at Bryce's sleeve. "Honey, our table's ready," she said, her voice barely above a whisper.

Bryce's gaze flicked to Diane as if he'd momentarily forgotten her presence, then hardened as it returned to Reed. For a moment, I thought he might say something else, might push back against Reed's warning. Instead, he gave us his practiced smile and nodded.

"Of course. Enjoy your dinner." He looked at me one last time, his voice dropping a register. "It really was good to see you again, Maliyah. Take care of yourself."

They turned to follow the hostess who had been standing to the side for the entire interaction. A young girl who looked like a deer in the headlights at the interaction she'd just witnessed.

Bryce moved Diane in front of him keeping her in his sights for the walk to their table. I watched them go, noticing how Bryce's hand found the small of her back, and how quickly she seemed to recover after she shrank slightly at his touch—I remember those days where I'd also experience the fear at the thought of him noticing a flinch or slight movement away from him.

Reed sat back down, but his posture remained alert, his eyes tracking Bryce's movement across the restaurant.

"You okay?" he asked, reaching for my hand again.

I realized I was shaking. "Yeah. I just... I don't think that was a coincidence."

"Neither do I." Reed's jaw was tight. "He knew we'd be here."

The thought sent a chill through me. How could he have known? We'd made these dinner plans this morning.

"How would he know that?"

Reed was quiet for a moment, thinking. "I don't know, but we need to stay alert."

The idea that Bryce might have been following any of us made my stomach twist.

"What do we do?"

"We finish our dinner," Reed said firmly. "We don't let him ruin our night. But tomorrow, I'm going to have a conversation with a few people, see what we can find out about his movements."

"That feels like an investigation."

"It's not—not yet, at least. But it's about to become one if he keeps this up." Reed's expression was grim. "That wasn't a coincidence, Maliyah. And the way he asked about the kids..." He shook his head. "That was a message."

I knew he was right. Bryce had always been subtle, always careful to maintain plausible deniability. But I'd learned to read between the lines, to hear the threats wrapped in polite conversation.

"Did you see Diane?" I asked.

Reed nodded. "Scared. And she had a bruise on her wrist."

"You noticed it too?"

He nodded and we sat in silence for a moment, both lost in our own thoughts. Around us, the restaurant continued its evening rhythm—couples sharing dessert, friends laughing over wine, normal people having normal dinners.

"I'm sorry," I said finally.

"For what?"

"For bringing this into your life. For—"

"Stop." Reed's voice was firm but gentle. "You didn't bring anything into my life. He did. And we're going to deal with him together, remember? As a team."

I managed a small smile. "As a team."

The server approached hesitantly, probably sensing the tension at our table. "Is everything alright? Can I get you anything else?"

Reed looked at me, raising an eyebrow in question.

"Actually," I said, "could we get the check? I think we're ready to go."

As we waited for the bill, I found myself glancing toward where Bryce and Diane were seated across the restaurant. They looked like any other couple having dinner—him leaning forward, talking animatedly, her listening with what appeared to be rapt attention. But I could see the tension in her shoulders, the way she kept her hands carefully folded in her lap.

"I wish we could do something," I said quietly. "About Diane."

Reed followed my gaze. "You know as well as I do that you need to want to be saved in order to accept help offered. Do you think she's ready for that?"

"I don't know." Taking a sip of my water, I pushed my chair out, "I'm going to run to the restroom before we head out."

"Can you wait til they bring the check and I can follow? I don't like the idea of you being out of my sight when that bastard is around."

"I think it should be okay. I won't be long. I promise. And I'll bring my phone with me, okay?" I leaned down and kissed his cheek.

Reed exhaled slowly, his shoulders dropping as he leaned back in his chair. His eyes followed me for a moment, then he gestured toward the restrooms with an open palm. "Go ahead, I'll be right here...watching him and keeping an eye out," he said quietly, already reaching for his phone to place it on the table between us.

I leaned down, kissed him quickly and went to walk to the bathroom.

Chapter 17:

Echoes

MALIYAH

As we walked to his car, Reed's fingers slid between mine, warm and strong—his calluses making my hand tingle. The rough pad of his thumb brushed over my knuckle, then traced a slow circle that sent electricity racing up my arm. My breath caught as the sensation bloomed in my chest, warm and unexpected—pulling me from my thoughts for a moment.

"You okay?" he asked once we were inside, engine idling.

"Yeah. Just... processing."

He pulled out of the parking spot, heading in the direction of my apartment.

"I talked to her," I said finally. "Diane. In the bathroom."

Reed's hands tightened on the steering wheel. "I wondered. Saw her head in the direction of the bathroom after you went. How did it go?"

I stared out the window at the passing streetlights. "I told her I'd been where she is. That she's not alone." I touched the scar along my hairline unconsciously. "Shared some of my experiences with Bryce."

Reed was quiet, letting me continue.

"She said Bryce told her I was unstable. That I made accusations to hurt him after we broke up." I laughed bitterly. "Of course he did. I'm not even surprised."

"Did she believe you?"

"I think part of her did. She didn't defend him, not really." I pulled a business card from my purse. "I gave her this," I said, holding up the glossy card with its delicate pink and gold lettering. "It's a business card for Serenity Salon, a little place down the street from the shelter. The phone number printed here," I tapped the embossed digits, "leads to a second on-call line we each take turns having forwarded to an app on our phones. When it rings, we answer with 'Serenity Salon, how may I help you?' The owner, Jenna—she had her own hard experiences—years of abuse. She actually came up with the idea years ago and the staff told me they've saved so many women. We've gotten eight women to safety this way in the past year alone."

"Shit. That's fucking smart."

"I thought so. I shared the idea with my old boss too. Anyways, I gave her the card—told her to either take it or even memorize the number and throw it away if she was nervous about him checking."

He nodded his head. "Good. That's the way to do it."

"Yeah, I hope she gets away from him. But really, I don't know." I closed my eyes. "She started making excuses for him. 'It's not always bad. Sometimes he's wonderful. He just gets stressed with work, and I know I can be difficult—'" My voice cracked. "The kinds of things I hear all the time now—words I've even said myself," I whispered.

His hand found mine again, squeezing tight.

I let silence fill the car again. Thinking about my conversation, replaying the words over and over again. "You know, she asked me if I was happy. With my new life."

"What did you tell her?"

"The truth. That leaving him was the best thing I'd ever done. That I have two beautiful children, a career I love, people who care about me." I looked at him. "That she could have that too."

"Do you think she'll call?"

"I don't know. She took the card. Whether she'll use it..." I shrugged helplessly. "She has to be ready."

Reed nodded slowly. "When Diane went to the bathroom, I don't think Bryce realized you'd already gone. Then he saw your seat was empty. He looked furious, and I think he even considered going after her."

"But he didn't."

"No. He wised up—realized I was watching." Reed's jaw tightened. "He kept checking his watch, timing how long the two of you were gone."

The thought made my stomach twist.

"But then Diane came back," Reed continued. "Leaned close to him, whispered something. And his whole expression changed. Went from ready to explode to looking like he'd won something."

"She probably told him I tried to turn her against him. That he was right about me being crazy or something."

"Would be smart," Reed said. "Help her stay safe."

"Yeah." But it still hurt, knowing Bryce had probably twisted my attempt to help into another victory for himself.

We drove in silence for a few minutes, the city lights blurring past the windows.

"Are you sorry you went after her?" Reed asked as we approached my neighborhood.

"No. I couldn't not try. Even if it makes things harder for me." I looked at him. "Even if Bryce sees it as me interfering in his life."

"Which he will."

"I know." The weight of that settled over me. "He knows where I work now. What I do. He'll see this as a threat."

Reed pulled up to my building and put the car in park. "Maliyah, I need you to promise me something."

"What?"

"Promise me you'll be careful. Extra careful. You know as well as I do that men like Bryce are unstable."

"I promise to be careful. But Reed, I can't live in fear. I did that for years with him. I won't do it again."

"I'm not asking you to live in fear. I just want you to keep your guard up and maybe, just maybe—" His blue eyes were intense in the dim light. "Let me help you stay safe. Please."

The vulnerability in his voice got to me more than any demand would have. "Okay. I know I might seem like I don't want your help. I'm just—I guess, it's just that I'm so used to doing this alone."

"You're not alone. I'm right here." He echoed.

He walked me to my door, his hand a steady pressure at the small of my back. Inside, I moved to the kitchen while Reed began his now-familiar routine—checking window latches, pulling curtains closed, testing the back door's lock.

I filled the electric kettle and pulled out my phone, seeing a text from Felicity.

Felicity: Kids are asleep. Movie was a hit. They want to stay tomorrow too.

Me: Tell them I love them. I'll pick them up in the morning—don't go trying to steal my kids from me.

Felicity: They love me more. I come with ice cream and their favorite cousin. Sorry Bish! J/k. Love you. Don't hurt me.

I laughed at her ridiculousness. Leave it to my sister to give me something to smile about.

Felicity: *You have a good time tonight? Did you make smoochies? Are you getting naked? Did he toot your horn?*

Me: *Are you drunk? High? Tell the truth. Should I come get my kids you maniac?*

Felicity: *Haha. Shut up. No. Just happy for my sister. Asshole. lol*

Me: *Haha. Love you too*

Felicity: Go have fun with Reed. The kids are happy and safe in bed probably dreaming of the sugar filled breakfast I have planned for them before their mom comes to get them! ;)

Me: Thanks. I'll remember that and pay you back ten-fold one day!

Felicity: xoxo

I looked up at Reed where he stood across the counter. He'd come into the kitchen and pulled down two teabags, setting one in each mug—tags draped over the edges. I hadn't even asked for tea yet, but there he was, anticipating. My smile came before I could think to stop it.

I set my phone on the charger and went to join him when a sharp knock echoed through the apartment.

Three deliberate raps against the door.

Reed's head snapped up, his hand moving instinctively toward his hip where his off duty weapon rested. "You expecting someone?"

"No." My voice came out thin, my pulse hammering in my throat.

"Wait here." His voice was low, controlled—the detective voice I'd heard him use at the restaurant.

He approached the door with careful, measured steps. Put his eye to the peephole. His body went rigid.

He looked back at me, pressed his index finger to his lips for silence, then jabbed it toward the kitchen alcove. I quickly moved out of sight of the door.

Reed's other hand hovered near his hip. The door hinges gave a soft whine as he twisted the handle and yanked it open in one fluid motion, his body angled sideways, shoulders squared.

Nothing. The doorway was empty.

The hallway was completely empty.

Reed stood in the doorway, body still coiled and ready, scanning left and right. The fluorescent lights hummed overhead, casting their harsh glow on worn carpet and scuffed walls. Nothing moved. No footsteps retreated down the stairs, no doors clicked shut, no elevator dinged its arrival.

Nothing.

"Stay back," Reed said quietly, stepping into the hallway.

I watched from the doorway as he moved to the stairwell door, checked it, then walked to the elevator. The indicator lights showed it hadn't moved from the ground floor.

He checked the other apartments on our floor—four doors, all closed, no sounds coming from within. He came back to me, his expression grim.

"No one."

"Someone knocked." My voice came out defensive, like I needed to prove I hadn't imagined it.

"I know." He ushered me back inside and locked the door, engaging both the deadbolt and chain. "Could have been a neighbor with the wrong apartment. Or kids playing around."

"At this time of night?"

His silence was answer enough. We both knew what we were thinking but neither of us wanted to say it out loud.

What if it had been Bryce?

But how could it be? We'd just left the restaurant all of half an hour ago. Could he have followed us here?

Reed moved to the window overlooking the street, peering down at the cars parked along the curb. "I'm calling this in."

"Reed, no. What are you going to tell them? Someone knocked on my door and left?"

He turned to face me. "I'm going to tell them that your ex-boyfriend, who has a documented history of domestic violence, may be stalking you. That tonight he made contact at a restaurant, made veiled threats about your children, and now someone's doing knock-and-runs at your apartment." His voice was firm, brooking no argument. "This needs to be documented, Maliyah. You need a paper trail."

I nodded, knowing he was right even as part of me wanted to pretend it was nothing. Just some kid, just a mistake, just paranoia.

But I'd learned a long time ago that ignoring warning signs didn't make them go away.

Reed made his call, speaking in low tones with whoever was on the other end. I moved to the couch and sat down, my legs suddenly unsteady.

Through the window, I could see the street below—cars parked along the curb, streetlights casting pools of yellow light, shadows between buildings.

Was someone down there? Watching?

Or was I being paranoid?

The kettle in the kitchen had gone silent—the water long since boiled and automatically shut off. I'd forgotten about the tea.

"I'll make fresh," Reed said, hanging up. "They're sending a patrol car to do a sweep of the area. They'll check the building, talk to the landlord about security footage if there is any."

"There isn't. My landlord is too cheap for cameras." I looked up at him, feeling the familiar burn behind my eyes—not from fear, but from sheer frustration. "I'm so fucking angry, Reed."

"I know." He crossed to me, pulled me up from the couch and into his arms.

"I'm angry at Bryce. Angry at myself for not seeing what he was back then. Angry at the whole damned world." My voice cracked. "I just want to feel safe in my own home. Is that too much to ask?"

"No. It's not." His arms tightened around me. "And we're going to make sure you are safe. I promise you that."

"You can't promise that."

"Then I'm staying tonight." His tone left no room for argument. "Couch is fine. I just need to be here."

Part of me wanted to protest, to prove I could handle this on my own. But a larger part—the part that was still hearing that knock echo in my mind, still imagining Bryce's smug smile at the restaurant—felt nothing but relief.

"Okay," I whispered. "Thank you."

He turned the kettle back on while I sank back onto the couch. Every sound made me tense now. Every creak of the building settling, every voice in the hallway, every distant siren. My body was on high alert, adrenaline making my hands shake.

Reed brought me tea, sat beside me, and we waited in silence for the patrol car to arrive.

Twenty minutes felt like hours.

When the knock finally came—official, authoritative—Reed checked the peephole before opening the door.

Two uniformed officers stood in the hallway. The shorter one, stocky with dark hair, introduced himself as Officer Santos. His partner, tall and lanky with sandy-blonde hair, was Officer Harrison.

They took our statements—the restaurant encounter, Bryce's veiled threats about my children, the pattern of contact since the farmer's market. When I mentioned the documented history from fifteen years ago, both officers' expressions hardened. I pulled up my phone, showed them the password-protected folder with hospital records, police reports, photos I'd kept all these years.

Santos and Harrison exchanged looks as they reviewed the documentation. Three broken ribs, ruptured eardrum requiring surgery, concussion, facial lacerations. The kind of injuries that spoke for themselves.

They suggested filing for a restraining order. Gave me the information for the victim's advocate office where I could find someone to help with the application. Explained the process: gather the evidence, file, prepare for a hearing. With my history and the recent pattern of contact, they thought I had a solid case.

"And if I get it?" I asked.

Reed's jaw tightened. "Then he has to stay away. No calls, no texts, and he can't try to get someone else to do it on his behalf either. Can't come near your apartment, the center, or the kids' school. And if he violates it, there are consequences."

Santos nodded. "Document everything between now and the hearing. Times, dates, witnesses. Vary your routine—don't make yourself predictable." He handed Reed his card. "We'll include this address in our patrol routes. Anything else happens, call 911 first, then reach out to me directly."

As I walked them out, Santos turned to Reed, "Take care, Detective. We'll keep an eye out tonight." After they left, Reed locked the door—deadbolt, chain, handle—and joined me in the living room.

"A restraining order," I said quietly. "I'm scared. Do you think that will just piss him off more?"

"I'm not sure we can take the chance to not try." He sat beside me. "I don't like the intentions this guy might have rolling around in his head."

I looked at him—at this man who'd been here for me, for my kids. Who'd come in and made sure my place was secure, that I felt safe. Who'd helped me talk to the officers without taking control. This man who I knew was already planning to sleep on my shitty couch just to keep watch tonight.

"Reed, you don't have to do all this."

"I know." His voice was soft but firm. "But I want to. I'm going to be right here with you."

His voice was quiet but certain, the kind that made the noise in my head finally still for a moment. His words were comforting. But they also scared me because I was starting to need them too much. Starting to rely on Reed being there, being my protection, being my safe place.

And needing someone meant they could hurt you when they left.

But sitting there in my living room, Reed beside me, I let myself believe—just for tonight—that maybe this time would be different.

That maybe this time, it wasn't too much to hope for someone to actually stay.

Chapter 18:

The Weight of Protection

MALIYAH

A week had passed since that night. For the last seven nights Reed had been sleeping on my couch, his presence a steady comfort in the darkness. Each morning he'd leave for work after helping me get the kids ready for school, then come back at night with takeout and that determined look that said he wasn't going anywhere.

I hadn't asked him to stay. After that first night, he'd simply shown up the next night with an overnight bag and his phone charger, settling onto my couch like he belonged there. Lucas had started calling the couch "Reed's bed," and Zoe had taken to leaving her stuffed animals arranged on his pile of linens during the day—her way of making sure he'd come back.

We'd fallen into a routine. Dinner together, homework help for Lucas, bedtime stories for Zoe. Then Reed would make sure we were locked up tight while I made tea, and we'd sit together in the quiet, talking about everything and nothing until my eyelids grew heavy. Every night, he'd tell me to go to bed. Every night, I'd see the glow from his phone in the living room as I drifted off to sleep.

It felt dangerous, this growing dependence. This need for him to be there. But I was too tired to fight it.

On Monday morning, I'd met with a victim's advocate, Maria Bonano, at the courthouse. Reed had offered to come, but I'd told him I wanted to do it myself. He'd already done so much, and I felt like I still had something to prove to myself.

Maria's office had been small, tucked inside the courthouse with no windows and a single fake plant—unsurprising given the complete lack of sunlight. She was younger than I'd expected—around my age, maybe mid-to-late-thirties—with kind eyes and a no-nonsense demeanor that immediately put me at ease.

"Okay, Ms. Davenport. Let's walk through this together." She'd spread the documents I'd brought across her desk—hospital records, photos from back when we'd been together—so violent-looking that they still made my stomach turn, the police report with its clinical description of that final time—the worst of them all. "This is good documentation. Very thorough."

I'd twisted my hands in my lap. "Is it enough?"

"It's more than enough for the petition. The question is whether the judge will grant a temporary order." Maria had made notes on a legal pad. "The prior assault is significant. The fact you needed surgery shows how severe it was. Add to it that you left the state for as long as fifteen years shows your fear was substantial."

"What about the recent contacts?"

"Absolutely. Multiple encounters so soon after you came back—the farmer's market, the restaurant, and the incident at your apartment building—that establishes a pattern." She'd looked up at me. "Has there been any contact since that Thursday night?"

"No. Nothing."

"Good. That may actually help. It shows he's capable of staying away, which would mean if he makes contact after being served, it could establish a deliberate violation." She'd pulled out a fresh form. "Let's start filling this out. I'll need specific dates, times, and details for every interaction."

For the next hour, I'd recounted everything. The way Bryce had looked at my kids at the market. Seeing him around. The casual menace he exhibited at the restaurant. The sound of that knock echoing through my apartment, the violation of knowing someone had forced their way into my building.

"And you're certain it was him?" Maria had asked about the knock.

"I can't prove it. But yes. I'm certain."

She'd nodded, writing. "Your certainty matters. It also helps that you're trained to recognize threatening behavior given your career."

When we'd finished, Maria had organized the papers into a neat stack. "I'll file this today. The hearing will be scheduled within ten days, probably next week. In the meantime, keep documenting everything. If he contacts you, if you see him, if anything feels off—write it down."

"What are my chances?" I'd needed to hear it again.

Maria had met my eyes. "Honestly? I'd be surprised if the judge doesn't grant the temporary order. Your case is strong. The prior violence, the geographic separation, the recent pattern—it all points to someone who poses a credible threat."

I'd felt something loosen in my chest. Not relief, exactly. But hope.

That afternoon, Reed texted me.

Reed: *How'd it go?*

Me: *Good. Advocate is going to file everything. Should hear back soon about the temporary order.*

Reed: *Great. Listen, I have an idea. Can you get someone to watch the kids tonight?*

Me: *Probably. Why?*

Reed: *I want to teach you some self-defense stuff. Basic moves that might help—just in case. I'd feel better if you knew some things.*

Me: *I've done some stuff with the Florida shelter, but it's been a while. I'll call Felicity.*

At seven, I met Reed at a small gym near the precinct. It was mostly empty—just a few people on treadmills and one guy doing pull-ups in the corner. Reed had reserved one of the private training rooms in the back.

"You didn't have to do this," I said as he held the door open for me.

"I know. But as hard as it is to consider, a restraining order is just paper. If Bryce decides to violate it, you need to be able to protect yourself until help arrives."

The room was lined with mats, one wall covered in mirrors. Reed had changed into athletic pants and a t-shirt. I felt suddenly self-conscious in my leggings and tank top—arm flab and all, but I put away my self-deprecating thoughts and committed to focusing.

"Okay," he said, moving to the center of the room. "First thing you need to know—the goal isn't to win a fight. The goal is to create an opening and get away. That's it."

"Got it."

"I want you to remember the acronym A.V.A.D.E.—Avoid, Validate: meaning validate his feelings and use empathy to de-escalate or distract him. Avert, so try to redirect or defuse before it gets physical. Defend—if it's unavoidable then defend yourself, and lastly, Escape."

I repeated the acronym back to him a few times, committing it to memory.

"Okay, let's go through some foundations. Most attackers rely on surprise and intimidation. They expect you to freeze or to be easily overpowered." He demonstrated a basic stance. "Your best weapons are the ones he won't expect—elbows, knees, the heel of your palm, your voice."

"My voice?"

"Yelling does two things. It can startle an attacker, and it draws attention. Never fight in silence if you can help it." He positioned himself in front of me. "Now, if someone grabs you from the front, like this—" His hands closed around my upper arms, firm but not painful. "What do you do?"

My breath caught. The room tilted sideways, Reed's face blurring into someone else's. My skin burned where his fingers pressed, and I could taste the copper tang of blood in my mouth, hear Bryce's low growl in my memory—"Don't you know how stupid you are? Are you too stupid to even know?"—feel the wall against my back, nowhere left to go.

"Maliyah." Reed's voice was gentle. He immediately released me, stepping back. "You okay?"

I nodded, swallowing hard. "Yeah. Sorry. Just... caught me off guard."

"Do you need a minute?"

"No." I shook my head firmly. "No, I want to learn this. I need to learn this."

Reed studied my face for a moment, then nodded. "Okay. But if at any point you need to stop, you tell me. Deal?"

"Deal."

He moved closer again, more slowly this time. "I'm going to grab your arms again. Remember, you're safe. This is practice. And I'll let go the second you ask me to, but I really want you to try and fight back."

This time, when his hands closed around my arms, I focused on him. On the concern in his eyes, the tension in his jaw. This wasn't Bryce. This was Reed. This was safe.

"Good," he said quietly. "Now, defend yourself. Bring your arms up fast and hard, breaking my grip outward." He demonstrated in slow motion. "Then step back and assess. Can you run? Do you need to strike? Always look for the exit."

We practiced the movement over and over. His grip got progressively stronger, more realistic. Each time, I broke free a little faster.

"Excellent. Now let's try from behind." He moved around me. "This is scarier because you can't see the attacker, but you have more options. If someone grabs you like this—" His arms wrapped around me from behind, pinning my arms to my sides.

My heart rate spiked. The mirror showed us—him behind me, so much bigger, so much stronger—

"Breathe," Reed said against my ear. "Feel where my weight is. Where are the weak points?"

I forced myself to think instead of panic. "I know this one. Miss Congeniality."

"Huh?" he asked.

"Yeah! Sandra Bullock taught all of us S.I.N.G.! Solar plexus, instep, nose, groin!"

Reed's eyes widened in recognition. "Right." His hands settled on my shoulders, positioning me. "Like this." He guided my elbow backward in slow motion until it hovered an inch from his solar plexus. His breath warmed my ear as he whispered, "Full force, this would knock the wind out of him." His foot nudged mine wider. "Now your heel—" I felt the gentle pressure as he tapped my instep against his. His fingers tilted my chin up slightly, our reflection catching in the mirror—his tall frame behind me, my eyes wider than I'd realized. "Head back here," he murmured, "or fist up—use the heel of your palm, not a closed fist. Then—" His hand slid down to my knee, raising it slightly. "And run. Don't look back. Take the chance to escape as soon as you get it."

"Escape."

"Escape." He released me. "Want to try it for real? I'll hold on, you break free. I promise I'll let you go once you execute the moves."

"Okay."

This time when he grabbed me, I didn't freeze. I knocked back, stomped down hard on where his foot would be—well, sorta hard since it's Reed and not the shit-bag. His grip loosened slightly.

"Good! Now the head—careful, just the motion—"

I snapped my head back, knocking just a bit into his nose until I heard him grunt.

"Perfect." He released me completely. "And?"

"Escape." I stepped away, putting distance between us.

"Exactly." He was breathing a little hard, a slight smile on his face. "You're a natural."

We spent the next hour running through scenarios. What to do if someone grabbed my wrist. How to use my keys as a weapon. The vulnerable
points on the human body—eyes, throat, groin, knees. Where to strike
for maximum impact.

By the time we finished, I was a mass of sweat and my muscles were
trembling, but I felt... different. Not invincible. Not fearless. But, even
I had to admit, I felt empowered.

"One more thing," Reed said, pulling two small canisters from his gym
bag. "Pepper spray. One for your purse, one for your keychain. Have you
ever used it?"

I turned the canister over in my palm, surprised by its lightness. "I had one
years ago, but it was this huge bulky thing that wouldn't fit in my purse.
This is tiny. Will something this small actually stop someone like Bryce?"

"It will. These little canisters pack a serious punch." He showed me how
to hold it, how to aim, how to spray in a sweeping motion rather than
a single stream. "It's effective up to ten feet, but aim for six to eight
for accuracy. Hold your breath when you spray so you don't catch the
blowback. Aim for the face, spray, and run. Don't wait to see if it worked.
Just go."

"Spray and run. Got it."

Reed handed me the canisters. "Practice taking it out of your purse. You
need to be able to grab it fast, without looking. Muscle memory."

I practiced the motion—hand in purse, fingers finding the canister,
thumb on the trigger—until it felt automatic.

"Good." Reed checked his watch. "We should probably head out. Don't
want Felicity to think I kidnapped you."

As I gathered my things, Reed caught my arm gently, pulling me in and
resting his palm on the side of my face while touching his nose to mine.
"I know this stuff is scary. But you did great tonight."

"I'm still terrified."

"That's okay. Fear can be useful if you don't let it paralyze you." He leaned
in for a short kiss. "The restraining order will help. And now you have
tools if you need them. That's all we can do—be prepared and hope we
never have to use any of it."

On the drive back to my apartment, I caught myself practicing the movements in my head. Break the grip. Strike the vulnerable points. Escape.

"Thank you," I said as Reed pulled up to my building. "For today. For
everything."

"You don't have to thank me." His expression was serious in the dim light from the street lamps. "I just want you to be safe."

"I know. But still. Thank you."

He parked and came upstairs with me. Felicity had already put the kids to bed, and she gave us both knowing looks before gathering her things to leave.

"They were angels," she said, kissing my cheek. "Lucas finished his homework without being asked, and Zoe made it into three of the five agreed-upon bedtime stories before she passed out."

After she left, Reed moved methodically through the apartment, his fingers testing each window latch with a soft click. I watched his shoulders relax slightly when the deadbolt slid home with a satisfying thunk. In the kitchen, the kettle whistled as I pulled down two mugs. The blanket and pillow I'd arranged on the couch still held the indent from where he'd lain the night before, positioned perfectly between my bedroom door and the apartment entrance.

"You should get some actual sleep tonight," I said, handing him a mug. "You must be exhausted."

"I'm staying—at least until the restraining order comes through." His tone left no room for argument. "Once that's official, once Bryce gets served and knows there are legal consequences, then we can relax a little. But until then—" He settled onto the couch, pulling the throw blanket over his lap. "I'm not leaving you and the kids alone at night."

Something warm bloomed in my chest. "Reed—"

"Please don't argue. Just accept that I'm a stubborn asshole who's going to camp out on your very uncomfortable couch until I know you're protected."

I smiled despite myself. "It's not that uncomfortable."

He shifted, and the couch let out a creak that sounded like a complaint. "My spine is finding places between these cushions I'm sure no one knew existed." He rotated his shoulder with a wince, but his eyes stayed soft, crinkling at the corners. "I'd sleep on a bed of nails if it meant being as close as this is to the front door."

We talked for another hour, our voices low, about everything and nothing. Work stories, childhood memories, the kind of random topics that come up when it's late and you're tired but don't want the conversation to end. Eventually, my eyelids grew heavy.

"Go to bed," Reed said gently. "I'll be right here."

"You sure?"

"Positive. Go."

I stood, then on impulse, bent down toward him. My fingers found the warmth of his stubbled jaw, rough like sandpaper against my fingertips. Our lips met, soft and tentative at first, then with quiet certainty. His breath caught—a small, vulnerable sound that rippled through the stillness of the apartment. I lingered there, feeling the steady thrum of his pulse beneath my thumb as it traced the sharp curve of his cheekbone. The faint scent of his soap filled my senses before I pulled away. My eyes stayed closed for a moment after, savoring the ghost of his touch.

I pressed my lips together, the warmth of our kiss still lingering there. "Goodnight, Reed." The words barely disturbed the air between us.

His eyes caught the dim light as he looked up at me. "Goodnight, Maliyah."

As I lay in bed, I could see the glow from the living room—Reed on his phone, probably scrolling through social media. Knowing he was there, knowing I wasn't facing this alone, made sleep come easier than it had in days.

Maria had said we'd hear about the temporary order by the end of the week. Three more days of Reed on my couch. Three more days of this fragile peace.

For the first time since seeing Bryce at the farmer's market, I felt something close to safe.

For the love of all things holy, let it last.

Chapter 19:

Paper Shields

MALIYAH

Thursday afternoon, my phone rang while I was in the middle of a staff meeting. Maria Bonano's name lit up the screen.

"Excuse me," I said to my team, stepping into the hallway. "I need to take this."

"Ms. Davenport? I have good news and a question. The court has an opening for a hearing tomorrow—Friday at ten AM. I know it's short notice, but if you can make it, we can get the temporary order in place immediately rather than waiting until next week."

My pulse hammered in my throat as I gripped the phone tighter. "T-tomorrow?" The word came out breathless before I steadied myself against the wall. "Yes, I can be there."

"Good. This will be a brief hearing—you'll need to testify about the assault history and recent contacts. If the judge grants the temporary order, Bryce will be served immediately, and then we'll have the full hearing for the permanent order in about ten days. Can you get off work?"

"Yes. Absolutely."

"Meet me at the courthouse at nine-thirty. We'll go over everything before we go in."

After I hung up, I leaned against the cool wall of the hallway, my phone still clutched in my hand. My heartbeat thudded in my ears. Tomorrow. The fluorescent lights buzzed overhead as I tried to swallow past the dryness in my throat. Less than twenty-four hours, and I'd be facing the judge, reliving my past, my words becoming permanent record.

I texted Reed immediately.

Me: *Hearing for TRO is tomorrow at 10 AM. I have to testify. I'm nervous.*

The response came within minutes.

Reed: *You've got this. What time do you need to be there?*

Me: *9:30 to prep with Maria. Hearing at 10.*

Reed: *I'll be there.*

Something in my chest loosened.

Me: *You don't have to come*

Reed: I'll be there. We'll plan when I get to your place tonight.

On Friday morning, Reed had left for work early—before I was even awake. He'd needed to get some hours in so he could take time out of his day for my hearing. He was already waiting on the courthouse steps when I arrived at nine-ten, two coffee cups in hand. He'd shaved, put on a suit, and the sight of him standing there—solid, present, real—made my eyes sting with unexpected tears.

"Hey," he said softly, handing me a cup. "Got your favorite."

"Thank you."

After kissing my cheek, he pulled back and studied my face. "How are you doing?"

"Terrified."

His hand found my elbow, warm through the fabric of my blazer. "That's allowed." His eyes, steady on mine, crinkled slightly at the corners. "When you're in there—" he paused, his thumb brushing a small circle against my arm, "—just breathe. Your voice might shake. That's okay. Let the judge see the real you and understand what you're going through."

Maria arrived moments later, and after introductions, she and I went inside to prepare while Reed waited in the hallway.

The hearing room was small—more like a large office than a courtroom. Judge Martinez sat behind a modest desk, her reading glasses perched on her nose as she reviewed the file in front of her. There was no witness stand, no jury box, no gallery of observers. Just a couple of chairs facing a desk, a court reporter in the corner, and harsh fluorescent lighting overhead.

"Ms. Davenport, please have a seat." Judge Martinez gestured to the chair across from her. "This is an informal proceeding, but you'll still need to be sworn in."

After the oath, the judge looked at me directly. "Tell me about your relationship with Bryce Callahan."

I gripped the edge of my chair, the wood digging into my palms as Judge Martinez nodded for me to continue. My voice started steady, describing how Bryce's temper first appeared six or so months in—a shattered glass against the wall when I'd been late for dinner because of an exam. Then came the grip on my wrist that left fingerprint bruises, the "accidents" that weren't accidents at all. I faltered when I reached that final night—the sound of my own ribs cracking, the split lip, my body broken and lying on the cold linoleum as I waited for the ambulance, certain I would die there on our kitchen floor as the world around me had gone quiet from my broken eardrum.

"And you left Massachusetts after that?"

"Yes, Your Honor. I moved to Florida. I was afraid of him." I could hear the wavering in my voice and the blood moving through my system—even my fingertips pulsed with the rush of nerves.

"You were gone for fifteen years?"

"Yes."

"And you returned approximately six months ago?"

"Yes. I wanted to be back here with my family. They'd been through some rough times so I came to help. I didn't want to be alone and away from them anymore. I wanted my kids to be raised with family around them."

Judge Martinez made notes as I spoke, occasionally asking clarifying questions. When I described the recent encounters—the farmer's market, the restaurant, the knock on my door and the broken entry door—she leaned forward.

"And how did these encounters make you feel?"

"Terrified. After fifteen years of feeling safe, suddenly he was everywhere. At places I go with my children. I'd thought that, after all this time, we'd be safe. I was wrong."

The judge reviewed the hospital records Maria had submitted, the photos, the police report. She asked about the timeline, whether I'd had any contact with Bryce during those years away (none), about the frequency of the recent encounters.

From start to finish, the whole hearing took less than thirty minutes.

Finally, Judge Martinez looked up. "Ms. Davenport, I'm granting the temporary restraining order. Mr. Callahan will be served today and must maintain a distance of five hundred feet. No contact, direct or indirect. A hearing for a permanent order will be scheduled within ten days where Mr. Callahan will have the opportunity to respond. You'll be notified of the date."

"Thank you, Your Honor."

Outside in the hallway, Reed stood with his back against the wall, phone clutched in one hand, the other jammed into his pocket. His head snapped up at the sound of the door. His eyes found mine, searching, then his shoulders dropped an inch. In two strides he was there, his arms enveloping me, his suit jacket rough against my cheek, his cologne mingling with the cold courthouse air.

"You did it," he murmured against my hair as he held me close.

"I did it." I let myself lean into him for just a moment. "Thank you for being here."

"Where else would I be?"

The permanent hearing turned out to be pretty uneventful. Bryce didn't even show.

Reed had offered to come again, but I'd insisted he didn't need to take more time off work. "I've got this," I'd told him. "And you'll be there when I get home."

He'd kissed me and made me promise to text him as soon as it was over.

The hearing itself was quick. Without Bryce, there was no one to object. When the Judge granted the permanent order, I felt something like vindication.

Me: *Permanent order granted. Bryce didn't even show. I'm okay. Heading home now.*

Reed: *I'll meet you there. I'm so proud of you.*

Six months. That's how long Reed and I had been together when everything changed. Two months had gone by since I got the protective order. Two months of peace, of routine, of letting myself believe Bryce was really gone. Reed came for dinner several times a week, helped Lucas with homework, played endless games with Zoe. Sometimes I let myself believe this was permanent.

Sometimes I'd catch him watching us—Zoe sitting with a picture book, Lucas showing him a new video game trick—with this look of wonder, like he'd stumbled into someone else's life. Then his phone would buzz or the clock would hit nine, and he'd start gathering his things. I'd find myself straightening his collar before he left, letting my fingers linger just a moment too long, memorizing the warmth of him, while my chest ached with all the words I couldn't say.

Things changed though. And I should have realized how undeserving I was of that happily ever after. It was a Tuesday evening in late Fall when I blinked and my happiness fell apart.

Reed had just finished helping Lucas with a pain-in-the-ass of a math assignment and had offered to wash dishes while I put Zoe to bed.

"You know," I said, coming back into the kitchen and wrapping my arms around him from behind, "you're getting pretty good at this whole family thing."

He turned in my arms, his smile soft. "Yeah?"

I stood on my toes and kissed him. "The kids love you. I love—" I caught myself, the word hanging between us like a soap bubble. "I love spending time with you." My cheeks burned as I turned away, busying myself with wiping down the already-clean counter. Reed smiled and I felt a warmth fill my chest. There was still something holding him back though, and I held back a part of me because of it. Just last Saturday, when Lucas had asked if Reed would coach his soccer team next season, Reed had ruffled his hair and changed the subject.

His expression shifted, became more serious. "Maliyah, I've been thinking—"

His phone buzzed. Then buzzed again. And again.

"Sorry," he muttered, pulling it out. His face changed as he read the messages. "Shit."

"What is it?"

"Officer down call. All hands." He was already grabbing his jacket. "I'm sorry, I have to—"

I swallowed the lump in my throat and stepped back, my arms crossing over my chest. "Go," I said, the word catching slightly. My fingers dug into my biceps as I added, "Be safe," hating the feeling of watching someone I cared about rush toward danger.

He kissed me quickly, fiercely. "I'll text you when I can."

Then he was gone, the door closing behind him with a soft click that shouldn't have felt so permanent. I stood frozen, aching inside with something deep I couldn't name—at least, not yet.

Chapter 20:

In an Instant

REED

The drive to Dorchester was short, but long enough to think about the way Maliyah had almost said it. I love—

She'd caught herself. But I'd heard it anyway.

And I'd felt it—that surge of panic I thought I'd buried, but intermingled with a depth I never thought I deserved. Because I still knew that loving me meant trusting I'd come home. What if Lucas and Zoe woke up one morning to learn the same lesson I had—that the people you count on can disappear without warning?

I gripped the steering wheel tighter, pushing the thoughts away. It wouldn't happen like that. John told me to keep trusting that I wouldn't end like my father—that I'd keep coming home to them. I'd been doing so much better, but shit like today's "officer down" call made the bitterness well up inside.

The scene in Dorchester was already controlled when I arrived. Paramedics loading Brick, a beat officer I'd worked with a few times, into an ambulance. The perp was already in custody in the back of a patrol car, and a perimeter was being maintained to keep onlookers out. The air still crackled with the aftermath of violence.

"Morrison!" My captain waved me over. "We need witness statements from the building. Brick went down responding to a domestic, but half these apartments won't even open their doors. Start with the third floor—that's where the call originated."

I nodded, grabbed my notepad, and headed inside.

I spent the next hour interviewing witnesses, documenting evidence, doing the job I'd done a thousand times before. The suspect's apartment had been a disaster—drugs, weapons. It was the kind of chaos that usually went along with a long rap sheet, not the clean one that had come up when Brick had been dispatched. Brick had unknowingly walked into a nightmare, and now he was in surgery.

As the night wore on, most of the scene was processed without any issues. One last apartment was on the list, "I'll take the last two apartments," I told John, my notepad already out. "Should be quick since no one's telling us shit here."

Apartment 3A answered—an elderly woman who'd heard shouting but nothing else. 3B was empty, no one home.

I knocked on 3C.

No answer.

I knocked again, harder this time. "Boston PD! I need to ask you some questions about the incident downstairs!"

Silence. But I could hear movement inside—shuffling footsteps, something scraping across the floor.

Probably another older tenant like 3A. "BPD. I just need a few minutes of your time."

More silence. Then, finally, the chain rattled and the door opened—barely two inches. A man's face appeared in the gap. I definitely hadn't expected a guy in his mid-thirties. Looking at him, he seemed nervous—eyes darting past me to the hallway.

"I don't know nothing about what happened."

"I understand. But you're a neighbor—you might have seen or heard something that could help us. Can you open the door?"

"No."

"Why not?"

"I just can't, okay?" He started to close the door.

I put my hand on the doorframe—not forcing, just preventing it from closing completely. "Sir, I'm just here to ask a few questions. Won't take more than a few minutes of your time."

The door suddenly wrenched open.

I saw the gun a split second before my training kicked in. I went for my weapon, already knowing I was too late. The first shot hit my vest—knocked the wind out of me, sent me stumbling back into the hallway wall.

The second one didn't miss.

White-hot pain exploded in my left armpit, radiating through my shoulder and down my arm. The impact spun me sideways. My weapon clattered to the floor as my left arm went completely dead, useless. I tried to reach for it with my right hand but my legs were already giving out.

I hit the floor hard, my head cracking against the floor. Warm blood pulsed from the wound with each heartbeat—too much, too fast. I could feel it soaking through my shirt, pooling beneath me, spreading across the cold floor in a way that made my vision blur at the edges.

Arterial—the word floated through my mind with detached clarity. Fucker had hit an artery. Shit.

I tried to press my right hand against the wound but couldn't reach it properly, couldn't get the angle right. The blood just kept coming, hot and slick between my fingers. My left arm was completely limp—useless.

Radio. I needed my radio.

My fingers fumbled for my radio, slippery with blood. I tried to press the button but my hand wouldn't cooperate. It didn't matter—I could already hear footsteps pounding up the stairs. The hallway tilted sideways.

Cold. Why was I so cold? My teeth tried to chatter but my jaw wouldn't move right.

"Jesus Christ—Reed!" John's coffee-soured breath hit my face as he leaned close, his hands already moving, one pressing into my armpit with brutal pressure that made me gasp, the other keying his radio.

"Officer down! Gunshot wound, arterial bleed—I need that bus NOW! He's losing too much blood!"

My voice coming out in a rasp "John—" My voice cracked. "Maliyah. The kids. If I don't—tell them—"

"You shut the fuck up with that shit. You stay with me, Morrison!" John's face appeared above me, pale and sharp. "You son-of-a-bitch! Don't you pull this shit on me. No fucking way you're going out like this!"

I tried to answer but my tongue felt thick, my lips numb. The pressure of his hands against the wound was excruciating—like hot irons pressed directly into torn flesh—but I knew he couldn't let up. Couldn't ease off even a little or I'd bleed out right here in this shitty hallway.

My vision tunneled further. Sounds became muffled, distant. More voices now, more hands on me, someone cutting my shirt away. A tourniquet being cinched high on my arm—agony that made me try to pull away, but I couldn't move. Couldn't do anything but lie there and bleed.

Maliyah's face flashed in my mind. The way she'd looked at me tonight, standing in her kitchen, about to say something that sounded a lot like love. And how I might never get to hear her say it. I should have known this would happen. I did know this would happen. I'd said it months ago. And I still let myself hope. So fucking dumb.

"Reed! Stay with me!" John's voice, sharper now, more desperate. "Ambulance is here, they're coming up—just hold on—"

But I was already slipping under, the darkness closing in from all sides. The last thing I felt was the paramedics taking over, practiced hands moving with efficiency, voices talking over each other in muffled words I couldn't quite make out.

And something in me broke. All the fear I thought I'd mastered came roaring back, sharper and more certain than ever. I'd been pretending. Playing house. And now Lucas and Zoe were going to learn the same lesson I did as a kid, and Maliyah would learn the lesson my mom did—that the man you count on can disappear in an instant.

And then, the darkness swallowed me whole.

Chapter 21:

Fractures

The morphine made everything soft around the edges, but not soft enough. My shoulder felt like someone had driven a railroad spike through it and left it there to rust. Even breathing hurt.

"Reed?"

Maliyah's hand wrapped around mine. Her thumb traced circles on my palm—the same movement she made when she was anxious, when she was trying to soothe herself as much as me.

"Hey." My tongue was thick, words slurring. "You didn't have to come."

She leaned forward, her brow creasing. "Where else would I be?" Her fingertips brushed my forehead, cool against the heat of my skin. Shadowy black mascara trails mapped the path of earlier tears down her cheeks, and when she blinked, her eyelids fluttered like she was fighting to keep them open. In the half-light, her pupils had swallowed almost all the brown of her irises. I tried to squeeze her hand back but my grip was weak. Everything was weak. "The kids—"

"Felicity has them. They're fine. They're safe." Her voice cracked on the last word.

Safe. Right. Safe because I'd almost given them the need for a lifetime of therapy. They'd counted on me. I should have known better than to let myself get attached—to let them get attached.

I pulled my hand away. Trying to push myself more upright against the pillows with only one arm was almost impossible—even using just the one arm lightning shot through my injured shoulder. The IV line tugged, the hair at the edges of the plastic bandage pulling.

"What are you doing? Lie down—"

"I'm fine."

Her voice was firm as she gestured at my bandaged shoulder. "You were shot. There's a hole in you where a bullet tore through muscle and bone, Reed."

"And they sewed me back up. I'm fine." I looked at the ceiling tiles instead of her face. Twelve tiles across. Water stain in the corner shaped like a snowman. "You should go home. Get some sleep."

"I'm not leaving you."

"Maliyah." I forced myself to meet her eyes. "You sitting here watching me sleep isn't helping anyone. You look exhausted."

She flinched like I'd slapped her. "I'm fine."

"You're not. And the kids will be up early, and you need to—" I waved my good hand vaguely. "I'm just going to sleep anyway. The nurses are here. There's nothing for you to do."

"I want to be here." And I want to be alone—looks like we can't all have what we want.

"You should go."

The words came out sharper than I'd intended. She sat back in the chair, her hand withdrawing from the bed rail where it had been resting.

"Okay." Her voice was small. "If that's how you feel."

"It is."

She stood slowly, gathering her purse, her jacket. Movements careful and precise like she was walking on ice. At the door, she turned back.

"I'll come first thing in the morning."

I nodded but didn't say anything. Couldn't promise I'd want her here in the morning either. Couldn't promise anything. Shouldn't have promised anything in the fucking first place—I just ruined everything.

The door closed with a soft click. I stared at it for a long time, at the scratched metal, the safety instructions, the biohazard warnings. My father's funeral had been closed casket. The gunshot had been to the head.

As a kid, I'd wanted to see anyway, to prove it was real, to prove he was really gone. My mother had said no. She'd held my hand so tight, I swear at times I could still feel her squeezing my fingers.

I closed my eyes and tried not to think about the kids. About Saturday mornings filled with laughter. About what I was walking away from. The morphine pulled me under before I could stop it. The hours ticked by with me in and out of consciousness—nurses coming in, interrupting my sleep every few hours to take vitals and give me more meds. So many interruptions that I couldn't even sleep the pain away.

John appeared in the doorway first thing the next morning—two coffees in hand and a smile that just pissed me the fuck off. He entered just as the nurse was leaving after taking my vitals—again.

"Brought you the good stuff." He held up a cup from the café down the street. "None of that hospital shit."

"Thanks." I took it with my good hand. The warmth felt real—solid. Something to focus on besides the pulling ache in my shoulder and the muddiness in my brain from all the morphine. *Gotta get off this shit as soon as I can. It makes me feel like my thoughts aren't right.*

John dropped into the visitor's chair and stretched his legs out. "So. You wanna tell me why Sarah got a call last night from Maliyah crying in her car outside this place?"

I took a sip of coffee. Too hot. Burned my tongue. "I sent her home."

"Yeah, I got that part. The question is why."

"She needed sleep."

"Reed." John leaned forward, elbows on knees. "You jackass. I've known you since we were kids. I was there when your dad died." His voice caught, jaw working as he swallowed hard. "I watched what it did to you. To your mom."

"So what?"

"So, I know what you're going to do. I know you're going to run. You sent Maliyah away because you're spiraling about your dad." John's voice tightened, and something in my chest constricted with it. "And now, like a dipshit, you're about to blow up everything good in your life—" He leaned forward, his eyes boring into mine until I had to look away, my throat burning with unspoken words. "All to prove that you were right to be scared all along."

My jaw clenched. The empty coffee cup crumpled slightly under my grip. "That's not—"

"Bullshit.

I opened my mouth to speak, closed it, then forced the words out. "I almost died last night." My voice caught on "died," betraying me. Part of me wanted her hand back in mine, while another part couldn't bear to see her face if it happened again.

"But you didn't."

"An inch closer—"

"But it wasn't. You're alive. You're going to recover." He exhaled sharply, running a hand over his face, his shoulders sagging momentarily before he straightened again. "And yeah, it was scary as hell, but that's the job, man. You knew that when you signed up—you can't give up on having a life though."

I tossed the crumpled coffee cup across the room, hitting the top of the garbage can. My hand shook as I closed my fist and pressed it against my thigh. "John, that's the damned point. *I* signed up. *Me! They* didn't choose this career. I can't do this to them."

"Do what? Your job?"

"Put them through—" My throat closed up. I had to stop, breathe, try again. "Do you know what it's like? Lying on the pavement, bleeding, knowing you might die, and all you can think about is the people you're going to leave behind?"

"No. But I know what it's like to see my partner on the ground after he got shot. To ride in the ambulance wondering if you were going to make it." John's voice was steady but his knuckles were so firm around his coffee cup, I was sure it would buckle under the weight. "And I know Sarah spent half the night yelling at me after she got off the phone with your girlfriend because you sent her away terrified that she almost lost you."

"She shouldn't have had to go through that."

"She chose to. She knew what she was signing up for."

"Lucas didn't. Zoe didn't." I looked at my hands. The IV port in my wrist. The scrapes on my knuckles from hitting the pavement. "They're just kids. They don't understand that people die. That I could die."

"So you're going to leave them first. Before they can lose you." John shook his head. "That's not protection, Reed. That's just making sure you hurt them on your timeline instead of fate's."

"It's different."

"How?"

"Because they'll get over me leaving. They won't get over—" I couldn't say it. Couldn't put into words the image of Lucas and Zoe standing together at my funeral—Maliyah hollow and broken like my mother.

John was quiet for a long moment. Outside the room, a cart rattled past. Someone's phone was ringing down the hall. Normal hospital sounds. Normal life continuing.

"My dad had a heart attack when I was sixteen," John said finally. "Remember?"

"Yeah."

"He lived. But for two weeks while he was in ICU, my mom had to decide whether to keep hoping or start preparing for the worst." He rotated his coffee cup between his palms. "You know what she told me later? She said those two weeks were the worst of her life, but she'd do it again. She basically said she'd take every moment of fear, every night crying in the hospital cafeteria, every morning wondering if this was the day—she'd take all of it for the twenty-eight more years she got with him."

"That's different."

"Why? Because they were married? Because she didn't have a choice?" John met my eyes. "Maliyah has a choice. She's choosing you. And you're about to tell her she chose wrong."

"I'm telling her the truth. That I can't—" The words stuck. "I thought I could do this. I really did. I thought I'd gotten past it. But I haven't."

"Work through it, Reed. Don't make a permanent decision based on temporary fear."

"It's not temporary," I yelled. Then quieter, I said, "It's not temporary. It's always been there. I just—" I gestured vaguely with my good hand. "I got good at ignoring it. Pretending. But last night stripped all that away and I can't—I can't pretend anymore."

John stood up, moving to the window. "You're going to do what you're going to do. I can't stop you. But I want you to really think about this. You're not protecting those kids by leaving. You're teaching them that people leave when things get scary. That love isn't worth the risk. Is that the lesson you want them to learn?"

He didn't wait for an answer. Just grabbed his coffee and headed for the door. Pausing, he asked, "Do you love her?"

I stared at him, feeling something inside me move, but unable to put it in words. Instead, I said, "It doesn't matter what I feel. It only matters that I'm not right for them."

John shook his head and turned away from me.

"John—"

He paused, looked back.

I opened my mouth, then closed it. My throat tightened. John stood there, waiting. I glanced down at the cup, steam no longer rising from its surface, and managed only, "Thanks. For the coffee."

"Yeah. Sure." His expression was disappointed, a mirror to the ache I felt inside. He walked out the door, closing it silently behind him.

I sat in the empty room and thought about my own weakness. About the way I'd avoid difficult subjects with the kids, never committing too much of myself. About Maliyah's face last night when I'd told her to leave. About laying on the floor in that apartment building, watching everything I'd wanted just disappear.

This was right thing—it's better if I let them live their lives without me.

Chapter 22:

What About Next Time

MALIYAH

Reed's apartment smelled like stale air and old coffee. The curtains were drawn despite it being two in the afternoon. Dishes in the sink. Mail piled on the counter. A prescription bottle on the coffee table, the label facing away. *Good Lord. It had been less than a week since he was released and this place looked like it had been taken over by a bunch of teenaged boys.*

"You should sit." I set my purse down, moved toward him where he stood by the window. "Let me—"

"I'm fine." But he wasn't. His skin had a gray tinge. Dark circles under his eyes. Hair unwashed, sticking up where he'd been sleeping on it. "You didn't have to come."

"I wanted to see you. It's been days since I've laid eyes on you."

He nodded but didn't move toward me. Just stood there, his left arm in the sling, his right hand shoved in his pocket. The space between us felt larger than the length of the room.

I crossed the room, each step on the hardwood floor echoing in the silence between us. My fingers found his—cold, limp, unfamiliar. His eyes fixed on some point beyond the window as my thumb traced the ridge of his knuckles, searching for the man I'd kissed goodbye that night. I croaked out, "Talk to me."

He let me hold his hand but didn't squeeze back. "What's there to talk about?"

"You've barely responded to my texts. You sent me home from the hospital. You—" I stopped, tried to control my voice. "You're shutting me out."

"I'm recovering."

"This isn't recovering. This is hiding." I gestured around the apartment. "Have you even been eating?"

"I'm fine."

"Stop saying that!" The words came out louder than I'd intended. I took a breath, tried again. "You're not fine. I can see that you're not fine. And I want to help but you won't let me."

He finally looked at me then. Really looked at me. And what I saw in his eyes made my stomach drop—resignation. Like he'd already made a decision and was just waiting for the right moment to tell me.

"What?" My voice came out smaller than I wanted. "What are you thinking?"

He pulled his hand away. Moved to the couch and sat down heavily. "I keep seeing it. Every time I close my eyes."

"The shooting?"

"No. After." He stared at his hands. "When I was on the ground, bleeding out—all I could think about was Lucas. He's so close in age to the age I was—I thought of him having to hear that I died. Just like I had to hear about my dad."

I sat beside him carefully. "But, Reed—you didn't die."

"This time."

"Reed—"

"What about next time?" His voice was raw. "What about the next call, the next traffic stop, the next time someone has a gun and I don't see it fast enough? What then?"

"Then we deal with it. Together."

He laughed, but there was no humor in it. "You say that now. But you didn't see my mother after. She was—" He stopped, swallowed hard. "She died a couple of years ago but she'd been dead inside since he died. Just going through the motions, waiting for it to be over. I can't do that to you."

"So what are you saying?"

The silence stretched. Outside, someone's car alarm went off. Stopped. Started again.

"I need—" He rubbed his face with his good hand. "I need some space. To think. To figure out—"

"Figure out what?" But I already knew. Could feel it in the careful distance he was keeping, the way he wouldn't meet my eyes.

"If I can keep doing this."

The words landed like a punch. "Doing what? Being with me?"

"Being with anyone. Having people depend on me. Putting myself in a position where—" He stood carefully, groaning as he moved. It took everything I had not to try to help him, but I just couldn't do it. I watched him move to the window, and while his good arm braced against furniture, I braced for his words. "I'm not cut out for this, Maliyah. I thought I was. I really did. But I'm not."

"That's not true." I stood too, moved toward him. "You're good with the kids. You're good with me. This is just fear talking—"

"Of course it's fear!" He spun to face me. "I'm terrified! Is that what you want to hear? That every time I leave for work I think about dying? How one wrong move can be the difference between life and death. I can't take the chance of doing to the kids what happened to me!"

"Reed—"

"You have to go." His voice was flat now. Cop voice. "I need time alone to recover. The pain meds make me tired, I can barely move my arm, and it's all just—" He gestured vaguely. "It's too much. I need space."

Every instinct screamed that this was wrong. That space was the last thing we needed. But I also heard the finality in his voice.

My purse strap twisted in my fingers as I fumbled to pick it up, my hands betraying me with their trembling. "Don't do this, Reed." My voice cracked. I thought about movie nights. About pancake breakfasts. Our trips to the park. Festivals and markets. All those moments over the last six months when I'd believed—this is it. He could be the one. "You were there. Every step. Every day. But you were never really committed, were you?"

He didn't respond. He just looked away, unable to look me in the eyes.

"I'll give you a couple days. I know you're scared. I know what happened was terrifying. But you need to figure this out, Reed. My kids and I aren't fucking disposable." My purse strap slipped off my shoulder. I didn't bother adjusting it. My feet felt heavy, each step toward the door requiring conscious effort, like I was walking through water.

"You'll need to figure it out soon, though," I said. "I won't let you pop in and out of my kids' lives." Grabbing the handle, I paused, not even looking back anymore. I leaned my forehead on the door and said, "You're so worried about what would happen to them if you died. But what you're doing right now—this is you leaving them just the same. The only difference?" My voice trembled. "This one is completely your choice."

The door closed behind me and I stood in the hallway, staring at the scratched paint, trying to breathe around the tightness in my chest.

He wasn't going to call.

I knew it even if I couldn't admit it yet.

Chapter 23:

Wishes

MALIYAH

It had been weeks since Reed and I split. I stood in my kitchen making lunches for the kids and realized I'd gone an entire morning without thinking about him—without missing him.

Progress, I told myself. This was progress.

A small hand tugged at my sleeve, and I looked down to find Zoe standing there, one sock striped purple, the other dotted blue, with a pink tutu fluffed out over her navy leggings. She pointed toward the fridge, her eyes wide and hopeful. "Mama, can I have the strawberry yogurt?"

"We're out of strawberry. How about vanilla?"

"But I don't like vanilla."

"You liked it yesterday."

"Yesterday was yesterday." She crossed her arms, her expression so serious it almost made me smile.

"How about I put some strawberries in the vanilla yogurt?"

She sighed dramatically but accepted this solution—which let's be real, probably has less sugar—something my kid definitely doesn't need. Small victories.

Lucas shuffled in, backpack already on, hair sticking up on one side. He glanced at the empty chair where Reed used to sit drinking coffee when he'd come over. When our eyes met, he quickly looked away, hitched his backpack higher on his small shoulders.

A week after I'd told him "Detective Reed needed to focus on his job," he'd stopped saying Reed's name entirely. His small shoulders hunched forward slightly as he bent to tie his shoe, the gesture so adult-like on his small frame that something twisted painfully behind my ribs.

"Ready?" I asked, grabbing my purse and the lunch bags.

"Can we get donuts on the way?" Lucas asked hopefully.

"It's Tuesday. We get donuts on Saturdays."

"But what if we got them on Tuesday this time?"

"Nice try. Let's go."

The morning routine was familiar, comforting in its predictability. Drop Lucas at the bus stop, then the drive to Harbor House Road where Zoe's daycare was in-house. I'd thrown myself into work, taking on extra tasks aimed at fundraising—a job that is never finished in this world.

Some of the team had noticed me throwing myself into work. "You're doing too much," Danya, one of the social workers, said yesterday, catching me in the office at seven PM. "You should go home. Rest."

But home meant thinking. And thinking meant remembering Reed's face when he'd said he needed space. Remembering how easily he'd let me go.

When the kids were busy with their activities, work gave me another focus.

I was halfway to Harbor House Road when I noticed the car behind me. A dark sedan, staying two cars back. Nothing unusual about it—Boston traffic was always heavy. But something made me check my rearview mirror again.

Still there.

At the next light, I changed lanes. At first, the sedan stayed in its lane. After the next light though, it switched lanes and came up behind me again.

My pulse picked up. I told myself I was being paranoid. That heartbreak was making me see threats where there were none. But I'd spent years learning to trust my instincts about danger, and my instincts were screaming.

I took a sudden right turn, looping back toward my apartment instead of continuing to work. The sedan went straight. I breathed a sigh of relief. I turned left at the next corner planning to go back around. Looking behind me moments later, and I swear the same sedan was back. Am I losing it?

My hands tightened on the steering wheel. I pulled out my phone, voice-dialing Felicity while keeping my eyes on the mirror.

"Hey, you okay?" she answered.

"I think someone's following me."

"What? Where are you?"

"Heading back toward my place. Dark sedan, can't see the plates from here. And I can't see into the front windshield from my angle." I made another turn. This time, the car stayed with me. "Definitely following."

"Call the police."

"And tell them what? A car is driving on the same streets as me?" I pulled into my building's parking lot. The sedan drove past, not slowing. I caught a glimpse of the driver—male, hoodie, baseball cap, sunglasses. Could have been anyone.

Shit, I forgot to look at the license plate.

"Maliyah?"

"It drove past. I'm probably just paranoid."

"After everything with Bryce, you're allowed to be paranoid." Felicity's voice was firm. "You still have that restraining order. If you think it's him, call the police."

"I didn't see his face clearly. It might not have been him."

"But it might have been."

I sat in my car for a long moment after hanging up, watching the street. No dark sedan. No sign of anyone watching. Just normal morning traffic, people heading to work, life continuing all around me.

You're just being paranoid, Maliyah. Had to be.

I drove to work and tried to forget about it.

That night, I triple-checked the locks before bed. Pulled up the camera app on my phone, cycling through the four feeds—living room, hallway, both kids' windows facing the street. Everything quiet. Everything normal.

I was overreacting. The car had been a coincidence. I was jumpy because of Reed, because my defenses were down, because I was exhausted from single-handedly holding my life together.

I fell asleep with the phone on my nightstand, camera app still open.

The sound that woke me wasn't loud. Just a soft scrape, metal on metal. My eyes opened in the darkness, heart already racing.

The doorknob. Someone was trying the doorknob.

I was out of bed before the thought fully formed. Gun case. Nightstand drawer. Fingers on the lock, twist, grip the handle. Safety off.

I crept to the door on quiet feet, gun raised. Put my eye to the peephole.

Empty hallway. Fluorescent lights humming. Nothing.

But I'd heard it. I knew I'd heard it.

I stood there, barely breathing, listening for another sound. Thirty seconds. A minute. The seconds ticked by. Nothing.

I slid down with my back against the door and stayed there, gun in my lap, watching the darkness of my apartment. Twenty minutes passed before I could make myself move to the kids' rooms.

Finally, when I could force myself to move, I headed over to the kids' bedrooms and settled myself on the floor, back resting on the wall between their doors. No way I was getting back to sleep now.

Maybe I'd imagined it. Stress, exhaustion, paranoia—take your pick.

But I wasn't moving away from my kids' rooms—not a chance.

By Saturday, I'd had enough time and space to start to feel comfortable again—questioning if it had been a dream or my imagination.

It was Lucas's birthday and, in all honesty, it was the one bright spot in the weeks since everything fell apart.

I'd been planning it obsessively, pouring energy into something I could actually control. Dinosaur cake from the bakery. Streamers in green and blue. A handful of kids from his class whose parents had RSVPed yes. Felicity and Caden. Macy, who'd insisted on bringing party games.

We held it at Felicity's, where they had a huge backyard compared to my apartment.

The place was chaos by noon—kids running everywhere, Zoe trying to "help" by rearranging the napkins every five minutes, Lucas's classmates hyped up on juice boxes and anticipation. Normal birthday chaos. And it was amazing.

Only one exception—I kept catching Lucas glancing at the door.

"Time for cake!" Felicity announced, carrying the T-Rex monstrosity I'd spent too much money on. Seven candles flickered on top, casting dancing shadows across Lucas's serious face.

"Make a wish, baby," I said, crouching beside him.

He stared at the candles for a long moment. Too long. His jaw tightened the way it did when he was trying not to feel something.

Then he closed his eyes, scrunched up his face in concentration, and blew.

All seven flames went out in one breath. Everyone cheered. Zoe clapped so hard she nearly fell off her chair.

"What'd you wish for?" one of his classmates asked.

"Can't tell," Lucas said quietly. "Or it won't come true."

His eyes flicked to the door one more time. Then back to the cake, like he was forcing himself not to look again.

The party continued. Games were played. Presents were opened. Lucas posed for photos when Felicity shoved her phone in his face. He was happy—everything a seven-year-old should be.

But I knew my son. I knew he still missed him. I knew he was thinking about Reed.

After the guests had gone, Felicity and I started cleanup duty. Things quieted down, but Lucas appeared to still be having fun. He and Zoe were going through all the presents, chucking the boxes and wrapping paper while packing up the contents to take home.

Once we got home, the kids went through the steps to get ready for bed and I did the same. I found Lucas in his room just before bedtime. He was sitting on his bed, holding the watch I'd inherited from my father—the one I'd given Lucas last year. He turned it over in his small hands, not really looking at it.

"Hey, birthday boy." I sat beside him, the mattress dipping under my weight. "You okay?"

"Yeah." He didn't look up.

"Lucas."

He was quiet for a long moment. His thumb traced the edge of the watch face.

"I didn't wish for LEGOs," he finally said.

My chest tightened. "No?"

"I wished—" His voice cracked. He swallowed hard, tried again. "I wished he'd come. I kept thinking maybe he'd show up. Like a surprise." He finally looked at me, and the hurt in his eyes nearly broke me. "But he didn't. So I guess wishes are stupid."

I pulled him into my arms, feeling his small body tense and then slowly relax against me. He didn't cry. My boy who used to cry over everything had learned to hold it in. I wasn't sure if that was growth or not at this stage.

"I'm so sorry, baby."

"It's not your fault." His voice was muffled against my shoulder. "You didn't make him leave."

No. I didn't. But I'd let him in. I'd let both of us believe he might stay.

"He said he'd take me to a game," Lucas continued, pulling back to look at me. "He said he was going to get tickets to a game—since I hadn't been to one."

I hadn't known that. Reed had never mentioned it to me. The thought of him planning something like that made the ache in my chest sharpen. It broke my heart to see my kid like this.

"I'm sorry he broke that promise, sweetheart."

"Why do grown-ups do that?" Lucas picked at a loose thread on his comforter, not meeting my eyes. "You always tell me not to make promises I can't keep. But grown-ups do it all the time."

I opened my mouth, then closed it. How do you explain fear and trauma to a seven-year-old? How do you make sense of something that doesn't make sense to you either?

"I don't know, baby. Sometimes people get scared. And when they're scared, they make bad choices."

"Was he scared of us?"

My breath caught. "No. Not of you. Never of you."

Lucas considered this, his fingers still working at that thread. Then, quietly: "Then what?"

I smoothed the hair back from his forehead—the cowlick that never stayed down, no matter how much I tried. "You know how his dad was a police officer?"

"Yeah."

"Well, his dad got hurt and didn't make it home one day. Reed was just about the same age as you when that happened."

Lucas's hands stilled. He looked up at me, something shifting behind his eyes. "Oh."

"So when Reed got hurt—" I paused, searching for the right words. "I think it scared him. A lot. Made him remember what happened to his dad. And he got worried the same thing might happen to you and Zoe that he went through."

Lucas was quiet for a long moment. His brow furrowed the way it did when he was working through a math problem. Finally, he said, "That's dumb."

A surprised laugh escaped me. "What?"

"It's dumb." He looked at me, fierce and certain in the way only kids can be. "Can we tell him it doesn't matter? That I'd take the chance?" His voice wobbled slightly. "Because me and Zoe want him more than we don't."

My throat closed. I pulled him against me, blinking hard.

"Oh, baby."

"Can we tell him, Mom?"

I pressed my lips to the top of his head, breathing in the little-boy smell of him—grass and sweat and the cheap shampoo he insisted on because the bottle had a dinosaur on it.

"It's not that simple, sweetheart."

"Why not?"

Because I'm too scared to reach out. Because he made his choice and I'm supposed to be strong and not care. I'm supposed to put my feelings aside and stop loving him.

"Sometimes grown-ups need to figure things out on their own," I finally said. "Even when other people want to help."

Lucas pulled back, jaw set. "That's dumb too."

I almost smiled. "Yeah. It kind of is."

He was quiet for another moment. Then: "I'm tired. Gonna go to bed, okay?"

"Okay, baby. Whatever you need."

I kissed my baby's forehead realizing I couldn't fix this brokenness. But I could be here. I could answer his questions, hug him in these moments and show Lucas that sometimes hurts happened, but I would be here to hold him no matter what.

Even if it meant doing it alone.

That night, after the kids were asleep and the apartment was quiet, I stood at the kitchen window staring at the empty street below.

Somewhere out there, Reed was probably sitting in his apartment. Did he know what day it was? Did he remember the plans he'd made, the promises he'd broken?

Did he care?

My phone sat on the counter. I could call him. Make him hear what he'd missed. Make him understand what his absence had cost.

But what would be the point? He'd made his choice.

A car stood out front of my apartment, idling. No one getting in or out. Dark sedan. Tinted windows.

My breath caught. I turned out all the lights to get a better look outside without the glare and I watched it as the driver started forward and turn the corner—disappearing into the night.

Probably nothing. Just paranoia. Just the weight of too many things gone wrong.

I checked the locks. Pulled the curtains closed. Checked the cameras.

And tried not to think about any of it—not Reed, not the sedan, not exhaustion of doing life alone, or the pain of giving my heart again only to have it burned to a crisp.

Tomorrow would be better. It had to be.

Chapter 24:

Watcher

MALIYAH

The morning after Lucas's birthday was quiet. No dark sedans. No shadows to follow me around. Then the flowers appeared.

I'd run out to grab lunch for the team—sandwiches from the deli down the street. Twenty minutes of waiting, small talk with the guy behind the counter, normal everyday stuff. When I got back to my car, arms full of bags, I unlocked it with the fob and climbed into the driver's seat.

As I reached to put the bags on the passenger seat next to me, my heart slammed against my ribs.

Petals. Dozens of them. A wrapped bouquet sitting on my passenger seat, ribbon-bound stems peeking from crinkled cellophane. More petals scattered across the leather, dusting the dashboard, nestled in the cup holders, wedged between seat cushions.

The car I'd locked. The car no one else had keys to.

I scrambled out so fast my legs betrayed me. The world tilted sideways as my body met asphalt, skin tearing against rough pavement. The sting registered somewhere distant as I pushed myself up, backing away from the open door. My heart hammered against my ribs as if warning me there might be something lurking inside worse than unwanted flowers.

My eyes darted across the parking lot. The woman loading groceries into her trunk. The teenager leaning against a pillar, scrolling his phone. The elderly man shuffling toward the pharmacy. Normal people. Ordinary people. Any one of them could be watching.

I called the police. Documented everything. Tried to keep my voice steady as I explained that someone had broken into my locked vehicle to leave flowers with a very specific meaning. I explained my restraining order. The officer who spoke to me sounded bored.

I forced myself to breathe through the conversation. Slow down. Think. While waiting for an officer, I looked over my car, still keeping my eyes out for things going on around me.

But I kept looking at the flowers—I recognized them. Unique. And a memory came with them. *"For my love. For the plans I have for us. A life of my affection and love."* He'd said those words years ago. On the last anniversary we'd had together. It was the last one but I remember thinking he was close to proposing. It wasn't long after that night when I ran away from Bryce.

The flowers were Blue Nigellas and I remembered that they symbolized deep love and affection, but he forgot that they were also supposed to symbolize harmony—a feeling I *never* had with him.

I looked back to my car at the flowers. No card. No note. But I knew. And I lost the contents of my stomach. Waiting for the officer to come, I sat on the ground next to my car. The smell of my own sick overwhelming my senses. And the tears ran. The feeling that I had lost all control over everything was too much to manage. I called Felicity, asked her to keep the kids for the afternoon and that I'd be by later to get them.

It was hours before the officer finally showed and I knew within moments that nothing would come of it. That I would be blown off and the report would be buried under a pile of paperwork.

Three days later, the coffee was waiting for me. I walked into Grind—the café where Reed and I had our first date, not that I let myself think about that—and the barista smiled brightly.

"Andi! Hi!" Recognition crossed over Andi's face when she met my eyes and beamed a smile at me. Caden's cousin, Andi was amazing.

"Maliyah! Swinging in for coffee? How are you!?"

"I'm great, thanks! How's it going here?"

"Fantastic! You'll never believe it. I'm closing on this place next week. Bought it from the owners."

"No freaking way. That's amazing. Congratulations!"

"Thank you! It's funny, I saw your name on the mobile order list and almost wondered if it was the same Maliyah."

I hit a wall of cold in that moment. "What do you mean? I didn't order yet."

"No?" She picked up a coffee from the mobile order area and showed me the cup. "French vanilla latte, extra cream. For Maliyah. Is that your normal order?"

My usual. The drink I'd ordered a hundred times. The drink Reed used to have waiting for me when I was running late.

"Who called it in?"

She checked her tablet, brow furrowed. "It came through the online system. Just says 'for Maliyah.'"

I reached for it, the cup shaking in my trembling hands. I barely registered the heat against my palms. I fumbled with my wallet, dropping a five on the counter even as the barista said, "It's already been paid for—"

"I gotta go. I'll catch you later, Andi."

I was out the door before I could hear her response. Outside, I dumped the entire contents into the trash, watching the steam curl up and disappear. Then I stood there, scanning the street, my heart pounding so hard I could feel it in my throat.

I called the non-emergency line again. Same bored voice. Same polite dismissal dressed up as concern. But I knew it was more than they were making it out to be. I knew it was him. I knew he was watching me.

Officer James came to my apartment that evening. He was maybe thirty, clean-shaven, with the kind of neutral expression they must teach at the academy. He flipped open a fresh notepad like he was starting from scratch—which, of course, he was. Different officer every time. No continuity. No context.

"Start from the beginning," he said.

So I did. Bryce. The restraining order. The car following me. The sounds of someone trying to get in at night. The flowers in my locked vehicle. The coffee.

I watched his face as I talked. Watched the subtle shift from professional interest to something closer to skepticism. I knew how it sounded. Thin. Circumstantial. The paranoid ramblings of a woman going through a bad breakup.

"I know how this sounds," I said. "But I know Bryce. This is exactly how he operates. Small things. Quiet things. Things that make me doubt myself. That's the whole point—he wants me to feel crazy."

Officer James's pen stopped moving. "I understand your concern, ma'am. But we're dealing with incidents that could be attributed to anyone. Or no one." He ticked them off: "An unidentified vehicle. A doorknob that might have been tried, with nothing to verify. Anonymous flowers. A coffee order with no name attached. There isn't enough to show he violated the order."

"The flowers were in my locked car."

"Is it possible you left it unlocked? Even for a moment?"

I stared at him. "No."

He nodded slowly, the way people do when they don't believe you but are too polite to say so. "Like I said, without concrete evidence linking these events to your ex..." He let the sentence trail off.

"So there's nothing you can do."

"I can increase patrols in your area. Note everything in the report." He met my eyes with practiced sympathy. "If there are more incidents, we can send someone to talk to him directly. But Ms. Davenport—be vigilant. If you see him, if you have any proof, call 911 immediately."

After he left, I checked every lock. Every window. Cycled through the camera feeds until my eyes burned.

Then I pulled up my messages. Scrolled to Reed's name. My thumb hovered over the text field. I typed: I need—

Deleted it. Typed: Something's wrong—

Deleted that too. I stared at our last exchange. Weeks old now. The silence between us a wall I didn't know how to breach. Part of me wanted to call him, hear his voice, let him tell me I wasn't crazy. He'd come running. I knew he would.

But then I remembered his face when we last spoke. The careful distance in his eyes. He'd made his choice. And I wasn't going to beg.

I locked the screen. Unlocked it. Went back to the cameras. I'd have to handle this alone.

Outside my window, the street was empty. But somewhere out there, Bryce was watching. I could feel it. And sooner or later, he was going to make his move.

Chapter 25:

Silence

REED

I wasn't right for her. I knew this. But it didn't stop me from feeling it—the pain. I shut everything and everyone out. I didn't see any other options.

So, when John called, I let it go to voicemail. When Sarah texted asking if I was okay, I sent her a thumbs up. Nothing else.

I stuck with my PT and I kept improving. When the doctor finally cleared me for desk duty, I went back to work with feelings of relief from the silence constantly surrounding me. I buried myself in paperwork, volunteered for every shit assignment nobody wanted. Anything to stay busy.

A week went by. Then two. I didn't reach out—didn't stop me from drafting messages and deleting them at a ridiculous frequency. But really—what would I even say? She deserved better than anything I could offer. This was the kindest thing I could do. Let her move on without dragging it out. That's what I told myself.

I knew Lucas's birthday was coming up. I'd put it in my calendar months ago. Got tickets for us to go to a game in April that I was going to give him. His first in Boston.

I kept meaning to delete the reminder, but I couldn't. Just because I wanted her to move on from me didn't mean I could move on from them. The weeks kept passing before John let me have it.

"You look like shit and I'm over watching you play the self-pity game."

"Thanks, man. It's not self-pity. I'm just focused."

"Whatever. Listen—we need to get you out of the house and do something, man."

"I'm fine."

"You're not fine. You're a zombie who happens to go to work daily." He crossed his arms. "When's the last time you ate something that wasn't from a fast food joint or vending machine?"

I didn't answer. Couldn't remember, actually.

"That's what I thought." He grabbed his jacket. "Come on. We're getting lunch. Real food. And you're going to tell me what the hell is going on in that head of yours."

I should have said no. Should have made an excuse about reports that needed finishing or calls I had to make. But the truth was, I was tired. Tired of the silence. Tired of the emptiness. Tired of pretending I was handling this when I clearly wasn't.

"Fine," I said. "But you're buying."

At the diner, I pushed eggs around my plate while John demolished a burger. He let me sit in silence for approximately three minutes before losing patience.

"So. I get you guys broke up. I get that—really. But are you going to tell me what actually happened? Because I'm at the point where I might just start guessing."

"Nothing happened."

"Bullshit. You were practically living at her place. Now you won't even say her name." He pointed a fry at me. "Spill."

I set down my fork. Stared at the congealed yolk on my plate. "I ended it."

John rolled his eyes. "Yeah, I gathered that much, genius."

"Then why are you asking?" I stopped, tried again. "Fuck, man. Listen. I can't be what she needs."

"Oh. Yeah. That's what she told you?"

The question hit harder than I expected. "It doesn't matter."

"It absolutely matters." John leaned forward. "Reed, I've known you for most of our lives. I watched you build something real with her. With those kids. And then you just—what? Walked away because you got scared?"

"I. Got. Shot, John."

"I know. I was there. I was the one pushing down on the fucking wound to keep you from bleeding out. Remember?" His voice was sharp, then softened. "But you made it. You're here. And instead of being grateful for that, you're using it as an excuse to blow up your life."

"It's not an excuse. It's reality." I shoved my plate away. "It was a sign. What are the chances I'd experience almost the exact same thing my dad did? It was a sign! And a chance to save Lucas and Zoe from going through what I did."

"What the fuck? You think it was a sign? Why the hell didn't you think it was a sign that you *didn't die* then! Why didn't you consider that it was a sign that you should dig in? Not fucking run! You *didn't* die like your dad." He jabbed a finger toward my chest, where beneath my shirt lay the puckered scar tissue. "That right there—that's a physical sign that you're alive and healthy. It's a sign that you could actually be there for them!"

"That's not it—"

"How the fuck would you know?" John's voice rose, drawing a glance from the waitress. He lowered it again. "You pray about it? Meditate? Do some chakra shit or something? Feng shui yourself? Do anything other than think you know all and have all the answers? Talk to Maliyah about it? Talk to me? No! You thought you knew best, so you decided for everyone how it would be. You made your choice. All. By. Yourself."

The words landed like blows. I couldn't argue because he wasn't wrong.

"You think you're protecting them," John continued. "But all you're doing is proving that people can't be trusted to stay. Reed—is that really what you want?"

I thought about those kids. About Maliyah. About the way it felt to be with them—to have something real with them.

"No," I said quietly. "It's not what I want."

"Then fix it."

"It's too late."

"It's been a few weeks or so. That's not too late. That's barely the beginning." He threw some cash on the table. "But if you keep going like this—isolating yourself, refusing to talk to anyone, pretending you're fine when you're clearly falling apart—then yeah. Eventually it will be too late."

I didn't respond. Just sat there, staring at the untouched food on my plate, knowing he was right and having no idea how to fix it.

Finally I said, "You know feng shui is like for furniture or something, right?"

John flipped me off, his eyebrows raised in that way they do when he knows he's right. "Fuck you, professor," he said, leaning back in his chair with a smirk that made me want to punch him. "What, you think that invalidates my point? Congratulations, dipshit. The point. Still. Stands."

I exhaled slowly, shoulders slumping. "Yeah. I guess it does." My lips twitched into the ghost of a smirk—not because anything was funny, but because John had always been able to call me on my bullshit. The smirk faded as quickly as it appeared, replaced by something heavier. I met his eyes across the table, a silent acknowledgment passing between us. He was right, and we both knew it.

John's words followed me around for days. Every time I reached for my phone to call her, my hand would freeze mid-air, paralyzed by the certainty I'd only make things worse.

Then, on Saturday morning the calendar notification popped up on my screen. *Lucas's Birthday - 4:00 PM*

I stared at it for a long time. Seven years old. My serious little man was turning seven. *Fuck*—not *my* little man. *What the fuck was I doing?*

I should delete the reminder. Should have deleted it weeks ago. But I couldn't bring myself to do it—like erasing the notification would some-how erase him from my life completely. As if he wasn't already gone.

I dismissed it instead. Let the screen go dark.

The apartment was too quiet. I turned on the TV just for noise, some old basketball documentary I didn't give two shits about. Paced to the kitchen. Opened the fridge. Closed it. Paced back. Back to the kitchen again. Grabbed a beer and dropped on the couch to stare at the TV.

Time passed, numbing something inside me and, before I knew it, the sun had set. Then, I thought about them—that somewhere across the city, a party was probably wrapping up. Cake and candles and kids heading home after a day of running around. Maliyah owning her success like a queen. Lucas having blown out candles, making a wish. Zoe had probably spent the party running around in some princess outfit, excited for all the shenanigans and causing more herself.

What did Lucas wish for? I sat forward from my spot in the couch, head in my hands.

Don't think about it. Don't fucking think about it.

But I couldn't stop. Couldn't stop picturing his face when he'd realized I wouldn't be coming. Couldn't stop imagining Zoe asking where I was, Maliyah having had to come up with some excuse. Couldn't stop won-dering if Lucas had given up on me yet, or if some small part of him was still wishing me to come through the door. And Maliyah—God, I missed her more than I had any right to. I could see her in my mind, the smile. I could feel her soft hands and almost taste her lips. Remember how it felt to have her arms around me—the smell of her shampoo, softness of her curls against my face.

That's when I felt it—a single tear breaking free, carving a hot path down my stubbled cheek. I wiped it away with my fingers, surprised by the unfamiliar sensation. Looking at the moisture on my hand, I sat in wonder—I couldn't remember the last time I'd actually cried. With actual tears. The weight in my chest had become a physical pressure, constricting my ribs until something had to give.

And my whole body wracked as I let it all go. No holding back this time. No one here to see me lose my shit. I'd lost Maliyah, the kids, my dignity. I'd lost my family. The one I never thought I'd have in the first place. My body was hot with anger and brokenness. I needed them back. I don't think I can survive this life without them. I didn't *want* to survive this life without them.

How, though? How did I even begin? Where did I even start? I leaned back on the couch, pressing my fingers into my eyes, trying to stop the tears but completely at a loss. It wasn't possible.

The angry buzz near my ear jolted me upright, my hand slashing through empty air as I fought an imaginary insect. Harsh morning light assaulted my eyes through blinds I'd forgotten to close. My mouth tasted like stale beer and regret, tongue stuck to the roof like sandpaper. Empty bottles stood sentinel on the coffee table, casualties of last night's breakdown. The buzzing continued—not a bee, but my phone vibrating against the hardwood floor where it must have fallen. I fumbled for it, squinting at the screen through sleep-crusted eyes: six missed calls from John, his concerned face flashing on my screen for the seventh time now.

My phone vibrated again. A text this time—John.

You alive? Since your ass didn't answer my calls, I'm expecting a text back. Send proof of life or I'm showing up with a boom box and standing outside to serenade your ass.

Me: *Fuck. Fell asleep. Don't do that. You don't want to give me evidence to send around the department.*

John: *Well fuck. Look who's alive. How you doing today, asshole?*

I thought about the night last night. The feeling of missing Lucas's birthday. Of missing all three of the most important people who'd come into my life in a long time. The constriction in my chest that was quickly taking over again.

I typed back: *Not good.*

John: *You want company?*

I almost said no. Almost kept it all to myself—drown in sorrow alone. But I had to start somewhere.

Me: *Yeah—but tomorrow. I'm covering for Macky today and need to get ready—pulling a double.*

John: *Okay. I'm off today. I'll come over tomorrow for the game.*

Monday night John showed up with a six-pack and a pizza I didn't ask for. He took one look at my face and didn't say a word. Just walked past me, set the food on the coffee table, and dropped onto the couch.

We sat in silence for a while. The basketball game droned on. I picked at the label on my beer bottle, shredding it into tiny pieces.

Finally, John spoke. "It was his birthday the other day."

"I know."

"You didn't go."

"No. That would make his party about me. Wouldn't be fair to him or Maliyah."

He nodded slowly, like he was working something out. "You going to keep doing this? Torturing yourself?"

"No. I don't want to keep doing this. But—I don't know where to start."

"Look, man." John leaned forward, elbows on his knees. "I'm not going to sit here and tell you it's going to be easy. You fucked up. You hurt people who didn't deserve it. That's on you."

"I know."

"But you're not dead. And neither is what you had with them." He grabbed a slice of pizza, took a bite, talked around it. "But, you've got me. You've got people. So, let's fucking figure this shit out."

I stared at the TV without seeing it. "What if I can't? What if it's already too late?"

"The answer will always be no if you don't ask the question. Every. Single. Time. And at least if you do something, you'll have tried—even if you fail." He shrugged.

The words settled over me like a weight. He was right. He'd been right at the diner, and he was right now. Doing nothing was still a choice—and it was the coward's choice.

"I don't even know where to start," I admitted.

"I know you don't." John finished his slice, wiped his hands on his jeans. "But, like I said, we'll figure it out. Not tonight. Tonight, you eat some pizza, drink some beer, and stop being such a miserable bastard. Tomorrow is soon enough to start figuring shit out."

I almost smiled. Almost. "That your professional advice?"

"That's my 'I'm smarter than you' advice." He shoved the pizza box toward me. "Eat. You look like hell."

I grabbed a slice. It tasted like cardboard, but I forced myself to chew. To swallow. To do something other than fall apart.

John stayed until ten. We didn't talk much—just watched the game, drank beer, existed in the same space.

After he left, I sat with my phone in my hand.

Maliyah's contact open on the screen—again. It's become a ritual, just staring at our conversation history.

What would I even say?

I typed: *I was wrong.*

Deleted it. Tried: *I miss you.*

Deleted that too. Tried: *Can we talk?*

I've done this before—when I broke it off with her. My thumb hovered over the send button, feeling the memory settle in and the punch to my gut right along with it.

She'd have every right to say no. She'd probably already moved on, realized she was better off without me. What if I'd burned that bridge so thoroughly there was nothing left but ash?

I set the phone on the coffee table. The apartment was quiet. Too quiet. I picked up the phone again.

I know I don't deserve another chance. But I need you to know I was wrong. About everything.

Deleted it. *I've been miserable without you. Without Lucas and Zoe. I know I did this to myself, but—*

Deleted that too.

Nothing I wrote sounded right. Everything felt either too much or not enough. Too desperate or too casual. An excuse or an apology that would never be sufficient for what I'd done.

I opened a new message.

I'm sorry. Can we talk? I know I don't deserve it, but I've been working through some things and I really hope you see this and say yes.

Simple. Direct. Left the ball in her court. My thumb hovered over send.

Tomorrow. I'd send it tomorrow. Give myself tonight to be sure, to pre-pare for whatever her response might be. One more night to work up the courage I should have had weeks ago. Tomorrow I'd stop being a coward. Tomorrow I'd fight for what I'd thrown away. Even though I know I don't deserve them.

I set the phone on the nightstand, Maliyah's contact still open, that long fucking message sitting unsent in the text field. I closed my eyes, but sleep wouldn't come. Just her face. The kids' laughter. The joy I felt when I was with them—with her.

I reached for the phone again. Stared at the words. Tomorrow was a cow-ard's answer. Tomorrow was what I'd been doing for weeks—waiting for the perfect moment that would never come.

My thumb hovered over send. Then pressed down. The message disap-peared from the text field. Delivered. I set the phone face-down on the nightstand and closed my eyes, my heart hammering against my ribs. No taking it back now.

Chapter 26:

I Need Help

MALIYAH

The morning light hit me hard—too bright, too sharp. Every sound felt amplified. The refrigerator hum felt louder than usual. The radiators clanged deeper. Even Zoe's laughter from her room, usually the best sound in the world, made my chest tighten.

I hadn't slept much. I'd stayed up late letting anxiety get to me—watching the cameras obsessively. My screens swapped from footage to my messages with Reed. I'd hovered over our text-chain half the night, wanting to tell him that something was wrong. Wanting to ask for help. But the thought of hearing the tired sympathy in his voice stopped me. Or him not even answering.

I was falling apart from the inside out. Panic crashed through me, washing away any rationality. Every anxious thought multiplied into ten more, each worse than the last.

I must have dozed at some point though. When I woke, I was still sitting up, my phone on my lap. Looking at the screen, I'd seen a notification that I had a message from Reed. My heart soared. Had he known I was thinking of him? Had he heard about my calls to the department or conversations with all the different officers?

Just as quickly, though, my heart plummeted. Unable to bring myself to open it, I'd thrown my phone on the bed like it was on fire before starting to get ready. I couldn't do it. I couldn't give him a piece of myself or let him see me like this. I had no pieces left and no peace inside.

"Mommy, my shoes don't match," Zoe announced, appearing in the kitchen twenty minutes later while I was making their lunches. She was wearing one black patent Mary Jane and one matte black one.

"Close enough," I said absently, my mind focused on what to do next. How to protect my kids.

I turned to find her frowning at me, arms crossed. "You said shoes have to match."

"I did," I said, forcing a smile. "And you're right." I crouched, helping her switch out the matte one. "Now they match."

She smiled, satisfied, then skipped to the table where her brother was hunched over a bowl of cereal, stirring it until it turned soggy.

"Lucas, eat," I said.

He didn't look up. "Do you think Reed would come to my game if I asked?"

The question caught me off guard. My throat closed. That was the first time I'd heard him say Reed's name in several weeks. "No, honey. Reed's... busy with work right now."

His spoon hit the side of the bowl with a sharp clink that echoed through the kitchen. Lucas's shoulders tensed, his eyes flashing beneath his dark lashes. "You don't know that!" The words burst from him as his fist tightened around the spoon, milk sloshing dangerously close to the rim. His voice dropped to something smaller, almost pleading. "You don't know if you don't ask. I bet you didn't even ask if he'd come to my birthday. I bet you didn't!"

I gripped the counter edge until my knuckles whitened, avoiding his eyes. My voice came out thinner than I wanted. "Honey, I—" The words stuck. I swallowed hard and busied myself wiping invisible crumbs from the counter. A car horn blared outside, making me flinch. I didn't have an answer, so I left the words unsaid.

What could I say? It's all my fault. I'm sorry? Me too? I didn't ask. I wouldn't ask.

He didn't say anything else. Just pushed the bowl away, put his elbow on the counter and rested his head on his hand. He turned his face from me and stared at the wall—I knew he was trying not to cry, or maybe he was crying and wouldn't let me see.

Something inside me cracked. Reed's absence had left a hole in this house that I couldn't fill, and I felt a tear drop from my eye. It's unfair. Everything that we're going through. When does it stop?

On the way to Lucas's school, I stopped at a red light and caught sight of my reflection in the mirror: eyes ringed with exhaustion, lips pressed tight. I looked like someone bracing for impact.

Even the mothers in line at school drop-off looked at me like they knew something was wrong. One actually asked me if they could help me with anything, that I looked "haggard." I wanted to call her a bitch, but she wasn't wrong. I did look haggard.

When I pulled into the parking lot at Harbor House Road, I didn't get out right away. I sat there, hands gripping the steering wheel until my knuckles turned white.

The events of the last few weeks haunted me—the coffee, every creak in the house, the flowers. I swore there were things in my house that had been moved around. When I checked the footage, there was nothing on it. The cops were no help. I'd stop calling them with any new issues if I couldn't prove it was him. They thought I was just some paranoid crazy woman.

Zoe's voice broke me out of my thoughts. "Mommy? Can we get out now? I wanna get to art class." Shit. How long had I been sitting here? I ushered her out of the car, walked us inside, and dropped her off with her teacher. Keeping my shoulders squared, I headed over to my office, trying to look like someone who wasn't falling apart.

"Morning," Danya said, handing me a stack of folders. "You okay? You look..." She hesitated. "You look like you didn't sleep."

"Didn't," I said. "We had a long night."

"With the kids?"

"With everything."

She gave me a look that said she wanted to ask more but didn't. "Well, your donor meeting's at noon. I can reschedule if you're not up for it."

I shook my head, gripping my travel mug so tightly my fingers ached. "No. Keep it." I needed the distraction—even if just for an hour in a room full of people who couldn't possibly know all the crazy going on in my life. A moment of normalcy would be wonderful.

But as the morning wore on, the unease in my chest grew heavier. Every time the door opened, I turned too quickly. Every time the phone rang, my stomach clenched.

Then, just after eleven, the front desk called through the intercom. "Maliyah, remember how you asked the other day about any strange cars hanging around? Well, I think there's one outside."

I was already halfway to the door.

The monitor showed the front parking lot. A black sedan parked across the street. Same make. Same tint. I could swear it was the same damn car.

"It's been out there for about an hour. No one got in or out and there isn't a ride share sign or anything."

"Did you get a plate?" I asked.

"Too far," the receptionist said. "It's just been sitting there. You know, we've been getting a few calls with dead air today too. I answer but no one is there. I just thought there was an issue with the connection. Now, everything just feels weird."

I swallowed hard. "Call it in. Tell them about the calls and the car out front. Let them know I think it's the same vehicle I reported last week."

She nodded, picking up the phone. I stayed frozen, staring at that grainy image until my reflection in the glass—wide eyes, tight jaw—looked like someone else entirely. Should I be the one to call it in? Yes. But did I want it to be someone else so they wouldn't think it was me—the crazy lady—again? Yes.

The cruiser showed up fifteen minutes later. When they pulled up to the car, they got out and knocked on the window. From where we stood, the window rolled down, but it was impossible to see who was in the car. The cop stood there, talking and checking their ID. I saw them wave the car on and then head over to walk our way.

The officer's shoes made a soft-soled noise on the tile as he came in, one hand resting casually on his belt. "Ms. Davenport?" he asked, glancing around the lobby like this was just another errand on a checklist. "Everything alright?"

"I swear that's the same car," I said. "The same one I've reported to you guys before."

He nodded slowly, flipping open his notepad. "We ran the plates. Belong to a rental out of Quincy. Guy's license checked out. He says he was waiting for a client. Real estate agent."

"Did you confirm that? Isn't that weird? A real estate agent using a rental and sitting across the street from a women's shelter?"

He shrugged one shoulder, tapped his pen against his notepad twice. "Guy had all his paperwork. Real estate license number, business card." His gaze drifted past me to the window where the car had been. "Can't arrest someone for sitting in a legal parking spot."

My stomach dropped. "He's watching this building. He's watching me."

"Ma'am, I understand you've had some trouble recently—"

"Trouble?" My laugh came out brittle. "I have a restraining order. You can't even imagine what I've been through."

The officer's pen hesitated mid-scratch, but his face stayed neutral. "And that order hasn't been violated, technically speaking. There's no proof he approached you or made contact. Or that he's behind all the things you're reporting to us."

"Because he's smart," I snapped. "Because he knows how to make me look crazy."

His expression softened, pity slipping through the professionalism. "I'll file a report and pass it along to the domestic liaison unit, alright? We'll keep an eye out."

He left a card on the desk and walked back toward his cruiser. Outside, the sedan was gone. Just like that. Vanished.

Danya turned to me. "You should go home. Get some rest."

"No. I have work to do. I'd prefer the distraction. Can you let me know when the donors arrive?"

Danya nodded, giving me a look that said she wasn't convinced, but she didn't push.

Home. The word made me nauseous anyway. Work was better. Work meant I didn't have to think about how to keep Zoe and Lucas safe, at least not for the rest of the day.

By the time Zoe and I left Harbor House at the end of the day, the weather was freezing. I was exhausted, but my earlier meeting had been highly successful—a significant check for the center that will fund beds into Spring. The knowledge of this impact lifted my spirits, however briefly.

I took a deep breath and filled my lungs with cold air—it had that raw edge of coming snow. I watched every car in my rearview mirror on the way to Lucas's school, half expecting the dark sedan to reappear.

It didn't. I'm not crazy. I know he's out there. I know he's watching.

Lucas came running out of the building with his backpack half-zipped and his jacket unbuttoned. He grinned when he saw me, but the moment he noticed my face, his smile faltered. "Mom? You okay?"

"Of course, honey. I'm fine. Just had a long day." I lied automatically. "Hop in, buddy."

I waited until we were on the highway before saying, "We're going to Aunt Felicity's tonight, alright?"

Zoe gasped. "Sleepover?"

"Something like that."

Lucas frowned. "But it's a school night."

"I know. I'll talk to your teacher. I just... need to take care of a few things." My voice was calm, controlled, but my hands were gripping the steering wheel so tightly they ached.

He watched me in the rearview mirror for a long time before saying quietly, "Is it because of him?"

I almost missed the exit. My throat closed, the words caught somewhere behind my teeth. "Who?"

"The bad guy—Bryce," he said. "I heard you on the phone last week. You told Aunt Felicity you thought he'd done something."

I forced a smile into the mirror. It's so easy to forget about little ears and how they hear things you'd never expect. "It's just a precaution, honey. I'm keeping everyone safe."

Zoe hummed to herself in the backseat, unaware. Lucas kept watching me like he didn't believe a word I said.

Then I heard his voice, quietly say, "I bet Reed would take care of it."

Felicity opened the door before I'd even knocked. "You look like hell," she said bluntly, pulling me into a hug.

"Love you too."

She glanced over my shoulder toward the car that was running with the heat on. "The kids?"

"Sleeping," I said. "I didn't want them to hear us talk."

Her expression softened. "Okay. Let's sit."

We sat on her front porch steps, bundled in coats, while keeping the car in sight.

The porch light spilled across the driveway, soft and gold against the dark. My SUV idled quietly and through the windshield, I could see Zoe was still fast asleep in her car seat—her head tilted at an awkward angle that made me want to go fix it. Lucas was in his booster seat beside her, chin tucked to his chest, lying on top of his backpack that he was clutching.

Watching them should have eased the knot in my chest. It didn't. The longer I sat there, the tighter it pulled.

My brother-in-law, Caden, emerged from the house with two mugs of tea, steam curling into the cold air. He handed one to each of us with a quiet nod before heading back inside.

"Start from the beginning," she said softly.

I told her everything. The car. The flowers. The coffee, and more. Everything—I held nothing back. Her hand tightened around the mug, knuckles white, but she didn't interrupt. Why hadn't I already told her all of this? I knew the answer though. There was something inside me that was still afraid that maybe I was just being paranoid.

When I finished, my voice barely worked. "I sound insane, don't I?"

She shook her head. "You sound scared. Which is fair. But you're not insane, Maliyah. If you think he's out there, then he probably is. I wish you would have told me what was going on before now."

My throat burned. "The cops think I'm just paranoid."

"The cops don't live your life." She glanced toward the kids again. "You did the right thing bringing them here. They'll stay with us tonight. You stay, too."

"I can't."

"Maliyah—"

"I need to go home," I said, forcing the words out before she could stop me. "If I don't, I'll spend all night wondering if he's there. I just... I need to see for myself."

She stared at me like I'd lost my mind. Maybe I had.

"At least call Reed," she said finally. "You don't have to tell him everything, just—let him know what's going on. He'll listen."

I looked down at my hands wrapped around the mug, steam curling into the cold air. "I haven't spoken to him in weeks. He won't care. And I can't just run to him because I'm falling apart."

"You're not falling apart," she said softly. "You're trying to survive. Stay here Maliyah. Let us be here for you. We have an alarm, cameras, the works. It's safer here."

I looked back toward the car. Zoe was still asleep but Lucas had woken up. He was blowing fog on the window and tracing shapes into it. For a moment, I saw Reed sitting in front—his arm draped behind the headrest, eyes on me the way they used to be. I blinked hard and looked away.

"I brought stuff for them but nothing for myself. Even my work stuff is at home. But you're right." I sighed in resignation. "Let me go grab my stuff and I'll come right back," I said.

"Maliyah—"

"Please. Don't argue with me."

She pressed her lips together, then nodded once. "Fine. But you text me the second you get there. And if anything feels off—anything—you call 911 first, not me."

"Got it."

I helped her get the kids out and in the house.

"I'm coming with you," Caden said, forcefully.

"I'll be fine. Honestly, nothing's happened so far. I'd rather both of you stay with my kids and keep them safe. Leaving Felicity here with just the kids and Macy isn't a good idea given everything that's happening."

"Then call Reed on your way," he said.

"Honestly—"

"No. Maliyah, I mean it. You call him or I'm coming. The cops won't listen, but Reed's a cop. At minimum he'll offer some protection. What happened between you guys doesn't matter when we're talking about your safety. Please. Do this. For me."

I sighed. Giving up, I finally agreed. "Okay. I'll call him."

I pulled out of the driveway, her porch light shrinking in my rearview mirror. The street was quiet—too quiet. Every shadow felt like it was watching.

My phone sat in the cupholder, Reed's contact already pulled up from this morning when I'd seen his message and couldn't bring myself to open it.

I told Siri to call Reed.

It rang once. Twice. Three times.

"Hey, this is Reed Morrison. Leave a message."

Of course. Of course he didn't answer. My throat tightened as the beep sounded.

"Reed, it's me." My voice came out steadier than I felt. "I know I have no right to call you. I saw you sent me a text earlier. But I—" I swallowed hard. "Something's wrong. Bryce is... I know he's been following me. Watching me. The officers I've spoken to won't do anything because he's smart enough to stay just on the right side of legal, and I can't prove it's him. But *I know* it's him."

I stopped at a red light, checking my mirrors. Empty street behind me. Empty street ahead.

"The kids are safe. They're with Felicity. I just... I needed to tell someone who would understand." My voice cracked. "I needed to tell you. I'm going home to grab some things, then I'm going back to Felicity's."

The light turned green.

"I'm sorry. For calling. I shouldn't have. I—Um—bye Reed." I ended the call before I could say anything else I'd regret. Something about it just felt so—final.

My phone screen dimmed, still showing the unread message from Reed. I still couldn't make myself read it.

The drive to my apartment took a little more than fifteen minutes. I parked in my usual spot, scanned the lot twice. No dark sedan. No one watching. The pit in my stomach eased.

The building was quiet as I climbed the stairs. My neighbor's TV played through the door. The aromas of garlic and tomatoes hung in the air as I ascended the stairs. Normal. Everything was normal.

I unlocked my door, flipped on the lights. Everything looked exactly as I'd left it. I shot Felicity a quick text: *"Made it to my place."*

I moved quickly—overnight bag, toothbrush, clothes, laptop. Grabbed the kids' stuffed animals. Zoe's elephant, Lucas's dinosaur. My gun was already in my purse, but I checked the safety by instinct, though I knew it was on. I never leave home without it and I never leave the safety off. Not since I'd started carrying.

It took me half an hour to get changed and grab everything I could.

Felicity: Zoe's upset—says she needs Lani, her elephant????

Ha! Feeling accomplished as I looked down at the bag, Lani was lying right on top. The covert spot where the Harbor House tracker was stashed was facing me. If I didn't know where it was, I'd never guess.

Me: Already got it. It's the elephant that the shelter gives away. #mom-forthewin

Felicity: Awesome. On your way back?

Me: Almost. I'll grab some ice cream on the way too.

Felicity: Sweet. My sweet tooth is raging. Get me bubblegum flavor.

Me: gross. What are you? Five???

Felicity: STFU don't be jealous of good taste. Finish up and get back here!

Me: Fine. I'll get you and my 4yo the same thing... be there in a bit

I was smiling as I shut all the lights and closed the door behind me. I locked the deadbolt and started making my way toward the stairs. I couldn't help but really appreciate my sister. We would both do just about anything for each other. I'd even get her bubblegum ice cream. Ridiculous, I thought as I chuckled to myself.

As I walked toward the stairs, I was stashing my phone in my purse and almost bumped into someone standing at the top of the stairs.

Backing up, I said, "Oh, sorry, I—"

My breath stopped. *No. Not him. Not now.*

"Hello, Maliyah." Bryce's voice was calm, pleasant. Like we'd just run into each other at the store. "I think it's time we talked. Don't you?"

Chapter 27:

The Message

REED

I rubbed my eyes as I looked around and realized I'd fallen asleep on the couch. The muted glow of the TV left flashes on the walls of my living room—some late-night talk show I didn't remember turning on. My neck ached from the angle I'd been sleeping in. Looking at the clock, I saw it was late.

I'd come home from work, hours ago, heated up leftover Chinese food I hadn't eaten, and apparently passed out before taking a bite. The container sat on the coffee table. Nothing like room-temperature, congealed lo mein. An empty glass of water sat next to it, a ring of condensation at its base—the ice long melted.

This was my life now. A pathetic, half-lived existence. Empty.

My phone buzzed on the cushion beside me. I grabbed it, squinting at the bright screen. A text.

John: *You still alive?*

If that's what you want to call it.

Me: *Yeah. Fell asleep on the couch.*

John: *Exciting life you're living.*

I didn't respond. The asshole wasn't wrong.

I was about to set the phone down when I noticed the voicemail notification. One new message. Looks like it came in over an hour ago.

I swiped to see the details.

Maliyah.

My heart stopped. Then started again, too fast. I sat up, the blanket I didn't remember getting sliding off my lap, landing on the floor by my feet. My thumb hovered over the play button. I paused. Once I listened, there'd be no going back. Fuck.

Man up. She'd called. After weeks of silence, after I'd sent that text this morning that she hadn't responded to, she'd called. My nerves buzzed through my body. My fingers felt electrified as I reached for the play button.

I pressed it and hit speaker—needing to hear her voice alive, in this room with me.

"Reed, it's me."

Her voice hit me like a physical punch to my gut—familiar and wrong at the same time. Strained. Tired. Scared. Was she nervous to talk to me too? *Fuck. Just hearing her voice—*

"I know I have no right to call you." *You do. You have every right to call me.* "I saw you sent me a text earlier. But I—" A pause, like she was gathering courage. "Something's wrong. Bryce is... I know he's been following me. Watching me. The officers I've spoken to won't do anything because he's smart enough to stay just on the right side of legal, and I can't prove it's him. But I know it's him."

The room seemed to drop twenty degrees. My legs moved before my brain caught up, launching me off the couch so fast my knee banged against the coffee table, sending my glass of water, and the half-empty container of lo mein, crashing to the floor. *Shit.*

"The kids are safe. They're with Felicity. I just... I needed to tell some-one who would understand. I needed to tell you. I'm going home to grab some things, then I'm going back to Felicity's."

A pause. Background noise—a car, traffic sounds. My mind went from freaking out in hearing from my girl—because she was my girl—to fo-cused and clear. I'm a fuck-up and don't deserve her, but the prospect of something happening to her—no. I can't—I won't let anything happen to her.

"I'm sorry. For calling. I shouldn't have. I—Um—bye Reed."

The message ended. I stared at the phone, my hand shaking.

She'd called over an hour ago. In all that time, she'd been dealing with this while I was passed out on my couch like a fucking idiot.

Bryce. That motherfucker. He'd been silent—no contact or issues after the restraining order.

This is my fault. The realization hit me like a fist to the sternum, crushing the air from my lungs and sending ice water through my veins. Every second I'd wasted feeling sorry for myself was a second he'd been out there, watching her, waiting. And now she was alone.

I hit callback before I was even conscious that I'd done it. It rang once. Twice. Three times. Four.

"Hi, this is Maliyah. I can't come to the phone right now—"

I hung up and immediately called again. Same result. Voicemail.

I called a third time—this time it went straight to voicemail. It didn't even ring—her phone was either off or dead. My chest tightened. She said she was going home, then back to Felicity's. Maybe she was driving. Maybe her phone was on silent. Maybe—

I pulled up Felicity's contact and pressed call. It rang four times before she answered, slightly breathless. "Reed?"

"Is Maliyah with you?"

A pause. "No. She went home to get some things. Didn't she call you?"

"She did. I missed it. When did she leave?"

"It's been maybe an hour and half now. She let me know when she got there, said she was gathering her stuff. We were texting and said she was going to get ice cream on the way back here. I didn't expect she'd be back for another ten or so minutes given the time it takes to get to her place, get the ice cream, and get home." She was rambling at this point but I could sense the change in Felicity's voice, when fear sharpened her tone as she asked, "Didn't she call you? Reed, what's going on?"

"She left me a message. Telling me about Bryce following her. He's stalking her, Felicity." I was already moving; I'd grabbed my keys and coat and made my way to the door. "I'm trying to call her back but she's not answering, and now her phone is going straight to voicemail."

"Oh my God." Felicity's voice went thin. "Reed, if he's there—"

"Already on my way. I'm calling it in." I exited my building, my unmarked car already in sight. "Felicity, I need you to stay there in case she shows up. The kids need you calm."

"But I should come—"

"No. Stay with the kids. If she comes back, call me immediately."

She made a sound that might have been agreement or a sob. "Just find her. Please."

I was in my car, engine starting, phone connected to Bluetooth. "I will."

I hung up and called John while I pulled out onto the street. He answered, "Change your mind about getting out of the house? I'm down for a drink."

"Maliyah might be missing."

"Wait. What?"

I explained what had happened, catching him up.

John responded quickly, saying, "Okay. I'll call it in and meet you there."

"Okay. I'll see you there." Disconnecting the call, I tried Maliyah's number again.

Straight to voicemail again. Maybe it died.

Or someone had turned it off for her.

The drive to her apartment should have taken twenty minutes. I made it in twelve, lights going, running two red lights, and pushing my speedometer past eighty on the highway.

The entire time, Maliyah's voice played on a loop in my head.

Something's wrong. Bryce is following me.

I needed to tell someone who would understand. I needed to tell you.

She'd called me. She'd reached out for help. And I'd been fucking sleeping.

Every fear I'd had about my job, about dying and leaving her alone—all of it was bullshit. Because the real danger wasn't me getting shot. It was me being too much of a coward to be there when she actually needed me. I'd gone complacent after the TRO was issued. He'd been silent for so long. How could I be so stupid.

I pulled into her parking lot, scanning for her car. There—her SUV, parked in a spot near the building entrance. I breathed a sigh of relief. Maybe she was still upstairs. My gut said something different, though, given the time that had passed. And I was instantaneously alert.

I jumped out of my car before the engine fully died, my hand automatically going to my weapon as I approached the building, walking by her car first—nothing out of the usual there.

The front door's security lock was broken—the strike plate hanging loose, fresh scratches on the metal. Someone had forced it. FUCK!

I drew my weapon and pushed through the door. Approaching the stairs, I scanned the area. Nothing. I slowly ascended the stairs, making my way to Maliyah's apartment, listening for any other sounds.

The landing was empty. Moving toward Maliyah's door, I saw her keys were lying on the floor, half the distance from her door to the stairwell. Her telltale "Best Mom" keychain, with faded gold plating, pointing out. The sounds of a blaring TV came through a neighbor's apartment. If there'd been a struggle, no one heard it.

My heart launched itself into my throat. I needed to focus. I wouldn't be any good to Maliyah if I panicked. My training kicked in and I approached her door. Entering, I cleared the apartment quickly, moving methodically from room to room. As I cleared the final room, I heard John's voice call out for me. "Morrison!"

Holstering my weapon, I started toward the front living room. "Here," I called out in response. "I've already cleared the area."

"Saw a set of keys on the ground near the door."

"Yeah—Maliyah's. I motioned to Officer Marquez behind John. "Can you secure the scene and get the evidence documented?" Marquez nodded once, already pulling latex gloves from her pocket as she stepped back into the hall.

I scanned the living room—couch cushions still perfectly aligned, kids' books and crayons neatly stacked on the coffee table, not a single thing out of place. Even in the kitchen, dishes in the dish rack and the counters were clear. Whatever happened, it hadn't happened in here.

I tried calling Maliyah's phone again. Still straight to voicemail.

John stepped forward, "Reed, you're too close to this."

"Get the fu—"

"Listen, man, I know you're not going to just back off, but you're going to need to let me take the lead here."

Officer Marquez's voice broke in, "Detectives, we've got something." I gave John an eye, pushing past him as I followed Officer Marquez. She brought us to the back stairwell which leads to the rear of the building.

A trail of debris was scattered all along the floor of the landing. A purse, phone face-up with a shattered screen, and a tube of lipstick were front and center. Scattered around it—receipts, granola bars, tissues, and a dozen other small things. But my eyes were drawn to what I saw smack dab in the middle of it all. A gun. Maliyah's gun. So she was unarmed now.

The punch to my gut was unreal. Leaving Marquez to preserve the scene, John and I returned to Maliyah's apartment. We needed to plan and act now. I couldn't stand around hoping for a solution.

John's voice pulled me out of my thoughts. "Reed, man. Let me take over. We get this guy, you don't want him trying to get off on a technicality."

I looked at him. Seeing the genuine concern on his face, I knew I needed to trust him. I *did* trust him. My partner for years, friend for longer than I could remember.

"Yeah man, alright. I'll step back while you lead." Rushing on, I said, "but I'm not stepping away."

"I wouldn't expect it of you. At least this way, I can keep an eye on your ass."

"I'm calling her sister now."

"Alright, let's step in the other room and we can call her together."

We moved over to the kitchen. I tapped *call* on Felicity's contact card, and put it on speaker.

"Reed. Did you find her? Is she still there? What's happening?" Felicity was understandably panicked.

"She's not here, Felicity. Her keys and her car are both still here, though. Is Caden with you?"

"Yes. Why?"

"You're going to need him."

"I'm here Reed."

"Guys, John's here with me."

"Hi Felicity, Caden." They knew John—barbecues, double dates, back when my life made sense. John's face was strained with the news he was about to deliver.

Felicity responded, "John—what's going on here, guys? Where's my sister?"

"Felicity, there was a struggle outside Maliyah's apartment. We don't have a lot to go on right now, but we are placing an APB out for Bryce Callahan. We have to assume at this point that she's missing and was likely abducted."

Felicity's voice and cry out was guttural. I heard Caden's voice in the background, low and trying to steady her, and that was it — that was the sound of a family falling apart.

I dropped my head. Stopped breathing. Felt the pain constricting my heart. Her brokenness was my own. Maliyah had been calling me and I'd been fucking sleeping.

Felicity's sobs were the only sound John and I could hear. But I didn't get the luxury of breaking down. This was my world. This was where I make a difference. And I would burn his world to the ground to find my woman. There was no place on this earth that motherfucker could hide that I wouldn't find him.

And once I had her back. Once I had all of them back. I'd never let them go again. No matter the consequence. No matter the struggles. They were mine, and I was theirs. For better or fucking worse.

Bryce Callahan better get ready because he made a big fucking mistake coming for Maliyah. And I was all too happy to help him see that.

Chapter 28:

Taken

MALIYAH

The eerie calm when he said my name and told me it was time we talked made my skin crawl. My hand was already moving toward my purse, fingers searching for the grip of my gun or the pepper spray. Anything. But Bryce was fast—he'd always been faster than me when it mattered. And he was so close to me right now, that his speed mattered.

It took him less than two strides to close the short distance I'd put between us when I'd stepped back. His hand clamped around my wrist just when I got my hand on the handle of my weapon. But he squeezed so hard that I reflexively opened my hand and dropped the gun back into the depths of my bag. His free hand wrapped around the front of my throat. When he applied pressure along my trachea I felt the urge to cough. He was showing me that he held the power in this moment.

His cheek scraped against mine, each bristle of stubble catching and lifting individual strands of my hair. The sound—like sandpaper—filled my ear as he pressed closer, his nose tracing my cheek and face. My stomach turned, as I heard his deep inhale. When his lips brushed the shell of my ear, I felt the wet heat of his exhale dampen my skin."Now, now," he said softly. "Let's not do anything stupid. I just want to talk."

I swallowed back the acidic burn climbing my throat. "Let. Go. Of. Me." Each word came out clipped but steady, belying the violent tremor I felt inside as my stomach clenched and twisted. My free hand curled into a fist at my side, nails digging half-moons into my palm. "You're violating the restraining order. The police will—"

"The police aren't here, Maliyah." His grip on my wrist tightened even more, pulling my hand from my purse as he twisted just slightly, causing me to cry out. "And by the time they arrive, we'll be long gone." Still whispering, he pulled back a bit. "You and me, Maliyah. Just like old times. Like it should always have been."

"I'm not going anywhere with you."

The smile in his voice never wavered. "Yes, yes you are, my love."

Fuck this. I drove my knee up hard, aiming for his groin. He twisted at the last second and my knee connected with his thigh instead. Not enough. But it gave me space—half a second where his grip loosened.

I yanked my wrist free and ran. Not toward the front stairs—he was blocking the way. Instead, I ran deeper into the hallway, down past apartment 3C, toward the rear stairwell. I was screaming the whole way there, banging on the door as I passed. "Help! Someone help me! Call 911!"

My neighbor's TV was still playing through the door. *Please let her hear me. Please!* I reached for the stairwell door, but suddenly I felt Bryce's hand in my hair. For a suspended moment, I was airborne, my arms flailing uselessly, before he drove me down. My back crashed against the hallway floor, the impact knocking the air from my lungs in a single violent rush.

My purse dropped off to my side. Bryce's hand covered my mouth as he hovered over me, muffling my screams.

"Shh, shh," he whispered against my ear. "Stop fighting. You're only making this harder on yourself."

I bit down on his palm as hard as I could, tasting blood.

He cursed and his grip loosened enough for me to twist in his arms. My elbow connected with his jaw—a solid hit that snapped his head back. He staggered, and I flipped over on the floor, scrambling away on my hands and knees.

My purse. I needed my purse. It was right there, a few feet away, my gun visible through the open top.

Bryce's foot came down on my ankle, pinning it. Pain shot up my leg and I screamed again, hoping someone—anyone—would hear.

Reed's voice echoed in my head, *"Never fight in silence if you can help it."* So, I screamed. Louder than I had ever screamed before.

"Enough." His voice had changed, losing that pleasant veneer. This was the Bryce I remembered. The one who'd give me nightmares until I could make myself forget. The one who ultimately put me in the hospital. "You're coming with me whether you cooperate or not. It's your choice how much this hurts."

I twisted, kicking at his knee with my free foot. He grunted but didn't let go. Instead he dropped down, his weight pressing me into the floor, one hand fisting in my hair and pulling my head back.

"I didn't want it to be like this," he said, his breath hot against my face. "I've been patient. I've been trying to show you how good we could be together. The flowers, the coffee, watching out for you—I was being romantic. But you just keep running."

"Because you're insane," I spat. "You've been stalking me. I'm not interested in—"

His fist connected with the side of my face and the world went white with pain. My vision blurred, ears ringing. I curled into a ball, trying to protect myself. I heard him get up and felt his hand curl into my hair while he pulled me up to standing with him. I attempted to make myself into dead-weight but the pain in my head was too much to bear when he pulled on my hair.

Through the haze, I felt him grab my purse, and saw him pull out my phone. My phone was vibrating—someone was calling. Felicity?

"We don't need any interruptions, do we, sweetheart?"

He dropped my phone and stomped on it, shattering the screen and breaking it. I saw him pocket my wallet then he bent to pick the phone up off the ground, dragged me along to the back stairwell where he dumped out the contents of my bag onto the floor just inside the door. My phone clattered across the ground. My gun—I saw it and tried to lunge for it, even with him holding onto me. I didn't care. I needed that gun.

"Tsk, tsk, tsk, sweetheart. You won't be needing that," he said as he slammed my head into the doorjamb.

The pain that broke through my haze had me screaming out again—this time the scream was ripped from me in a way I'd never felt my voice respond. I felt myself almost throw up it was so blinding. Everything was spinning as he walked me back toward the front stairs, passing my apartment.

He reached down and grabbed my duffel bag that I'd dropped when I first noticed him. He slung it cross-body over his shoulder, saying, "We'll bring this with us. You'll need some clothes for a while where we're going. I'm so glad you packed in preparation for our trip." He kissed the side of my head, suddenly, he was lifting me, throwing me over his shoulder like I weighed nothing. I wanted to fight, begged my voice to scream out, but my head was pounding and my body wasn't responding the way it should. With my head hanging upside down, I felt the blood rush in my ears and I think I blacked out for a moment.

When I opened my eyes, he was leaning me against the side of a dark sedan, the trunk already open.

"No," I managed to say, the word slurred. Tears streaming down my face. "No, please—"

"Shh. This will be easier if you just relax."

He dumped me into the trunk like a piece of luggage. Threw my duffel bag in after me. The trunk slammed shut, plunging me into darkness. I tried to lift myself up on my elbows but my head swam. I searched the bag, hoping to find something, anything I could use as a weapon. My fingers closed around something soft. Zoe's elephant. The one from Harbor House Road with the tracker inside.

The car started moving. I clutched the elephant to my chest, my only connection to my kids, to safety, to the life I'd been trying to protect. The tracker. Felicity had the app. So did Caden. I'd made sure of it after Carmen gave us the stuffed animals—one for each kid, both with trackers. Lucas had the dinosaur. Zoe had the elephant.

I'd grabbed both stuffed animals for them when I'd been packing. I couldn't find the dinosaur as I felt around for it. Doesn't matter. I have the elephant. Small—less than a foot high, this little toy might be the only way anyone could find me.

If Felicity realized I was missing. If she thought to check the app. If the tracker was even working this far from the city.

So many ifs. Too many.

The car turned, accelerated. I could feel us getting on the highway from the smooth speed, the lack of stops. He was taking me somewhere. Somewhere he thought no one would find us. I had to stay conscious. Had to stay alert. Had to find a way out.

But the darkness and the motion and the pounding in my head were pulling me under. I fought it, biting my lip until I tasted blood, digging my nails into my palms.

Stay awake. Stay alive. Lucas and Zoe needed me to stay alive.

I remembered hearing somewhere that you could get out of trunks these days with a latch or something. I reached toward the back of the trunk, feeling for a release latch, my fingers brushing against the plastic tab, but the energy it took was too much for me and I lost the grip.

Reed. I thought of him, remembering how I'd called him. He'd gotten my message by now, hadn't he? He'd know something was wrong. He'd come looking.

Unless he didn't care anymore. Unless he'd deleted the voicemail without listening. Unless—

No. I couldn't think like that.

The darkness pulled me under. I couldn't keep my eyes open anymore. It was too much. I tried. Thought of my kids, of my sister, of Reed. Nothing could keep me lucid though. And slowly I gave up the fight. It was too much energy to waste. I knew I'd have a chance again, and I needed to conserve.

Time became meaningless in the trunk. Minutes or hours—I couldn't tell. I drifted in and out, darkness pulling me under again and again. Eventually, the car slowed, then stopped. I heard the car door open and close.

I gripped the elephant tighter, shoved it deep into my bag where he wouldn't see it immediately. Positioned myself as best I could in the cramped space, ready to fight the moment that trunk opened.

The lock clicked. The trunk lifted.

Cold air rushed in. Stars overhead—so many stars. We weren't in the city anymore.

Bryce stood silhouetted against the night sky. Behind him, I could make out the dark shape of a large house. I recognized where we were. Bryce's parents' house on the Cape. Isolated.

"Welcome home," he said, reaching for me.

I kicked out hard, catching him in the chest. He stumbled back and I scrambled out of the trunk, my legs barely holding me. Everything spun but I forced myself to stay upright. I wasn't giving this mother-fucker an inch without a fight.

He recovered faster than I'd hoped, grabbing for me. I swung wild, connecting with his jaw. He grabbed my wrist and twisted. Pain shot up my arm.

"Inside," he growled, dragging me toward the house. "Now."

I dug my heels into the driveway, but he was stronger. Always had been. He pulled me up three porch steps, through a door he must have already unlocked.

The interior was dark but familiar. We'd come here often when we were together. I could see furniture shapes, but they looked different from what I remembered.

He threw me forward and I hit the floor hard, palms scraping against polished wood. Before I could get up, he was on me, flipping me over.

"I tried to be nice," he said, straddling my waist, pinning my arms with his knees. "I tried to do this the right way. But you never could just cooperate, could you?"

I bucked, trying to throw him off. He shifted his weight, pressed down harder.

"Why are we here?" I demanded. "What do you want?"

"Sweetheart, you know my parents' house is nice and quiet. It will give us the time to reconnect without the interruptions." He gestured around at the darkness. "You know how far away our closest neighbors are. There's no one to hear our discussions while we get reacquainted. We wouldn't want anyone to misunderstand the effort it will take to remind you of your place by my side."

"What about Diane? Don't you have Diane? Bryce—you should be with your wife."

"Shut up! Diane is a memory. She was there for me while I waited for you to come home. You should be *thanking me* for being so patient! It doesn't matter. Diane isn't a problem for us."

His words froze my blood. Diane "isn't a problem"? The implication hit me like another blow. My pulse hammered in my throat as I pictured what he might have done to her. If he could do that to his wife, what was he planning for me? My children's faces flashed before me—I would never let them grow up without their mother. Something primal surged through my veins, drowning out the pain.

My throat burned raw as I unleashed a primal scream. I bucked up with every ounce of power I had left in me, driving my hips upward until my spine felt like it could break. And then I did something I shouldn't have, but I couldn't stop myself—I spat in his face, and it landed across his cheek and eye. His lashes blinked rapidly as my saliva dripped down toward his snarling lip.

And with this act, his expression changed—something cold and dangerous sliding behind his eyes. The same look I still saw in my nightmares and no matter how hard I fought, I knew what was coming—it was inevitable.

His fist. It came at my face with a speed I'd never seen before. I turned my head at the last second and he caught my cheekbone and eye socket instead of my nose. Pain exploded across my face.

Another hit, this one to my jaw. Stars burst across my vision. I couldn't reach him with my hands pinned, but I could still move my head. I snapped it forward, trying to headbutt him. Missed. His fist connected with my eye and the world went dark on one side.

"Stop," he said, hitting me again. "Just stop fighting."

But I couldn't stop. If I stopped, I was dead. If I stopped, I'd never see Lucas and Zoe again. If I stopped, I'd be giving in. I'd be giving up.

I thrashed beneath him, trying to get leverage, trying to free my arms. My hand touched something on the floor—the corner of a rug, maybe. I grabbed it, pulled hard. Bryce shifted slightly as I pulled—his balance was thrown off. Not a lot, but just enough.

With a desperate twist, I yanked my arm free and clawed upward. My fingers found his left eye—wet, yielding—and I dug in despite the agony in my wrist. Not deep enough. His howl echoed through the room as he jerked backward, protecting himself from further damage. In that instant, I summoned every ounce of strength left in me, my back bowing off the floor in a violent arch that sent him tumbling sideways, one hand pressed against his injured face.

I rolled, tried to stand. My legs wouldn't hold me. I crawled instead, heading for where I knew the door was.

His hand closed around my ankle and dragged me back.

"No!" I screamed, kicking at him. "Let me go!"

He flipped me over again, and this time when his fist came down I couldn't avoid it. It caught me square on the temple. The room tilted. Sound became muffled, distant. Another hit. Another.

I tasted blood. Couldn't see out of my right eye anymore and the left was wavering too. My body was at war with itself—flames licking up my wrist, my face a crumbling ruin of bone and flesh, my toes numb blocks of ice. Every inch between screamed its own warning that my fading mind could no longer understand.

And then, through the haze, I saw him pull back his fist one last time, and I knew this moment could very well be my last.

I prayed to God not to take me yet. To let me see my kids again. To give me strength to overcome this evil. I prayed one final time and I hoped. I hoped that my voice didn't fall on deaf ears.

Just before darkness swallowed everything.

Chapter 29:

Just a Reach

MALIYAH

Cold. I was so cold. My face felt wrong—swollen, throbbing. Every breath sent shards of glass through my ribcage. Every movement, no matter how slight, caused lightning bolts of pain to radiate from my core to my fingertips.

I tried to open my eyes but only one would cooperate—and not all the way. The other was swollen completely shut, and even blinking felt like I had sand in both eyes.

Slowly, my surroundings came into focus with my working eye. Hardwood floors. A stone fireplace. Large windows showing nothing but darkness outside.

My fingers twitched beneath the weight of fabric. My body was unable to move more than a few inches in any direction. The fleece blanket pressed against my chin and was fully tucked around me, but I was already cataloguing the best way to get out of it. I could smell his cologne on it, the odor cloying at me and mingling with the metallic tang of blood—probably both mine and his.

The absurdity of the care that he'd tucked me in with—him beating me unconscious and caring for me afterward—would have made me laugh if my ribs didn't feel like they were broken.

I tried to sit up and immediately regretted it. Pain shot through my entire body, sharp and white-hot.

"Easy now."

Bryce's voice came from nearby. I turned my head—slowly, carefully—and saw him sitting in the winged back chair near where my head was situated on the arm of the couch. He'd cleaned up. Changed his shirt. Put something on his nose, which was swelling where I'd hit him. His eye was red and swollen from where I had tried to claw at it. The blood vessels had popped—it was disgusting to look at yet so fucking satisfying.

"You got me good," he said, almost admiringly. "I like this new fight in you. Gives us something to make up for afterward."

I tried to speak but my jaw screamed in protest. Broken? Dislocated? I couldn't tell. But it was wrong.

"Don't try to talk yet. Just rest." He stood, moved toward me. I flinched and he paused, holding up his hands. "I'm not going to hurt you again. Not if you behave."

He crouched beside the couch, reaching out to brush hair from my face. I jerked away and fresh pain lanced through my skull.

"We have time now," he said softly. "Time for you to remember what we had. What we will have again. My parents' beach house—no one knows we're here. No one will bother us. We can finally talk without all the distractions. Without those kids always needing you."

Those kids. Lucas and Zoe. The elephant. Where was the elephant? I tried to look around but moving my head made the room spin.

"What are you looking for?" Bryce looked me in the eye. "They aren't here—yet. We need to get settled first. Then we can bring them to live with us in my home. They'll have a lot to learn, I'm sure. But I'm committed to setting them on the right path."

My throat closed up. The room shrank around me, walls pressing in as my heartbeat thundered in my ears, each pulse sending fresh agony through my broken body. I couldn't swallow. Couldn't breathe. I saw evil in this man and a terror I'd never known before—not for myself, but for what those hands might do to tiny fingers that trusted. Ice water seemed to replace the blood in my veins, freezing me from the inside out. I would *never* let this psychopath near my kids. I would kill him first.

"In the meantime, I'm sure it's hard for you to be away from them. I found these when I unpacked your duffel bag in our bedroom earlier." He held up Zoe's stuffed elephant and Lucas's dinosaur.

He set them both on the end table, on the other side of his chair, out of my reach.

So close, yet unreachable. Those trackers inside them were my only hope now, my silent SOS. I stared at the stuffed animals, aching to clutch them against my broken body. Their worn fabric would smell like my babies—Zoe's strawberry shampoo, Lucas's citrus. In that moment, those small reminders of my children were the only tether keeping me from surrendering to the darkness pulling at the edges of my consciousness.

"Get some rest," Bryce said, standing. "We'll talk more in the morning when you're feeling better. I'll make us breakfast. You always loved my omelets, remember?"

He went back to his chair, lying back with his feet stretched out on the coffee table in front of him.

I lay there in the darkness, pain radiating through every inch of my body. I stared at the elephant and counted my breaths. Stay alive. I have no idea how long I waited—a moment, a lifetime. It needed to be enough.

So, I kept counting my breaths. In. Out. In. Out. I counted his the same—listening for the steadiness that would tell me he's sleeping. Mine were more shallow, constricted by the brokenness inside me.

Each breath sent fire through my ribs. The right side of my face throbbed with my heartbeat. My jaw felt wrong—dislocated maybe? Or just completely broken. I'm not a doctor, but I can tell you if one were here now, I don't think they'd have a very positive outlook on healing me without long-term damage.

Pain had its own language and I was fluent. Pain meant I was here. Pain meant I was alive. And I planned to stay that way.

Bryce was finally asleep. His head tilted back, mouth slightly open. The soft sound of snoring mixed with the sound of the heated air rushing through the vent nearby.

I thought of Reed. How different they looked when they slept. Bryce slept like he hadn't a care in the world, like no one would dare cross him enough to wake him. Reed slept like he was always on guard, ready to stand and protect.

Reed had probably listened to my voicemail by now. Probably felt guilty. Probably started an investigation that would take days to find me.

If he even cared enough to look. No. I couldn't think like that. Couldn't let despair win. Because I know, if I knew anything about Reed Morrison, it's that he would protect and serve to his last breath—no matter what.

I don't know how long I have though, and I won't just sit and wait like a damsel in distress. I was alive which meant I could still fight.

The coffee table was eye level from where I lay. Glass. Thick. A top surface and another lower glass shelf underneath.

The lower shelf held a few decorative objects. Things his mother had prob-ably chosen to make the beach house feel sophisticated. She was always so kind. I never understood how Bryce had come from a sweet woman like Moira Callahan. There were a few books. A crystal bowl. A small wooden box.

And a figurine. Heavy bronze, from the look of it. An abstract female form—all angular planes and sharp edges. Maybe ten inches tall. From where I sat, the base appeared wide and solid—heavy. The top came to several pointed protrusions—her hair flowing off to her side, the tips of her ends creating a collection of sharp barbs.

Modern art. Expensive. Weighted. Sharp. My pulse kicked faster despite the pain. A weapon. Just over an arms-length away. Right there. Within reach if I could just move—just stretch.

Bryce still snored softly in his chair. His arms were crossed over his chest, head lolled to one side. I just needed him to stay asleep—just long enough.

I assessed the distance again. The couch to the coffee table. It felt like it was an ocean away, but it wasn't. It was a reach—a painful one, but I'd crawl through the desert with no water to have even the chance of survival.

I could do this. The tips of my fingers escaped the blanket, paving the way for my hand and arm. Each millimeter had been a battle won in silence. Now came the real war—shifting my broken body without a sound. With-out waking him.

I waited. Counted his breaths. Listened to the rhythm of his snoring. If I lived through this, I swore I'd do everything in my power to make sure women like me didn't have to rely on luck or timing or which detective picked up the case.

The heat coming through the vents was loud—it sounded almost like waves. I prayed it was loud enough to cover my grunts and heavy breathing. Reed's voice echoed in my head from that day at the gym: "Use every advantage. Sound, distraction, anything."

Okay. I had sound. I had distraction—he was asleep. What I didn't have was time. He could wake up any second. Could decide to move me. Could decide to finish what he started.

I had to move now. I shifted my weight slightly. Fire exploded through my ribs and I bit down on my split lip to keep from crying out. The taste of blood filled my mouth.

Bryce's snoring continued, unchanged.

Another shift. I rolled onto my side, the blanket catching on my elbow before I was finally able to break free of the prison it had represented. My vision went white at the edges. Sweat beaded instantly across my forehead, and bile rose in my throat. Every pain in my body exploded—it felt like I had broken glass inside me. I bit my tongue until I tasted copper, anything to keep from making a sound.

I would not let him win. I would not die here. I would not let Lucas and Zoe grow up without me.

I could do this. I had to do this. The thought crystallized in my mind as every cell in my broken body hummed with a determination that let me push past the pain. My children's faces flashed in my mind—Zoe's dimpled smile, Lucas's serious eyes. They needed their mother to come home.

My hand reached out toward the coffee table. The shelf underneath was right there. The bronze sculpture caught the dim light from the windows. So close.

I pushed myself forward—just an inch—and white-hot pain lanced through my ribs. A new pain in my shoulder I hadn't noticed before exploded. My vision grayed at the edges. I froze, barely breathing, waiting for the agony to subside enough that I could think.

Bryce shifted in his chair. I went completely still—panting as quietly as I could. My hand extended toward the table, my body halfway off the couch, ribs screaming. If he opened his eyes right now, he'd see me. He'd know.

Stay asleep. God, please stay asleep. A tear slipped from the corner of my eye, trailing across my temple before falling. The tiny splash it made against the hardwood seemed deafening as I hung suspended between couch and floor.

His breathing evened out again. The soft snore resumed. Focus. Just a few more inches.

I braced my other hand on the floor and pushed. The movement sent lightning through my entire torso. There was something very wrong with my shoulder. The single tear soon had followers—a steady stream of them rolling down my face, but I didn't stop.

My fingers brushed the edge of the coffee table's lower shelf. So close. I stretched further, my hand sliding under the shelf. Almost there. I could feel the cold metal against my fingertips. Then, my hand closed around the base.

Heavy. Fuck, it's heavier than I'd expected—a good and bad thing. The bronze was solid. Substantial. I pulled it slowly toward me, the bottom must be felted as it slid smoothly along the shelf.

Something else on the shelf shifted. The crystal bowl. I'd bumped it. It tipped, started to fall.

My other hand shot out—pure instinct—and caught it an inch from the floor. Pain exploded through every inch of my body with the sudden movement and I bit down on my cheek to keep from screaming.

I couldn't breathe. Couldn't move. Both hands occupied—one holding the sculpture, one holding the bowl. Frozen. All of this while I tried to balance my body and not collapse.

Bryce's snoring stopped. The chair creaked as he shifted.

I stayed perfectly still, holding both objects, not breathing. My arms were shaking. My one shoulder ready to give out entirely. Any second I was going to drop something or collapse or make a sound and it would all be over.

Bryce's lips moved, forming half-words that tumbled from his sleeping mouth. My name—or something close to it—slipped between his unconscious breaths.

Again, I heard the wood groan beneath his shifting weight. Then his breathing evened out. Deepened. The soft snore resumed. I almost cried—not from pain this time, but from relief.

I carefully—so carefully—set the crystal bowl on the floor. It made the tiniest sound against the hardwood but the heating vent was pretty loud—almost like white noise—and he didn't stir.

The sculpture was still in my other hand. Cold bronze. Sharp edges. Heavy enough to do real damage. Heavy enough to kill.

The thought didn't scare me. It should have. I'd never killed anyone. Never even imagined it. But as I clutched that bronze sculpture, feeling its weight, I knew with absolute certainty: if I got the chance, I was taking it.

No hesitation. No mercy. What he'd just done to me—all of it led to one certainty: if I didn't stop him, he'd do it again. He'd kill me. I couldn't take that chance. Not with my life. Not with my kids. This ended now. One way or another.

I pulled my lifeline closer, tucking it against my body under my side. The bronze was cold against my broken ribs but I barely felt it. The pain was background noise now. I had a weapon.

I couldn't get back onto the couch without making noise. So I stayed on the floor, pulling my legs down behind me as quietly as I could—positioning myself to look like I'd shifted in my sleep. Fallen. The blanket had slid down with me. My body angled slightly toward the coffee table.

If he noticed, he might think I was trying to escape. I'm not though—I'd never get far enough. So, let him think that.

The sculpture was hidden under my side, pressed between my body and the floor. Accessible. Ready. I tested my grip on it. Could I reach it quickly if I needed to? Yes. Even with broken ribs, even barely conscious, I could grab it and swing.

I just needed an opening. One chance. And I wouldn't miss. I took a moment to focus on breathing through the pain. Counted the seconds. Listened to the air blowing and Bryce's snoring and my own heartbeat.

Time passed. Minutes or hours, I couldn't tell. Pain had its own timeline. Bryce's breathing changed.

The snoring cut off mid-breath. A beat of silence followed, then the soft creak of leather as weight shifted forward in the chair. My pulse hammered in my throat as I heard the unmistakable sound of bare feet touching hardwood. *He's coming.*

His footsteps whispered against the hardwood before I felt him hover over me. I kept my eyes closed, though. Kept my breathing even despite the agony it caused.

His hand on my shoulder, shaking me. Not gentle. I had to respond. If I didn't, he'd get suspicious.

My eye opened—the one that still worked. My brow furrowed and I looked around, parting my lips—as if confused. His face hovered above mine. Backlit by the dim light from the windows. I couldn't read his expression.

He noticed I'd moved. I could see it register—the way his eyes tracked from the couch to where I lay on the floor, wedged between the coffee table and the couch. He wouldn't think of me having fallen. He'd think it was an escape attempt. Any excuse to hurt me. I knew this. I just knew it, so I braced for fallout.

One hand tightened on my shoulder. Not painful. Not yet. Just pressure. A reminder.

"Trying to go somewhere, were we?" His voice was soft. His other hand reached forward brushing hair out of my face. Everything about him was almost... gentle.

That made it worse somehow. I didn't answer. Couldn't. My jaw wouldn't cooperate and I didn't trust my voice. The heavy weight of my own way out of this nightmare was clutched against my ribs, hidden beneath me.

He didn't know. Didn't see it. Thought I was too broken to be a threat. His mistake. I stared up at him. I said nothing.

My vision wavered. My head spun. And I waited. I waited for him to act. For him to make his move. For my opening.

Chapter 30:

Finding Her

REED

The apartment felt like a crime scene because it was one. Yellow tape across the doorway, evidence markers scattered across the hallway carpet, Officer Marquez's camera flash illuminating the scattered contents of Maliyah's purse every few seconds.

I stood in her living room, staring at the kids' books stacked neatly on the coffee table. A purple crayon lay on top, the paper wrapper peeled back from use. Zoe's favorite color.

I stepped into the hallway and called the precinct. "Detective Morrison, badge 4137. I have a suspected kidnapping, active scene and need CSU." After I provided the address, the desk sergeant confirmed. Units were en route.

"Morrison." John appeared in the doorway. "Neighbor in 3A finally answered. Elderly woman, deaf in one ear. Says her TV was up loud but she thought she heard something in the hall but didn't check. Said she saw a man matching Callahan's description with a dark sedan out front. Didn't see him leave."

I nodded, but the information felt distant. We already knew it was Bryce. The voicemail had told us that. The restraining order history told us that. The forced entry and scattered evidence told us that. It was merely confirmation.

What we didn't know was where he'd taken her. My phone vibrated. Felicity's name flashed on the screen."Reed, did you find her? Tell me she's okay."

I moved to Maliyah's bedroom, closing the door on all the listening ears surrounding me. My jaw clenched so tight the tension shot into my shoulders. "It's been half an hour, Felicity." The words came out like gravel.

"Where is she?!" Her voice broke on the last word.

"We're working on it. I've got a BOLO out on Bryce Callahan and his vehicle. Every cop in Massachusetts is looking for that car."

"That's not good enough!" Her voice cracked. "She called you, Reed. She asked for help and—"

I gripped the phone so hard my knuckles went white. "I know." My voice cracked like a whip in the quiet bedroom. I caught my reflection in Maliyah's mirror—jaw clenched, eyes wild—and forced a deep breath. "Felicity," I said, softer now. "I know."

She was quiet for a moment. I heard Caden's voice in the background, low and soothing.

"Wait," Felicity said suddenly. "Reed, the stuffed animals. You know—the kids stuffed animals they got from the shelter. Maliyah picked it up from the apartment. They both have GPS trackers. Did you see them at Maliyah's? Could she have them with her?"

My heart stopped. "What?"

"Yeah—remember she was grabbing stuff from the apartment? She grabbed the stuffies for the kids. I have the app on my phone and iPad—Caden does too." Her voice pitched higher, words tumbling out faster. "Maliyah had us install it. Shows their location right down to the street address. Oh my God, why didn't I think of this sooner? My hands are shaking so bad I can barely unlock the damn screen!"

"Can you access it right now?"

"Caden's coming back in. Hold on." Rustling, muted conversation. Then Caden's voice came on the line. "Reed, I've got the app open. Both trackers are active and showing a location."

"Where?"

"Dennis Port. Cape Cod. It's been stationary for a while now."

Dennis Port. My fingers trembled against the screen as I logged into our precinct's database, each loading circle another second wasted. "Come on, come on," I hissed through clenched teeth, the taste of adrenaline metallic in my mouth. I logged in and pulled up Bryce's file on my phone—thumb leaving smudges as I frantically scrolled through his history to known addresses.

My heart stuttered when I saw it—Richard and Moira Callahan. 247 Oceanview Drive, Dennis Port, MA. Isolated beachfront property. Perfect place to try and hide away.

"Text me the exact coordinates from the trackers," I said. "And keep that app open. If it moves, you call me immediately."

We will. Reed—" Caden's voice cracked slightly before he cleared his throat. His exhale was audible through the phone. "Bring her home."I gripped the phone tighter, my knuckles white against the dark screen. "I will."

I disconnected and turned to find John in the doorway. "We've got her. Cape Cod. His parents' beach house."

John's expression sharpened. "Let's move."

I jabbed at my phone as we hit the stairs, connecting with Dennis Port dispatch. After a brief exchange, they patched me through to Sergeant Walsh.

I gave him the essentials—active kidnapping, victim abducted from Boston two hours ago, GPS tracker placing her at 247 Oceanview Drive. Suspect Bryce Callahan, white male, early forties. I needed units on scene immediately.

Walsh knew the property. Big place on the water, Callahan family owned it, usually empty this time of year. He could have two cars there in fifteen minutes but warned me the house had multiple exits—beach access, side doors. If Callahan wanted to run, he'd have options.

I told him to establish a perimeter and keep eyes on every exit. We were forty minutes out.

In the parking lot, John grabbed our go-bags while I called Captain Martinez. His message was clear: do this by the book or he'd bury my badge himself. No cowboy shit.

John drove. I pulled up the tracker on my phone—still stationary at the house. She was there.

"You good?" John asked.

"No."

The hour-long drive stretched into eternity. I tapped my fingers against the door in rhythm with the windshield wipers slicing through the flurries that had started falling. We weren't moving fast enough. I stared at the GPS dot on my phone until my vision blurred, as I thought about Maliyah's voice in her message: "Something's wrong," she'd said. And I'd missed it.

"You're here now," John said. "Focus. She needs you focused." He was right.

Walsh texted an update: *In position. House dark. No movement. Sedan matches description.*

Ten minutes later, we pulled onto Oceanview Drive. John cut the headlights. Two Dennis Port cruisers sat dark a hundred yards back, officers positioned to watch the exits.

Walsh met us, keeping his voice low. No movement since they'd arrived. They had eyes on all exits.

We moved toward the house in formation, staying low, using the landscaping for cover. The ocean was loud—waves crashing against rocks below the bluff. Good. It would mask our approach.

The house loomed ahead, dark and silent. We reached the side door. Locked.

John drew his weapon. I did the same. The door splintered open. We stepped into the darkness.

Chapter 31:
Goddess Rage

MALIYAH

"Come on." His hand closed around my upper arm. "Let's get you back on the couch where you belong."

He pulled me up and pain exploded through my ribs. White-hot, blinding. I bit down on my tongue to keep from screaming, tasting copper. My vision went gray at the edges.

Don't drop it. Don't let the weight get the better of you.

Somehow I tucked the bronze statue against my body as he yanked me to my feet. The weight of it pulled at my muscles, its edges digging into my palm. I clutched my side with it, the pain in my ribs providing the perfect cover for what I was really holding.

He positioned me on the couch, standing over me. His hand held the side of my face with a tenderness that made my skin crawl.

"There," he said. "Isn't that better?"

I couldn't answer, but nodded my head as if I were cooperating. I couldn't talk, and my whole body was screaming. I felt a sob rip through me as I thought about whether I would be permanently damaged by what he'd done to me. I needed help.

Bryce settled back into his chair. Crossed his arms. Watched me with that expression I remembered too well—possessive, satisfied, like I was a belonging he'd misplaced and finally recovered.

"You know," he said conversationally, "I've thought about you every day for all these years—fifteen years, Maliyah. Every single day. Did you think about me?"

I closed my eye. Tried to find somewhere else to be. Somewhere that wasn't here, wasn't this.

"I asked you a question, Maliyah."

When I didn't respond, he leaned forward, elbows on knees. "Diane's pretty, isn't she? Sweet. Obedient." His voice dropped. "But she wasn't you. She would never have been you."

My stomach turned.

"I tried," he continued, as if we were having a normal conversation. As if he hadn't just beaten me nearly to death and dragged me to a beach house to—what? Keep me? Kill me? "I really did try to forget you. Move on. But then I saw you at that farmer's market with your kids—" His eyes darkened. "—and I knew. It was like no time had gone by. You were always meant to be mine."

Just wait, I told myself. *Just wait for the right moment. Don't move too fast. Don't react.*

"I brought you here because this is where we should have been all along," he said, gesturing around the beach house. "You, me, the ocean. Remember when we used to talk about living at the beach someday? Having a place like this?"

I didn't remember that. Or I'd buried it with all the other poisoned memories.

"We can start over," he said, and the delusion in his voice was complete. Absolute. "I'll make you understand. You'll see—this is where you belong. With me. The way it was always supposed to be."

He actually believed this could work. Believed I would just... what? Accept this? Stay with him willingly? Be his new wife? Broken and complacent? *Fuck him.*

His delusion made him more dangerous than ever.

I tried to assess my situation through the haze of pain. My body's brokenness was at the forefront of my mind, but my spirit's strength was greater, and both would feed my rage.

"You're quiet," Bryce observed. "That's okay. You don't have to talk yet. We have time." He leaned back in his chair. "All the time in the world now."

A sound.

A thud from somewhere outside the room. Faint but unmistakable.

Wood splintered as the door burst open. Even before I saw him, I knew—Reed had come for me. The certainty of it hummed through my battered body like electricity through a wire.

Bryce's head snapped toward the hallway. "What the—"

My heart stuttered as Bryce reacted. Hope and terror mixing until I couldn't tell them apart.

Bryce stood abruptly, moving toward the doorway. Listening.

Another sound. Closer now. Whispers of footsteps.

"Stay quiet," he hissed at me. "Not a fucking sound."

He crossed back to the couch in three strides. His hands closed around my neck from behind, fingers digging into bruised flesh as he dragged me up by my hair. Standing me in front of him like a shield as he positioned himself with his back to the wall.

I couldn't breathe. Couldn't move. The pressure on my windpipe was immediate and crushing as his hand wrapped around to the front of my neck, tucked under my chin.

The sharp edges of my way out stung against my ribs—ready to act on my behalf. But his hands were choking me and I couldn't—

Flashlight beams swept across the hallway visible through the open door.

"Police!"

Reed.

Reed's voice.

It really was him. I wasn't imagining it. I'd been right. He came. He actually came.

Relief crashed through me so hard it felt like drowning and I was barely holding it together. But Bryce's hands tightened and the relief turned to panic. I couldn't breathe. Couldn't get air. My vision was tunneling, darkness creeping in from the edges.

"Not a sound," Bryce whispered in my ear. "Or I snap your neck right now."

The flashlights were getting closer. Footsteps in the hallway. Multiple sets.

The door opened.

Reed stood in the doorway, weapon drawn, flashlight mounted. A silhouette behind him that, by the shape I knew was his partner and best friend, John. Other officers flanked them, but the flashlights were blinding me.

I could see however, that there were several guns pointed at us.

At Bryce.

But I was in the way.

Someone hit the lights and Reed's eyes met mine. I saw everything in that instant—shock at my injuries, rage at Bryce, desperation because he couldn't shoot without hitting me.

I tried to hold it together, but the look on Reed's face brought tears out. A hot trail burned down my right cheek while my face throbbed, the salt stinging where skin had split beneath the swelling and along my cheek.

Reed's voice cracked, "Bryce." His voice faltered. He swallowed hard, then squared his shoulders. "Bryce Callahan." Reed's body was a coiled spring. The muscle beneath his stubbled jaw twitched once, twice, as he kept his gaze locked on Bryce. "Let her go," he commanded, each word precise and controlled. Not once did his eyes flicker toward mine, as if looking at my broken face might snap what little control he maintained.

Bryce's hands tightened, cutting off my thoughts. I made a sound I didn't recognize—choked, desperate.

"Put the guns down!" Bryce's voice was shrill. Panicked. "Put them down or I'll snap her neck right here!"

"You don't want to do that," Reed said. His voice was calm. Too calm. The way you talked to someone on a ledge. "Bryce, listen to me. You're surrounded. There's no way out of this except—"

"Shut up! Just shut up!" Bryce's breath was hot against my ear. His fingers dug deeper into my throat. "She's mine! She's always been mine and you can't—"

His grip shifted slightly as he yelled at Reed—spittle landing on my face.

His hand shifted just a fraction.

My lungs screamed for air. Black spots danced across my vision. If I didn't move now, I was going to pass out.

Or die.

Reed's voice from that day in the gym echoed through my oxygen-starved brain: Solar plexus, instep, nose, groin. S.I.N.G., Maliyah. You can do this.

I could do this.

I had to fucking do this.

Now.

Solar plexus.

Could I even do it? Every breath sent shards of glass through my ribs, my shoulder screamed with each tiny movement, and my wrist throbbed in time with my racing pulse. Every movement was agony.

But Reed's voice was clear in my head: *Fight, Maliyah. Don't give up.* So I did it. I drove my elbow back into his solar plexus—using the arm that didn't feel like it was being ripped from my body.

Pain exploded through my torso, sending lightning through my entire body—I felt the impact. Felt his body curl slightly. Felt the air whoosh from his lungs in a surprised grunt. He thought I was too broken to fight. *Surprise.*

His grip on my throat loosened. Just a fraction—just enough.

Instep.

I stomped down on his instep with my heel. Found the top of his foot and brought all my weight down. Hard.

Bones crunched under my heel.

He stumbled, crying out. And his balance shifted—his grip on my throat grew lax.

I sucked in a desperate breath of air. My vision cleared slightly.

Nose.

I snapped my head back into his face. Felt the impact reverberate through my skull—adding to the concussion, making the room spin and spots appeared in my vision—but I felt something crunch. I wasn't sure if it was his nose, but I didn't care. I broke something and I'd take what I could get.

His hands released my throat completely.

I could breathe.

Groin.

I turned—agony ripping through my body as I pivoted—and saw his face. Contorted in pain and rage and shock.

This man. This man who had tried to take my strength. Tried to take my freedom. Tried to take my life. This man who terrorized me. He would kill me if I didn't end this right now.

So, I drove my knee up into his groin with every ounce of strength I had left.

For Lucas. For Zoe. For every woman he'd ever hurt. For Diane. For all of it. For me!

The impact connected and he doubled over with a sound that didn't seem human. A high-pitched wheeze of pure agony. His hands went to his groin, face twisted in pain.

And the goddess was still in my hands. Heavy, sharp edges, solid in weight. She was ready to defend. Ready to stand up. Ready to end this. And I was ready with it.

Bryce's body faltered and, while the back of his neck exposed, I felt his hands reach forward. He moved to grab me around my legs and I realized I had *one chance.*

It was him or me.

This ended now—it ended with him.

As I felt his grip on me take hold, I brought it down with everything I had left.

The blunt bronze base struck the back of his head with a sickening thud. The impact reverberated up my arms—bone meeting metal, the shock of it traveling through my broken body—and for a split second everything stopped.

Then he howled—a sound of shock and rage. He pulled me in, grappling, clawing, trying to bring me down. Footsteps pounded toward us, but there wasn't enough time.

He was grappling for me, clawing at me. My responding cry was guttural—ripped from the depths of my being. In my hands I still held onto my final chance. This time, the spears of the statue's hair—long tendrils of metal, curved and firm—pointed outward.

I raised it again, and with every ounce of my strength, I brought it down on him—bringing it down onto the evil that had been haunting me. Haunting my dreams. And this time, the statue embedded itself in his neck and spraying me with the warm mist of his blood. The impact reverberated in my arms, and with it I felt his last breath exhale.

And once it was done, he collapsed on top of me, crushing me under his dead-weight. We fell to the ground together, and, upon impact, I lost all sense of being. The surrounding voices became distant fragments of a life I thought I'd earned. That I deserved.

I saw my children's faces, heard their voices, and felt their arms embrace me. I heard the words of a life I thought I'd almost lived—Reed's voice call out "Maliyah!"

Everything was going gray at the edges, and finally, after what felt like a lifetime, the darkness closed in—taking my pain. Taking me.

Chapter 32:

The Rhythm of Breath

<u>**REED**</u>

Bryce's dead weight pinned her to the floor. The sight of Maliyah trapped beneath him sent me sprinting across the room, my legs burning with a speed I didn't know I possessed. Before John could stop me, I'd thrown Bryce's body aside with enough force to send him rolling across the floor. My hands still burned with the satisfaction of it, with the need to put distance between this monster and Maliyah. His vacant eyes appeared fixed on eternity, and for one savage heartbeat, I imagined flames licking at his soul in whatever darkness waited beyond this room.

Maliyah lay motionless on the floor, each shallow breath a victory. My rage transformed into something worse—a cold, sickening terror that clawed at my insides before hardening back into fury at the sight of what that monster had done to her.

I took inventory of what he'd done to her. One eye had swollen completely shut. The other remained closed—I hoped she was somewhere peaceful in her mind, because reality would be brutal when she woke. Blood masked the true extent of her injuries, but I could make out the purple-black bruising beneath the crimson smears on her face, her arms, everywhere her skin showed through torn clothing.

I dropped to my knees beside her. "Maliyah." My voice cracked as I pressed trembling fingers against her neck, searching. There—faint but steady beneath my fingertips. "Stay with me, sweetheart. Please stay with me."

"Medic!" John's voice behind me. "We need a bus now!"

Footsteps thundered through the house. The trauma team swept in with equipment, voices overlapping. I stepped back—forced myself to let them work—but I couldn't look away. Not from her. Never again.

"Sir, are you riding with us?" The paramedic looked at me expectantly.

"Yes." I climbed in before anyone could object.

Maliyah lay strapped to the gurney, unconscious, IV already placed. The paramedic had said something about shock and trauma—a mercy, maybe, that she wasn't awake for this. I took the jump seat near her head. The doors slammed shut and we were moving, siren wailing.

"Maliyah." I kept my voice low even though she couldn't hear me. "I'm here. I'll be right here with you every step of the way."

The paramedic rattled off vitals to the hospital. Because of the extent of her injuries, we were taking her to Mass General in Boston. I caught fragments. Blood pressure low but stable. Respirations shallow. Each word hit like a fist. I took her hand—careful of the IV line. Her fingers were cold. Limp.

John would have called Felicity by now—told her we'd found Maliyah, that we were en route to MGH. I knew she'd meet us there. The thought brought a small measure of relief. Maliyah would need her sister.

The siren wailed. The road stretched on. I kept talking to her anyway. Told her where we were going. That she was safe. That I wasn't leaving.

The trauma bay was chaos. Blue scrubs, overhead lights, a doctor calling orders.

"Officer. You'll have to wait out here. Family only." A nurse looked at me.

"Detective. And I am family—she's my fiancé." The words came out before I could think. I knew I didn't have the right. I also knew they would stick to the rules with Maliyah. I swallowed hard, taking it down a notch, "And her sister is already en route—she's Maliyah's next of kin."

At the nurse's nod, they let me follow as they moved her into the trauma bay. I stayed close, just outside the treatment area where I could see but wouldn't be in the way.

"Reed!"

I turned. Felicity rushed through the emergency entrance. Her hair was messy, no makeup, clothes thrown together. She looked frantic. "Where is she?"

"Trauma bay. They're assessing her now."

Felicity pushed past me, heading straight for the curtained area. A nurse intercepted her. "I'm her sister. Felicity. I'm next of kin."

The nurse checked something on a tablet, then nodded. "Come with me."

Felicity grabbed my hand, pulling me with her. We stood together at the edge of the treatment area. The doctor examined Maliyah with gentle hands, occasionally making notes.

"Get portable X-ray in here," someone called. "And book CT—full trauma protocol."

The X-ray machine arrived within minutes. They positioned it, took images, moved it again. Felicity's hand gripped mine tighter with each flash.

"Taking her to CT," a nurse announced.

We followed the gurney through hallways. Felicity kept pace beside it, one hand on the rail. I stayed just behind, giving her the space to be the sister Maliyah needed.

Outside the imaging suite, we waited. Felicity paced. I sat, elbows on knees, watching the closed doors.

"Tell me what happened," she said quietly.

I told her everything. The beach house. Bryce. The fight. How Maliyah had saved herself. Felicity's eyes filled with tears, but she didn't let them fall. Thirty minutes later, they wheeled Maliyah back to the trauma bay. We followed.

Dr. Pettit stood at a computer, studying the scans. He turned to examine Maliyah again, occasionally referencing the images. "Significant facial trauma—left orbital fracture, mandibular fracture requiring surgical repair. Severe bruising and petechiae around the neck consistent with strangulation. Three rib fractures on the left side. Right shoulder shows signs of rotator cuff strain, possibly a partial tear—we'll monitor it, but it shouldn't require surgery. Right wrist has significant swelling but no fracture."

Felicity made a small sound. I put my hand on her shoulder.

"Call ortho—that jaw needs open reduction and internal fixation. Prep an OR."

"Surgery?" Felicity asked.

Dr. Pettit looked at her. "Yes. The jaw fracture is displaced. We need to stabilize it surgically."

"How long?"

"Two to three hours for the jaw repair. We'll place plates and screws to stabilize the fracture, then wire it shut for healing. The orbital fracture looks stable—we'll monitor it, but I don't think it needs surgical intervention."

A nurse adjusted Maliyah's IV, added something to the line. "Pain medication."

Time blurred. Nurses moved around us, prepping equipment, drawing blood, checking monitors. Felicity stayed close to the gurney. I hung back, knowing my place wasn't at Maliyah's bedside. Not yet. Maybe not ever.

Dr. Pettit returned with another doctor in surgical scrubs.

"This is Dr. Carter, our maxillofacial surgeon. She'll be performing the repair."

Dr. Carter studied the scans on a tablet. "The fracture is displaced but clean. Good candidate for ORIF. We'll go in, reduce the fracture, place titanium plates and screws for stability, then wire the jaw shut. Six weeks wired, then we'll reassess."

"Risks?" Felicity's voice was steady, but I heard the fear underneath.

"Standard surgical risks—infection, bleeding, anesthesia complications. Specific to this procedure, there's a small risk of nerve damage affecting sensation in her lower lip and chin. But the fracture needs to be stabilized or it won't heal properly."

Felicity nodded.

"We're ready to take her back," Dr. Carter said. "OR's prepped. While we have implied consent in life-threatening situations. I do want to try to get her agreement." Dr. Pettit leaned over the gurney. "Maliyah? Can you hear me? We need to talk about your surgery."

Nothing. He tried again, louder. "Maliyah?" Nothing.

He rubbed her chest round and round, calling out her name again. Her right eye fluttered. Opened just a crack. My heart lurched.

"Maliyah, I'm Dr. Pettit. You're at Mass General Hospital. Can you understand me?"

Her eye moved—searching, unfocused. Then found me. What escaped her throat wasn't language but a raw, animal sound—half-whimper, half-moan—that cracked something fundamental inside my chest. Tears slipped from the corners of her eyes, tracking silver paths down her temples into her hair.

Felicity stepped closer, taking Maliyah's hand. "I'm here, Mali. Reed's here too. You're safe."

Maliyah's fingers twitched against Felicity's. Then her eye found me again.

"I'm here." I moved closer. "I'm right here."

"Maliyah," Dr. Pettit said gently. "You have a broken jaw that needs surgery to repair. We need to do surgery to fix it—put in plates and screws to hold the bones together. Then we'll wire your jaw shut so it can heal. Do you understand?"

Her eye closed.

"I know you're in pain," Dr. Carter said. "The surgery will help. We'll stabilize the fracture and get you on proper pain management. But we need your consent. Can you nod if you understand and agree?"

Maliyah's eye opened again. Found Felicity first, then me.

I saw everything in that look. Terror. Pain. Exhaustion. And something else—something that looked like a question.

"It's okay," Felicity said softly. "They're going to help you."

Another sound escaped Maliyah—smaller this time. Broken.

"'Ids?" The word was barely recognizable, slurred and weak through her damaged jaw.

"The kids are with Caden," Felicity said immediately. "They're safe at our house. They're okay."

"'afe?"

"Yes. I promise. They're safe."

Her eye closed again. Tears continued to escape, following the trails marked before them. Her chest hitched once, twice, her breath catching in her throat as her fingers curled into the hospital sheet. She shook with the effort of holding herself together.

"Maliyah," Dr. Pettit said. "Can you nod for me? Do you consent to the surgery?"

For a long moment, nothing. Then the smallest movement of her head. Up and down. Barely there.

"Good. Thank you. We're going to take good care of you."

They started moving. Unlocking the gurney wheels. A nurse turned toward Felicity and me. "Only one person can accompany her to pre-op. Who should we plan to take back with us?"

Felicity didn't hesitate. "I'm her sister. I'll go."

The nurse nodded, making a note on her tablet.

Maliyah's hand shot out—grabbed mine with surprising strength. Her eye opened wide, frantic.

"'eed—" The sound was garbled, desperate.

I leaned close. "I'm here. I'm right here."

"'ease—" Her breathing hitched. "'on' 'eave—"

Please don't leave. The words I didn't deserve to hear. The trust I'd broken.

"I won't." I brought her hand to my lips, kissed her knuckles gently. "I'll be right outside. Felicity will stay with you. I'll be right here when you wake up. I promise."

"'omise?"

The word twisted something in my gut. All the promises I'd broken. All the ways I'd failed her.

"I promise, Maliyah. On everything I am. I'll be here." Her eye held mine for another moment. Searching for the lie. For the escape route I'd always taken. I didn't look away. Finally, her fingers loosened. She let go.

Felicity squeezed my shoulder as they wheeled Maliyah past me. "I'll take care of her."

I nodded, unable to speak. I followed as far as they would let me. Maliyah's eye stayed on me until they turned the corner. Then she was gone.

I stood there for a moment, staring at the empty hallway, her broken voice still echoing in my ears. *Please don't leave.* I'd already left once. Walked away when she needed me because I was too scared to stay. Not this time. Never again. I turned and walked to the surgical waiting room. I sat down in a plastic chair and pulled out my phone.

John had texted: She okay?

Me.: *In surgery. 2-3 hours.*

John: *You staying?*

Me: *Yeah.*

John: *Need company?*

Me: *Not right now.*

John: *Copy. I'll get the paperwork taken care of.*

Me: *Thanks, man.*

I set the phone down. Leaned forward, elbows on knees, and let my head drop into my hands. Two to three hours. I'd wait. However long it took. I'd made her a promise. And this time, I wasn't going to break it.

Chapter 33:

The Words of Silence

MALIYAH

I knew three things when I came to: I was alive, I hurt everywhere, and by the sound of soft snores, someone was in the room with me.

The beeping came into focus first. Steady, rhythmic. A monitor tracking something—my heartbeat maybe? Then the smell: antiseptic, sterile, that unique hospital scent that clings to everything.

I tried to open my eyes. The fluorescent lights overhead stabbed into my skull even through my closed eyelids. My head pounded with a rhythm that matched my heartbeat—relentless, brutal. Only one eye cooperated. The left stayed stubbornly closed. I knew it was because the lid was too swollen—the pressure behind it was sharp and wrong.

Through my open eye, the room took shape slowly. White ceiling tiles. Fluorescent lights dimmed low. An IV pole beside the bed with clear bags hanging from it, tubes running down to my arm.

Slumped in a chair by the window, his chest rising and falling rhythmically with each quiet breath, was Reed Morrison—the source of those gentle snores.

I took the time to look him over. His neck was resting at an uncomfortable angle. His clothes were wrinkled, blood-stained by the look of them. Dark stubble covered his jaw. He looked... haggard.

I tried to speak. My jaw wouldn't open. My chest constricted, lungs suddenly unable to fill. The walls of the room seemed to press inward, the ceiling lowering inch by inch, and I could feel sweat beading along my hairline as my good eye darted frantically around the shrinking space.

I tried again, harder this time. Nothing. My jaw was locked shut, held by something I couldn't see. Wires. Metal. I could feel them now, taste the metallic tang in my mouth. My breath came faster. The monitor's beeping accelerated. I knocked over the water and jug on the table next to me.

Reed's eyes snapped open.

"Maliyah. Sweetheart." He was on his feet, moving toward the bed but stopping short of touching me. "You're okay. You're in the hospital. Your jaw is wired shut from the surgery, but you're safe."

Safe. Was I? Was I really safe? I tried to sit up. Pain exploded through my core—ribs, I remembered now. Broken ribs. I fell back against the pillow with a sound that wasn't quite a moan, muffled behind my clenched teeth.

"Don't move too fast." Reed's hand hovered near the call button. "Let me get the nurse."

He pressed it before I could object—not that I could object, or would object for that matter. I couldn't speak. I couldn't open my jaw. I couldn't do anything but lie here and hurt. Then panic hit.

I clawed at my face, desperate to force my jaw open. But my left arm hung useless in a sling, fingers immobilized in a splint, while my right hand caught in the web of IV tubing. Trapped. My jaw remained sealed shut, metal wiring biting into bone. My lungs seized. The walls closed in. I couldn't move, couldn't speak, couldn't draw breath—

A sound ripped out of me. Guttural. Animal. It vibrated against the metal wiring, rattling my teeth and sending white-hot pain through my jaw.

The nurse appeared within seconds—middle-aged woman with kind eyes and quick hands. "It's okay, honey. It's okay." She caught my wrists gently but firmly, holding them away from my face. "You're at Mass General. Just breathe through your nose. Slow breaths. You're going to be okay."

I couldn't. My chest heaved. The monitor's beeping accelerated into a frantic rhythm.

"Look at me," she said, her voice steady and calm. "I'm Carol. You're safe. Your jaw is wired shut from surgery—that's why you can't open it. It's supposed to be like that. You're not choking. Your airway is clear."

Her words filtered through the panic slowly. Wired shut. Surgery. Supposed to be like that.

"Good," Carol said as my breathing started to slow. "That's good. You've been awake a couple times already, but you were pretty out of it then. This is probably the first time you're really aware of what's happening."

I stared at her. Tried to ask how long. Made some kind of sound that didn't form words.

"Your jaw's wired shut," Carol repeated gently, checking the IV line. "Six weeks minimum. I know it's disorienting. You have a concussion too. That's why the lights are dimmed. You might feel foggy, nauseous, dizzy. That's normal."

"I'm sure you have things you want to say. For now, we have a tablet you can use to communicate, but you can always use your phone too."

She produced one from somewhere, set it up on the rolling table, positioned it within reach. Opened a notes app and handed me the stylus that was attached with a cord.

My right hand shook as I tried to balance the tablet. My left arm was useless in its sling, so I had to rest the tablet against my thigh, making the stylus harder to control. I erased my writing three times before I turned it toward her.

How long here?

"You came out of surgery this morning," Carol said. "About six hours since you woke up in recovery, but you were pretty out of it then."

I tapped the screen again, my hand steadier now. **Bryce?**

Carol glanced at Reed. He stepped forward slightly, still maintaining distance.

"He's gone," Reed said quietly. "You don't have to worry about him anymore."

I stared at him. At the exhaustion in his face, the careful way he held himself. Like he wanted to come closer but knew better.

I killed him. The words sat there on the screen. Stark. True.

Reed's eyes softened. "Self-defense, Maliyah. Nothing more." His voice dropped to nearly a whisper. "If you hadn't fought back—" His jaw tightened, and he swallowed hard. "I wouldn't be sitting here now."

I turned to Carol. Easier than facing Reed's words. Carol adjusted something on the IV. "Your pain medication is due. This will help you sleep."

No. My fingers were clumsy but insistent as I wrote. **Too fuzzy. Want to be awake.**

"Honey, you need rest—"

Less meds. Please.

Carol glanced at Reed. He squared his shoulders. "Don't look at me. She wants less medication. Her body, her decision."

"I'll talk to Dr. Pettit," Carol said. "But you need some pain management. The ribs alone—"

IV Tylenol. No narcotics.

Carol looked at me in surprise. "They don't usually like to prescribe just IV Tylenol—it's significantly more expensive."

I tapped the tablet again, emphasizing this. Erasing it, I then wrote:

Narcotics itchy, foggy, and bad dreams. IV Tylenol. I'd fought this battle before—after Lucas's C-section. The nurse then taught me IV Tylenol works just as well for me without the fog or nightmares.

Carol sighed, "I'll see what we can do." She made a note on her tablet. "Are you hungry? Thirsty?"

I hadn't thought about it. But now that she mentioned it, my throat was dry, scratchy.

Water.

Carol held a cup with a straw to my lips. The thin plastic slipped through the gap in my wired teeth, but water dribbled down my chin at first. Swallowing sent pain shooting through my jaw, but the cool liquid soothed my parched throat.

After she left, silence filled the room. Just me and Reed and the monitors.

I shifted against the pillows, trying to find a position that didn't hurt. My left shoulder throbbed with every breath, the sling keeping my arm pinned against my chest. The splint on my wrist felt like dead weight. I couldn't hold the tablet and reach my face to wipe away tears at the same time. I felt like I couldn't do anything without help.

Reed reached forward and helped me shift. I didn't even complain—I just let him. What other choice was there?

He settled back into his chair. He didn't try to talk or ask any questions. He was just... there.

I closed my eye. Exhaustion pulled at me despite the fear of sleeping, of not being alert. My body didn't care about my fears—it demanded rest.

When I woke again, the light had changed. The sun had set completely, leaving only the dim glow of the monitors and the light from the hallway filtering under the door. The room tilted slightly when I opened my eye, and I had to wait for it to steady.

Reed was gone, leaving the chair empty.

Relief and something else—something I didn't want to name—twisted in my chest.

Then the door opened and he appeared with two coffee cups.

"Felicity's on her way," he said, lifting the coffee cup to show he'd picked one up for her. He settled back into the chair, saying, "I texted her that you were more alert."

I reached for the tablet.

You don't have to stay.

He looked at me for a long moment. "I know."

But he stayed anyway.

Why are you still here?

Silence stretched between us. His bloodshot eyes never left mine, his knuckles white on the chair's armrests. When he finally spoke, his voice caught, broke, and roughly, he said, "There isn't anywhere else in this world I would rather be than right here with you."

His words cracked something open inside me. I looked away, blinking back tears. Not yet. I couldn't face this—couldn't trust—not now.

Twenty minutes later, Felicity burst through the door like a hurricane, eyes red-rimmed, makeup smudged. She took one look at me and her face crumpled.

"Oh, Mal."

Reed stood. "I'll give you two some time. Need to grab something to eat anyway."

He left before I could type anything.

Felicity sank into the chair he'd vacated, taking my hand gently. "How are you feeling?"

I gestured to the tablet. She leaned closer so she could see.

Like hit by truck. Driven by a fucking psycho.

Felicity's laugh was half sob. "Dark humor. That's a good sign."

How are my babies?

Her expression shifted. "They're okay. Worried about you. They want to visit."

Everything in me seized up.

No.

"Mal—"

No. Don't bring them here. I can't.

My fingers trembled so badly I could barely hold the stylus. My chest tightened until it felt like my broken ribs were crushing my lungs. I erased, tried again, my heart hammering against my bandages.

Can't see me like this.

"You're their mother," Felicity whispered, her voice cracking. "They need to see you're alive."

Went away for work. Emergency trip.

I looked at her, pleading. I knew what I must look like. I'd seen my reflection after Bryce before. My babies shouldn't have to remember their mother this way. The thought of their faces seeing me—it cut deeper than anything.

Please! Not like this. Look like monster.

"You don't—"

Stop. My choice. Don't argue. They shouldn't see this in real life.

Felicity stared at the tablet, then at my face. Her eyes welled up. "What do I tell them?" she whispered, voice breaking. "They keep asking for mommy."

Away for work. That I love them.

Tears streaked her face. "Maliyah, this recovery will take months. Your kids will beg for you. They need their mother." She squeezed my hand gently. "And you need them."

NO! Just until bruising goes down. Until my eye can open. When I won't scare them.

She blew out a breath, calming and dropping her head. "Okay." Felicity squeezed my hand. "Okay. I'll handle it. But Mal, you can't hide forever. They're going to want to see you eventually."

I know. Not hiding. Just don't want to scare them. Too young to see something like this.

"All right. I got you." Then, Felicity paused. The silence became deafening.

WHAT?!

"You know...Reed hasn't left," Felicity said after a moment. "Since they brought you in. He's been here the whole time."

I looked away. Didn't type anything.

"I know you're angry at him. You have every right to be. But he's been—"

Already left before. The words appeared on screen before I could stop them. **When things got hard, he left.**

"He came back."

Kidnapped. His job. And for emphasis, I underlined the last part over and over again.

Felicity's hand landed on my shoulder, lightly but firmly. "Is that really what you think?"

I didn't answer. Didn't know how to answer.

Felicity sighed. "He cares about you. I can see it. Whatever else is true, that's true too. He told them he was your fiancé so he could stay with you. That's not what cops do. That's what someone who cares does."

My mouth would have dropped open if it hadn't been wired shut. My good eye widened, and I felt my pulse quicken in my throat. Reed appeared with coffee, freezing when he saw Felicity. Fiancé? Is he crazy?

"It's fine," Felicity said. "I need to get back to the kids anyway." She kissed the top of my head softly, avoiding the bandages. "I'll come back tomorrow. Call if you need anything."

She left. Reed took the chair again and silence fell on the room.

I watched him until sleep took me. When I woke, it was dark out. They'd hooked up the Tylenol while I slept. Reed was still there. I reached for the tablet, my movements slow and clumsy.

Don't you have work?

"Took leave," he said simply.

For how long?

"As long as you need."

I stared at him. At the exhaustion in his face, the stubble, the wrinkled, blood-stained clothes.

Why? Because you're my fiancé?

Reed's eyes widened. He rubbed the back of his neck, a flush creeping up his throat. "They wouldn't let me stay unless I was family," he said quietly, not meeting my gaze. "I couldn't—" His voice dropped even lower. "I couldn't stand the thought of you waking up alone." I let that sit with me, not sure how to respond—or if I even *could* respond.

You don't have to do this.

"I know."

Then why are you here?

He was quiet for a long moment. "Because I want to be."

I didn't type anything else. Just closed my eye and pretended to sleep. As I lost the battle and sleep took me, though, I thought I heard a quiet whisper, "One day, it won't be a lie."

The nightmare came around three AM. Bryce's hands around my throat, squeezing, squeezing. I couldn't breathe, couldn't scream. My jaw was sewn shut and I couldn't get air and he was laughing—

I jerked awake. The monitor was beeping faster. My good eye flew open, scanning the dark room for threats. Reed was standing beside the bed, not touching me, hands carefully visible.

"You're safe," his voice was low and steady. "You're in the hospital. He's dead—that fucker is gone forever. You are safe, sweetheart." The beeping from the monitors slowed just a bit as I listened to his words.

He wasn't saying anything I didn't already know. Logically, I knew Bryce was gone. But my nightmares didn't seem to care. I started thinking about him again and the inability to open my mouth sent my monitors flying again. My heart was racing.

I reached for the tablet with shaking hands. Pain shot through my left shoulder as I tried to reach for the tablet, the sling restraining my movement. I grabbed it awkwardly with my right hand alone.

Can't breathe.

Reed hit the call button immediately. A new nurse appeared within a minute, checked my oxygen levels, adjusted the tube under my nose and softly rubbing my forearm. "Panic attack," she said gently. "Perfectly normal after what you've been through. Your oxygen is fine. Try to breathe slowly. In through your nose, out through your nose."

I tried. It took several minutes before my heart rate slowed. The new nurse offered more pain meds. I shook my head. I didn't want to be loopy. Didn't Carol tell her?

Tylenol only.

"Are you sure about that?"

SURE

She nodded, updated the whiteboard with "Donna," left fresh water and a protein shake, then disappeared. Reed settled back in his chair.

"You want me to call someone?" he asked. "Felicity?"

No. She's asleep and has the kids.

"Okay."

He didn't try to comfort me. Didn't offer platitudes. Just sat there in the dark, a solid presence against the shadows.

I wanted to tell him to leave. That I didn't need him.

But I was so tired.

And maybe—just maybe—some small part of me was glad he was there. I didn't type that though.

I tried to find sleep again, knowing the nightmares would probably come back. Maybe having him here for a little while wouldn't be so bad. Not forever though. I didn't know that I would ever again have forever.

Chapter 34:

Small Victories

REED

I woke up with my neck screaming and my back reminding me that hospital chairs weren't designed for long-term sleep. Day four. Maliyah was still asleep, monitors beeping their steady rhythm.

The bruising on her face had started to change—less angry purple, more sickly yellow-green around the edges. Dr. Pettit said that was good. It was progress and there were no signs of infection.

As I stared at her, though, the fading bruises only highlighted what lay beneath—all the broken bones he'd left behind but with less swelling. I could see everything. Everything she felt.

Her survival was nothing short of a damned miracle—a sign of her strength and resolve.

I stood carefully, joints protesting. My shirt—unchanged for two days—bore deep creases from the chair. One quick armpit check confirmed it: I reeked. Like a locker room after double shifts.

Yesterday's nurse had brought me a washcloth, soap, and a bin—without me even asking for it. That was a sign in and of itself. Now it was even a day later and the "bath" I'd tried to take with the supplies hadn't done a damn thing. *I was ripe.*

I needed to shower. Change clothes. Get my shit together and get things ready for Maliyah. But first, more coffee.

I'd memorized the hospital by now, which vending machines worked and which didn't. The cafeteria opened at six and shut down for an hour to prep for lunch and again before dinner.

There was a decent coffee shop two blocks away that opened at five-thirty. I'd timed my trips to coincide with nurse shift change—never gone more than twenty minutes. Never leaving her alone longer than necessary.

The coffee shop guy knew my order now. Two large black coffees. One with cream and sugar that I'd bring back for Felicity when she came this morning.

When I got back to her room, Maliyah was awake. She tracked me as I entered but she didn't reach for the tablet. Just watched.

"Morning," I said, settling back into my chair. "How'd you sleep?"

She reached for the tablet.

Okay. You?

"Great. That chair's basically a luxury mattress—not as high-end comfort as your couch, of course."

The corner of her mouth twitched. Almost a smile. Not quite. But close enough to count it as a win.

Carol, on days again, came in with her morning routine—vitals, medications, the standard protocol. She'd ask about pain levels, check the wires in Maliyah's jaw, help her clean her teeth with this weird sponge thing, and then update the whiteboard with the day's plan.

"You're doing really well, honey," Carol said, checking Maliyah's oxygen levels. "Dr. Pettit will be by later, but everything looks good. Bruising is improving. Ribs are healing nicely. We might be able to talk about discharge soon."

Maliyah's eye widened slightly. She grabbed the tablet.

When?

"That's up to Dr. Pettit. But if you keep improving like this? Maybe a couple days—as soon as the worries about infection and your head trauma are clear."

After Carol left, Maliyah stared at the tablet for a long moment. Then she wrote something but didn't turn it to show me. Just kept looking at it.

I didn't push. Didn't ask. Just drank my coffee and gave her space.

Breakfast arrived—another chalky vanilla protein shake. I prepped it with a straw and offered it to her. Maliyah's gaze flicked between me and the bottle. She took it reluctantly, winced through several swallows, then pushed the half-finished drink away and turned toward the window.

"Want me to see if they have chocolate?" I asked.

She considered this, skeptical at first, then nodded in resignation.

Please.

"Be right back."

I found Carol at the nurses' station. She returned with two chocolate protein shakes, winking as she handed them over. "Don't tell anyone where these came from, they're supposed to be in the gastro unit," she whispered.

When I brought them back, Maliyah's good eye actually lit up slightly. She reached for one immediately, managed to drink nearly the whole thing.

Better. Thank you.

Two words that made my morning. Around ten, I stepped out to make calls. Kept Maliyah's room in view through the window as I dialed.

Felicity answered quickly. "How is she?"

"Better. Bruising's improving. Possible discharge in a few days."

"Thank God." Her relief was audible. "Lucas is getting suspicious. Says his mom wouldn't leave without telling them."

"Smart kid."

"I know." She sighed. "What now?"

"Video call? Good lighting, careful camera angle. Maybe bring concealer so she feels better about them seeing her."

Silence on the other end. Then: "That's actually a good idea. Think she'll go for it?"

"Don't know. But I'm going to suggest it—see how she feels."

"Okay. I'll tell the kids it's just Mom checking in from her work trip." A pause. "Reed? Thanks for staying. For everything."

"You don't have to thank me."

"Yeah, I do."

Next call was to John.

"Morrison, where the hell are you?" His voice was loud, familiar. "Captain's been asking. And I haven't heard from you for a couple days."

"Still at the hospital."

"It's been four days, man."

"I know how many days it's been."

John was quiet for a beat. "When are you coming back?"

"I've got three months of paid leave saved up. Haven't taken a vacation in four years. I'm using it."

"Three months? You're taking three months?"

"At least two. Maybe more."

"Holy shit. You're serious about her."

"Yeah, John. I am."

"The captain's not going to like this."

"The captain can deal with it. I've got the leave. I'm taking it." I watched through the window as a nurse checked Maliyah's vitals. "She needs help. And I'm going to be there."

"Alright. I'll handle the captain. But Reed? Don't fuck this up. Don't do what you did before."

"I won't."

"You better not."

After I hung up with John, I called Harbor House Road. Got transferred three times before reaching the office manager—said her name was Delilah. After explaining that I was calling to help with Maliyah's leave process, the office manager's clipped "Yes?" transformed into a lingering "Oh!" Her voice dropped half an octave, softened at the edges. The rapid keyboard clicking in the background paused. "How is she?"

"Healing. Slowly. She's going to need significant time off."

"Of course. Her position is safe. With state medical leave, she's covered for up to twenty weeks while she recovers."

Relief hit me. "Thank you. She can't talk on the phone. Is it okay for her to email with you guys?"

"Definitely. Maliyah is family here. We take care of our own. You tell her not to worry about anything. I'll send her an email and we can do everything electronically."

"Great. I will."

"And Detective? Thank you for finding her and caring for her. I'm sure you can understand that what she went through—well, it's something that resonates deeply here."

"She saved herself. I just showed up at the end."

"You showed up. That matters."

After the calls, I went back to the room. Maliyah was dozing, the tablet resting on her lap. I settled back into my chair and pulled out my phone.

Texted Felicity: Can you meet me tonight? Need to talk about logistics.

Her response came immediately: Sure. 7 PM? Hospital cafeteria?

Perfect.

Around two, Dr. Pettit came for rounds. Maliyah was awake, alert. He examined her, going through the motions from head to toe.

"Everything looks good," he said. "Overall, you're healing well. Even your jaw is progressing well. I know it's hard, but the wires will need to stay in for about six weeks."

Maliyah grabbed the tablet.

Discharge?

"If you keep improving like this, probably tomorrow or the day after. We'll monitor you another day or two. My biggest concern is the concussion combined with your wired jaw—as I mentioned the other day, there's a real aspiration risk if you get nauseous and can't open your mouth. I want to see your concussion symptoms improve before we send you home."

Had he mentioned that? I felt like the last week had been a whirlwind and I was having a hard time keeping everything straight. I can't imagine how Maliyah must be feeling about it too.

I think I forgot that.

"That's not surprising. There's been a lot going on."

So, when I go home. Are there things I need to do?

Dr. Pettit pulled up a chair. "You'll need significant support. Liquid nutrition multiple times daily—protein shakes, broths, smoothies. Medication management. Wound care for your face. Assistance with showering, until your ribs, shoulder, and wrist have healed more. You also can't drive until your vision returns fully."

Maliyah wrote: **I can manage. Sister nearby.**

"With all due respect, this is more than one person can handle alone, even with family close by. You'll need consistent help for at least the first two weeks."

I leaned forward. "What about overnight? Is there a risk of complications?"

"There's always some risk. Infection, complications with the jaw wires, difficulty breathing—with her panic attacks happening almost nightly, you can expect that will continue for a bit. Having someone there to monitor, to call for help if needed—that's ideal."

Maliyah's expression shifted. She knew where this was going.

I'll be fine.

"She won't be alone," I said firmly. "I'll be there." Maliyah's head whipped toward me. She grabbed the tablet, wrote furiously.

No. You're not staying with me.

"Yes, I am."

No. My kids will be there.

"You said you wanted your kids to stay with Felicity until you're ready for them to come home. You need help, and I'm going to help you."

Don't need help.

The words sat on the screen between us. Dr. Pettit looked between us, cleared his throat.

"I'll leave you two to work this out. But, Ms. Davenport, you do need help. Whether it's Detective Morrison or someone else, this is not a recovery you should do alone and I can't release you safely without a support system at home." He stood. "I'll be back tomorrow."

After he left, Maliyah stared at me.

You can't just decide to move in.

"I'm not moving in. I'm staying temporarily to help you recover." I thought I exercised remarkable strength by not tacking on, *once you recover, we can decide who's moving in with who—or if we should get a whole new place.*

It feels weird.

"I did say it was temporarily. And Felicity agrees with me." *Take that. Even your sister knows I'm not giving up.*

Her eye narrowed. **You talked to my sister first?**

"I talked to her about logistics. About what you'd need. We just want to make sure you're safe." I leaned forward. "Maliyah, you can't lift anything heavy—you only have the use of one arm and hand. You can't even open your drinks without help yet. You can barely get in and out of bed without someone helping you up. Add to all of that the concussion—sweetheart, you need someone to be there."

Not your help.

"Why not?"

She didn't say anything. Just looked away.

"Is it because you don't trust me? Because you think I'll leave again?" I did my best to keep my voice steady, but my own heart hurt at the knowledge of how much of an asshole I'd been. "I'm not leaving. I took medical leave from work. Two months. I'm here for as long as you need me."

Her face was a vision of surprise. Her fingers trembled slightly against the edge of the tablet as she turned it toward me. The screen glowed with two words and a question mark: **Two months?**

"Yeah. I told them at minimum two. But I have more than three available if I need to take more. I'm not going anywhere, Maliyah. Never again."

She stared at me.

You can't put your life on hold for me.

"I'm not putting my life on hold. I'm living it. Right here, right now, with you."

Reed—

"I'm staying, Maliyah. At your apartment. On the couch, at the foot of your bed—wherever you want me. But I'm staying. You can be pissed about it. You can ignore me. You can make it as difficult as you want." I looked her in the eyes and enunciated clearly and firmly, "But I'm not leaving you to do this alone."

She looked at the tablet for a long moment. Then wrote slowly:

I'm terrible company.

"I don't care."

I'm not entertaining you.

"Don't expect you to."

No promises. About us. About anything.

"I'm not asking you for promises, but I'll make you one—you can't get rid of me easily. I'm going to be there to support you at every turn." I leaned forward, the chair creaking beneath me. My voice softened as I added, "No matter how mean you are to me." I felt my face shift into that expression I've learned made me look like a kicked retriever—eyebrows lifting slightly, bottom lip jutting forward just enough to catch the overhead light.

She studied my face, searching for something—trying to hide the quirked corner of her lips. Not fast enough for me to miss it though!

Fine. You can stay in Lucas's room while he's at Felicity's. You leave when I'm better.

"Lucas's room it is." I prayed she missed my complete avoidance of the latter requirement. I needed enough time to win back her trust before I just put it all out there. Needed to help her fall back in love with me.

She turned away, clearly done with the conversation. But she didn't look angry anymore. Just exhausted.

Within minutes, her breathing had evened out—asleep again. The conversation had drained her. I pulled out my phone and texted Felicity:

Me: *She agreed. I'll move my stuff in tomorrow.*

Felicity: *Good. She needs you, even if she won't admit it. This will give you time to win her back. Don't. Fuck. Up.*

Me: *Copy that. She passed out already again before I could talk about a call with the kids.*

Felicity: *Okay. Maybe we can talk to her about it later.*

Me: *Sounds good. Was hoping to head out and shower/change before coming back for the night.*

Felicity: *On my way to relieve you.*

I turned back toward my future, watching her doze. She'd almost smiled at me more than once today. It wasn't forgiveness—I was a long way off from that. But it was a victory, and even small victories count.

Chapter 35:

Small Things

MALIYAH

The discharge papers sat on the rolling table—medications, wound care, PT exercises, and follow-up appointments. "Wound check and jaw assessment next week," Carol said with a brightness that scraped against my nerves. "You'll be free to go after Dr. Pettit's visit."

Free. The word tasted bitter. Free to return to an empty apartment. Free to wait for Reed to inevitably leave. Free to communicate through scribbled notes instead of my own voice. *Some freedom.*

Dr. Pettit arrived minutes later, echoing Carol's instructions while checking his tablet. "Follow-ups scheduled: one week for wound check, six weeks for potential wire removal—pending healing." In the corner, Carol's barely-concealed eye roll gave me the day's only smile.

I nodded, turning my tablet his way: **Understood. Thank you.**

Dr. Pettit rattled off warning signs. "Fever, swelling, discharge from the wires. Breathing issues, chest pain, severe panic attacks—call immediately." He looked directly at my half-open, still-blurred eye. "I know you're independent, but you need help. Accept it."

I wanted to argue. Wanted to type that I'd been handling things on my own for years, that I didn't need anyone, but I was so tired. Tired of being in pain. Tired of always being the strong one, of doing it alone.

I will.

As Carol helped me struggle into the clothes Felicity had packed, I closed my eyes and saw myself weeks from now—no longer burdened by this pain and fully healed. No help needed. The fantasy vanished when pain shot through my ribs, my wired jaw clenching with a sound I barely recognized as my own. Soon enough, this would be nothing but a memory.

The wheelchair appeared—hospital policy, apparently. I couldn't even walk out on my own two legs. I was wheeled through the maze of hospital corridors and out the automatic doors where cold air bit at my face. Reed crouched before me, his eyes level with mine. Unwinding the soft gray scarf from his throat, he draped it carefully around my neck, tucking the soft fabric against my bruised skin to create a barrier between me and winter's bite.

His gaze burned into mine, hot enough to melt the winter air between us. His fingertips grazed my cheekbone as he pulled away, leaving a trail of fire across my bruised skin. My heart slammed against my broken ribs. He turned and strode toward a sleek black sedan that the valet practically leapt from—not his usual car, I realized through my haze. Bigger. Newer.

"Borrowed it from a friend," he said before I could write the question. "More room. Smoother ride."

Of course he had. He helped me into the passenger seat with careful hands, mindful of my pain points, adjusting the seat back so I could recline some. As he reached across me to buckle my seatbelt, the scent of his shampoo—cedar and something citrusy—clouded my senses. I wanted to lean into him and push him away all at once, my fingers curling into fists on my lap as I fought the urge to touch the stubble along his jaw. When he glanced up, our faces inches apart, I couldn't look away.

He stepped back, his eyes still burning through me, and closed the door gently. I looked at him through the window. He hadn't moved. His palm pressed against the top of the window, fingers splayed, as if he might push through it to touch me. His jaw tightened, a muscle twitching beneath that same stubble I almost ached to touch.

Those eyes—damn those eyes—held mine with an intensity that made my chest ache worse than my ribs. I turned away first, my fingertips rising involuntarily to my wired jaw, suddenly conscious of how I must look to him. When I glanced back, his expression had softened into something that made my stomach flutter traitorously.

The drive home was quiet. Reed kept his speed steady, avoiding potholes, taking turns slowly. Every bump still sent pain shooting through my body, but it could have been worse. I watched out the window as Boston passed by. I loved the cobblestone streets, the narrow roads lined with red brick row houses pressing close together, some more than a hundred years old. Fall foliage had already come and gone, robbing the trees of their colorful leaves, but many were already being decorated for the upcoming holidays.

We passed a corner bodega with faded awnings, about twenty Dunkin's
with their orange and pink signs glowing, a small park where the playground was filled with kids, even as cold as it was. The streets narrowed
as we turned off Broadway, triple-deckers and apartment buildings lining
both sides in an unbroken wall of brick and vinyl siding. The number 11
bus hissed past us going the opposite direction, and I caught a glimpse of
passengers staring out at the gray afternoon.

All of it familiar. All of it different now. My building appeared—three stories, red brick, squeezed between identical structures on a one-way street.
No different from a dozen others we'd passed, except this one was mine. I'd
climbed those stairs to the third floor a thousand times without thinking.
Now they looked insurmountable.

Reed parked as close to the entrance as possible and he came around to help
me out. "Take your time," he said. "One step at a time. I'm right here."

I stood outside, looking at the entry door. My fingers curled into fists at my
sides, nails digging half-moons into my palms. The world tilted slightly, and
I squeezed my eyes closed, in the darkness, I saw Bryce closing the trunk lid,
heard the sounds of my breath echo off the small space.

My jaw clenched against its wires, sending a spike of pain through my
temples. My breath came quick and shallow, each inhale catching on my
broken ribs. My name floated through the panic. "Maliyah." Reed's voice,
low and steady.

I blinked. His face swam into focus, eyes level with mine as he crouched
slightly. The crease between his eyebrows deepened as his gaze held mine,
unwavering, while his hand hovered an inch from my arm, close enough
that I felt its warmth but not its weight.

I nodded at him, grateful for a moment for my inability to speak—anything
to not to have to voice my fears. He ushered me forward and I could swear
I'd felt the lightest brush of his lips on my hair when he'd stood up straight.
Glancing at him though, his focus was straight ahead—on the door in front
of us.

The stairs took forever. Reed stayed beside me, one hand hovering near my
elbow, his touch vacillating between hovering and a light brush—ready to
catch me if I stumbled. By the time we reached my floor, I was breathing
hard, ribs screaming, and we'd only had to pause twice.

He unlocked my door—already had a key, apparently—and held it open. I
stepped inside, and stopped.

My apartment looked the same but different. The furniture hadn't moved.
The photos on the walls were untouched. But there were changes everywhere.

In the kitchen, the counter was lined with protein shakes. Not just a few
bottles—at least a dozen different varieties. Chocolate, vanilla, strawber-

ry, cookies and cream, coffee—was that fruity pebbles? There were some brands I'd never seen, some that were familiar. A brand-new Ninja blender sat beside them, shiny in its brand new state.

I was in awe, and I reached for the refrigerator door as he still hovered over me, protective instincts humming through him. I opened it to find a variety of premade shakes, broths in glass containers labeled with dates, electrolyte drinks, and—tubs of Greek yogurt?

On the counter: a basket of straws in different sizes. Insulated cups with easy-grip handles. Bottles of medications all lined up. Beside it, a printed chart showing what to take when. I turned slowly, cataloging everything.

Fresh flowers on the coffee table—simple daisies, nothing overly fragrant. A tablet stand positioned beside the couch. The couch had been moved, so instead of being parallel to the TV, it was now turned a bit—almost caddy-corner to it.

You moved the couch?

He blushed a bit, saying, "Yeah...I got a wedge pillow for the couch so you'd be comfortable," he said, rubbing the back of his neck. "But then you'd have to turn your head to watch TV, and that'd strain your ribs and shoulder, so...I moved it."

At his explanation, I looked at the couch closer and noticed a complicated wedge thing positioned into the side of it and extra throw blankets and pillows were folded along the opposite side.

My fingers tapped away on my phone again.

You did all this?

Reed stood there, hands stuffed in his pockets now, as he watched my reaction.

"Wanted you to be comfortable." His voice cracked, suddenly shy.

It's too much.

"It's not enough."

I didn't know how to respond to that. Didn't know how to process the amount of thought that had gone into this. He hadn't just thrown together some basics. He'd considered everything. What I'd need. What would make things easier. What would help.

Where's your stuff?

"Lucas's room. Want to see?"

I followed him down the short hallway. The bedroom door stood open. His duffel bag sat neatly in the corner. A few shirts hung in the closet. Toiletries organized on the dresser, but not spread out—contained.

"I can move to the couch if you'd rather," Reed said. "Or if you need me closer at night—"

Lucas's room is fine.

He nodded. "Okay. Your room is—"

I rolled my eyes and smirked. **I know where my room is.**

But I let him follow me there anyway.

My bedroom looked mostly the same except for the additions: a wedge pillow on the bed for elevated sleeping. A heating pad plugged in and ready. A foot warmer—still in its package but placed deliberately at the foot of the bed.

Foot warmer?

"Well, I know your feet get cold at night. Thought it might help."

He'd remembered. Of course he had.

On my nightstand: photos of Lucas and Zoe in new frames. My phone charger with an extra-long cord so it would reach easily. A small nightlight plugged into the outlet.

I don't need a nightlight.

"In case you wake up disoriented. So you can see where you are."

I wanted to argue. Wanted to say I didn't need any of this, that he was overstepping, that this was my apartment and he couldn't just come in and change things.

But I was staring at photos of my children, and my feet did get cold at night, and I'd woken up disoriented in the hospital more times than I could count. I sniffed, feeling tears burn my eyes.

Thank you.

Two words that didn't feel like enough but were all I had.

"You should rest," Reed said. "It's been a long morning."

Felicity's coming at six. Video call with the kids.

His expression shifted—surprise, then something that looked like pride.

"You're doing the call?"

You were right. They need to see me.

Then, I added: **And I need to see them.**

"Want me to help set it up?"

I nodded. **That would be nice.**

And then—breaking every post-op rule Dr. Pettit had given me—I forced out a strained, barely-there "Thanks." It hurt like hell, but the moment called for my real voice.

Chapter 36:

More Than All the Stars

MALIYAH

The hours until six o'clock dragged. I tried to rest but couldn't. Tried to watch TV but couldn't focus. Kept looking at my phone, at the photos of Lucas and Zoe, wondering if this was a mistake.

What if they were scared? What if Lucas saw through all of it and knew I was lying about the work trip? What if Zoe cried?

At five-thirty, Felicity arrived with a makeup bag.

"Okay," she said, spreading supplies across my bathroom counter. "Let's make you feel a little more like yourself."

The concealer helped. She applied it carefully around the worst of the bruising, blending and layering it so the sickly yellow-green was less obvious. My left eye was still swollen partially shut, but at least my right eye looked relatively normal.

"You look beautiful," Felicity said, squeezing my shoulder gently.

I looked like someone had beaten the shit out of me and tried to cover it with makeup. But it was better than before.

Reed had set up the iPad on the kitchen table, white wall at my back, and angled so there was a light behind me, casting me in a shadow—witness protection lighting for the win. He moved to the living room, giving us space but staying close enough to help if needed.

Hopefully this would make sure my face was less visible.

Felicity had told them I was sick and wouldn't be able to talk, so Caden was with them and would help read my chat messages for me.

"Ready?" Felicity asked, iPad set up on the table.

No. But I need to do this.

I hit call. The screen flickered. Then Zoe's face filled the screen, taking up the entire frame.

"Mama!"

Her voice—that sweet, high-pitched four-year-old voice—broke something in my chest. Tears burned behind my eyes before I could stop them.

I waved, tried to smile around the wires. Opening a chat window on my phone so I could keep the FaceTime screen on my iPad, I texted Caden who was standing off to the side:

Hi baby. I miss you so much.

Caden read it aloud, his voice steady though I could sense he was shook up. He'd stayed with the kids so Felicity could visit me in the hospital—this was his first time seeing me because of it. I could sense his shock and his rage was clear as day. Guess the lighting didn't work as well as I thought it would.

Lucas appeared beside Zoe, pushing into frame. His face was serious, guarded. My observant, cautious boy.

"Aunt Fliss said you're sick. But when I'm sick, I can still talk. How come you can't?" he asked immediately.

Leave it to kids to have no filter.

I got hurt at work. Doctors had to fix my jaw. But I'm okay. I promise I'm okay.

"You don't look okay," Lucas said flatly.

God. My smart, honest child.

I look scary, I know. But it doesn't hurt as bad as it looks. And I'm getting better every day.

"Does your face hurt?" Zoe asked, leaning so close to the screen that I could only see her forehead.

A little. But the doctors gave me good medicine.

"Are you coming home soon?" Lucas's voice was smaller now, younger.
Vulnerable in a way he rarely showed.

My fingers shook as I typed:

**Soon. As soon as I can. But I need you to be patient and help Aunt
Felicity and Uncle Caden. Can you do that for me?**

"Yeah," Lucas said. "I can do that."

"I'm being really helpful!" Zoe announced. "I helped make pancakes yesterday and I only spilled a little!"

That's my girl.

"Mommy?"

I nodded at her to tell me what was on her mind.

She whispered, "Will you be mad if I tell you that Uncle Caden's pancakes
are better than yours?"

I exaggeratedly threw my hands up, trying to get a giggle out of my kids.

My thumbs flew across the screen: **Lies! LIES! My pancakes are the
BEST!**

But as Caden's eyes darted from my message to the children's eager faces, his
mouth curved into that mischievous grin I'd seen a thousand times. Instead
of reading my protest, he cleared his throat dramatically and announced,
"Your mom says she already knew this and is actually glad you've finally
discovered how much better my pancakes are. She says mine have the
perfect golden-brown edges that she can never quite achieve."

My eyes popped open wide enough to make my bruised skin sting, and I
frantically texted him, thumbs practically smoking: You will pay for that!

I shot Caden a death glare over the iPad, but of course, my sweet traitor
of a daughter—oblivious to the adult conspiracy unfolding—just nodded
her little head, her dark curls bouncing as she said, "Oh! Okay, well that's
good then!" Her gap-toothed smile beamed through the screen, innocent
and completely unaware of the betrayal.

*This was absurd. I needed to regain control before Caden corrupted my
children further.*

Changing topics! How was school this past week?

I talked to my kids for a few more minutes, though they did all the talking.
Their words blurred together. I caught fragments—Zoe's library stickers,
Lucas's fall schedule—but exhaustion dragged at me like an undertow.

There was a pause in the chatter and I tried to focus back in. "Mama?"

Yes, baby?

Zoe's quiet voice came through. "Can we go home now? I miss you and I want to be home with you." My throat closed up—or tried to. I couldn't sob with my jaw wired shut, couldn't make the sounds my body wanted to make.

Soon, sweetheart. Soon

Zoe pressed her small palm to the screen. "I love you, Mama." I matched her hand with mine, screens and miles between us.

I love you both so, so much. More than all the stars.

"More than all the stars," they echoed together. The screen went dark. And I broke.

Silent tears streamed down my face, painful against the bruises. My jaw throbbed as the tears fell; the pain was sharp, but not sharp enough to stop them. I couldn't sob, couldn't cry out, could only sit there with my chest heaving and my body screaming and my heart shattering.

Felicity moved toward me on one side, Reed on the other. I could tell neither wanted to overwhelm me. They each placed a hand on my shoulders, gentle and grounding.

Felicity kneeled in front of me. "Hey. You remember when we were kids, and dad used to travel a month or two at a time for work?"

I nodded, confused at why she was bringing it up.

"Remember how mom would take us for adventures and take pictures of us? Then when dad got home, we'd have all these pictures we would share with him of what we did. And he would do the same for all the things he did."

I wiped my face carefully with tissues Reed handed me.

Where are you going with this?

"Let's do that now." Felicity said, encouragingly. "I'll take the kids around while you're recovering, and send you daily videos. You can talk to them every night about what we did."

I straightened my shoulders slightly, my breath coming a little easier as I imagined Zoe's gap-toothed smile in short videos and watching Lucas's antics and laughter. I looked at my sister—really looked at her—and felt the weight of what she was offering. Sniffling, I pulled her into a tight hug.

Felicity held me for a while, whispering comfort and love in my ear. We'd been each other's only family since losing our parents a decade ago. I knew without a doubt that I could trust her to care for my kids while I recovered.

When it was time, I walked her to the door, slow and stiff—but determined. The apartment fell silent after she left—just me, Reed, and the weight of everything I couldn't say.

Chapter 37:

When the Dark Comes

MALIYAH

After Felicity left, the apartment felt too quiet. Just me and Reed and the weight of everything I couldn't say.

He stood near the door, hands in his pockets, watching me with that careful expression he'd perfected over the past week—concern wrapped in patience, waiting for me to fall apart or push him away. Maybe both.

The silence stretched between us until it became uncomfortable.

"You should eat something," Reed said finally. "Keep your strength up."

I reached for my phone. **I'm not hungry.**

"How about a smoothie. You barely touched your protein shake."

The number of protein shakes I need to drink in order to have enough calories in a day makes me gag.

Fine. Could you make me a PB & chocolate?

He moved to the kitchen, and I heard the refrigerator open, the sound of him putting ingredients into the Ninja and soon after the loud grind of the blender.

I closed my eyes for a bit, trying to chase away the headache that came with using both my eyes—though my one eye was opening more recently, it was still blurry and painful to blink.

I felt Reed's hand lay lightly on my shoulder and opened my eyes to see him holding out a glass with the shake. He handed it to me like this was normal. Like we did this every day.

I drank. Rich chocolate and perfect peanut butter—nothing like the hospital's bland concoctions. Before I realized it, I was slurping air from an empty glass.

I guess I was hungrier than I thought. That was good!

"I'll put that one down as a favorite, then." Reed took the glass while sporting a sheepish smile, and brought it to the kitchen.

He called out, "You ready for your meds? Knock once for yes, or twice if you want to hold off."

I'd forgotten about the evening medications. The chart he'd made was still on the kitchen counter, each compartment in the organizer labeled with the day and time. Friday. 8 PM.

I knocked once. Better off just getting it out of the way. He brought measured cups with all my liquid meds in them. All of them taste like ass, but since I can't swallow pills, my choices are limited.

"Need anything else?" Reed asked.

No. Going to bed.

"Okay. I'm going to hang out here for a while," he said, motioning to the couch. You can text or bang on the wall if you need anything."

You don't have to keep checking on me.

"I know."

But we both knew he would anyway. Reed hesitated at the entrance to the hallway. Like he wanted to say something. Like there were words building behind his careful expression that he couldn't quite voice.

I waited, phone in hand, ready to respond to whatever he needed to say. But he just nodded. Turned away.

Getting ready for bed took longer than it should have. Changing into pajamas was a painful exercise in frustration—soft cotton pants and a loose t-shirt that I had to maneuver around my ribs. Each movement pulled. Each breath reminded me of what Bryce had broken.

Going into the bathroom, I closed the door and looked in the mirror—really looked, alone for the first time without Felicity's gentle hands or reassuring words to soften what I saw.

I stared at my reflection—yellow-green discoloration, swelling that I knew had reduced but to my own eyes, I looked disfigured. Stitches ran in various parts of my face, my left eye still wouldn't open completely, and my bottom lip was still swollen.

I looked like someone had beaten the shit out of me. Because someone had.

I reached for my toothbrush and saw something I hadn't noticed before—where my toothbrush would normally sit was instead a children's toothbrush. Next to it was a brand new Waterpik. I sniffed, trying to hold back the tears. I couldn't though.

I sat on the toilet, looking at these additions Reed had obviously left for me. I laid my head in my hands, torn between a helpless feeling and one of utter gratitude. He made it so hard to keep my distance.

Buck up, Maliyah. Get control of yourself.

So, I stood up, shook it off as best I could and went about brushing my teeth as best I could with the wires. I washed my face carefully around the bruises and took one last glimpse of myself in the mirror before turning away. There was nothing I could do now about how I looked, so there was no sense in dwelling on it.

I left my bathroom feeling a sense of loss. Loss of the woman I used to be. Loss of the face I wasn't sure I'd ever see again. As I entered my bedroom, I pulled up short in surprise.

The door swung open to a changed room. Folded pillow shams on the chair. A black cord ran beneath my bed where I discovered an electric foot warmer already heating—waiting for my perpetually cold feet.

Reed had positioned another wedge pillow against the headboard, my other pillows arranged around it. I brushed my hand across the soft cotton as I lowered myself onto the bed. My shoulders relaxed as I settled into the perfect angle that relieved my ribs. I pictured Reed testing each position, making sure everything was just right.

I turned to my nightstand. A metal water bottle with a curved straw caught the light. Next to it stood my medication—cap already loosened—beside a protein shake. Against the wood grain lay something new: a large black e-reader with a folded note bearing my name in Reed's blocky handwriting.

Thought you'd appreciate how big the Kindle Scribe was. Maybe it will help with eye strain. Check your email for a gift to help you get started with loading up on some reading materials.

I sat on the edge of the bed and just stared—caught in a place of confusion. All these things, all this careful consideration, this wasn't the man who ran because he was afraid. My mind and heart had a hard time reconciling the two seemingly different men that existed in Reed.

I lay against the wedge pillow, picking up my new Kindle, and just held it. I lacked the mental energy to read, so I leaned back and rested my eyes, hoping to fall asleep.

And couldn't sleep. Every sound was amplified in the quiet. The refrigerator humming from the kitchen. The heat kicking on with a soft whoosh through the vents. Footsteps in the apartment above mine—someone walking from room to room. A car door slamming outside, followed by voices and laughter that faded as people walked away.

I was hyperaware of Reed in the other room. Could hear him moving around through the thin walls. Water running in the bathroom. The creak of the bed frame when he lay down. And...nothing. No sleep came. Just silence.

The apartment didn't sound like the hospital. No hum of electronic monitors or my IV pumps. No nurses' footsteps in the hallway. No bright lights bleeding into the room from the cracked door, or the annoying sound of machines notifying staff that someone's medication had run out.

Just darkness. And quiet. And my own breathing. The nightlight Reed had plugged in cast a soft glow across the room. My throat tightened. I blinked rapidly, fighting tears that burned behind my eyes.

I tried to sleep. Really tried. Closed my eyes and focused on breathing. In through my nose—one, two, three, four. Out through my nose—one, two, three, four. But my mind wouldn't shut off.

Running from Bryce in the hallway outside my apartment. Being shoved into his trunk. Being trapped in the beach house. The weight of his hands around my throat. The bronze goddess heavy in my hands. The sound it made when it connected with his skull. The crack of his skull against the table right after. All of it on repeat in my mind. In my soul.

I forced my eyes open. Stared at the ceiling. Counted the shadows cast by lights from outside. Time passed. I don't know how long. Maybe an hour. Maybe two. Finally, exhaustion won. My eyes drifted closed. And the nightmare came.

I'm in the trunk again. Dark. So dark I can't see my own hands in front of my face. The space is too small, pressing in on all sides. My jaw broken even in my dreams, stealing my voice.

I try to move. Can't. I try to scream. Can't. I can hear my own breathing—fast, shallow, panicked. The sound echoes off the walls, getting louder and louder until it's the only thing I can hear.

Then hands. Bryce's hands. Around my throat. Squeezing. He's stealing my voice and now he's stealing my breath. Nothing I do lets me pull in any air. No sounds now but his laughter—that terrible laugh that makes my skin crawl.

"Did you really think you could kill me?" His voice comes from everywhere and nowhere. "Did you really think you could get away?"

The trunk lid opens. Light floods in, blinding. I squeeze my eyes shut against it but can still see the brightness through my eyelids. Bryce's face appears above me. Smiling. Blood running down his forehead where the statue connected. Still smiling.

"You're mine, Maliyah. You will always be mine."

His hands tighten around my throat. I try to fight. Can't move. Can't breathe. Can't—

I jerked awake, arms flailing. Gasping. Or trying to gasp. My jaw was wired shut and I couldn't get enough air through my nose. Each attempt to breathe sent pain exploding through my ribs. The panic was immediate, overwhelming, all-consuming.

I sat up—agony shooting through my left side. I began pounding on the wall behind me. The room spun. I couldn't catch my breath. Couldn't orient myself. Was I in the trunk? The hospital? Home? Where was I?

My door slammed open and Reed came in, moving quickly toward me. No hesitation. Like he'd been waiting for this.

"Maliyah." He knelt in front of me, his voice cutting through the panic. "Look at me."

I tried. Couldn't focus. Couldn't—

"You're safe." He moved closer, his hands visible, open, non-threatening. "You're in your apartment. Your bedroom. He's not here. He's dead. You're safe."

He reached forward, hand on either side of my waist as he started running them toward my back, putting firm pressure. Not intimate—not in a way that would freak me out. Instead, he was moving his hands up and down, soothing like a parent would do for a scared child.

I wanted to believe him. I wanted to nod—to respond. But I couldn't get enough air. Couldn't—

His hands moved up to the back of my neck, massaging the base of my skull as he said, "Breathe with me." His voice was steady and calm as he leaned his forehead against my temple. "In through your nose. Count of four. One, two, three, four."

I did all I could to follow his pattern. Failed.

"Again. One, two, three, four. Hold it. Two, three, four. Out. Two, three, four."

His voice became an anchor. His right hand still massaging my nape, his left arm wrapping around me in safety. I held his bicep like a lifeboat in the chaos. I followed the count. Slowly—so slowly—the panic began to recede. My breathing steadied. The room stopped spinning.

We sat there, his hand down from my nape to rub my back again. Round and round it went, in circles hypnotizing the fear away. He whispered in my ear, "You're safe. I'm here." Repeating himself, over and over again.

I have no idea how long we sat there like that, his whispers settling into the spaces between my pounding heart, my breathing beating a steady rhythm. The nightlight cast long shadows across the wall, shifting imperceptibly as minutes that felt like hours passed.

Finally settled, I grabbed my phone. **Can't breathe right. Ribs hurt.**

"Want me to call the doctor?"

I shook my head. **Just need a minute.**

"Okay. I'm here. Take your time."

But the dark was too much. The room felt too big and too small at the same time. The silence pressed in on me from all sides. I couldn't be alone with it. Couldn't face another hour of lying here waiting for the nightmares to come back.

My fingers shook as I typed: **Can you stay?**

He whispered something I couldn't quite make out, but I thought it almost sounded like "forever."

But when I sought his eyes out in question, he said, "For sure," instead. He moved toward the chair by the window. "I'll just—"

I shook my head and patted the bed. **No. Not the chair.**

He stopped. Glanced at me after reading my message. In the dim glow from the phone, I could see the conflict on his face. The careful consideration of what I was asking and what it might mean.

"Maliyah—"

Please. Just for a while.

He studied my face. Then nodded slowly. "Okay. But you tell me if this isn't right. If it's too much."

It's fine. It wasn't fine. Nothing was fine. But I needed... I didn't know what I needed. Reed carefully lay down on top of the covers beside me, with his back against the headboard.

"Is this okay?" he asked quietly.

I nodded. Then, hesitantly, shifted closer. Felt his arm come around me, mindful of my ribs, holding me like I might break. Maybe I was already broken. But this—this helped. I grabbed my phone one more time.

This doesn't change anything. Don't get ideas.

Reed was quiet for a moment. Then: "I know. Just here to help you sleep."

I should type more. Set more boundaries, establish more rules, or maybe just tell him I changed my mind. But I was so tired, and his heartbeat was steady against my ear as I curled into him as much as my ribs would allow. His arm was warm around me. His breathing was even, reliable.

I typed one more thing: **Thank you.**

He didn't respond with words. Just tightened his arm slightly around me—a gentle squeeze that said *I've got you*.

The scent of his t-shirt—clean laundry and something indefinably him—surrounded me. The warmth of his body seeped through my pajamas, chasing away the cold that had lived in my bones since that night. His breathing was steady, a rhythm I could match, could use to ground myself.

My eyes drifted closed and, for the first time since waking up in that hospital, I felt safe enough to let go. I fell asleep in his arms.

Chapter 38:

The Warmth of First Light

REED

I woke to the warm pressure of Maliyah's head nestled against my chest, her breath whispering across my skin, and the soft weight of her hand resting on my torso. For a moment, I didn't move. I was afraid to even breathe or take the chance of disturbing whatever fragile peace we'd found in the dark hours of the night.

While my arm was around her, I did my best to keep her secure—careful of her litany of injuries. The nightmare that had sent her spiraling last night seemed distant, a shadow that had passed—for now.

Morning light filtered through the curtains, soft and gray. Just past dawn, the apartment was still quiet except for the distant hum of early traffic and Maliyah's steady breathing.

I should move. Should create distance before she woke up and remembered she was supposed to hate me. Should give her the space to regret asking me to stay.

But she was warm against me. Safe. And I'd spent too many nights alone in my apartment, staring at the ceiling, remembering what it felt like to hold her.

I wasn't ready to let go. Not yet, and if she'd let me, not ever.

She stirred slightly, and I felt her tense—that moment of waking confusion before memory caught up. Her breathing changed, no longer the deep rhythm of sleep but the careful awareness of someone trying to figure out where they were.

"Hey," I whispered, keeping my voice low. "You okay?"

She nodded against my chest, then reached for her phone that had fallen to my side from her hand while we slept. I waited while she typed, trying to hold back the excitement at how she still hadn't pulled away from me.

Better. Thank you.

"Nightmare?"

Yeah.

I moved my hand to her hair, fingers threading through the tangles with gentle patience. "Want to talk about it?"

She shook her head, and I didn't push. Telling me about it meant remembering what she'd dreamt—what she'd gone through. She'd done enough of that already.

We lay there as the room grew lighter. Minutes passed—maybe ten, maybe twenty. Neither of us moved to break the contact. I memorized the weight of her, the scent of her shampoo, the way her fingers curled loosely against my chest.

This might be all I got. This one morning. This brief moment before she remembered all the reasons to push me away. Minutes ticked by while I remained as still as my body would allow. Until her hand moved to her phone again.

You stayed.

"Yeah."

All night.

"All night."

Why?

My thumb traced a gentle line along her temple, just below the still-healing bruises, being careful of her sutures. The question hung between us, loaded with everything unsaid. I could give her the easy answer. Because she'd asked. Because she'd had a nightmare. Because it was the decent thing to do. All things that wouldn't scare her away.

But I was done with easy answers. Done with half-truths that protected me from her rejection—a well-deserved one at that.

"Because you needed me, and I wanted to be here with you. I wanted to hold you through it. To give you a piece of myself that could maybe help you feel safe," I said quietly.

The silence stretched. I could feel her processing, deciding whether to accept that or push for more.

And then I realized—this was it. This was the moment. If I was going to do this, if I was going to fight for another chance, I had to stop waiting for the perfect time. Had to stop being careful.

Had to tell her the truth. "Maliyah, I need to say something." She waited, her body still against mine, her breathing shallow.

"I was wrong. About everything." The words scraped out of me, rough with sleep and emotion. "When I got shot, I convinced myself I was protecting you and the kids by pushing you away. But I was just protecting myself. From getting hurt. From having to face my own fear."

I felt her start to reach for her phone, but I caught her hand gently. "No, let me finish. Please." I shifted so I could see her face, could look her in the eye while I said this. "You told me I was choosing to leave, that I was doing to them exactly what I'd been afraid that losing me would do. You were right. I was so terrified of dying and hurting you that I hurt you anyway. While I was still alive. While I still had the choice."

My hand cupped her cheek, so gentle I barely touched the damaged skin.

"I'm not going to lie and say I'm not still scared. I am. Every day. But it's a different kind of scared. Watching you fight to stay alive, seeing your strength—" My voice cracked, and I had to stop, swallow hard against the tightness in my throat. "You almost died, Maliyah. And I wasn't there. I wasn't there because I'd been too much of a coward to stay."

She grabbed her phone, her fingers moving quickly. **You found me.**

"Barely. And it was almost too late." My thumb brushed across her cheekbone, feather-light. My voice broke. "The truth is, this job—it's dangerous. I know that. And I can't lie and say I'll never be afraid again." I brushed my thumb across her cheek, feeling her warmth beneath my skin. "But what terrifies me now isn't what might happen if I stay. It's what I know will happen if I leave. I lost you once because I ran—almost lost you for good. I won't make that mistake again—not when every day without you felt like drowning. I will fight every day to be worthy of what you are giving me."

What am I giving you?

"Another chance." The words were barely a whisper. "A chance I don't deserve but I'm going to spend every day trying to earn."

I watched her face as she processed this. Saw the conflict there—the part of her that wanted to believe me warring with the part that remembered how easily I'd walked away before.

Reed—

"I hurt you. I hurt Lucas and Zoe." The admission burned like acid. "They were starting to trust me, and I walked away like their dad did. It wasn't something I was ready to hear, to understand, but I get now that I was proving that men can't be counted on." I shook my head, my jaw tight with self-recrimination. "Being scared doesn't make that okay. Nothing makes that okay."

She stared at me for a long moment. At the sincerity in my eyes, the guilt I couldn't hide, the desperate hope I was trying to keep buried.

Then she typed, slowly and deliberately: **Is this why you're here now.** She made a motion toward her own face.

"Is what why I'm here now?"

Because you feel guilty that you weren't there? That Bryce took me?

"What? No! No! Maliyah, no. That's not it. While almost losing you gave me the strength and opportunity to stand up straight, I was already committed to earning you back before that. This I swear."

I don't want you to want us out of guilt, Reed.

"Not even a little bit, Maliyah. *Yeah*—I feel guilty for being a dick. I feel bad for breaking your heart when it was entirely my fault. I broke my own damn heart while I was at it. But that's not why I'm here. I'm here because I can't imagine life without you."

So you're saying you want to do this? To be here?

"I am. And I'm not going anywhere. Not unless you tell me to."

Don't make promises you don't intend to keep.

The words hit me like a physical blow. Not because they hurt—because they were more than I deserved. More grace than I'd earned.

"I can do that," I said, my voice rough.

I can't promise you anything, Reed. I can't promise to pick back up. I'm in a weird place and I don't know how I feel about everything right now.

"I get it. I just want to be here for you. If you'll let me."

We were quiet again. The morning light had grown stronger, painting the room in shades of amber and gold. The warmth of first light after a long, dark night.

Finally, she shifted in my arms, wincing slightly as her ribs protested.

"Careful," I said, my hand steadying her. "You need your meds soon. And definitely another shake."

She made a face, and I couldn't help but smile. "I know. They're terrible. But you need the calories." I started to sit up carefully, trying not to jostle her. "I'll go make coffee. Maybe see what I can scrounge up for breakfast."

Wait.

I paused, looking into her eyes. In the morning light, with her hair mussed from sleep and even with the bruises fading on her face, she was the most beautiful thing I'd ever seen.

Thank you. For staying.

"Always," I said, then caught myself. "I mean—as long as you want me to."

She nodded, then typed one more thing:

Like I said, no promises...I'm not ready to forgive you yet. But I'm not pushing you away either.

Relief crashed through me so hard I had to close my eyes for a second. It wasn't forgiveness. It wasn't even close to forgiveness.

But it was more than I deserved. More than I'd hoped for. "That's more than I deserve," I said quietly. "I'll take it."

I stood carefully, tucking the blankets back around her before heading to the kitchen. My hands were steady as I started the coffee maker, pulled out mugs, grabbed the chocolate protein shake from the fridge.

But inside, I was shaking. *I would not do a dance in the kitchen. I would not act like a fucking moron.* On second thought, *fuck it.* A slight slide and turn in my socks on the kitchen floor didn't feel like overdoing it. I could celebrate a little without getting ahead of myself.

Eye on the prize, Reed. I needed to keep her and the kids in focus, not losing sight of the fact that I had a long road ahead to win all of them back. But, in the meantime she was giving me another chance and I wasn't going to fuck it up this time.

I had an idea. Taking coffee and adding it to a chocolate protein shake with ice, I hoped it would make it more palatable. Tasting it, I was impressed enough to make one for myself, in solidarity with my girl. I loaded everything onto a small tray—two iced protein coffee shakes and her measured medication doses.

My mind kept replaying her words. *I'm not ready to forgive you yet. But I'm not pushing you away either.* I knew winning the trust back from Lucas and Zoe was going to be a major undertaking too.

I'd failed them. While Maliyah was an adult—she could understand fear, could rationalize my choices even if they hurt. But the kids? Kids didn't understand nuance. They understood presence and absence. Promises kept and promises broken.

I'd let them down. I knew this was obviously going to take more than an apology. It was going to take time. Consistency. Proving that I meant it when I said I wasn't going anywhere.But first, my goal is helping Maliyah get through today. Then tomorrow. Then the day after that.

One day at a time. I carried the tray back to her room and paused in the doorway.

She was sitting up against the wedge pillow, phone in hand. Even with her hair in a messy bun and wearing just an oversized shirt and leggings, she was stunning. One leg lay exposed on the covers while she'd bunched the stolen comforter across her lap, using it as a stand for her phone.

I caught myself staring at her. Even with purple-yellow bruises and stitches mapping her face, she was beautiful in her vulnerability—a living testament to survival.

I've never known anyone as strong as Maliyah. After everything Bryce took from her—her voice, her safety—she's still standing. Not broken. I want to be the one who helps her rebuild, not because she needs me, but because she deserves someone who won't walk away again.

The words sat heavy in my chest—three simple words that felt impossibly complex after everything we'd been through. I had no right to expect her to believe me, not yet, but I would spend every day proving it until she did. Until Maliyah knew, without a shadow of doubt, that she was the center of my world.

She glanced up, caught me watching, and her hand rose halfway to her face before stopping. Her eyes darted away as her shoulders tensed. Something twisted in my chest—I wanted to be the man who made her forget those injuries, who showed her that nothing could dim how beautiful she was to me.

"I have a surprise for you. The best of both worlds—mocha latte!"

At her surprised look and small quirk of her lips, I acquiesced, "Okay, chocolate protein shake with coffee. But, you know—same difference."

Skeptical as my girl was, she wasn't giving an inch, and rolled her eyes while nodding toward the nightstand. Instead of putting it on the nightstand though, I handed her the glass saying, "just try it. You may be surprised!"

She rolled her eyes but held out her hands. I watched as she took a cautious first sip, nose scrunched in anticipation. Her eyes popped open. She took another sip, then met my gaze with a surprised smile.

"Better than expected?" I asked.

She nodded, then reached for her phone. **This is a winner! Thank you.**

I couldn't help the swell of satisfaction that rose in my chest. My smile stretched wide as I settled onto the edge of the bed beside her, both of us sipping our drinks in tandem.

Neither of us spoke for several minutes, but there was nothing awkward about it—just the quiet rhythm of two people who didn't need words to fill the space between them.

Finally, she typed: **What time is it?**

"Almost seven."

You should sleep. Real sleep, not on my bed.

"I'm okay."

Reed.

There was something in the way she typed my name—even just seeing it on the screen—that made my chest tight.

"I'll sleep later," I said. "Right now, I want to make sure you're settled." I picked up the dosage cups with her meds in them and handed her the first one. "Time for the morning cocktail of joy."

She wrinkled her nose but held out her hand for the small cup of liquid medication. I watched her swallow each dose one by one, her face twisting at the taste.

"All done," I said, taking the empty cups. "Need anything else? More pillows? Different blanket? An online order form for your next made-to-order protein shake?"

The corner of her mouth twitched. Almost a smile. **Just tired. Going to try to sleep more.**

"Okay. I'll be in the living room if you need anything. Just text or bang on the wall."

I will.

I turned to leave, but a soft sound from her throat stopped me. I turned back.

Thank you. For everything. For being here.

"I'll be here," I said quietly. "As long as you need me." Turning toward the door, I whispered under my breath—"forever, hopefully."

I left the door cracked and headed back to the living room. Sitting on the couch, I pulled out my phone. Seven AM. Felicity would be getting the kids ready for school soon. I should text her, let her know Maliyah was okay after the nightmare.

Me: *She had a rough night but she's doing better now. Nightmare.*

It wasn't long before the three dots started jumping and Felicity's message came through.

Felicity: *Poor thing. How are YOU doing?*

Me: *I'm okay. Just want to make sure she's comfortable.*

Felicity: *You're good for her, Reed. I believe you when you say you're not going to run again. Just keep showing up. She'll get there.*

I stared at that message for a long moment before responding.

Me: *Thank you. I don't deserve your faith, but I'll keep proving myself. I'm trying to show her. That's all I can do right now.*

Felicity: *That's all she needs. Keep showing up.*

Reed: *I will. I'll keep you posted on how she's doing.*

I leaned back on the couch and looked around the apartment. The morning light was streaming through the windows now, making everything look softer, more hopeful.

This was going to be a long road. Weeks of recovery for Maliyah. Months of rebuilding trust with her. And even longer with Lucas and Zoe—if they'd even give me the chance.

But I was all in. Finally, completely, terrifyingly all in.

Back then, I'd stood in front of Maliyah and promised I was all in. The words had felt true when they left my mouth, but they'd been hollow—a promise made by a man who didn't understand what he was promising. Now, with her bruised and healing under my watch, I finally grasped what those two small words demanded of me.

All in meant staying when it was hard. When she had nightmares. When she couldn't forgive me yet. When the kids looked at me with confusion or hurt. When the fear crept back in and whispered that I should run.

All in meant showing up. Every day. No matter what. All in meant trusting that I'm enough for them and they know they're more than enough for me.

This was going to work. It had to work. Because losing her once had nearly destroyed me. I wasn't going to survive losing her twice. And I sure as hell wasn't going to put Lucas and Zoe through that again. So, I'll keep showing up. One day at a time. I'd show them every day that I will always be all in.

Chapter 39:

The Sound of Home

MALIYAH

This apartment was driving me insane. The walls seemed to inch closer every day, and time had become this strange blur where Tuesday felt exactly like Friday, which felt exactly like Sunday. When I caught myself actually looking forward to having the physical therapist bend my limbs into painful positions just for the change of scenery, I knew I'd hit rock bottom.

I was on the couch, legs curled under me, staring at my phone. The silence was suffocating. I missed my kids—their shouting, their footsteps, the clatter of dropped toys, their calls of "Mama!" Even their bickering over the remote would've been welcome now.

Reed was in Lucas's room working on something for John—I think the quiet had even gotten to him, but he didn't seem to want to leave me alone, so he found ways to do work here instead of completely losing his mind while taking leave.

He was moving in by stealth. More clothes appeared in the closet each week. His toiletries had migrated from a travel bag to permanent spots on the counter—"just easier," he claimed. Sure. He was planting his flag. It's like he'd quietly moved in—and somehow, despite everything, I found myself getting used to the weight of his presence.

Part of me resented it though. Who gave him permission to just take over my space? I never actually said yes—I was just too exhausted and broken to push back.

Now that the fog was lifting and my strength returning, I couldn't ignore it anymore.

What I craved more than anything, though, was my children—the beautiful hurricane of them. Their sticky hands and endless questions. The weight of them against me. I wanted to be Mama again, not this fragile thing everyone tiptoed around.

And I needed Reed to leave—at least for a few hours. I needed some damn privacy to think.

I stood up from the couch, walked to Lucas's room, and knocked on the doorframe. Reed looked up from his laptop, concern immediately crossing his face.

"Everything okay? You need something?"

I held up my phone.

I need you to leave for a few hours.

His expression shifted. "Leave? Like go to my apartment?"

Or anywhere. I just need you gone for a while.

"Is everything okay? Do you need something I can—"

I'm fine. I just need space. Real space. Not you in the next room.

He was quiet for a moment, and I could see him processing. Even see the hurt across his features. "Oh. Okay. Yeah. I can do that. How long?"

A few hours. I'll text you when you can come back.

"Alright." He grabbed his jacket from the coat rack—my coat rack. "I'll just... I'll go. Text me if you need anything before then."

I nodded, relieved he wasn't pushing.

After he left, I sat there staring at the closed door. Then I pulled out my phone and texted Felicity.

Me: *Reed's gone for a few hours. Can you bring the kids over? I need to see them in person. The daily videos and phone calls are great, but not enough. I'm ready and if I don't see them I think I'll lose my mind.*

Felicity: *Finally! Yes! We'll be there in 30.*

I looked around the apartment. Reed's coffee mug was sitting by the sink, he had a book on the end table, and even his phone charger was plugged into the living room wall.

For fuck's sake. There was evidence everywhere that he'd made himself at home. Huffing out a breath, I got moving.

I rushed around the apartment, scooping up Reed's belongings—his watch from the bathroom counter, a sweatshirt draped over the couch arm, his laptop charger. I shoved everything into Lucas's closet, then gathered what remained in his room and hid that too. My heart raced as I scanned the living room one more time. Something still felt off, like I'd overlooked some obvious trace of him that would give everything away the moment my children walked through the door.

I grabbed a few coloring books and some things for the kids to play with, feeling the excitement building inside my chest at the thought of finally holding my babies. When I stepped into the kitchen to grab something to drink, I heard the front door open.

Dropping my cup down on the counter, I turned and ran from the kitchen heading to the door, my heart jumping as I rushed to meet the kids.

Felicity came in first. "You look better," she said, walking in.

I kissed her on the cheek and then all but shoved her to the side.

"Mama!" Zoe launched herself at me before anyone could stop her.

I caught her, scooping her up despite the dull ache in my ribs. She was warm and solid and real in my arms. I buried my face in her hair, breathing in the scent of her shampoo. I was as close to sobbing as a reasonable person could get without blubbering and snotting all over my kid's hair.

God, I'd missed this. Missed them. Missed everything about them.

The tears came hard, streaming down my face as I held her. It had been weeks. Weeks since I'd held my baby girl. Every day I doubted myself in keeping them away, not letting them see how bad I really was. I knew it was worth it to protect their nightmares, but my heart almost didn't survive the separation.

"Mama, you're squishing me," Zoe said, but she didn't try to pull away.

I loosened my grip just enough, pressing kisses to the top of her head, her cheek, anywhere I could reach.

Lucas hung back near the door with Caden, more cautious. Watching me with those serious eyes that were too old for seven. But I could see the emotion there too—the way his chin trembled slightly, the way his hands clenched at his sides.

I set Zoe down carefully, my vision blurry with tears, and held out both arms to Lucas.

His first step was slow. Tentative. then all at once—he rushed into me, wrapping his arms around my waist so tight it hurt my ribs and jarred my shoulder. I was sure physical therapy would be great this week—but I didn't care. I didn't care about anything except holding my babies.

Both of them. My babies.

I sank down to the floor right there in the entryway, pulling them both onto my lap even though they were too big for that now. They were too heavy for me, but I didn't fucking care. I wrapped my arms around them and let myself cry—really cry—for the first time since coming home.

"Don't cry, Mama," Zoe said, patting my face with her small hands. "You're okay now. We're home."

But that just made me cry harder. Because we *were* home. They were here in my arms. And just a few weeks ago I'd been so scared I'd never see them again.

Lucas buried his face against my shoulder, his small body shaking. He was crying too, trying to hide it, trying to be strong.

"It's okay, buddy," I managed to get out, my voice muffled and broken around the wires. "It's okay to cry."

"I thought—" His voice cracked. "I thought you weren't coming back."

My heart shattered. I held him tighter, rocked them both like I used to when they were babies.

Felicity was crying too—I could hear her sniffling from where she stood by the door. Caden's hand was on her shoulder, his eyes bright.

We stayed like that for a long time. Me on the floor with my kids in my arms, all of us crying, all of us holding on like we'd never let go.

Finally, I pulled back enough to look at them. Really look at them.

"You look different," Lucas said quietly, his voice muffled against my shoulder. "Better than on the video calls."

I pulled back enough to look at them, then reached for my phone, texting Felicity who read it aloud. While Lucas could read simple sentences, Zoe wasn't there quite yet.

I'm getting better every day. The doctors say I'm doing really well.

"Can you talk yet?" Zoe asked, tilting her head up at me.

I shook my head, pointed to my jaw.

Not yet. It's too hard and hurts to try too much. Maybe a few more weeks. But I can hear you. Tell me everything.

And they did. Zoe's words tumbled out in a rush, her hands gesturing wildly as she described Miss Alice's classroom and the butterfly that had landed right on her finger before flying away. "And Aunt Felicity let us have ice cream for breakfast one time but she said not to tell you," she confessed, then clapped her hand over her mouth.

Lucas sat closer to my uninjured side, his voice softer as he filled me in on baseball practice and the fantasy books with dragons that he'd started reading. "I missed our apartment," he admitted, eyes downcast. "And you." Then he mentioned Madison from his class, how fun she was and that she shared her cookies with him. My eyes found Felicity's across the room, and I couldn't help the knowing smile that spread across my face.

I kept touching them—smoothing Zoe's hair, adjusting Lucas's collar, just making sure they were real. That this wasn't another dream I'd wake up from.

When I was finally able to pull myself away from them, we moved into the living room where Caden and Felicity settled into the chairs, letting the kids have the couch with me. We'd been sitting there for maybe ten minutes when Zoe suddenly scrambled off the couch and started looking around.

"Mama, where's all your stuff?" She pointed toward the entryway. "There's boy shoes by the door."

My stomach dropped. Dammit.

I'd missed the shoes. Reed's running sneakers, tucked against the wall by the door.

Lucas's head turned, following her pointing finger. His eyes landed on the shoes, then slowly swept the room. I watched his expression change as he took inventory—the jacket I'd missed on the back of a chair, a pair of reading glasses on the sideboard. *Come on!*

"Is someone living here?" Lucas asked, his voice careful. Controlled.

Felicity jumped in smoothly. "Your mama has a friend helping her while she recovers. That's all."

"What friend?" Lucas pressed, his eyes coming back to mine. Too knowing. Too smart.

Just someone making sure I'm okay.

"Is it Detective Reed?" Lucas asked directly. Not a guess. A question he already knew the answer to. "The shoes look like his shoes."

Damn. My smart, observant boy.

I looked at Felicity, then at Caden. Thought about lying. Thought about making something up.

But Lucas deserved the truth. Even if it was complicated.

Yes. Reed has been helping me. But that's all. He's just helping.

"So he's here?" Zoe's face lit up like Christmas morning. "Can we see him? I made him a picture!"

No. He's not here right now.

"But he was here." Lucas wasn't asking. He was stating. Processing. "He's been staying here."

Lucas—

"It's okay, Mama." But his voice was flat. Careful. "I just wanted to know."

The withdrawal in his expression broke something in me. He was protecting himself. Already assuming the worst because he remembered what it felt like when Reed left.

He's been helping me recover. That's all. I needed someone big to help and Reed is big, right?

His head tilted to the side at that—considering.

"Does he sleep here?" Zoe asked, innocent and curious.

In Lucas's room. Just until I'm better.

"And then he'll leave again," Lucas said quietly. Not a question. A certainty. "Like before."

The resignation in his voice. The acceptance.

My baby boy had already written Reed off. Had already protected his heart because I hadn't protected it the first time.

Lucas, I don't know what's going to happen. But right now, what matters is that I'm getting better and you're here with me.

Felicity caught my eye, concern written all over her face. I shook my head slightly. Not now.

"Who wants to tell Mama about the pizzas we made last night and how Aunt Felicity made one with chocolate and peanut butter!?" Caden jumped in, changing the subject.

Lucas hesitated, but took the bait, and thank God, the conversation moved on.

But I caught Lucas glancing at those shoes again. At the jacket. Taking inventory of Reed's presence in our space.

My boy was too smart. And too hurt.

We spent the next hour coloring, playing games, just being together. Zoe sat plastered against my side, like if she let go I might disappear again. Lucas stayed close but more reserved, watching me like he was still making sure I was real.

Every few minutes, Zoe would pat my face gently, careful of the healing injuries. "Does it hurt, Mama?"

Not too much anymore, baby.

"Good. I don't like when you hurt."

My throat tightened. I pulled her closer, kissed the top of her head.

Eventually, Zoe started getting restless and Lucas was beginning to fade. It had been good but exhausting for all of us.

"We should probably head out," Felicity said gently. "Let your mama rest."

"Can we come back tomorrow?" Zoe asked, her bottom lip already trembling.

Definitely. I'm starting to feel so much better. Maybe by the weekend

"Okay! Yeah!" She threw her arms around my neck. "I love you, Mama."

I love you more than all the stars.

"More than all the stars!" she echoed.

Lucas hugged me too, but more carefully. "Bye, Mama."

Bye, baby. I'll see you soon. I promise.

As they were putting on their coats, Lucas turned back. "Mama? Can you tell Detective Reed hi from me? If you see him?"

The question hit me like a punch to the chest.

Of course, sweetheart.

He nodded, then followed Felicity and Caden out the door. Just as I thought he was gone, his small face reappeared in the doorway. "And tell him thank you? For being big so he could help you." Then he was gone, the door clicking shut behind him before I could respond.

After they left, I sat in the too-quiet apartment alone. Surrounded again by quiet.

I thought about my babies and how I'd ended up here—separated from them, surviving Bryce. The system had failed us repeatedly, just as it fails countless others daily. I'd always believed my place was in shelters, not advocacy. But tonight, something shifted. Why couldn't it be both? Maybe it was time to not just support survivors daily, but to also fight for real change: better funding, taking protective orders seriously, actual accountability. Something had to give.

I knew I should probably text Reed. Tell him it's okay to come back.

But I didn't. Something was unfolding in my mind—a plan, a purpose—and I needed the quiet to think it through.

Chapter 40:

The Geography of Unseen Scars

REED

I sat there, staring at the front door of Maliyah's apartment, keys in hand, not moving.

I need you to leave for a few hours. Not "Can you give me space?" Not "Would you mind?"

I need you to leave. The difference felt significant. Final, almost. I pulled out my phone, checked the time. 10:47 AM. She'd said a few hours. I hadn't even asked if she'd text me when I could come back. When I could come back. Not if. I held onto that. Had to hold onto something.

My car was parked down the street. I walked to it slowly, unsure what to do next. For weeks I'd barely left her side—working from Lucas's room, sleeping on her couch to be there when the nightmares came. And they always came. God, if I could kill Bryce again, I would. If I could erase her memories, I would. I would do anything to have been there that night, to have answered my damn phone, to have never walked away.

But I couldn't change the past. So I need to keep moving forward. I sat in my car and stared at my phone. No new messages. Christ, I was pathetic. I had a feeling she was with the kids, that she was finally ready to let them come home—but she wasn't ready for me to be part of that reunion. My chest tightened. I had no right to feel hurt by it—hell, I was the reason they'd been separated in the first place. I'd walked away when she needed me most, and now I was paying the price. Still, knowing I deserved it didn't make the exclusion any easier to swallow.

I started the car, pulled out into traffic without any real destination in mind. Just drove. Let muscle memory take over while my brain spiraled. What if this was the beginning? What if asking me to leave for a few hours became asking me to leave for a day, then a week, then permanently? My phone sat in the cup holder, the dark screen mocking me. Still nothing. It had been all of twenty minutes, but I couldn't stop myself from obsessing. I needed to shake it off though.

I turned onto Memorial Drive without thinking, following the curve of the Charles. The water was gray today, choppy with wind. A few stubborn rowers cut through the current, their movements precise and determined. Crazy. You couldn't pay me to be out there—where the water was opaque and the things under the surface were questionable at best.

I should go to my apartment. But the thought of being that far away, of not being able to get back to her quickly if she needed me, made my chest tight. *What was I supposed to do for a few hours?* And without meaning to, I found myself in Brookline.

I parked across the street from my childhood home, engine still running, staring at the doubled-decker. The shutters were dark green now, not black. Window boxes with fall mums. The oak tree had grown, reaching toward my old bedroom. A trellis climbed the side wall.

The sun glanced off my bedroom window where I'd hidden from Mom's vacant stares. Depression and anxiety broke her—terms we never used then. We buried her pain in silence, ashamed instead of understanding. Now as a cop, I recognize what I couldn't name as a child, how darkness once kept hidden finally finds the light.

I cut the engine. Sat there in the sudden silence. This was where I learned people vanish—first in an instant, then over years. I still see Mom's face when the officers came. The way she crumpled, strings cut. That sound she made—not scream, not sob. Something primal. Broken.

And then the quiet that came after. It was a terrible, suffocating quiet that never learned sound again. Before Dad died, she would hum while she cooked—she had a beautiful voice and perfect pitch. After he was gone, the humming stopped. The cooking stopped. Eventually the conversations stopped too. She spoke less each year until her silence filled the whole house—the laughter and music were gone.

My mother had died two years ago, though the woman who'd raised me vanished long before that—the day they buried my father. I remember her kisses when I was small. Then quick embraces. Then nothing, once my face began mirroring his and my footsteps followed as well.

That's what love and loss had done to her, and that's what I'd been so terrified of doing to Maliyah. But Maliyah wasn't my mother. And Lucas and Zoe weren't me. I sat there, letting that sink in. The past had shaped me, but it didn't have to dictate my future. I put the car in drive and headed to the next stop.

Mount Hope Cemetery was quiet. I parked near the main entrance and walked the familiar path to the graves. Left at the giant memorial. Past the bench where I used to sit when I needed to think. Up the small hill to the plot my mother had bought after my father died.

Two headstones. Side by side now, though hers was newer—shinier.

JAMES MORRISON April 27, 1957 - November 23, 1996 Beloved Husband and Father Boston Police Department End of Watch: November 23, 1996

CATHERINE MORRISON March 13, 1960 - August 2, 2023 Beloved Wife and Mother Reunited at Last

I stood there, hands in my pockets, staring at the names. "Hey, Dad," I said quietly. "It's been a while." The wind picked up around me just a bit—lightly tousling my hair, the cold biting into my cheeks.

"I fucked up. Pretty badly." I sat down on the grass between the two stones, my jeans soaking through as they quickly became cold and damp. "Maliyah. She's amazing. Funny, sweet, kind, amazing mom, and beautiful. She's so beautiful, Dad. And she makes this sound when she laughs hard—half snort, half giggle—brings a smile to my face even as I think about it now. She has these two incredible kids, Lucas and Zoe."

I pulled up some grass, ripping the blades to pieces as I fidgeted. "I fell pretty hard for them, you know. Didn't think it was possible. Guess I didn't really want it to be possible since, well—you know. But I let myself believe I could do it—take a chance. And then sure enough, I got shot. Not bad, just a shoulder wound—not like you."

I cleared my throat, my fingers finding the scar tissue beneath my shirt. "When I was bleeding out on that floor, all I saw was you. I saw Lucas and Zoe standing at my grave. I saw Maliyah going hollow like Mom did." I glanced at the other headstone. "Sorry, Mom." My voice broke. "So I ran. Convinced myself hurting them now was better than destroying them later."

My throat burned as I fought back tears. "But I was wrong. I hurt those kids anyway. And Maliyah—" I swallowed hard. "I made her feel like she wasn't worth fighting for."

I looked back at my mother's headstone. I stared at my mother's name etched in stone. "Mom, I—" My voice caught. "I'm sorry I wasn't enough." I traced the letters with my eyes, feeling the anger I'd carried for years shift into something else. "I hate that you stayed but weren't really there. And yet—" I swallowed hard, surprised by the tears. "Part of me understands it wasn't a choice. Doesn't make it any easier though."

I pressed my palm against the cold marble. "I won't repeat history. I won't abandon them again—not while I still have breath in my lungs. I can't." My hand trembled. "But God, I'm terrified I won't be able to get them back."

I stood up, brushed off my jeans. "I'm going to fight for them. Not because I'm not scared—I'm terrified. But living without them hurts worse than dying ever could."

I laid my hands on their stones, feeling the cold bite into my fingers. "I love you both. Always did—even when it was hard. Even when it hurt. That never changed."

I walked back to my car, feeling lighter somehow. Clearer. My apartment felt foreign when I walked in—stale air, mail piled under the slot, dust everywhere. I'd barely been here in weeks, only stopping to grab essentials before rushing back to Maliyah's. After a quick shower to warm my cemetery-chilled bones, I dressed and retrieved the box I'd shoved onto my closet's top shelf after Mom's funeral.

Inside: photo albums. My father's dress uniform badge. A folded flag from his funeral. Letters my mother had written to him after he died—I'd found them in her nightstand drawer after she passed. I sat on my bed and opened the first album.

My parents in their youth—late teens, maybe early twenties. Yellow-tinted seventies photo, white border faded with time. Their wedding day: Dad in dress blues, Mom in a simple white dress, wildflowers woven through her hair. Both grinning like co-conspirators.

I kept moving through the album. Me as a baby. My dad holding me, that proud father look on his face. My mom laughing at something off-camera. Beach day: me at six with a half-collapsed sandcastle, Dad's hand steadying the tower, Mom's smile genuine. Little League. Backyard barbecues. Me and John with gap-toothed grins.

The last photo in the album: my parents and me at a Halloween party, mom dressed like a police officer with a mustache and dad looking like James Dean with a pack of cigarettes rolled in his short-sleeved white shirt. Me standing between them, in a cowboy hat and boots with fake pistols and a sheriff's badge, missing one of my front teeth. All of us smiling.

It was less than a month before he was killed. I took that photo out carefully, held it up to the light. My fingers shook as I laid it beside me. I took out several more photos. Me and my dad at a Red Sox game. My parents dancing at someone's wedding. My mother, before—bright-eyed and laughing. And after—hollow, distant, fading. The progression of loss, captured in four-by-six glossy paper.

I found my father's badge, ran my thumb over the number. 4137. The same badge number I'd requested when I joined the force. The number that connected me to him, reminded me daily why I'd chosen this job. And why I'd been afraid of it.

I closed up the box, laying my hand on the top. This was the family I wanted to build—lasting though. True. Love in every form. I carefully put everything back, storing it away again. I felt better about things. I have a ways to go, but there was something different in me—in my heart.

My phone buzzed.

John: *How are things going?*

Me: *Okay. She's recovering. Doing good.*

John: *Drinks soon?*

Me: *Yeah.*

John: *Good. Text when you've got the time.*

Me: *Will do.*

I pocketed my phone and headed back to my car. I drove aimlessly for a while. Past Maliyah's apartment building—I slowed down but didn't stop. Caden and Felicity's car was out front though, so my guess is I was right.

She'd needed her kids. Good. She needs them and they her. I kept driving. Found myself heading toward the North End, circling endlessly until I found a spot. Finally parking down the street from a small Italian market I'd visited a hundred times.

Giuseppe looked up as I entered, his face breaking into a smile. "Detective Morrison! It's been too long."

"Hey, Giuseppe."

"How is your lady? John came in, told me about what happened. Terrible business."

John was my best friend, but he was a teenaged gossip at heart. "She's recovering. Getting stronger every day."

"Good, good." His expression grew serious. "And you? You're taking care of her? Doing okay?"

I didn't know how to answer that. "I'm trying. I felt like that was the right answer for all of his questions in one."

He studied my face for a long moment. "My father used to say that love without risk is not love at all. It's just safe. And safe is boring. And doesn't keep you warm at night." He pumped his eyebrows suggestively at the last, making me laugh—and I think I even blushed a bit.

"Yeah, yeah, old man."

Giuseppe hunched his shoulders and raised his fists. "I'll give you an old man!" His wedding band flashed as he jabbed at the air, apron strings swinging.

I shuffled toward him, fists raised in mock defense. Giuseppe landed a slow-motion punch to my gut. I staggered back, knocking a bag of rigatoni to the floor. "Help! Senior citizen brutality!" I called out. An elderly woman glanced up from the cheese counter, rolling her eyes when Giuseppe winked at her.

I left the market smiling and carrying a giant bag of goods with Giuseppe's words echoing in my mind. He's right—safety doesn't keep you warm at night. I pulled my phone out of my pocket. Still no text from Maliyah.I checked the time. It had been well over three hours since I'd left. How long was "a few hours"? When would she text? What if she didn't?

I drove to a coffee shop, ordered black, and sat with my phone face-up, waiting. Finally, I texted Maliyah.

Me: *Is it safe to come back?*

My phone buzzed moments later.

Maliyah: *You can come back now.*

Five words. No elaboration. No indication of how it had gone. I didn't care that she hadn't said anything else though. She wanted me to come back.

I stood up so fast I nearly knocked over my chair, and I was out the door in seconds.

Me: *OTW*

No response.

I strangled the steering wheel as a third light turned red. An elderly woman inched across while I drummed my fingers. Green. Two blocks. Another red.

She opened the door immediately. Alone. Her face blotchy, eyes red-rimmed but dry. She looked exhausted, relieved, and unreadable.

"Hey," I said quietly. "You okay?"

She nodded, stepped back to let me in. She held up her phone. **Sit down. We need to talk.**

My stomach dropped. This was it. She was going to tell me to leave. I sat on the couch. She took the chair opposite me. And started typing.

Chapter 41:

In Truth, Alone

MALIYAH

Reed took his seat on the couch, facing me. His eyes searched my face, trying to read what was coming. He knew something had shifted. He just didn't know what. I looked down at my phone and stared at the cursor blinking in the text field. My fingers hovered over the screen. How did I even start this?

Something had changed. Something inside of me was different after seeing my kids—after feeling like I was finally almost on the other side of my recovery. I didn't feel like I was making all the right decisions at this point.

I'd realized, sitting there after they'd left, that I'd been letting everyone treat me like I was broken. I'd spent the past few weeks hiding behind Reed, using him as a shield against the dark, against the memories, against my own damn ability to stand up.

I started typing. **You can move out now.**

His whole body went rigid. "What?" The word came out rough, like I'd punched him.

I need space. To figure things out. To heal without leaning on you.

He leaned forward, elbows on his knees. "Maliyah—"

I'm not angry. I just need to do this on my own.

"Come on!" The words snapped out of him, sharp and sudden.

I blinked, looked up from my phone. Reed never yelled. Never challenged me like this, especially not since everything happened.

He stood up, paced to the window, and leaned his forehead against it, like he was searching for words and patience. Time ticked by before he spun back to face me, heartbreak written all over his face. "Why do you think I'm here?"

Confused, I looked at him and shook my head. Honestly, I don't know if I could answer his question. I wasn't sure I did know why he was here and, in realizing this, I don't know if I had the emotional bandwidth to dissect it even if I tried.

When I couldn't answer, he continued, his voice low and intense. "I'm not here because you're weak, Maliyah. I'm here because you're strong—strong enough to fight off a monster when most would've broken. I'm here because you're incredible, not because you need me. I'm here because I already knew how I felt and I know how I feel. I'm here because the thought of living without you breaks something inside me."

My throat tightened. I forced myself to put my fingers back to the keyboard on my phone.

I don't know how to feel right now. It's not about strength or weakness.

He moved closer, not crowding me but making sure I could see his face, the intensity in his eyes. "It feels like you are scared to let me back in."

My fingers stilled on the screen. He wasn't wrong. But he wasn't entirely right either. **Maybe. Maybe it's all of it. Maybe I need to know I can be alone before I can choose not to be.**

He ran a hand through his hair, the gesture so familiar it made my chest ache. "You really want me to leave?"

I nodded.

"Okay. Obviously it's your decision. But know that I already know you are independent. I already know you can do this alone—and I think so do you." He looked me right in the eyes. "You don't trust me. I know it. And I deserve it, but at least be honest about it."

The words hit like a slap. I stood up too fast, my body protesting a little, reminding me that while I'm recovering there are still some lasting impressions of Bryce on my body, not just my mind. I walked to the kitchen and got some water to cool off, leaving Reed to watch me. When I was steady, I typed with shaking fingers.

You're right. You left me. You LEFT. And yes, I'm angry about that. And yes, I am still trying to figure out if I can trust you.

I paused, trying to find my words. **This is not about you, though. It's about knowing I can face my nightmares without you here. Knowing if I choose to really let you back in, it won't be because I was too scared to be alone.**

Each word I typed felt like ripping off a bandage, painful but necessary. **And it will have to be if and when I regain my trust in you—and when I can believe you won't just take off again.**

We stared at each other across my small living room—him by the windows and me on the other side of the kitchen bar top. The late afternoon sun slanted through the window, coming through the sheer curtains, bringing a glow to the room. The faucet dripped in the kitchen—three drops, then silence, then three more—telling me I hadn't shut it off completely when I'd poured my water.

"How long?" His voice was quieter now, controlled.

I don't know.

"That's not fair."

Fair? None of this is fair. But it's what I need.

He laughed, but there was no humor in it. "What you need. What about what we need? What about rebuilding us?"

Reed. There is no us right now. There's you feeling guilty about everything and me feeling broken. There is both of us pretending that's enough to build on.

"So you're just giving up?"

No.

I shook my head. I needed him to get where I was coming from, but I also felt exhausted by all the tapping on my screen.

I need to know I'm choosing you because I want to, not because I'm scared to be alone. And that you're choosing me, not your guilt. Understand?

He stood there for a long moment, hands clenched at his sides. I could see the war on his face—the urge to fight harder against the need to respect what I was asking.

"Okay," he finally said, but the word came out sharp. "Okay, if this is what you need. But I'm not disappearing. I'm not walking away again. And I am not here because of responsibility. I am here because of us. I was coming to earn you back before he even took you, and I will prove it to you."

I looked at him, surprised at that. What did he mean by that?

"I texted you the night before he took you. I was coming back. We never found time to talk about it, and maybe today isn't that time, but you should know—I'm not here out of guilt. I'm here because there is nothing in this world that could tear my focus from you. I want you back, Maliyah. Without fear. Without question, and I will prove it to you—come hell or high water."

He moved toward me in the kitchen, coming within a hairsbreadth of me. He reached for me, running his hands through my hair on either side of my face. His fingers locked behind my neck as he pulled me toward him, and we stood there foreheads touching.

My lips had parted in surprise and my breath caught. My heart raced as his eyes bore into mine. My breathing increased and my pulse thrummed as I felt his breath mingle with mine. He leaned forward touching his lips to mine lightly, oh so lightly. I could tell he was trying to be careful, to test the waters and make sure he wasn't hurting me.

He wasn't hurting me—not one bit. Pain was the furthest thought from my mind. Instead, I felt a gentle warmth spreading through me—a quiet want I wasn't sure I'd ever feel again. His lips barely brushed against mine—almost nuzzling. He was careful of the metal framework still holding my jaw together. The tenderness in his restraint made my chest tighten.

His hands moved with deliberate care, one lightly cradling the back of my head, the other resting at the small of my back. He held me close enough to feel his heartbeat, but with enough space to remind me he was conscious of my healing body. The wires in my mouth made any real kiss impossible, yet somehow this careful dance of almost-touching felt more intimate than passion.

I closed my eyes, focusing on the simple miracle that I could still feel anything gentle at all after everything that had happened. For just a moment, the constant ache receded, and I remembered what safety felt like. His lips barely grazed the corners of my mouth before traveling up along my cheek, following the faint ridges where stitches had once been. When his nose brushed against my temple and his breath warmed my skin through my hair, I found myself swaying toward him, chasing that forgotten feeling of shelter.

Then he was gone. The sudden absence of his touch left me off-balance, my body still leaning into the space where he'd been. I stumbled forward, catching myself against his chest. His hands steadied me at my elbows. My cheeks burned, but I straightened myself. Pride would have to wait.

His voice was gravelly as he said, "You know what? I know I broke your trust. I'm working on regaining it—showing you that I will be here." He swallowed hard, Adam's apple bobbing. "I will stand with you and by you. I told you I'm not afraid to be all in, and I mean it. You have every part of me and the only thing that scares me is the thought of losing you."

With each word he spoke, hairline fractures spread through my walls. Not painful—like ice at first thaw. I couldn't name what was happening inside me with his gravitational pull constantly tugging. That's exactly why I needed distance. I needed to hear my own thoughts, feel my own heartbeat, and breathe air that wasn't warmed by his presence.

So I stepped back. And then again, and even as we were both breathing heavy from what had to be the most passionate experience of my life, the coldness of the space began to seep into my bones. I felt the loss of his touch and the loss of his embrace somewhere inside of me that I wasn't sure I could reach. And yet, I took another step back—our gaze still locked.

And there he remained, leaning back now against the kitchen counter with his hands on the edge alongside himself. I'd pulled away so much so that I was almost outside of the kitchen entirely. I was torn—desperately wanting to be back in his arms, but knowing I needed this separation for myself. For my kids.

I just need time. I need to breathe on my own. I need to see for myself where I stand. And you need to be okay with that.

He nodded, looked down at his feet as if wearing the weight of the world on his shoulders. And while I felt for him, I absolutely couldn't give him this. It was for me. And I'm just not ready for more right this moment. Whether he was or wasn't okay with that couldn't be my focus. So I left it at that. Feeling like there were no more words to explain myself, I turned and began to make my way to my room.

Then I stopped though, debating, and then deciding. I went back to the kitchen, grabbed some essentials from the cabinet and fridge, and then turned back around without comment to Reed. This time I did make it to my room, closing the door quietly behind me. I couldn't watch him pack without my heart betraying me.

I retreated to the bathroom and shut the door behind me. The clawfoot tub beckoned. I uncorked the wine I'd grabbed from the kitchen, poured just enough to taste, and set my phone to play something soft. Tonight, I'd allow myself this small indulgence.

Tonight was for me. Tomorrow I would deal with everything else that waited, but for now, I think I deserved a damn break.

Chapter 42:

At The Table

REED

I stood there for a minute, outside Maliyah's—staring at her door. Flipping my car keys in my hand, my feet felt frozen, though my heart was still racing from everything that just happened.

She'd asked me to leave. Asked me to move out. Admittedly, I'd hoped she wouldn't realize I'd slowly moved in. At least until she was willing to admit she loved me and forgave me for being an absolute fucking idiot.

I sighed, turning away, and made my way down the stairs. I had my overnight bag slung over my shoulder—it wasn't everything, since I'd brought things over a little at a time. One bag couldn't hold it all. A sign maybe that I wouldn't be completely gone from her life.

Honestly, I knew this day would likely come. I just hadn't expected it to hurt this much.

I threw the bag in the trunk and sat in my car. My breath clouded in front of me as I stared at her building, fingers gripping the wheel, though the engine was still off. Only after my teeth started to chatter did I realize how long I'd been sitting there.

I pulled out my phone, staring at it—unsure of what to do next. My apartment. I should go to my apartment. Except the thought of walking into that space—silent, empty, and musty—made my chest tight.

I texted John: *O'Malley's. 20 minutes.*

His response came immediately: *Already there. Rough day?*

Something like that.

I started the car and drove.

O'Malley's was exactly what I needed—dark, loud enough to drown out thoughts, and filled with off-duty cops who knew better than to ask questions or else they would learn turn about was fair play.

John was at our usual table in the back corner, two beers already waiting. He took one look at my face and slid one across to me.

John leaned forward, elbows on the table, studying my face. "Damn, Morrison. You look like someone just told you Santa isn't real."

"She asked me to move out."

John lifted his beer and took a long pull. "Yeah? Well, shit. Sounds like our girl wised up and realized what a pain in the ass you are." His eyes crinkled at the corners as he studied me over the rim of his glass, mouth quirking up just enough to show he was giving me shit, but not enough to make me want to punch him.

I drank half the beer in one pull. "She just needs some space. To figure things out. To get past all the shit she's been dealing with—without leaning on me."

"And you're here because...?"

"Because I don't know what the hell else to do tonight that doesn't land me on my couch with countless beers." The words came out rougher than I intended.

"That's because you're an idiot."

I looked up, ready to tell him to fuck off, but he was grinning.

"Morrison!" Macky's voice boomed across the bar before I could respond. "Got the look of a man drowning your sorrows. Count me in for a front row seat."

Joe "Macky" McLoughlin slid into the booth next to John, his perpetual grin firmly in place. Behind him came Jaxson Williams, ducking slightly under low support beam, his shoulders nearly filling the space as he moved through the crowd. People shifted out of his path without him saying a word, just a slight turn of his body and they made way. He settled his weight into a chair that looked too small beneath him, his movements unhurried but precise.

"Great," I muttered. "The whole damn squad's here for my misery."

"Actually," a softer voice said as Gloria Velazquez appeared with Luis Rodriguez behind her, "we saw you over here and missed your ugly mug. But... sounds like you need a woman's opinion and I wouldn't trust these knuckleheads with anything important."

John looked up indignantly. "I'm a fount of wisdom, I'll have you know."

Gloria squeezed in next to me, her dark hair pulled back in its usual neat bun, glasses sliding down her nose as she looked John over with a critical eye. "Yeah. Sure. Keep telling yourself that." Turning to me, as she studied my face with an intensity that made me feel like she was plucking out all my secrets. "My guess? You got woman trouble."

"That's one way to put it," I said.

Luis dragged a chair over from another table, the legs scraping against the floor. "So you and that woman you've been seeing—Maliyah, wasn't it?—things went sideways?" His words carried the musical lilt of his Puerto Rican heritage.

"Yeah."

Macky whistled low. "Man, you don't do anything halfway, do you?"

"What's that supposed to mean?"

"Means you picked someone who's probably seen every excuse, every empty promise, every 'I'll change baby, I swear' speech in the book." Macky leaned back, somehow managing to look relaxed despite the serious topic. "And she's not buying your bullshit routine."

"I don't have a bullshit routine—"

"Don't you though?" Jaxson's deep voice cut through my protest, calm but firm. His dark eyes held mine with the kind of steady patience he'd probably perfected raising four kids. "Son, I know you've taken leave to help her out. But hear me—I've been married to Kayla for thirty years. You know what I learned early?" He leaned forward, ready to lay some truth out, "Taking care of someone when they're down? That's the baseline. That's not love. That's just being a decent human being."

I blinked twice, my mouth half-open with words that evaporated on my tongue. The beer bottle froze halfway to my lips. *Damn.*

"That face says it all, man." He leaned back with those words, staring at me—waiting for my response.

"I am not baseline, man," I said. "She asked me to leave. To give her space. So I'm giving her some time to breathe before I come crashing back." I felt the corner of my mouth lift in a half-smile, the stubble on my jaw pulling tight against my skin. My fingers tightened around the cold glass, condensation dampening my palm. "She won't be getting rid of me that easily. I may have been a grade-A dumbass, but—as I'm sure John'll tell you—I turned that badge in for something better—a backbone."

"A backbone," Macky repeated, deadpan. "That what we're calling it now?"

"Better than what I'd call it," Gloria muttered, pushing her glasses up.

Luis grinned. "At least he admits he was a dumbass. That's progress, no?"

"Baby steps," Jaxson rumbled, the corner of his mouth twitching. "Real *small* baby steps."

"You guys done?" I asked.

"Not even close," Macky said cheerfully. "We've got all night and at least three more rounds of giving you shit scheduled."

"Not helpful, guys," Gloria corrected. "While, I'm sure we could all make a list, I've got my nieces for a sleepover tonight. So, let's cut the shit and actually help the dumbass."

John guffawed, almost choking on his beer. "Well, looks like G's spoken. Must mean we all have to jump."

Gloria narrowed her eyes and pulled a pen from her bag, clicking it twice against her palm. She reached for a napkin, drew a perfect line down the middle, and wrote "JOHN" in block letters at the top of one column. "I've got a photographic memory for your screw-ups, I'm happy to start a list about you and refocus my attention," she said, pen hovering over the paper.

My shoulders shook as John's face scrunched into that familiar scowl, his fingers snatching the napkin from Gloria's hand so fast she blinked twice. He wadded it with deliberate precision, flicked his wrist, and sent it sailing past my ear. I caught myself mid-chuckle, realizing how good it was to have an actual laugh bubble up.

"Alright, alright. Back to fixing my screwups—John's would take too long, so let's focus."

"Asshole." John's laugh was contagious for everyone at the table.

"Back to the point," Macky said, bringing us back around. "First step is admitting you have a problem."

"The problem being I fell in love with a woman who's too good for me?"

"That's not a problem," Jaxson said, his deep voice carrying the weight of three decades of marriage. "That's called having good taste. I think the actual problem is you're trying to prove yourself the wrong way."

I took another drink. "Enlighten me then, Sensei. Because from where I'm sitting, I've spent weeks making sure she had everything she needed. And I'm afraid I'll never be—" I stopped, shook my head.

"Dude, you what? Got her fed," Luis said, rolling his eyes. "Fluffed some pillows? Washed some dishes?"

"Laundry," Gloria added. "I'm betting he did some laundry too."

"So?" I looked around the table. "What's wrong with taking care of someone?"

"Nothing," Jaxson said. "And I'm sure it helped her, but that's just doing what she needs done. Where's the romance? Where's the action that shows her you see her as your partner, not a patient?"

Macky leaned forward, grin fading into something more serious for once. "When I worked DV, this woman—black eye, split lip—looked me dead in the face after I promised we'd protect her. She said to me, 'I don't need another man telling me what he's gonna do for me. I need to know what I can do for myself.'" He tapped his index finger against the table with each word. "Never forgot that."

"She runs a shelter," I said slowly. "She helps women escape abuse and rebuild their lives."

"So you know what she values," Jaxson said. "Question is, what are you going to do about it?"

I stared at my beer, thinking about Maliyah. About her strength. About how she'd fought Bryce even when she was terrified. About the work she did every day, helping women find their own strength.

"She doesn't need me to take care of her. Shit, she saved her own damn self," I said quietly.

"Right," Gloria said.

"She needs—" I looked up. "She needs to know I understand what she's fighting for."

"Now you're getting it," Macky said, signaling the waitress for another round.

"But how do I show her that without making it about me? Without it looking like I'm trying to buy my way back in?"

Luis tilted his head. "What does the shelter need?"

"Everything, probably. It's a nonprofit."

"No," Gloria corrected. "What do the women there need? Not money. Not things. What do they need to feel like they won't be victims anymore?"

The answer came to me and Gloria at the same time.

"Self-defense classes. Tools to help them survive. To feel strong. To feel empowered," I said.

Macky sat up straighter. "Now that's a start."

"We should have it be taught by both men and women," Gloria continued, already pulling out her phone. "Bring in some female officers who know what we're doing. The women don't need a bunch of guys telling them how to throw a punch."

"Regular sessions," I added, the pieces falling into place. "Not just one-time. Ongoing. So they learn the skills but also build confidence over time."

"I know at least a dozen guys who'd volunteer for logistics," Macky said. "Equipment, funding, scheduling. Hell, my wife would probably want in on this too."

Jaxson nodded slowly. "Kayla used to teach women's self-defense. Before the kids came. She'd probably love to get back into it." He pulled out his phone. "Chief may be an obstacle—red tape and all that shit, but put together a solid plan and he'll sign off."

"Shit yeah. Lot of red tape," Luis pointed out. "You'll need to get official permission."

"Yeah." I straightened up. "I don't want to lean on Maliyah. She's on medical leave anyway. This needs to be real—about the women there, not about winning her back."

Macky raised an eyebrow. "Even though that's exactly what you're hoping it'll do?"

"It's not about that. Or, shit—well not *only* about that." I looked around the table at these people—all of them already pulling out phones and making notes. "It's about showing her that she's important and I not only understand what's important to her, but I want to help with it too."

"A convenient side benefit," Gloria said with a small smile.

"The best kind," Macky agreed.

"So we're doing this?" I asked.

"Hell yeah we're doing this," Macky said. "I'm not letting you mope around for the next month drinking bad beer and feeling sorry for yourself. This is much better."

"Plus," Gloria added, "it's actually a good idea. Even if your motives are questionable."

"Hey! My motives are pure," I protested, my voice rising slightly at the end, betraying me.

Everyone at the table looked at me.

"Okay, mostly pure."

"Thirty percent pure," Luis offered.

"That's generous," John muttered.

"Forty," I argued. "At least forty percent."

"We'll give you thirty-five and call it even," Jaxson said, the hint of a smile playing at his lips.

Gloria was already typing rapidly on her phone, her glasses sliding down as she focused. "I'm texting someone who probably has a contact at the shelter."

"Tonight?" I asked. "It's after ten."

She didn't even look up. "Meh. Monica never sleeps. She'll answer." Her phone buzzed almost immediately. "Looks like she already answered. Said she'll meet tomorrow at eleven."

"That fast?"

"Menopause. The woman never sleeps anymore." Gloria showed me the text. Five pairs of eyes suddenly found fascinating things to look at—the ceiling, the table, our drinks. John cleared his throat. Macky shifted in his seat. I became intensely interested in peeling the label off my beer bottle.

Fastest way to shut a table of men up? Talk about menopause or periods. Fastest way to get murdered? Comment on it, after a woman talks about it.

Macky pulled out a napkin and started writing, breaking the awkward silence before one of us says something stupid and didn't live to tell about it. "Okay, ahem. Yeah, so—Gloria will work on getting a shelter contact. We're going to need mats, pads, maybe some training dummies. Reed—it's your baby, so we'll generously leave the paperwork to you."

"I'll handle finding some volunteers," Jaxson said, his deep voice cutting through the planning chaos.

"I know some officers who speak Spanish and Haitian Creole," Luis added. "Make sure all the materials are accessible. A lot of these women, English isn't their first language."

I looked around the table, the stress across my shoulders loosening. "You guys are really doing this with me."

"Of course we are," Macky said, like it was obvious. "What else are we going to do? Let you sit around and be pathetic?"

"I wasn't going to be—"

"You were absolutely going to be pathetic," John interrupted. "I saw you after shit fell apart with Maliyah before when you broke up—wasn't pretty. I refuse to watch that happen again."

"This isn't a breakup," I said firmly. "She asked for space. That's different."

"Sure," Macky said, clearly humoring me. "Space. Got it."

"Let's make this good," Gloria warned. "We can't do half-assed."

"I don't do half-assed!"

Macky snorted. "Except with relationships apparently."

I flipped him off.

"See?" He grinned. "Already feeling better."

He wasn't wrong. For the first time since I'd walked out of Maliyah's apartment, I didn't feel like I was drowning. I felt like I had a direction. A purpose that wasn't just waiting around hoping she'd take me back.

"What about Maliyah?" Luis asked quietly. "When does she find out?"

"I don't know, man," I said. "I feel like if she hears it from me, she'll think it's about us."

Jaxson studied me with those patient eyes that had probably seen through every excuse his four kids had ever tried. "You really mean that."

"Yeah. I do." I finished my beer. "Look, if this works—if we actually get women the tools to feel safer, to feel stronger—that matters whether Maliyah and I ever figure our shit out or not."

"And if she does find out and thinks you're just doing it to impress her?" Gloria asked.

"Then I'll deal with that. But at least I'll be doing something that actually helps people instead of just playing nurse."

"Nurse," Macky repeated, shaking his head and laughing. "I didn't know that was your kink, man."

"Shut it, asshole!"

The whole table erupted, and something cracked open in my chest—a sound I barely recognized coming from my own throat, my shoulders shaking as I leaned back in my chair. My face actually hurt from smiling.

"Alright," Jaxson said, standing up and somehow making it look graceful despite his size. "I need to get home before Kayla sends a search party. But Morrison?" He clapped a hand on my shoulder, heavy and warm. "You're on the right path, man. And I'm here for it."

"Thanks, Jax."

A simple nod, and he was off.

Luis stood too. "This is going to be good, bro."

"Agreed," Gloria said.

Macky was the last to get up, leaving cash on the table for his share. "You got this, Reed. *We've* got it with you." Not one to wait for a response, he turned and left.

By the time everyone had left for the night, I found myself sitting alone, the remnants of my beer in hand. The idea of going home to my empty apartment sucked. But it would give me some time to plan. To get ready. To think of other ways to show Maliyah where my heart is.

My fingers drummed against the tabletop as I stared at the empty glasses left behind. I'd give her the distance she asked for, but sitting still had never been my strong suit. There was a difference between respecting boundaries and giving up entirely.

I paid my tab, grabbed my jacket, and headed out into the cold night air. I had work to do, and my musty-ass apartment would have to do for now.

Chapter 43:

Shared Scars

MALIYAH

The morning after Reed left, I woke to find a text from him telling me to "check the front door." When I opened it, I found a thermos—somehow I just knew it would be fixed exactly how I like it. Alongside it sat a cup of blended Greek yogurt and a side of honey.

He must have dropped it all off before dawn. My lips had twitched, then curved upward, the muscles in my cheeks pulling tight enough that my jaw ached slightly from disuse. I couldn't wait to have my words back, to hear my own voice, to speak to my kids and tell them I love them. I thought to myself *four more days*. The countdown was running through my head constantly.

The next morning, there were grocery bags by the door when I opened it following another text from Reed. So far, he texted me throughout each day, letting me know he was thinking of me. Messaging short little notes about what was going on, or something funny he'd noticed.

I'd respond, but I couldn't seem to make myself say much. Maybe because I was tired of messaging. Tired of still not being able to speak. Tired of how every message I typed made Bryce's face flash in my mind—he'd stolen even this simple act from me, turned it into another reminder of what he'd done.

In this delivery, he'd included a ton of soft foods—yogurt, soup, the expensive smoothies from Whole Foods that actually didn't suck too bad. There was some weird gel-pad for the face, and a sudoku book. My fingers itched to grab a pen and dive into those little numbered squares.

This morning—day three—Felicity had shown up with her arms full. She barged in before I could stop her, hip-checking me aside as she made a bee-line for the kitchen counter. Her phone buzzed in her pocket. She rolled her eyes as she unloaded her bags. "Betting it's Reed again. Seven-thousandth text today. 'Is she eating? Are the kids overwhelming you? Have the kids gone home yet?'" *Tomorrow*, I thought, *and not a day too soon.*

She pulled out her phone, thumbs flying across the screen. "Your one or two-word answers aren't cutting it for him, May-May. Look." She thrust the screen in my face—showing me how often he was checking on me with her. Nothing crazy, just asking if she needed help, if she could just check on me, do the kids need anything. *Good Lord.*

I busied myself with putting things away, avoiding her gaze as she sighed. "I'm here now. I'll report back. Maybe then I can actually use my phone for something other than Reed's hourly welfare checks." She snorted, rolling her eyes dramatically, but the corners of her mouth twitched upward and her dimples appeared as she glanced down at her phone again, thumbs hovering over the screen.

She'd brought some foods for me and—bless her heart—a stack of tawdry romance novels...discreet covers be damned! *Give me a bodice ripper to break the tedium!*

"Figured you'd be going stir-crazy with nothing to do, you should get out of the house. It's not like you're an invalid," she'd said, setting them on the coffee table before I quickly swept them up and hustled them over to my room.

I went to Stop & Shop yesterday.

"Good! Great! I'm so proud of you!"

I snorted and shook my head. **I got gasps from people I walked by, and one lady asked me if I needed help running from someone. I guess. I thought my face was better than it is. Guess I'm just a fucking train wreck.**

At this, I paused. My throat tightened, vision blurring as I stared at the kitchen counter. Without thinking, my fingertips found the raised ridges that ran down the side of my face, the permanent signature Bryce had left on my skin.

While my stitches had been removed weeks ago, it was only after Reed was gone that I found my fingertips constantly tracing the raised scars. I kept wondering what my face would look like long after the healing—would the scars remain forever?

She stared at me, assessing my face. I knew what she saw—the pockets of blood in my eyes had almost completely resolved. The droop in my eye had finally improved where it was almost invisible. The bruising had finally disappeared. To her, I was sure I looked almost normal.

My sister would say I had made great strides. The rest of the world would still say I looked like I got the shit kicked out of me. The scars that ran the length of my face. The blood in one of my eyes still there. The eye socket he'd busted still looked... off. My clenched jaw made my face look shorter. I was a living picture of fucked up.

I turned my head slightly, letting my hair fall forward to hide the raised textures on my face. Providing the perfect opportunity to avoid her stare, I moved around the kitchen. She dropped it without speaking. My sister knew me. She knew I wasn't ready to talk.

So, she did what I needed her to do—chattered incessantly. And I listened without hearing. It was perfect. It was comfortable. Half an hour later, with promises to respond to Reed when he asks how I'm feeling, she left.

The quiet surrounded me as I poured myself some bone broth, allowing the rich liquid gold to warm me from the inside. I was settling in with my cup, and one of my new books, when the doorbell rang.

My whole body went rigid. Nobody rang the doorbell. Felicity had a key. I didn't think it would be Reed since he seemed to be better at the "drop and text" approach.

I still hadn't moved by the time it rang again. I crept to the door, trying to see through the peephole without making a sound. A woman stood in the hallway, but I couldn't make out her face. She was looking down at something in her hands.

My phone was on the coffee table. Too far to reach without leaving the door. But the baseball bat Reed had insisted I keep by the door was right there, leaning in the corner.

The woman knocked. "Maliyah? It's Diane. Do you remember me?"

Oh, shit.

Diane. Bryce's wife. *My God. I'd forgotten about her.* And guilt pierced my gut. I'd been so wrapped up in my own healing that I'd completely forgotten to see what happened to her.

I peered through the peephole again. She was looking up now. The left side of her face had a tinge of yellow-green bruising, but otherwise she looked okay.

My hands shook as I undid the locks. I opened the door but kept the chain on.

"Hi," she said softly. Her voice was hoarse. "I'm sorry to just show up. I found your address in his phone."

She held up Bryce's phone.

"I know I shouldn't be here. But there is something in his phone I thought you would want to see and I realized—I needed to see you."

I closed the door to undo the chain, then opened it fully. We stood there looking at each other. Two women bearing the same signature—survivors despite the attempts to break us by the same man

I stepped back, gestured for her to come in.

It was then that I noticed the crutches. She wore a full skirt, so I couldn't see much, but I could tell that she was moving only on one of her feet. Letting her in, I relocked everything, then, with as much voice and clarity I could muster through the wires, I said, "Can I get you anything?"

"Water would be good."

I got us both water. When I returned, she was staring at her phone.

She held it up for me to see. "Bryce's."

At my nod, she continued. "I was in the hospital for two weeks," she said, her fingers absently tracing her throat as if remembering what he'd done. "Almost choked me to death the night he went for you. I remember the carpet burn on my back as he dragged me to the stairs." She rapped her knuckles against the plaster cast encasing her right leg—I couldn't see all of it, but the outline looked like it ran from mid-thigh to toes. "Three pins in my femur, shattered ankle. Still have a couple weeks to go in this thing."

I felt my pulse quicken, the memory of his voice slithering back when he'd spoken about her in past tense.

Her eyes went distant, reliving the memory. "Thank God for smart-home devices. As I laid there, at the bottom of the steps, I couldn't move and didn't have my phone. But I managed to tell Alexa to call 911." She sniffed, looking down at her leg and tracing the cast absentmindedly. "It was a couple days later when they told me he was dead. I was in the ICU—drifting in and out of consciousness—I'd had multiple surgeries. They said he'd kidnapped someone—you."

I nodded, my jaw aching from clenching my teeth against the wires.

"When they told me he was dead, all I felt was relief."

"You're human."

She showed me the phone. "He had everything about you. Photos, notes, your schedule. Pictures through your windows."

My hands shook as I took the phone from her hands and looked through it. Photos of me leaving for work. Lucas and Zoe at the playground. Reed's car outside. Notes about when Reed left me. Times when I was alone. The kids school schedules.

I couldn't read more. I handed the phone back as if it were on fire.

"The earliest photos are from months ago. Right after we ran into you."

The room tilted. He'd planned it for months. I'd known it—felt vindicated by it almost. After being told multiple times by the police that there was nothing they could do, I felt a righteous anger toward the system and all that it lacked for protecting those of us in these situations.

Her voice pulled me back to the moment. "I just—I wanted to say I was sorry. Sorry that I didn't realize he was coming for you."

"Not your fault," I managed again, my voice barely audible through the wires. "Good at hiding."

"I should have seen it." Her eyes filled with tears. "All those years. I thought it was my fault. That if I just tried harder, if I was better—"

I reached for my phone, typing quickly—my face hurting too much to try to verbalize again.

You couldn't have known. I thought the same as you when I was with him.

She read it, wiping at her eyes with shaking hands. "The police told me what happened. That you fought him. That you—" Her voice broke. "That you ended him."

I nodded slowly, watching her face for any sign of anger or blame.

"Thank you," she whispered.

The words hung in the air between us. Thank you. For killing her husband. For ending her living nightmare—our living nightmares.

I'm sorry you had to go through this. That he hurt you too.

"I tried to leave him," she said suddenly. "After that night at the restaurant, after what you said—it stayed with me. I'd hidden some clothes away, thinking I would get out. Then something changed. I know he thought he'd killed me. Left me for dead at the bottom of those stairs." Tears ran down her face as she shared her story.

"I woke in the hospital, not knowing what happened—my last memory of his hands at my throat and my world going dark. When the police told me what happened." She laughed bitterly. "Oh, the relief I felt. Almost joy really. It washed over me in that moment and I don't know if I've ever felt as safe as I did right then."

Where are you staying now?

"My sister's. In Connecticut. I drove down today just to see you. To give you this." She held out the phone. "I thought you should have it. For evidence or closure or whatever you need. The police already made copies of everything."

Nice of them to have copies and not shared all of this with me. I felt bitterness, but I tamped it down, knowing it wasn't helpful—knowing I didn't need it anymore. Looking at the phone though, I held my hands up, not wanting to feel the weight of it again. All those photos. All that planning.

Keep it or destroy it. I don't want it.

She nodded, taking it back and slipping it into her purse. "I'll get rid of it then. Wipe it and donate or something."

We sat there for a moment in the kind of silence only two people who'd survived the same monster could share.

"Can I ask you something?" Diane said quietly.

I nodded.

"Does it get better? The nightmares? The jumping at every sound?"

I thought about the past few weeks. About waking up screaming. About checking locks three times. About the baseball bat by the door that I still couldn't bring myself to move.

It gets different. Some days are better than others. But yeah, it gets better.

Diane nodded slowly, her fingers twisting the strap of her purse. "I had to identify him, you know? At the morgue." She said it matter-of-factly, like she was talking about picking up dry cleaning. "They asked if I wanted someone to come with me—my sister offered—but I went alone."

She looked up at me, her eyes dry. "I thought I'd feel something. Relief, maybe. Or fear. Or anger. Something. Even joy." Her voice dropped to almost a whisper. "But I stood there looking at him on that table, and I felt... nothing. Like I was looking at a stranger. Like I'd never known him at all."

I waited, letting her process.

"Is that wrong?" she asked. "That I felt nothing?"

I shook my head slowly, then reached for my phone.

Not wrong. It's survival. Your mind is protecting you from the monster he was.

"I kept thinking I should cry. That someone should cry for him." She gave a bitter laugh. "But I couldn't. I just signed the papers and left—turned his body over to his family."

I sat there, offering the only thing I could—silent understanding. In that moment, words felt inadequate, even intrusive. So we existed together in the quiet aftermath of survival, two women who'd escaped the same storm, now sitting in its wreckage.

"I'm going to therapy," she said, breaking the silence of the moments that had ticked by. "Starting next week. My sister found someone who works with women like me—like us."

Good. That's really good.

"What about you?"

I hadn't thought about therapy. Hadn't thought about anything beyond getting through each day, getting these wires out, getting my voice back.

Maybe. Eventually. I don't really know.

Diane stood carefully, holding her side, seeming like a mirror of myself. "I should go. I've taken up enough of your time."

I walked her to the door, unlocking it slowly.

She paused in the doorway. "If you ever need to talk—someone who gets it—my sister gave me a new number. Would it be okay if I texted it to you?"

Yes. Please.

She pulled out her phone, and I gave her my number. A moment later, my phone buzzed with her contact information.

"Thank you again," she said. "For everything. For fighting back. For surviving. For giving me the power to believe I could too."

She turned toward the door, her shoulders hunched as she moved carefully on crutches. When she looked back, her mascara had drawn thin black rivers down her cheeks, and her hand lingered on the doorframe for three heartbeats before she stepped through.

I closed the door, locked it, and slid down to sit on the floor with my back against it.

Bryce had been planning this for months. Taking photos. Watching me. Watching my children.

And if he'd succeeded—if Reed hadn't found me—no one would have ever known.

I'd spent weeks thinking about what Bryce had taken from me. My voice. My sense of safety. My ability to trust. But he hadn't taken everything. And he hadn't won.

I pulled myself up, locked the door one more time for good measure, and went back to the living room. Just days until these wires came out. Until I could start living again without flinching at my own reflection. I could wait just a little longer. I'd survived worse.

Chapter 44:

Without Nightmares

MALIYAH

I stared at myself in the bathroom mirror. *Tomorrow. Tomorrow these wires came out.* I would *not* freak out or let fear speak into me. I would *not* wonder what would happen if the doctor said that I hadn't healed enough. I was ready for this to be done—to get back to living.

I turned away from the mirror and went through my nightly routine on autopilot. I pulled on the faded blue flannel bottoms with the fraying drawstring that had seen me through two pregnancies, tugging the matching top over my head, relishing in the ability to stretch with less pain these days. The soft, well-loved, fabric slid against my skin like a familiar embrace.

Walking into my bedroom, I flipped off the bathroom light and gravitated toward my phone where it sat on the nightstand. The screen sat there—dark and mocking. Reed had texted earlier—something about a meeting running late, hope I was having a good evening. I'd responded with a thumbs up emoji because that's all I could manage lately. Every text felt like effort I didn't have.

But tomorrow. Tomorrow I could call him—*would* call him. I want to speak to him instead of typing one-word responses like some kind of automated system. Hard as it was to admit it, I missed him.

I pressed my palm against my stomach, right where that hollow ache lived—the one that flared whenever I thought of Reed—of his smile, then immediately I'd remember the feeling of him leaving. What if I let him in again, only for him to leave? But I knew I was lying to myself—I'd already let him in. I'd already taken the chance.

I stared at the dark screen, my index finger hovering over the screen as I contemplated waking my phone to text him. *No. Stick to the plan. I'd wait until the wires were out.*

I climbed into bed, pulled the covers up, and stared at the ceiling. The apartment was quiet except for the occasional creak of the building settling and the muffled sound of someone's TV through the wall. Normal sounds. Safe sounds.

My mind wandered to Lucas and Zoe. They'd video called earlier today—like every day now. Their faces filled my screen with gap-toothed grins and excited chatter about school and soccer practice and Zoe's new best friend Charlotte who apparently had the best snacks. I'd typed responses, speaking small amounts when I had the energy. I'd shown them drawings, made silly faces that pulled at my healing jaw.

"When can we come home, Mama?" Lucas had asked.

Soon, baby. So soon.

And I'd meant it. I was going to surprise them tomorrow—I'd show up at Felicity's with my jaw finally free, ready to scoop them into my arms when they burst through the door from school. I'd imagined a million times what it would feel like to watch their faces as they realized I had come to take them home.

I rolled onto my side, tucking my hands under the pillow. Tomorrow couldn't come fast enough. But what if—

No. I wasn't doing that. Wasn't playing the hypotheticals game where my mind spun out worst-case scenarios.

I closed my eyes and focused on my breathing. In through my nose, out through my mouth. The meditation app Felicity had downloaded for me played softly from my phone—some woman with a soothing voice talking about releasing tension and trusting the process.

Sleep found me somewhere between the third and fourth breathing exercise. I woke to the sun cracking the horizon, a sliver of light streaming through my bedroom window. No nightmares.

The realization hit me as I blinked awake, my body relaxed instead of coiled tight with fear. No dreams of hands around my throat. No visions of Bryce's face looming over me. No darkness closing in.

Just sleep. Real, actual sleep. I lay there for a moment, letting that sink in. Then I grabbed my phone. Two hours until my appointment.

I threw back the covers and got up, my body protesting the quick movement. My ribs were mostly healed now, just the occasional twinge when I moved wrong. The bruises had faded completely.

The shower felt like the best of all luxuries—hot water pounding against my back, steam filling the bathroom. I took my time getting ready—unsure of what today's appointment would bring and afraid of letting hope burn too hot.

In the kitchen, I made myself a smoothie from the stash Reed had left. Mango pineapple today. I sipped it slowly through the straw, my jaw aching with the familiar pull of the wires.

Last time. This was the last time I'd have to do this. My phone buzzed.

Felicity: *Good luck today! Text me as soon as you're done. Love you!*

Me: *Will do. Love you too.*

Another buzz.

Caden: *You've got this, May-May. The kids are so excited to talk to you tonight.*

That tugged on my heart—in a good way. Tonight. Tonight I would pick up my babies and bring them home to me.

I finished the smoothie, rinsed the cup, and looked around my apartment. Everything was in its place. Clean. Organized. Ready. I grabbed my purse, checked that I had my wallet and insurance card, and headed for the door.

My hand closed around the doorknob. *Deep breath. You've got this.* I pulled open the door.

And there stood Reed. Leaning on the wall next to my door, two coffee cups in hand, wearing jeans and a henley that made his shoulders look impossibly broad. His hair was slightly messy, like he'd run his hands through it over and over again. On his face rested a hopeful but careful expression.

"Hey," he said, his voice soft in the quiet hallway.

I stared at him, my hand still on the doorknob, my brain trying to catch up. Reed. Here. With coffee.

He held up one of the cups. "Figured you might want company for the appointment. If that's okay. If not, I can just—" He started to lower the cup. "I can leave the coffee and go."

I shook my head quickly, stepping back to let him in. The smile that broke across his face was like sunrise. He came inside, and I closed the door behind him, my heart doing something complicated in my chest. He was here. He'd shown up.

"How did you—" I gestured at him, at the coffee, at everything, my voice barely working through space between my lips.

"How did I know about your appointment?" He set both cups on the counter and turned to face me. "Maliyah, I know when all your appointments are. I've known since the hospital." His blue eyes held mine. "I pay attention—I care."

The words landed in my chest and settled there, warm and solid.

He picked up one of the cups again and held it out. He stopped, looking uncertain and rushing through his words, "Is this weird? This feels weird. Am I making this weird? I'm making this weird."

I took the cup from him, my fingers brushing his, and shook my head and smirked at his nervousness. Not weird. The opposite of weird.

Speaking through the wires as best I could, trying to avoid slurring too much, I said, "Thank you for being here. I hadn't realized you knew about today."

At her words, something shifted in his expression—relief mixed with determination. "I know about all of them. The follow-ups, the physical therapy appointments you have next week, the one with the plastic surgeon in two weeks." He ran a hand through his hair. "I'm not trying to be creepy. Felicity keeps me updated. I just—I wanted to be here. If you wanted me here. If you needed anything."

The truth surprised me even as I whispered, "I want you here." And I realized that it was true. Standing here facing Reed as he held his coffee and watched me like I was something precious—I wanted this. Wanted him.

"Good." His shoulders relaxed. "That's good. Because I was prepared to camp out in the hallway, waiting for you to get back, if you said no."

I couldn't help it—I smiled. Really smiled, even though it pulled at my jaw and probably looked ridiculous with the wires.

But Reed's expression went soft, his eyes crinkling at the corners. "There she is."

My phone buzzed in my hand—an alarm I'd set reminding me to leave in fifteen minutes.

Reed glanced at it. "We should probably get going. Traffic might be bad."

I nodded.

He waited while I locked up, then walked beside me down the hallway to the stairs. His hand hovered near the small of my back, not quite touching but close enough that I could feel the warmth of him.

Outside, his car was parked in visitor parking, and he opened the passenger door for me before I could reach for it.

"Your carriage awaits," he said with a small smile.

I rolled my eyes but got in, the familiar smell of his car—coffee and that cedar soap he used—surrounding me.

He slid into the driver's seat, the leather creaking beneath his weight. The engine rumbled to life as he started the car, but he let it idle, his knuckles white against the steering wheel. When he turned to look at me, morning light caught the stubble on his jaw, highlighting the tiny scar near his chin I'd never noticed before.

"Whatever happens in there today," he said, his voice barely audible above the engine's purr, "whatever the doctor says—you've already survived the hardest part. This is just the next step."

He reached over, his calloused fingers enveloping mine. He squeezed—just once, quick, but I felt the warmth of his palm against my skin, the gentle pressure of his thumb brushing my knuckle. I curled my fingers around his and held on for a heartbeat longer than necessary, feeling the steady thrum of his pulse against mine.

Then he put the car in gear and pulled out of the parking lot, and I watched my building disappear in the side mirror. Today these wires came out. Today I'd get my voice back. Today I would start figuring out what came next.

And Reed was here—not because I'd asked, not because he felt obligated, but because he'd paid attention. Because he cared. That had to mean something. No—that *did* mean something. I settled back in my seat, the coffee cup warm in my hands even if I couldn't drink it yet, and let myself feel something I hadn't felt in weeks.

Hope.

Chapter 45:

Forward Motion

REED

Offices inside hospital waiting rooms all look the same. Same off-white walls, same uncomfortable chairs, same smell of disinfectant trying to cover up things even I didn't like to think about. Maliyah sat beside me, fingers drumming against her thigh—tap tap tap, pause, tap tap tap. I'd learned her rhythms over time. This one meant she was singing something in her head and keeping a beat going with it.

"Stop staring," she quietly muttered.

"Why?"

She scoffed, sounding annoyed.

I caught her gaze and held it. "Get used to it. I like looking at you. When the most beautiful woman in the room is sitting next to me, where else would I look?"

"She locked eyes with me, focused."

"Now who's staring?" I said with a smirk I couldn't prevent.

Scoffing again, she looked away after rolling her eyes, which only gave me more of a chance to study her face. The swelling was gone. But those thin scars along the side of her face—those would stay. She kept touching it, an unconscious gesture that made me want to hold her hand and tell her that I see her through them and I love what they represent—her survival.

I leaned close to her ear—close enough I knew she could feel my breath—and said, "I like your battle wounds, you know. Nothing more stunning than a warrior goddess. And, baby, that's exactly what you are."

She drew back, her eyes widening before narrowing again, her fingers twitching against her thigh. Her lips parted slightly, then pressed together in a thin line as she glanced away, then back to my face, searching for something. I kept my expression open, steady. Let her look all she wanted. I'm not running away.

"Miss Davenport?" A nurse appeared in the doorway.

Maliyah tossed the magazine onto the table harder than necessary. I stood first, offered my hand. She looked at it for a moment, her eyes dancing between mine and my hand before she finally took it. Her fingers were ice cold.

"You sure you're okay with me coming?" I asked as we followed the nurse.

Her grip tightened. Out of the corner of her mouth, she answered in hushed tones, "No, but you'll just make me tell you everything anyways. Easier this way."

If that's what she needed to tell herself, then who was I to question it. I was just glad she was letting me come.

The exam room was every medical room ever—paper on the table, old cupboards with a sink, fluorescent lights that made everyone look sick or wrinkled. Maliyah hoisted herself onto the table, wincing. Her ribs were mostly healed, but I could tell that sudden movements still hurt her.

"How are we feeling today?" The nurse—Janet, according to her badge—pulled up Maliyah's chart on the computer.

"Want a burger," Maliyah garbled out. "Real burger. I want to chew!"

Janet smiled. "I'm sure you do! Soon."

Janet took Maliyah through the motions, taking all her vitals and marking them down. "Okay, then. You just sit tight and Dr. Pettit will be right in."

The door clicked shut. Maliyah's heels started bumping against the table base. Another tell—this one was pure nerves.

"Hey." I moved closer but didn't touch. We were still figuring out boundaries. "It's going to be fine."

"Hmmmmmm."

"Listen. The x-rays last week looked good. Dr. Pettit said—"

"Hmmmmm." She cut me off, then softer: "Can we just wait to talk? It's hard for me."

I nodded, realizing how much I may have been pushing her. It couldn't be easy. The door opened before I could try to fill the quiet by saying something stupid.

"Good morning." Dr. Pettit entered, already pulling up images on his fancy tablet. "Ready to see how we're doing?"

"Ready to get these wires out," Maliyah said.

"Let's take a look first." He moved closer, gentle hands examining Maliyah's jaw. "Open as much as you can."

She stretched out her lips by maybe a centimeter. The wires held everything locked tight.

"Good. Let me get fresh images, then we'll make our decision."

The x-ray tech wheeled in a fancy portable machine. I watched Maliyah go rigid as they positioned it, her knuckles white where she gripped the table edge.

"Deep breath and hold," the tech said.

The machine clicked and whirred. Maliyah's eyes found mine over the tech's shoulder. I tried to look confident. Like I wasn't remembering her face six weeks ago—broken, swollen, barely recognizable.

Dr. Pettit studied the new images on his tablet. The silence stretched. Maliyah's hand found mine, squeezing hard enough to hurt. Finally, he looked up with a smile. "Beautiful. The fracture has healed perfectly. We can absolutely remove the wires today."

Maliyah made a sound—half laugh, half sob. Then the tears came, fast and sudden. She pressed her free hand to her mouth, shoulders shaking.

"Shit. Sorry. I just—" Her words came out muffled. "I didn't think—"

"Hey." I wrapped an arm around her shoulders, pulled her against my side, burying her face against my chest. "It's okay. You're okay."

"I know. I know. I just..." She nuzzled her face closer, wrapping her arms around me. "I was so scared."

Dr. Pettit handed her tissues, giving us a moment. "This is completely normal. You've been through significant trauma. These emotions need somewhere to go."

Maliyah nodded, wiping her face. Mascara smudged under her eyes. "Okay. I'm okay. Let's do this."

"The removal is straightforward," he explained, preparing his instruments. "I'll cut the wires and extract them. You'll feel pressure, maybe some pulling, but it shouldn't hurt."

"And after?"

"Soft foods only for two to three weeks. Your jaw muscles have been completely immobilized for a while—they need time to remember how to work. Soups, yogurt, scrambled eggs, mashed potatoes. Nothing that requires real chewing. No chips, no nuts, definitely no steak."

"But eventually?"

"Eventually, yes. Everything goes back to normal. Or as normal as can be given all you've been through."

Maliyah lay back on the table. Her hand stayed locked with mine as Dr. Pettit positioned the overhead light.

"Open as wide as you can," he instructed, wire cutters in hand.

The first snip made Maliyah flinch and me want to wrap her in my arms while she went through all of this. I rubbed my thumb across her knuckles, watching her face. Her eyes stayed locked on the ceiling tiles, jaw trembling. Snip. Snip. Each cut seemed to echo.

"Almost done," I murmured. "You're doing great." I brought her hand to my lips. I knew I was testing some boundaries, but I couldn't help it. I wanted to take all this from her, but since I couldn't I would settle for making sure she knew I was here.

"This is weird," Maliyah said through barely parted lips. "I can feel them moving."

He smiled. "Last one—then we extract."

Snip. The doctor's hand moved with precision as he extracted the final wire, metal sliding out—a sensation that made Maliyah's nostrils flare. Her chest barely moved, each breath coming in tiny sips of air.

"All done." Dr. Pettit stepped back. "How does that feel?"

Maliyah worked her jaw experimentally. The movement was tiny—muscles protesting after so many weeks locked in place—but her mouth opened. Just a crack. Just enough. Fresh tears spilled over, but she was smiling. Actually smiling.

"Holy shit," she whispered. "It works. My mouth actually works."

"Careful," Dr. Pettit warned, but he was smiling too. "Small movements only. And remember—soft foods. Your jaw needs to rebuild strength gradually."

He went over ice packs, jaw mobility exercises, and warning signs of infection. "Limit range of motion to quarter-inch increments for the first three days," he said, demonstrating with his thumb and forefinger while Maliyah nodded. I glanced at her face—that tight smile that meant she was already planning to ignore half of what she heard. My fingers fumbled for my phone, thumbs tapping frantically as Dr. Pettit mentioned something about pain meds and sleeping with her head elevated.

"Questions?"

"No. Nothing that I can think of right now."

Yeah, okay. I was sure we'd have a ton soon enough.

Dr. Pettit's pen clicked shut with a finality that seemed to punctuate their session. "Most patients remember their questions the moment they leave my office," he said with a practiced smile. He steadied Maliyah with one hand as she eased herself upright. "I want to see you back two weeks from today. And my office is just a call away if something doesn't feel right before then."

"Thank you." Maliyah's hand went to her jaw, fingers exploring the freedom. "Really. Thank you."

"You did the hard part. I just removed some metal."

We walked through the hospital corridors, Maliyah testing tiny jaw movements every few steps. Open, close. Open, close. Like a kid with a new toy.

"Stop that," I said. "You'll hurt yourself."

"I can't help it. Do you know how weird it is to suddenly be able to move something that's been locked for what seemed like forever?"

"I'm guessing pretty weird."

"The weirdest." She stopped walking suddenly. "Reed?"

"Yeah?"

"I'm starving. Like, actually starving. And I can theoretically eat real food. Sort of real food. Soft real food."

"Protein shake?" I said, holding back a laugh and dodging a swipe from her hand.

"Too soon!"

Laughing, I moved closer again and asked, "How about some chowder?"

Her face lit up. "God, yes. Chowder. With oyster crackers I can smash into it like I'm ninety years old."

"I know a place."

Twenty minutes later, we were sliding into a booth at a favorite spot for New England clam chowder. Nothing fancy—just a hole-in-the-wall that made the best clam chowder in Boston. Maliyah studied the menu like it was holy scripture.

"Look at all these options," she said. "Soup. Different soup. Other soup. I'm dizzy with power."

"Don't go crazy. Remember what Dr. Pettit said."

"Soft foods, I know. But look—after the chowder, they have a lava cake. That's soft!"

No objections here!

When the waitress came, Maliyah's eyes lit up. "Clam chowder, please," she said, her voice rising half an octave. The waitress's lips curved upward as she scribbled on her pad. I ordered a bowl for myself with coffee for the caffeine kick I needed, then watched Maliyah's fingers dance around her place setting—straightening her spoon, folding the corner of her napkin, unfolding it again. Her leg bounced under the table, rattling the silverware with each tap of her foot against the floor.

I tried to engage her in conversation, but no matter what, I could see her attention was split—more interested in watching the kitchen door while waiting for her food.

The waitress arrived with two steaming bowls. Maliyah froze, staring at the thick, creamy broth where chunks of potato and clam broke the surface. Her spoon trembled slightly above the bowl as she watched tendrils of steam curl upward. This was a huge moment for her. It seemed as though her excitement was now warring with anxiety.

"What's wrong?"

"Nothing. Just... this is the first real meal I get to choose to eat. The first one that isn't through a straw or so blended it's baby food." She picked up her spoon. "I'm having a moment."

"Have your moment." If she'd let me, I would have reached across and kissed her right then. The way she looked, the moment between us—this was what it was about. I wanted this moment forever with her, but I didn't want to steal it from her. I held back, watching her savor this milestone, finding my own joy in simply being the one beside her for it.

The first spoonful was tentative. She held it in her mouth, eyes closed, like she was memorizing it. The second one came quicker. By the third, she was making little happy sounds that made the couple at the next table smile, clearly taking her for a tourist.

"Oh my God," she said. "There are chunks. Actual chunks of potato. And clams. I can feel texture, Reed. Texture!"

The bliss on her face, the soft curve of her lips, the delicate line of her throat as she swallowed, the way her fingers curled around the spoon—it hit me like a physical force. "You're the sexiest woman I have ever known, Maliyah," I said, my voice dropping lower than intended. "Sweetheart, the way you're enjoying that soup right now is making me want to forget we're in a restaurant full of people."

Her mouth dropped open at my declaration, clearly not expecting it. I smiled wickedly. God, I'd missed this. Her.

"Better take a bite, Sunshine. Clam chowder doesn't go down well cold."

"Yeah. Okay, yeah."

A few minutes in, she finally took a break to let some words out, and what she said made my heart hurt. "Lucas has been asking about you."

"Yeah?" I croaked.

"He's got this school project about community helpers. Wants to in-terview a detective." She kept her eyes on her bowl. "I told him maybe you could help. If you want."

"I want." No hesitation. "When?"

"This weekend maybe? If you're not working."

"I'll make it work."

She looked up then, her dark eyes catching the light from the window. Her fingers tightened around her spoon. "He's still..." She swallowed hard, a muscle in her jaw twitching despite the pain it must have caused. "Be careful, Reed. You hurt him when you left. Hurt both of them."

"I know." The coffee I'd ordered tasted bitter suddenly. "Maliyah, I—"

"I'm not trying to make you feel guilty," she interrupted. "I just need you to understand. If we do this—if we try again—you can't run. Not from them."

"I won't."

"You say that now—"

"I won't," I repeated, firmer. "I know I fucked up. I know I hurt you all. But I'm here now. And I'll keep being here. It will take time, but you'll see. I'm not going anywhere."

She stirred her soup, quiet for a moment. "They need to see you first as a friend. Not us together—just friends."

"Yeah. Okay. Yeah. I can do that. That makes sense. Yeah." Christ, I was rambling. The excitement made me want to do jumping jacks. I couldn't remember when I was last this excited. "I want to make this right. With all of you."

"I know." She reached across the table, fingers brushing mine. "That's why I'm letting you try."

We sat there, her slender fingers resting over mine, the warmth of her touch spreading up my arm. Her dark eyes held mine, soft and unguarded in a way I hadn't seen in months. The restaurant's ambient chatter faded to background noise as she methodically worked through her chowder, each careful spoonful a small victory. Steam no longer rose from the bowl by the time she set her spoon down with a quiet sigh. I could see how, though she managed to finish half, the tightness in her newly freed jaw had become too much for her to ignore.

"Getting sore?"

"A little. But worth it." She leaned back, satisfied. "So damn worth it."

"Still want that lava cake?"

"Reed Morrison, are you trying to seduce me with food?"

I scoffed. "I'm not saying I'm *not* trying to seduce you with food."

The laugh I got from her at that made my heart practically leap out of my chest.

I flagged the waitress. "We need lava cake, STAT, ma'am. I've been told good things come to those who buy my friend chocolate!"

With a smile, the waitress headed off to put the order in. She ate lava cake slowly once it arrived, savoring each spoonful like it was the best dessert she'd ever had.

"I missed this," she said suddenly.

"Cake?"

"No. Well yes. But I meant this." She gestured between us. "Just... being normal. Having lunch. Talking about the kids. Not everything being about medical appointments or police reports or—" She stopped, shook her head. "Sorry."

"Don't apologize."

"I'm trying to move past it all. But sometimes it just... hits me. What happened. What almost happened."

"That's normal."

"I know that's normal." Her voice cut through the air around us, then softened. "Sorry. Again. I just want to stop being the victim, you know? I want to just be Maliyah who has lunch with... with you."

"Your friend," I said carefully.

She met my eyes. "For now. For today."

"I'll take it."

We finished lunch, talking about safer topics. The kids' school. Her gradual return to work. My cases. Normal things. By the time I paid the check—overruling her protests—some of the tension had eased from her shoulders.

Outside, the air was sharp. She pulled her coat tighter, and I resisted the urge to wrap my arm around her. I was pretty proud of myself for holding back.

"Thank you," she said as we reached the car. "For today. For being there."

"Always," I said, meaning it.

She studied my face for a long moment. Then she rose up on her toes and kissed me. Soft, quick, but real. I was so surprised that I felt my hand shaking.

"Do friends kiss in this new world?" I asked, a little scared to hear the answer.

She looked down, fingers tracing the collar of her coat. "They do today." Her eyes flickered back to mine, a hint of color rising in her cheeks despite the cold. She bit her lower lip, wincing slightly at the pressure on her still-healing jaw. "I didn't plan that," she whispered, her breath visible in the winter air between us. "Do you wish I hadn't done it?"

"Not a freaking chance."

Her face flushed. After a moment, she asked, "Will you take me home?"

"Anything you want."

"I'm going to get the kids from Felicity's in a few hours. I can't wait to tell them the good news." She touched her jaw again. "Maybe order pizza to celebrate, even if I can't eat it yet."

"Sounds perfect."

As I drove, she talked about what else she wanted to eat over the coming weeks. Soft pasta. Risotto. Maybe even tender chicken if she cut it small enough. The excitement and her rambling was the highlight of the car ride.

"Hey Reed?" she said as we pulled up to her building.

"Yeah?"

"This weekend. Come for breakfast. Lucas can interview you and you can spend a little time with the kids. See how things go." She paused. "I mean, if you want—as a friend."

"I want," I said. "I really want."

She smiled—careful still, jaw sore, but genuine. "Good. Don't fuck it up."

"I won't."

"You better not."

She climbed out of the car, then leaned back in. "Thank you. For showing up."

I watched her walk to her door, standing straighter than she had in weeks—tomorrow there would be more challenges. More healing. More trust to rebuild. But today she got a piece of herself back again. And I got to be part of it.

Chapter 46:

Home, Home

MALIYAH

My hand shook as I reached for Felicity's doorbell. It had felt like forever—a lifetime of garbled words through wired teeth, of typing on phones and tablets, of watching their confused faces on video calls. All leading up to this point.

The door swung open moments after I pressed the button.

"Aunt Maliyah!" Macy launched herself at me, arms wrapping around my waist. "Mom said you can talk now! Say something!"

I laughed—actually laughed without pain shooting through my jaw, though it was sore and tight, it didn't hurt anymore. "Hi, sweet girl."

"You said it! You really said it!" She pulled back, beaming up at me. "Lucas! Zoe! Your mom's here, and guess what!? She has a surprise!" She glanced up at me again, a conspiratorial smile spreading across her face, revealing the gap where her front tooth had been. "I didn't want to tell them and ruin it," she whispered, her voice dropping to that stage-whisper volume that only children seem to think is actually quiet.

The thunder of small feet on hardwood made my heart race. Then they were there—my babies—barreling toward me with shouts of "mom!" and "mama!"

"Hi, my loves," I said softly. My voice was still rough from weeks of limited use, but it was mine.

Zoe moved first, pulling back to look at me. "Mama?" Just that one word, barely a whisper.

"Yeah, baby!"

She dug back in, burying her head into my leg, and I held on for dear life while I pulled both of my babies away so I could get down on their levels and hug them to me.

As I knelt, Zoe's arms locked around my neck like a vise, her small fingers digging into my skin. Her face buried deep in the hollow of my shoulder, dampening my blouse with hot tears. Her whole body trembled against mine—each sob rippling through her tiny frame and into my chest.

"Shh, sweet girl. I'm okay. I'm here." I pressed my lips to her temple and inhaled the familiar scent of her sweet shampoo, rocking her gently from side to side.

Her whole body shuddered with each hiccup, her small hands framing my face as she stared at me with wonder-filled eyes still swimming with tears. "You can talk," she whispered, her voice cracking. "You can really talk again." Her fingers trembled against my cheeks. "I missed your voice so much, Mama. I missed it every single night."

Lucas hadn't said anything, but he was right there next to Zoe, squeezing me close. My sweet boy, trying so hard to be strong. I pulled back to look at him too, and saw his eyes were red-rimmed, jaw set in that stubborn way that meant he was fighting tears.

Bringing him back in, I said, "Come here, buddy."

I felt his resolve crack as I squeezed him to me.

"I'm sorry," I whispered into his hair. "I'm so sorry I was gone. I'm so sorry this happened."

"Not your fault," he mumbled against my shirt. "Just... don't leave again. Okay?"

"Never. I promise."

I sank down to the floor, ultimately sitting in the entryway, and pulled them both onto my lap. It didn't matter to me that they were too big for that now, too heavy for me—I didn't fucking care. I wrapped my arms around them and let myself cry—really cry—for the first time since coming home.

A flash—Bryce's boot hovering in slow motion before slamming into my ribs. The sound of bones snapping inside me. White-hot lightning shooting through my chest. His eyes, dead, as he smiled down at me, savoring my scream.

I crushed my babies against me so hard they squirmed, but I couldn't loosen my grip. Their presence was my anchor in this moment.

Fuck Bryce. His memory was unwelcome. He didn't get to intrude on this moment—on holding my children. On surviving to come home to them.

So, I pushed the memory away, shoved it down, and focused on what was real: Lucas's heartbeat against my chest, Zoe's fingers clutching my shirt, the smell of their hair, the sounds of their joy.

We were here. We were safe. He was gone.

"Don't cry, Mama," Zoe said, patting my face with her small hands. "You're okay now. We're home."

But that just made me cry harder. Because we were home. They were here in my arms. It wasn't all that long ago when I'd been so scared I'd never see them again.

"You're really better?" Lucas asked, moving back to study my face. Always smarter and more observant than most kids his age, I could see he was cataloging the changes.

"Getting there. The wires are out, which is huge. Still have to be careful for a while, but yeah. I'm better."

"Your face looks different," Zoe announced with four-year-old honesty. "Do you like your lines? Can I color on them?"

"My scars?" I corrected gently. "No, honey, you can't color on them. But they are healed and, in time, they will probably get lighter and lighter." I'd forgotten to put makeup on today and I hadn't considered how pronounced my scars would be to my kids.

"I think they make you look tough," Lucas said. "Like a soldier. Like a hero."

My throat tightened. Reed had said almost the same thing this morning. Warrior goddess, he'd called me. I pushed the thought away.

Felicity appeared behind the kids, eyes suspiciously bright. "So, I hear someone mentioned pizza?"

"PIZZA!" Zoe shrieked. "Can we really have pizza, Mama? Can you eat pizza now?"

"You guys can have pizza. I'll stick with something softer. But yes, let's celebrate!"

The next hour was beautiful chaos. Caden ordered three different pizzas and a pasta side dish for me. The kids talked over each other, telling me everything I'd missed. From homework projects to artwork, to Lucas's story about how he gave his "friend" Maddie his dessert the day before at lunch. And, of course, the tooth that Lucas lost earlier today which led to the all-important question: "Will the tooth fairy still come," he asked me. "You know, if I'm here at Aunt Felicity's"

I caught Felicity's eye over his head. She winked.

"Hmmmm. Well, I'm not sure, but she might have trouble finding you here."

At the disappointed look on his face, I continued, "You know, we could make it super easy for the tooth fairy to find you."

"Really?! How!?"

"Well, you could just come home."

Both he and Zoe paused and stared at me. Like they weren't sure what to say or do. My heart stuttered. Was this the right thing? Had I screwed up my kids? My mind started to spiral.

Until Lucas's eyes widened, his small hand freezing mid-air above his plate. "Really?" The words barely disturbed the air between us, his lips hardly moving. He swallowed hard, a muscle working in his jaw just like mine did when I was trying not to hope too much. "Like come home for good?"

"Yeah sweetheart. Like come home for good."

And suddenly pandemonium ensued. Both of my kids launched out of their seats to slam into me again. "Okay, okay!" I coughed, taken aback by the force— but I held on with everything I had in me. I wasn't taking any chances that I'd miss even a single moment.

We ate crowded around Felicity's dining room table, Macy showing Zoe some complicated hand-clapping game while Lucas talked incessantly about his research for his project. I tried not to think about Reed volunteering to help, but it was impossible.

"Mama, watch!" Zoe had pizza sauce all over her face. "I can eat a whole piece by myself!"

"Amazing, baby. Chew carefully."

"Are we really coming home tonight?" Lucas asked suddenly. "Like, to stay?"

"Yes. We're all going home tonight. Together."

"And tomorrow?"

"Tomorrow too. And the next day. And the day after that."

He nodded, seemingly satisfied, but I caught him watching me throughout dinner like he was afraid I might disappear if he looked away too long.

By seven, both kids were dragging. Zoe had curled up in my lap and Lucas was leaning against my shoulder, trying to pretend he wasn't tired.

"Let's head out," I said softly. "Get you two in your own beds."

"Do we have to?" Zoe whined. "I like it here."

"I know, baby. But don't you miss your room? Your stuffed animals?"

That did it. "Yeah, I do. It's just so faaaaaaaaaaar away." Her voice dropped off as her eyes drooped more and more.

Getting them into coats and shoes took another fifteen minutes. Hugs all around. Felicity squeezed me extra tight.

"You sure you're okay?" she whispered. "I can come help—"

"I know. But I promise, we're good. I've got this."

She pulled back, studying my face. "You do. You really do. Call if you need anything?"

"Absolutely."

The car ride home was quieter. Zoe fell asleep almost immediately, head lolling against her car seat. Lucas stared out the window, occasionally glancing at me in the rearview mirror.

"You okay, buddy?"

"Yeah. Just... it's weird. Going home. Good weird, but weird."

"I know it's been a lot of changes," I said carefully.

Lucas squared his small shoulders and lifted his chin. "It's okay. We're okay." His voice dropped an octave lower than his usual pitch, and he reached over to pat my hand twice, the same way I'd done to comfort him after nightmares. Seems my little man was growing up fast.

"We are pretty great, aren't we?"

"The best," he agreed.

Our apartment building loomed in the darkness. I parked, then gently shook Zoe awake.

"Come on, sleepyhead. We're home."

She blinked at me, confused. "Home, home?"

"Home, home."

Lucas carried Zoe's backpack, while I managed Zoe—her legs wrapped around my waist, arms draped over my shoulders. I'd get their bags out of the trunk in the morning. My fading strength was more and more evident with every step up to our floor, but I didn't care. I had my babies back.

"Bath time," I announced as we entered and I set Zoe down.

"Noooo," she groaned. "I'm too tired for bath."

"Quick bath. Then bed. We'll do hair tomorrow"

"Can you do bubbles?" She perked up slightly. "And the songs?"

"All the bubbles. All the songs."

Forty minutes later, both kids were clean, in pajamas, and tucked into their beds. I sat on the edge of Zoe's bed first, smoothing her curls away from her face.

"Mama?"

"Yeah, baby?"

"Are the bad things over now? The scary things?"

My chest tightened. "The scary things are over. You're safe. We're all safe."

"Promise?"

"Promise."

"Okay." She yawned. "Love you, Mama."

"Love you more than all the stars."

Her eyelids fluttered, fighting sleep. "Love you more than..." Her voice trailed into a whisper as her small fingers loosened their grip on the edge of her blanket. The last word—"moon"—dissolved into a soft exhale, her breathing already deepening into the steady rhythm of dreams.

I kissed her forehead, turned on her night light, and slipped out.

Lucas was still awake, sitting up in bed with a book.

"Lights out, mister."

"Five more minutes?"

"Two."

The corners of his mouth curled upward as he tilted his head to one side, eyebrows lifting hopefully. "Three?"

"Deal."

I sat on his bed while he read, just watching him. My serious, careful boy, who'd been forced to grow up too fast.

"Mom?"

"Hmm?"

Lucas's fingers traced the familiar dinosaur pattern on his comforter, his shoulders relaxing as he sank deeper into his own pillow while shifting his book on his lap. "I'm glad we're home."

"Me too, buddy. More than I could ever possibly explain."

When his three minutes were up, he marked his page and set the book aside. I tucked his blankets around him, kissed his forehead.

"Sweet dreams, my love."

"Mom?" He caught my hand as I stood. "We're really okay, right?"

"We're really okay," I assured him.

He nodded, satisfied, and closed his eyes.

I stood in his doorway for a moment, just breathing. My babies were home. Safe in their beds. I could talk to them, sing to them, tell them I loved them without struggling through wired teeth.

We'd survived.

My own bed felt too big after weeks in a hospital bed, then sharing space with Reed's presence always nearby. I changed into soft pajamas, careful of my still-tender ribs, and climbed under the covers.

The apartment was quiet except for the familiar sounds of home. The refrigerator humming. Heat clicking through the radiators. Zoe's white noise machine down the hall.

Normal sounds. Safe sounds.

I should have told them Reed was coming Saturday. Should have prepared them. But Lucas seemed so protective, so determined that everything must be fine as it was. And maybe part of me was still protecting myself too. Still holding back.

My phone buzzed on the nightstand.

Reed: *How did it go with the kids?*

I stared at the text. He hadn't pushed to come along. Just gave me space to be with my babies while somehow letting me know he was thinking of us. And he'd been excited for the weekend.

Me: *Good. They're asleep. Zoe demanded all the bubbles and songs.*

Reed: *Sounds about right. You okay?*

Such a simple question. Was I okay? My jaw ached from talking more today than I had in weeks. With everything that had gone on during the day, I was exhausted down to my bones.

But my kids were in their beds. I was in mine. We were home together.

Me: *Yeah. I'm okay.*

Reed: *Good. Sleep well, Maliyah.*

Me: *You too.*

I set the phone down, pulled the covers up to my chin.

Saturday, Reed would come for breakfast. Lucas would interview him for his project. It would be the first real test of... whatever this was we were building. Rebuilding? Yes—rebuilding feels better.

I thought about his face at lunch today. The naked hope when I'd said Lucas wanted to talk to him.

For weeks, he'd shown up. Not because he had to—he could have walked away after the rescue. Could have checked the hero box and moved on. But he'd stayed. Through the nightmares, the frustration, the anger I'd thrown at him.

He'd earned something. Trust, maybe. Or at least the chance to earn it.

What would it take to trust him completely? To stop waiting for him to run? To actually believe him when he said "always"?

I didn't know.

But lying there in my too-big bed, thinking about that kiss outside the restaurant—soft and uncertain and real—I realized I wanted to find out.

Tomorrow, I'd make a plan. Figure out how to tell the kids about Saturday. How to navigate Lucas's protectiveness and Zoe's attachment and my own battered heart.

Tonight, though, I just held onto this: We were home. We were healing. We were going to be okay.

And I realized—it was okay not to have all the answers right this minute.

Chapter 47:

Proving Ground

REED

I'd been awake since four-thirty. The red numbers on my bedside clock had glared at me through the darkness while I twisted in my sheets, my pulse thumping in my ears like distant footsteps. By five, I'd given up, thrown off the covers, and stumbled to the kitchen. Now my fingertips tapped against the ceramic of my coffee mug, making me think of Felicity tapping the beat to songs in her head as I watched the ripples move through the black liquid's surface.

Today was the day. Today, I would get to see the kids again. Talk to them. Spend time with them. I was freaking the fuck out—not the run-away kind of freak-out, though. It was a day-of-reckoning freak out.

I ran through everything again, the mental list that had consumed me since Maliyah had extended the invitation. *Breakfast. You can spend a little time with the kids. See how things go.* Translation: You have some work to do to get those kids to trust you again, Morrison.

The coffee was strong and bitter, exactly what I needed to kick my ass in gear. I'd already showered, already dressed in jeans and a navy Henley that I hoped screamed '*non-threatening-loser-who-needs-forgiveness.*' I looked like a guy trying too hard not to look like he was trying, which I guess was the entire point.

My phone sat on the counter as I waited. The sun hadn't even risen yet, so it was going to be a long-ass wait. In the meantime, I needed to work off this nervous energy that felt like it might vibrate me apart.

I pulled up my notes on the DV training program instead. Better to keep my mind occupied than to spiral into all the ways this morning could go sideways.

DV Prevention and Self-Defense Training: Learn the Basics from Your Local BPD Officers

The title needed work, sounded more like "win a date with a cop" auction, but the framework was solid. I'd spent a lot of time working on this after leaving Maliyah's place, mornings before work, stolen hours in between cases. Jaxson had come through with connections to two women's shelters, and Luis was already translating materials into Spanish, Haitian-Creole, and now Portuguese too. Gloria had introduced me to a trauma psychologist who specialized in DV survivor support, and she'd agreed to consult on the curriculum. I knew the centers usually have psychologists on staff, but I really wanted to do this separately, providing a consistent resource that could help multiple shelters instead of just one-offs.

As I got into it, I found that I really liked the work—the idea of helping women feel empowered. One woman learning to protect herself would make every hour worthwhile.

The training would run six weeks: ninety-minute sessions, twice weekly, designed so participants could join at any point. We'd cover recognizing all forms of abuse—isolation, financial control, gaslighting, using children as leverage. We'd navigate the legal system—restraining orders, police limitations, advocacy. I'd interviewed survivors with vastly different experiences to ensure we addressed both successes and failures.

Most importantly, we'd teach practical skills: de-escalation, safety planning, proper documentation for court. Women would see their experiences weren't unique, shameful, or their fault. The final sessions would teach practical self-defense—simple techniques giving women real options if their abuser appeared at work or their child's school.

I'd sent the initial proposal to Captain Martinez yesterday, flagging it as a community outreach initiative with potential for grant funding and partnership with nonprofits. He'd responded in his typical fashion: This looks solid, Morrison—your job to get it funded. Get me more details once you get everything together. Good luck.

In other words: Don't fuck this up, don't make my department look bad, but if it's successful I want to say I got to weigh in.

Also: Again, don't fuck this up. It's on you.

No pressure at all.

My fingers flew across my laptop as I added comments to the doc. An idea came to mind—*Childcare. Providing childcare that was meaningful could be a game-changer.* If we made it safe, accessible, and fun for the kids, maybe more women would come. Maybe give the kids some self-defense moves.

Kids as young as 3 or 4 could start with basic jiu-jitsu moves—focusing on defensive measures. *Hell yeah.*

This could really fucking matter. This could turn out to be something that would make a difference for women like Maliyah. For kids like Lucas and Zoe.

Maliyah wasn't just a case or a conquest. I'd abandoned her once because I was too selfish to see what I had. Not anymore. This version of me, sitting in my kitchen at the ass-crack of dawn, had learned his lesson the hard way.

I closed my laptop and checked the time again. Five minutes had passed. *For fucks sake. This was going to be a long morning.*

Maybe I could swing by the bakery, grab something good. Maliyah had said breakfast, which meant she'd probably make something, but showing up with fresh pastries wouldn't be the worst thing.

Chocolate croissants. Definitely chocolate croissants. And sticky buns. Maybe I could swing by... *Shit—maybe some of everything.* Winning her heart and influencing her kids through food—maybe I'd write a book about how to fuck it up and then win them back... Should probably work on actually winning them back first.

I grabbed my keys and headed out into the cold-ass morning.

A couple of hours later, I was sitting in my car a block from Maliyah's apartment, breakfast carefully balanced in the passenger seat, trying not to overthink the fact that I'd doubled back to my place and changed—twice—before leaving again. The navy Henley had felt too casual. The button-up too formal. Pats jersey was even more casual. Then I'd settled back on the Henley again because I looked good in it, and confidence mattered.

My phone buzzed.

Maliyah: *Still coming this morning?*

I smiled despite my nerves.

Instead of texting, I hit dial.

"Hey." Her voice was a mix of excitement and hesitation.

"Hey. Yeah, so, thought I'd just call. Hope that's okay." Fuck I was so nervous.

"Yeah! Of course! Sure! That's good! Yeah."

Her excitement was so clearly overdone that we both went completely silent. I dropped my head to the steering wheel. I'm such a moron.

I cleared my throat. "Yeah. Okay. So, I'm already around the corner."

"Oh! Really?"

Ugh. Just fucking say it, Reed! I stumbled over my words, "Yeah, I Um—I got kind of excited and was nervous. And I didn't want to be late. Plus I got changed a couple times. And I went to the bakery too. I just didn't want to come empty-handed. And they had some cool things there—they had a bear claw actually shaped like a bear claw, not just a mass of something, and I thought Lucas would like it. Plus then they had this pastry shaped like a flower and it has strawberries on it that I was sure Zoe would like. So I thought I would get both." No stopping me now! "And then I got worried that they would think I was trying to feed them crazy shit to convince them back into liking me, so I stopped and got donuts. Then I realized you would probably hate how much sugar I brought so I picked up some bagels. *Then* I thought about how many carbs there were in every—"

Reed!" Her voice cracked between a laugh and a shout, cutting through my spiral as I gripped the steering wheel tighter. I could almost see her shaking her head on the other end of the line, that little crinkle forming between her eyebrows. "Breathe!"

I took a big breath and let it out. Feeling some of the tension leave my shoulders.

"It's going to be okay," she assured me. "Lucas has already been asking a million questions. He's excited you're letting him interview you. So fair warning, I hope you're prepared."

"Ha! I am. I've actually prepared a statement. It's probably a little lawyerly. He's going to hate it."

"Good. He needs to show you that he's going to hate something about this."

That made me laugh. Actual, genuine laugh that probably looked ridiculous sitting alone in my car, but there it was. She got it. She got that Lucas needed to test me, needed to know that I wasn't going to crumble the second a kid gave me attitude.

"Can I come now? Or should I wait?"

"Come now. Don't just sit in your car. We're just hanging out watching Bluey for the seven-millionth time."

"Sweet. See you in five."

"Sounds good."

"Maliyah—" I called out before she hung up.

"Yeah?"

"Thanks. You know? For letting me be part of this. I know we have a ways to go, but thanks for taking this chance with me. I mean—even as friends."

Her silence made me a little nervous, at first. But then I heard her say, "The chance is yours, Reed. Help me believe in you."

"For as long as you'll have me."

"See you soon, Reed."

At that, she hung up and I stared at my phone. *The chance is yours*, she'd said. I felt like I could walk on water.

I hopped out of my car, figuring the walk would do me good. My hands were steadier now than they'd been all morning.

This was it. This was the moment where I could back up my words with action.

Walking up her steps with the multiple bags in my hands, I was torn between running to her door or pausing to plan what I'd say. The choice was taken from me, though, when Maliyah opened the door even though I still had about five feet to go. For a second, I completely forgot how to breathe.

She was wearing this soft light pink sweater that made her skin glow, and her hair was down, falling in waves past her shoulders. The bruising was completely gone now and the scars on her cheek had been covered by makeup, though I could still see faint creases in her skin that caught the light.

She was beautiful. Stunning. She'd always been beautiful to me, but like this—fresh and open, excitement in her eyes—she was something else entirely.

"Morning," I said, holding up all the bags like an offering.

Her eyes went soft with laughter. "You didn't have to—"

"I know. But I did anyway." I stepped inside, and the smell of something cooking hit me. The telltale scent of eggs, toast, probably bacon. "What are you making?"

"Nothing special, just the standard breakfast fare." She closed the door behind me, and I caught a whiff of her shampoo. Coconut. "Bluey is on and Zoe is engrossed. Lucas is working on something for school and pretending he isn't into the show anymore—pretending and failing."

I laughed. *Bluey rocks*. "Okay, well how much can I expect to be judged?"

"Extensively." A smile played at the corner of her mouth. "But really, it's not too bad. Just come in. Let's rip off the bandaid."

We walked in and I set all the bags on the kitchen counter. The smell of bacon made my mouth water as I noticed all the foods Maliyah had been preparing. The sound of cartoons played from the other room, Bluey's Australian accent drifting through the air.

Maliyah paused beside me, her fingers drumming once against the counter. "Ready?"

"Is it okay to say I'm nervous?" I admitted, which made her smile.

"Yeah—definitely. It's honest." She lightly touched my forearm and my pulse raced even higher than it already was. She started toward the family room, and I followed—pulse rushing, heart hammering, and gut churning. *I feel like I'm walking into the principal's office or some shit.*

As soon as we entered, two little heads swiveled toward me.

"Reeeeed!" Zoe shouted and launched herself at me. "You're back! You really came!"

I caught her easily, my chest tightening at how light she felt, how readily she trusted me to catch her. "Hey, princess. Of course I came back."

Lucas stayed on the couch, his fingers fidgeting with the corner of a throw pillow. He glanced at me, then away, then back again—like he couldn't decide if he wanted to look at me or not.

"Hi," he said, voice barely above a whisper. Then, louder, "Mom said you're really doing the interview."

"Wouldn't miss it." I set Zoe down gently. "I even prepared some answers, but you can ask me anything you want."

He bit his lip, a gesture so like his mother it made my chest ache. "Even the hard questions?"

"Especially those."

He pulled his knees up slightly—seemingly protecting himself even as his eyes sparked with interest. "I made a list," he admitted, then quickly added, "It's not done yet though."

"Take your time. We've got all morning."

Maliyah touched my elbow. "Why don't we all sit for a bit before breakfast?"

Lucas scooted over—not much, but enough to make space. When I sat down, he stayed curled in his corner, but I caught him sneaking glances at me during Bluey, his notebook clutched in his lap like armor he wasn't quite ready to put down.

Chapter 48:

Pinky Promises

MALIYAH

I watched Reed from the doorway as he sat with my kids on the couch, Bluey's bright colors dancing across their faces. The morning light filtered through the window, catching the way Zoe leaned unconsciously toward him while pointing out every detail about Bingo's antics. Lucas stayed curled in his corner, but I noticed how his notebook had migrated from death grip to resting loosely on his lap.

"Muffin!" Zoe exclaimed, bouncing slightly. "She's so much fun—well, even though she's kinda mean—but she's not really. You know? Because she just doesn't know how to play nice sometimes."

Reed held back a smile, responding, "I think we all sometimes forget how to play nice. It's good when we have people to remind us," Reed said, looking over at me. Our eyes locked for a moment before he focused back on the TV. That's when I caught the careful way he kept his hands visible, movements slow and predictable. He was trying so hard not to spook Lucas.

"Mom says that about me sometimes," Lucas admitted quietly, then looked mortified that he'd volunteered information.

Reed turned slightly toward him, not enough to crowd, just enough to show interest. "Yeah? Me too. My partner, John tells me I need to work on my people skills all the time."

"Do you?" Lucas asked, curiosity winning over caution.

"Probably. Well, maybe more than probably." Reed's honesty made Lucas's mouth twitch—almost a smile. "Especially when I'm nervous. Like right now."

Zoe's mouth formed a perfect O, her eyebrows shooting up toward her hairline as she tilted her head back to look at Reed. Her small hand reached out, patting his forearm twice like she was the adult comforting him. "You're nervous?" Her voice lilted upward, soft and wondering. "Why?"

Reed glanced at me briefly before answering. He rubbed his palms against his jeans, leaving creases in the denim as he moved his hands back and forth. "Because I really want you guys to like me again, and sometimes when you want something really badly, it makes you nervous."

The raw truth of it hung in the air. Lucas studied Reed with that too-serious expression, processing this admission from an adult who wasn't pretending to have it all together.

"I'm nervous too," Lucas said finally, voice barely above a whisper.

Reed's voice dropped to match Lucas's whisper. "That's okay." His eyes crinkled at the corners. "We can be nervous together." He extended his fist across the cushion between them, holding it steady in the air. Lucas stared at it, his small fingers curling into a loose ball. One Mississippi. Two Mississippi. Three. Then Lucas's knuckles brushed against Reed's—a butterfly touch—before his hand retreated to the safety of his lap, and his eyes darted to me before shooting over to the TV.

Something tightened in my chest watching them—this careful dance of reconnection. Reed wasn't pushing, wasn't trying to be Super Fun Guy or begging for forgiveness. He was just... present. Real. Nervous.

Lucas looked over at Reed again, asking, "Are you and mom like back together?"

My breath caught, wanting to run over and interject, but before I could do or say anything, Reed led the way.

"Friends. We're just friends right now." His eyes stayed locked on Lucas's, unwavering but gentle. "Is that..." The words hung in the air between them as Reed cleared his throat. "Is that okay with you?"

Lucas's fingers drummed against his notebook, one-two-three, one-two-three, while the cartoon played on unnoticed. The air in the room seemed to thicken. Finally, his small shoulders lifted in a half-shrug. "Yeah. I think so."

I could swear that a collective sigh shuddered through the room. Time ticked by, moments feeling like lifetimes. Part of me wanted to rush forward and hug Lucas for his bravery, while another part wanted to grab Reed by the collar and drag him outside to warn him not to hurt my son again. I'd never been in this position before—torn between hope and terror, between wanting this man in our lives and fearing what would happen if he left again. My hands trembled slightly as I gripped the doorframe, anchoring myself against the storm of contradictions raging inside me.

"Breakfast should be ready," I said softly, not wanting to break the spell or shout my uncertainties. What I did know though is that, in this moment, we needed to move forward. "Who's hungry?"

"Me!" Zoe jumped up immediately. "Can I show Reed how you taught me to set the table?"

"Sure, baby."

She grabbed Reed's hand without hesitation, her small fingers wrapping around just two of his, tugging him toward the kitchen with the determined strength only a child can muster. "You can sit in this chair here today," she announced, patting the back of a wooden chair. "That's where Aunt Felicity sits now that we moved all our chairs around since I get to sit in the regular chair instead of a booster one." Her chest puffed with pride as she straightened to her full height, chin tilted upward. "It's super cool, you know."

Lucas followed more slowly, following me closely, then pouring milk for himself and his sister.

In the kitchen, I'd pulled out our everyday, indestructible kid-friendly dishes—nothing special. Reed helped Zoe carry the plates over and the various bags of food while I brought over the eggs, bacon and some fruit. With this breakfast, I'd be a miracle worker to get my kids to eat anything that wasn't a carb given what Reed brought with him today.

"As you can see, I brought options," Reed said, unpacking the bags and putting the pastries on a large plate I'd put out. "Wasn't sure what everyone wanted."

Lucas's eyes locked onto the bear claw pastry, his hand hovering in mid-air. He glanced at me, eyebrows raised in silent question, his fingers twitching with anticipation. When I nodded, he plucked it from the plate with deliberate care, turning it slowly between his fingers.

"This is actually cool—it looks like a real bear's paw," he admitted.

I rolled my eyes. "That's about seventy-five grams of pure sugar and a guaranteed afternoon crash waiting to happen," I muttered, but couldn't help smiling at Lucas's careful examination of his treasure.

"And here's yours, Princess Zoe." Reed presented the flower-shaped pastry with its fresh strawberries arranged like petals.

"It's beautiful!" She clapped her hands. "Like in my fairy book!"

I served the eggs and bacon I'd kept warm, adding fruit to each plate because someone needed to be the responsible adult here. Reed caught my eye and mouthed "thank you" over the kids' heads.

For a few minutes, we just ate. The kids' usual morning chatter filled the space—Zoe narrating every bite, Lucas quietly dissecting his pastry working outside inward—I knew he was saving the most gooey parts for last. Normal. Easy. Like Reed had always been at our breakfast table.

"So," Lucas said suddenly, setting down his fork with determination. "Can I do my interview now?"

Reed wiped his hands on his napkin, giving Lucas his full attention. "I'm ready when you are."

Lucas flipped open his notebook, revealing pages covered in his careful handwriting. My heart clenched seeing how much thought he'd put into this.

"First question," Lucas read, adjusting his glasses. "Why did you leave?"

Oh, fuck. Did not see that coming! My kid went straight for the jugular. *That's my boy.*

Reed didn't flinch. His shoulders squared as he met Lucas's gaze directly. "I was stupid. I got scared," he said, fingers tightening around his coffee mug until his knuckles whitened.

Lucas made a note, the pencil scratching against paper. "Were you scared of us?"

"No." Reed leaned forward, elbows on the table. "You know my job?"

Lucas nodded, eyes never leaving Reed's face.

"When I was a kid, my dad was a cop too." Reed's Adam's apple bobbed as he swallowed. "I wasn't much older than you when he got hurt on the job and didn't come home to us."

"Oh. That sucks," his response was quiet—almost in awe with this news.

Reed's voice dropped to a rasp. "Yeah, buddy, it did." He rubbed his thumb over a small scar on his wrist. "And once I started to get really close to you guys, I got scared about something like that happening to me—of hurting you guys because of it."

"Oh," Lucas said again, his small fingers fidgeting with the spiral binding of his notebook.

"But you hurt us anyway," Lucas's voice dropped so low I had to lean forward to catch the words. "By leaving."

"Yes," Reed agreed. "I did. And I'm so sorry for that, Lucas. Running away hurt everyone, including me. It was the biggest mistake I've ever made." Reed paused, looking at me for a moment. His eyes bore into mine, "I thought of you guys every day. Not one day went by when you three weren't on my mind."

Lucas twisted his pencil between his fingers, the eraser tapping against his notebook in an uneven rhythm. Zoe sat frozen, eyes wide, darting between Reed and her brother until—a flash of movement—her small hand shot out and snatched a chocolate donut from the pile. My girl knew her priorities.

I reached over, pressed my lips to her temple where a wisp of hair had escaped her ponytail, and sliced the donut in half with the side of my fork. I whispered in her ear, "Half, my love. You've had a lot of sugar." I laid my head on top of hers, absorbing the moment while already anticipating the afternoon crash of managing two sugar-wired children and my own frayed nerves.

Her bottom lip jutted forward as she reached for the donut half I'd left on her plate. "Awwwww, darn." Chocolate frosting smeared across her fingertips as she gripped it, her tongue peeking out from the corner of her mouth in concentration—likely deciding how to make it last as long as she could.

"Do you still like my mom?" Lucas's voice pulled my attention back to the conversation at hand.

I brought my coffee mug up to my mouth, taking a sip, I stood up straight behind Zoe's chair, just watching the show.

Reed's eyes found mine across the table again. "Yes," he said, still looking at me. "More than anything."

Heat flushed my cheeks, but I couldn't look away from the certainty in his expression.

"Okay." Lucas made another note. "Do you want to be our dad?"

"Lucas—" I started, but Reed held up a hand.

"Wait." He looked at me, "Is it okay if I answer?"

I hesitated, nervous. His eyes were steady and he seemed to really want to respond to Lucas's question. I looked over at my kid, who seemed to really need to hear Reed's response.

At my quick nod, Reed focused back on my son, giving him the respect of a real answer. "I want to be whatever you and Zoe will let me be—whatever you need me to be. If that's just a friend who comes around to hang out, then that's okay. If it's more than that someday, I'd be honored to be more than your mom's friend—more than your friend. But that's not just my choice—it's yours, and Zoe's, and your mom's too."

Lucas considered this, tapping his pencil against the notebook. "You won't leave again?"

"I won't leave again," Reed said firmly. "Never again, if I can help it. Even when things get hard or scary, I'll stay and work through it."

"Promise?"

"I promise."

"Pinky promise?" Zoe piped up, extending her tiny finger between them.

Reed's large finger curled around Zoe's tiny chocolate-smeared one, leaving a faint brown smudge on his skin. His eyes never left hers as he gave their joined pinkies a gentle shake that made her giggle. "Sealed," he whispered loudly, like they were sharing a not-so-secret-secret.

Lucas watched this exchange, then slowly, deliberately, offered his own pinky. Reed linked it with his free hand, and for a moment they stayed like that—connected by the most sacred of childhood vows.

"Okay," Lucas said, closing his notebook. "You can be our friend...for now."

Reed beamed like it was Christmas morning. "Thanks, buddy. I won't let you regret it."

"Okay. I have more questions, but I need to think about them first, and I still need to interview you for my project."

"Take all the time you need," Reed said. "I'm not going anywhere."

Lucas nodded and focused on his breakfast, but he kept sneaking glances at Reed when he thought no one was looking. The walls weren't down, not completely, but there were cracks now. Places where light could get in.

"Can we play a game after breakfast?" Zoe asked, strawberry juice on her chin. "All together?"

"What kind of game?" Reed asked, napkin already in hand to wipe her face.

She grinned. "Candy Land! I always win."

"She cheats," Lucas stage-whispered.

"I do not!"

"You do too! You always peek!"

"That's not cheating!" Zoe protested.

Reed laughed—a real, genuine sound that filled my kitchen. "Well, I've never played. Someone will have to teach me."

As the kids dissolved into their familiar bickering, Reed helped clear plates without being asked. Our hands brushed as we both reached for Lucas's cup, and he caught my fingers briefly, squeezing gently.

"Thank you," he murmured. "For this chance."

I squeezed back before letting go. "Friends, Reed. Don't waste it."

"I won't."

And watching him gently referee my children's debate about Candy Land rules while loading the dishwasher, treating their passionate debate about Queen Frostine with complete seriousness, I started to believe him.

Maybe second chances could work. Maybe broken things could be rebuilt stronger. Maybe trust could be rebuilt.

The morning sun painted golden stripes across my kitchen floor, and Reed Morrison was teaching my daughter the proper way to shuffle the cards while my son watched. It wasn't perfect. We had work to do—conversations to finish. But this was joy. The laughter echoing through the apartment helped me see that sometimes, this kind of joy was worth a thousand words. Actually, it was priceless.

Chapter 49:

The Love Bug

REED

Captain Martinez's office at Boston PD headquarters smelled like burnt coffee and old gym shoes—a combination that usually meant something was about to piss me off. I'd been sitting here for twenty minutes, watching the Captain flip through my proposal while Gloria sat beside me, her tablet propped on her knee. Out of the corner of my eye I could see flashes of some word puzzle she was working through. Her lips twitched upward at something on the screen, then quickly reset to professional neutrality when Martinez glanced our way.

"Community outreach," Martinez said finally, setting the papers down. "Self-defense for domestic violence survivors."

"Yes, sir."

"Six-weeks long?"

"Yes, sir. All on a volunteer basis. As you can see, multiple shelter locations have put their hands up to get involved."

He leaned back in his chair. "Morrison, you do realize this is going to be a paperwork nightmare?"

"I'm prepared for that."

"Are you?" He snatched up the proposal again. "Liability waivers. Insurance. Coordinating multiple nonprofits to actually get their shit together."

He tossed the papers down, leaning forward until I could smell the coffee on his breath. "And you want to do this on top of your regular caseload?"

Gloria cleared her throat. "Actually, Captain, aside from myself, I've already got seven female officers interested in teaching. Three have martial arts backgrounds, one even teaches at her gym already. We've also got buy-in from the community policing unit."

Martinez's eyebrows rose as he tossed the paperwork back down and crossed his arms over his slightly bulging belly. "You've been busy."

"It's a good program," she said simply. "Women teaching women. Building trust between the community and the department. The optics alone—"

"I don't care about optics," Martinez cut her off, though his tone wasn't harsh. "I care about whether this actually helps people and whether my officers can deliver it without creating more problems."

"With respect, sir," I leaned forward, "these women already have problems. We're trying to give them tools to help deal with them."

He studied me for a long moment. "This wouldn't have anything to do with the fact that your girlfriend runs one of the shelters on your list?"

Heat crept up my neck—Martinez calling her my girlfriend when we were still firmly in the 'friends' zone stung more than I'd admit. I kept my voice steady, though. "She's on medical leave. We're working with Delilah, the office manager. Maliyah won't even know about it until she returns to work."

"She doing okay?" Martinez asked.

"She's getting better," I said simply.

Martinez nodded and sighed. "Glad to hear it." He paused, paging through all the documents again. "Fine. You've got provisional approval. But—" he held up a hand as I started to speak, "—I want weekly reports. Any incidents, any complaints, any hint that this is going sideways, and you'll have a lot to answer for. Understood?"

"Yes, sir."

"And Morrison? This better not interfere with your active cases."

"It won't."

He waved us out. In the hallway, Gloria bumped my shoulder. "That went better than expected."

"It did." She put a hand on my arm. "He's just worried about things going wrong and needs to pretend to hate the idea. You know he's a big teddybear underneath it all though, right?"

I scoffed just as my phone buzzed. Text from Maliyah.

Kids and I going to the library Saturday. Just us, Felicity and family. Zoe is doing a sort of playacting skit. Do you want to come?

I stared at the message, my thumb hovering over the screen as something squeezed beneath my ribs. Three weeks, two days since I'd hooked my pinkies with Lucas and Zoe over breakfast. Weeks of careful distance—my hands trembling when I reached for the remote during movie night, hoping to brush against Maliyah's—like a teenager on a date night. Her laugh a touch too loud when Felicity's husband told jokes when we all went out to the Frog Pond on the Common. Always surrounded by chattering coworkers, giggling children, friends of friends who filled every silence with conversation.

We hadn't shared a quiet dinner alone, just the two of us. No goodnight kisses at her door after the kids went to bed. When our hands accidentally brushed reaching for popcorn during movie night, she'd pulled back first, her smile not quite reaching her eyes. But I'd wait—keep showing up for school projects and family outings until the day she didn't scoot away a bit when I sat next to her on the couch.

Wouldn't miss it, I texted back.

Gloria peered over my shoulder. "Things going good?"

"Yeah. They are," I said, realizing that, in all honesty—while things were slow, they were real. "We're working on it. Lucas lets me help with homework now. Zoe..." I smiled despite myself. "Zoe asked if I'd teach her to ride her bike."

"That's good, right?"

"Yeah." I pocketed my phone. "It's good."

We headed toward the community resources office a couple blocks away where Monica waited—Gloria's contact who worked with several shelter networks. She stood up from her desk, and I had to tilt my chin upward to meet her eyes. When she extended her hand, silver bangles clinked at her wrist, and her handshake could've cracked walnuts. My knuckles compressed against each other as she squeezed, and I found myself flexing my fingers after she released them, checking that everything still worked.

"Officers," she greeted us, gesturing to chairs around a cluttered desk with paperwork on one side that was piled as high as her shoulders. "Gloria's told me about your program. I have questions."

"Shoot," I said.

"First—are you ready for some of these women to be resistant to cops leading the show? Half of them have had police dismiss their complaints, arrest them instead of their abusers, or fail to enforce restraining orders."

I'd expected this. "Part of what we'll be doing is working to build trust with them. Won't be automatic—I get that. That's why we're starting with female officers only. Why we're coming to them, in a place where they can feel safe. It's why participation is completely voluntary."

Monica made a note. "Schedule?"

"Flexible. Whatever works for the shelters. Evening sessions, weekend options. We adapt to them."

"Childcare?"

Gloria jumped in. "Some of the shelters already have established childcare programs with vetted staff. For those that don't, we've discussed coordinating with the staff that work for other shelters and having them shift some of their hours over on a volunteer basis. Not looking to reinvent the wheel."

Monica's expression softened slightly. "Good. I'm glad you've thought this through. Too many programs come in wanting to 'save' these women without understanding the infrastructure already in place or other options that could be made available."

She grilled us for another hour—liability, curriculum, instructor qualifications, trauma-informed approaches. By the time we left, my head was spinning, but she'd agreed to work on helping us get some additional funding for not just this six-week session but for an ongoing program.

"Holy shit. Something sustained and going beyond what we'd originally planned," Gloria said as we walked to our cars.

"I know. It's fucking huge."

"High bar you've set here, man. This isn't something you can just throw away in the future. This is commitment, Reed."

I laughed, surprising myself. My fingers tapped against the folder in my hands, already dog-eared from constant opening and closing. The calendar on my phone had blocks of color stretching months ahead—blue for training sessions, green for shelter visits. Last night, I'd caught myself sketching out a graduation ceremony for the first cohort, complete with certificates I'd designed at 2 AM. "I'm in this, Gloria. It's not a whim."

"I gotta say, I thought at first it would be some cockamamie plan to get your girl back." She unlocked her car. "But you've really dug in here. I'm impressed and I like seeing you in this light. It's cool to see you this excited. I hope this all works out for you, Reed."

Gloria leaned on the roof of the car, forearms flat against the metal. Her eyes locked onto mine, steady and unflinching, like she was reading something written in fine print across my forehead. With a nod, she said, "That includes winning back your girl for good. I think you've earned something good, Reed. The whole team's here for you—whatever it takes to show her who you really are when it counts."

Back at my apartment that evening, I spread out the program materials across my kitchen table. Lesson plans, legal documents, volunteer schedules. My laptop showed dozens of open tabs—research on everything I needed to make this program work.

Lucas had asked me during homework help yesterday: "Why do people hurt other people?"

Such a simple question. Such an impossible answer.

I'd told him that sometimes people were hurt themselves and didn't know how to handle it properly. That it was never okay but understanding why didn't mean accepting it. He'd nodded seriously, his small forehead creasing with those same worry lines his mother gets, then nervously asked if I would come to his school and talk to his class.

He'd explained that his class thought his project with my interview had been "cool" and the class wanted me to come in so they could meet me. His fingers had fidgeted with the corner of his math worksheet the whole time, folding and unfolding it into a tiny triangle, like he was afraid I might say no.

My heartbeat kicked up, a rapid thrum against my ribs. I remember biting the inside of my cheek to keep my smile from popping too big. "Sure, bud. Anything you need," I'd said, voice steady despite the sudden dryness in my throat. My hand had tensed against my leg, holding back the fist pump I'd have made if I were alone—the kind reserved for touchdowns or winning the jackpot. Later, alone in my car, I'd pounded the steering wheel, shouted like the G.O.A.T. after winning the Super Bowl, and grinned like an idiot all the way home.

My phone rang breaking me out of my memory. John.

"You eat today?" he asked without preamble.

"Coffee and a protein bar counts."

"It absolutely does not. I'm bringing Chinese. You can tell me how shit went with Martinez."

"Yeah, okay."

"Heard Luis has half the Hispanic Officers' Association signed up to volunteer. Macky's got equipment donations lined up. Even Brennan from Murder/Homicide wants in, and that woman hasn't volunteered for anything since the Reagan administration."

I sank into a chair. "It's getting big."

"That's good, right?"

"Yeah. Just..." I rubbed my face. "What if it gets too big for me to handle and I fail because it got out of control?"

"Guy, you're not alone, right?" John's voice was dry. "It's getting big, yeah, but I think that's because it's something we've all realized we needed but no one has stepped up to do shit about it before now. So don't be an asshole and let fear get in the way of success."

"When you put it like that—"

"Look, I'll be there in twenty with some food. Text me your order. You can angst about your fears of success and all that dumb shit over egg rolls."

He hung up. I looked back at the spread of papers. If we stayed on schedule, next week, we'd start training volunteers. In a month, we'd actually be teaching.

My phone lit up with another text. Maliyah again.

Zoe wants to know what your favorite butterfly is. It's apparently very important.

I smiled, quickly googling butterflies—I knew shit about them.

Typing back: *Tell her Zebra Swallowtail* because who doesn't like a butterfly that could also be a Zebra?

Three dots appeared, disappeared, appeared again.

Maliyah: *She says that's acceptable. Also, Saturday—10am at the main library.*

Me: *I'll be there.*

A pause, then:

Maliyah: *She's making you a picture. Fair warning—heavy glitter involvement.*

Me: *Can't wait,* I replied, meaning it.

My finger hovered over Maliyah's last message, the corners of my mouth lifting involuntarily. I'd already set three calendar alerts for Saturday's library trip and bookmarked butterfly facts to casually drop into conversation with Zoe. The kitchen table—once home only to takeout containers and case files—now held program drafts alongside a drawing Lucas had given me last week, and coloring page of a princess Zoe had made for me.

The doorbell rang. John with Chinese food and probably more grief about my life choices. I gathered up the papers, making room for takeout containers and whatever wisdom he'd dispense between bites of egg roll.

"Morrison, you look fucking good," he announced, pushing past me with bags of food.

I beamed. "Thanks, man. I fucking *feel* good."

"You got the bug, huh?"

I grabbed plates while he unpacked containers. My eyebrows furrowed, "What bug? I just told you I'm great."

"Not a sick bug, dumbass." He piled lo mein onto a plate. "The looooooooooooooooooooove-bug!"

I ducked my head, rubbing the back of my neck where heat crawled up like ivy. My lips twitched, teeth clamping down on the inside of my cheek to keep from smiling too wide. I busied myself with the containers, focusing on the steam rising from the lo mein.

This time last year, I'd have changed the subject, made some crack about work. Now? My egg roll hovered over the tiny plastic cup, sauce dripping. I dunked it again—the wrapper was already soggy—and took a bite instead of answering, letting the heat crawling up my neck speak for itself.

"Yeah—you got that love-bug!" John's laugh was contagious.

"Fuck you, man. Nothing wrong with catching the bug."

We ate in companionable silence for a few minutes. Then John set down his fork.

"You look good happy, man."

I looked at him. Saw in his eyes what he meant. Saw the honesty in them and how much he really cared.

"It's because I am happy. Nothing's solved yet, but I'm fucking overjoyed that I even have a chance at a life with her. With them. With all of them." I said it—and I meant it.

Chapter 50:

Taking Flight

MALIYAH

Zoe's voice pitched high with alarm from the backseat. "Mama! They're falling again!" She twisted in her booster seat, small fingers grasping at the glittering monarch wings slipping toward the floor—the same wings that had kept me up until 2 a.m. with a hot glue gun burning my fingertips.

"They're fine, baby—just sit still." I caught her eyes in the rearview mirror. "Remember what we practiced?"

"I'm a monarch butterfly and I fly to Mexico for winter!" She bounced, her feet kicking out and accidentally popping the wings again. "Oh, no!"

Lucas, nose buried in a book, rolled his eyes and rescued the wings, tucking them safely beside him. "It's called migration, Zoe. And you're supposed to explain about the four generations."

"I know that!" She stuck her tongue out at him. "Miss Rachel said I just need to remember the important parts."

"All the parts are important. It's science, Zoe!"

"Kids." I pulled into the library parking lot, already half-full at 9:45. "Let's just focus on getting inside without destroying Zoe's costume, okay?"

My phone buzzed in the cup holder.

Reed: *Got us seats in the first row. Getting mean-mugged by a mom and a kid dressed like something that looks like a caterpillar...maybe??*

I found myself smiling before I could stop it, my thumb already moving to text back: *Just parked. Get ready for the butterfly diva.*

In the last few weeks, Reed had shown up with Lucas's favorite mint chocolate chip ice cream after his math test, picked up picture books to help Zoe learn about her butterfly role, and most recently had to learn all about SpongeBob after Lucas had slept at a friend's house where he'd seen it for the first time and thought it was 'the coolest'. Each time he appeared at our door, I'd catch myself holding my breath a little less, my shoulders dropping a fraction lower than the time before.

"Is Reed here?" Zoe asked, apparently having developed supernatural psychic phone-reading abilities.

"Yes."

Zoe's face lit up. "Yes!" Her hands shot to the glittery pipe cleaners wobbling above her head, fingers pinching and adjusting them with the concentration of a surgeon. "Can you see if they're even? I need them to look perfect for the pictures Reed promised to take, before I go on stage."

I smirked at my little diva as I parked and killed the engine. "Everything looks perfect. Let's go."

I wedged my hands under Zoe's armpits and tugged. Her puffer coat squeaked against the car seat, refusing to budge. "Arms up," I whispered, my breath clouding in the freezing cold air. She raised them like a touchdown referee while I pulled again, my lower back protesting.

Lucas stood beside me, Zoe's wings clutched carefully in one hand, duffel dangling from the other, his eyes rolling skyward as Zoe finally popped free with a vinyl squeal. Other families were streaming toward the entrance, kids in various states of costume—flowers, bees, even one ambitious oak tree.

"There's Macy!" Zoe took off running, wings flapping behind her.

"Zoe! Don't run! Be careful!" But she was already gone, joining her cousin at the library entrance where Felicity stood with Caden and their crew.

Lucas fell into step beside me. "Mom, are you feeling okay?"

I glanced down at him. "Of course, baby. Why?"

"You keep touching your face." He studied me with those too-observant eyes—when did my little boy grow up? "Where the scars are."

My hand dropped immediately. I hadn't realized I'd been doing it—running my fingers along the thin lines that remained. I'd been doing it less and less these days. Reed always made a point to lightly touch them whenever he said goodbye, right before he would whisper in my ear, 'Goodbye, warrior goddess.'

"Just a habit," I said. "They don't hurt anymore."

"Good." He took my hand, squeezing tight. "You look pretty today."

"Thanks, buddy." My voice came out rough.

We caught up to the chaos at the entrance. Felicity grabbed my arm the moment we got close.

"You look good," she said, her nurse's eye doing a quick assessment. "Like a badass, as a matter of fact. Ready to get back to work in a couple days?"

"Monday," I said, puffing out a breath, knowing she'd understand.

Her eyes narrowed slightly, head tilting when she asked, "Nervous?"

"It's time. I've been cleared, and Delilah needs to get back to her actual job instead of covering for me."

"But are you—"

"I'm ready." I straightened my shoulders, feeling the truth of it. My ribs didn't ache anymore. My jaw worked perfectly. The nightmares had faded to occasional whispers. "I need to be useful again. I need my normal."

Felicity pulled me into a quick hug. "Good. The shelter needs you. There are a lot of women there who need your backbone and your understanding."

"Speaking of normal," she added with a sly smile, "Reed's inside looking particularly un-normal. Man's practically vibrating with nerves."

"He's just excited for Zoe."

"Right. Just Zoe." Her knowing look made me blush.

"Can we please just go watch my daughter be a butterfly?"

Felicity's laughter followed us into the library's children's section, which had been transformed into a small theater. Rows of chairs faced a makeshift stage area decorated with paper flowers and twinkle lights. Parents clutched phones and cameras, younger siblings squirmed, and the noise level suggested barely controlled chaos.

I spotted Reed immediately—first row center, just like he'd said. But Felicity was right. His knee bounced rapidly, fingers drumming against his thigh, shoulders tight with tension.

Lucas saw him too and marched over, but instead of his usual defensive positioning, he crossed in front of Reed and slid into the seat next to him on the opposite side, placing Reed between himself and me. My breath caught as I watched my son's shoulders relax against Reed's side.

"You okay?" I heard Lucas ask Reed.

Reed startled, then gave Lucas his full attention. "Yeah, buddy. Just—big day."

"It's only a library show," Lucas said. "Zoe's been practicing."

"I know." Reed's eyes found mine as I approached. "Still feels important."

Recovering from my shock, I slid into the other seat beside Reed. I felt his warmth along my side, a line of heat where the narrow chairs forced us together. "You came."

"Wouldn't miss it for the world." His voice dropped lower. "How are you? Really?"

Instead of deflecting like I'd done for weeks, I let him see the truth. "You know—I have my good days and bad days. Today's good. Great, actually."

"Yeah?"

I touched my face again, caught myself, dropped my hand to my lap. Reed's hand twitched like he wanted to reach for mine.

"Your battle wounds aching?" he asked quietly.

"No. Just unconsciously touching them," I said, trying for light.

"Whatever. They're proof you're a badass. Touch them if you want to. They're yours," he said. Then, even quieter, "I think they make a warrior goddess like you that much more beautiful."

Heat flooded my face. Lucas looked between us with interest rather than suspicion.

"Are you two gonna be weird the whole time?" he asked. "'Cause Zoe's show is starting soon."

Reed laughed—a real, surprised sound that made something loosen in my chest. "We'll try to contain our weirdness."

"Good." Lucas settled back, leaning back into Reed, apparently satisfied.

Felicity's family filed in, Macy clutching a book she'd found to take home with her. As she chattered about the show order, I felt a gentle pressure from Reed's shoulder as he leaned a little into me.

"So," his words close enough that his breath stirred my hair, "Monday?"

I nodded. "Yeah. Time to get back to work. I need the full time distraction."

"How do you feel about it?"

"Terrified," I admitted. "Excited. Ready. It's been too long since I felt useful."

"You've been healing. That's not the same as useless."

"I know. But I miss it—the work, the purpose. Making a difference." I glanced at him from the corner of my eye. "You get that."

"I do." Lucas pulled away from Reed, excitedly talking with Macy about something. Reed took this opportunity to shift closer to me, casually draping his arm across the back of my chair our connection points multiplying. "You know the DV program I've been telling you about?" I nodded. "Well, looks like we get to start coordinating and training volunteers next week."

"Reed! That's amazing news!" My smile stretched wide enough to make my cheeks ache. I laid my hand on his knee without thinking, squeezing gently.

I watched a flush rise up his cheeks. "Yeah. Gloria and her team are doing the hard work of training and teaching. I'm just logistics." But pride colored his voice. "Twenty-two volunteers so far. Three shelters participating."

"That's amazing." I turned to face him more fully. "Really. That's going to help so many women."

"That's the idea." He held my gaze. "Maybe when you're settled back at work, you could come observe? Give feedback?"

A small flutter of excitement bubbled up in my chest. "I'd like that. I'm sure I could break away and go observe where you guys are training."

"Might be easier than you think. Harbor House signed up too." My eyes popped just as the library's lights dimmed, saving us from talking more about it. Miss Rachel took the stage, and soon we were immersed in the controlled chaos of children's theater.

When Zoe strutted out in full butterfly glory, Reed shifted away and sat forward, engrossed. He filmed her entire performance, cheering when she nailed the migration explanation and laughing when she improvised a dance.

The whole room erupted when Zoe explained that monarch butterflies "have to pack their tiny suitcases" for Mexico each winter. Reed also captured the moment when she compared the migration to her own family's move from Florida, complete with a dramatic reenactment of herself slumped over, "Are we there yet?"

"Did you see the part where I flew?" Zoe asked after the show concluded, one wing askew but spirits high.

"Best monarch butterfly in the house. You're the greatest story teller I've ever seen," Reed assured her, helping reattach the rogue wing.

She threw her arms around him without hesitation, and I watched something soft and surprised cross his face—like he still couldn't believe his luck.

"Hot chocolates?" Felicity announced. "Celebration requires sugar."

As we filed out in our usual pack, I found myself walking closer to Reed than necessary. When Zoe grabbed his hand and mine, swinging between us, I didn't tense up or make excuses.

"This is the best day," she announced. "I was a butterfly, and now hot chocolate, and everyone I love is here!"

Lucas took my free hand. "Mom's going back to work Monday," he informed Reed. "She's the boss again."

"She never *stopped* being the boss," Reed said, catching my eye over the kids' heads.

We all headed to the Grind coffee shop—a little spot in Southie that Caden's cousin Andi runs. When we walked in, Andi had already pushed a couple tables together for us, prepared for our arrival.

She and another barista appeared seconds later with a tray of hot chocolates and slices of cake, shooting Felicity a knowing grin. "Heard there was a star actress in the building," she said, setting a whipped-cream-topped cup in front of Zoe with extra flourish. "This one's got extra marshmallows for the best performance award."

Zoe beamed, and Andi winked at me before disappearing back behind the counter. I sat beside Reed instead of maintaining careful distance.

Felicity leaned over and swiped her fork through the corner of Caden's cake. "So, Monday. You feeling ready?" she asked me while Caden's mouth fell open in mock outrage. "Woman, that's theft!" he protested, pulling his plate closer. Felicity just shrugged and licked caramel from her fork, already eyeing his dessert for her next targeted attack. "Mine's chocolate. Yours has all that gooey caramel. A woman needs variety to survive, Caden."

Laughing at my brother-in-law's offended expression, I answered, "As ready as I'll ever be." I straightened in my seat, "I've hidden long enough. The women at the shelter need stability, and I need—" I gestured vaguely. "I just need to be me again."

"You never stopped being you," Reed said quietly. "But you needed a little time to heal first."

"Speaking of the shelter," I said, "Reed just told me his DV self-defense program is coming to Harbor House too."

Felicity's eyes sparkled. "Oh, you mean the new self-defense program that mysteriously got full funding and approval?"

"Yes—that one!" I turned to Reed, who suddenly found his mug fascinating, as a blush rose up the sides of his neck. "Though, why he didn't brag to me before that it would be at Harbor House too, I don't know."

"It's for multiple shelters. Harbor House is just one of them."

"Reed—"

"It's not about us," he said quickly. "Or not just about us. It's about—" He gestured helplessly. "It's about women like you. Strong women who've survived shit they shouldn't have had to. They deserve to feel powerful. To know they have options. And I wanted it to be a surprise for you when you came back." His voice dropped lower, eyes meeting mine with that earnest intensity that made my chest tighten. "I didn't want you thinking this was just some calculated move to win you over. It's bigger than that."

"See?" Zoe announced to the table. "I told you Reed was smart."

Everyone laughed, breaking the intensity of the moment. But under the table, I let my hand find his, our fingers tangling briefly—a squeeze of gratitude, of recognition, of something more I wasn't quite ready to name.

"Dance party when we get home?" Zoe asked around a mouthful of cake.

"After all this sugar?" I groaned.

"Reed has to come," Lucas declared, surprising everyone. "He doesn't know about dance parties."

"I don't think—" Reed started.

"You have to," Lucas insisted. "It's how we shake off the heavy days, and crazy ones, and fun ones, and cool ones—I guess all the ones! And Mom going back to work is kind of heavy and happy at the same time, so we need an extra big dance party."

I looked at Reed, no longer trying to hide my smile. "You heard the man. Dance party attendance is mandatory."

"Then I guess I better learn some moves."

"I'll teach you," Zoe promised excitedly. "I've been working on a butterfly dance! We could do it together!"

As we finished off our desserts, I caught Felicity watching me with that big sister look—proud and protective all at once. She mouthed "good" when Reed wasn't looking.

She was right. This was good. I was ready—for work, for normal, for whatever came next. For the first time since Bryce, I felt like myself again. He'd left scars, yes—but I was stronger now in every place he'd tried to break me. That was my doing, not his. My family was my foundation, my home, my everything. But maybe, just maybe, Reed had done enough to show he deserved to be part of that foundation.

Chapter 51:

Full Circle

MALIYAH

"Lucas, where's your Chromebook?" I called out, shoving a granola bar into Zoe's lunchbox while simultaneously trying to find my work ID badge. First Monday back, and if I couldn't get us in gear, we'd definitely be late.

"I don't know!" came the muffled response from his room.

"Check your backpack!"

"I did!"

"Check again!"

Zoe appeared in the bathroom doorway, a white foam ring around her lips, toothbrush still clutched in her tiny fist. For once, I hadn't needed to stand over her counting to sixty or desperately promising her something as a form of bribery.

"Mama," she said, words muffled around the mint paste, "can I wear my butterfly wings to school?" Behind her, the purple and pink glitter-covered wings leaned against the bathtub where she'd propped them.

"No, baby. Regular clothes today." I glanced at the clock. 7:32. Shit. "Go get dressed, please. The pink outfit is on your bed."

The telltale sound of spitting and rinsing made its way to my ears. "I don't want pink!"

"Please, sweetie! Just this once, can we do the pink without making it a thing?"

The knock at the door made me freeze, coffee mug halfway to my lips. Who the hell—

I peeked through the peephole and immediately yanked it open, finding Reed in all his glory—standing there in his work clothes, badge already clipped to his belt, holding a carrier with coffees and a white paper bag that smelled like heaven.

"Thought you might need backup to start out your day," he said, that half-smile making my stomach flutter.

"Reed Morrison, I could kiss you right now."

"Please do."

I laughed, but his eyes darkened, pupils dilating just enough that my breath caught. The corners of his mouth twitched upward in that way they did when he was holding something back. My shoulders relaxed at the sight of him—I hadn't realized how tense they'd been since he'd left the other night after our living room dance party, leaving the lightest touch of his lips on my cheek. Text messages throughout the day yesterday couldn't replace the warmth of his physical presence.

Puffing out a breath of air, I opened the door all the way to let him in. "Kids are in meltdown mode. I can't find my badge ID for work. Lucas lost his Chromebook. Zoe suddenly doesn't want to wear pink."

"Divide and conquer?" He stepped inside, setting everything on the counter. "Coffee's yours—extra shot, shot of vanilla. Breakfast sandwiches for everyone."

"When did you—"

"Lucas, buddy! Let me help." Reed called out, already making his way toward Lucas's room. "Were you reading before sleep last night? Did you check under your bed?"

A pause, then: "Found it!"

Reed caught my eye over his shoulder with a knowing smile, then raised his voice to reach my daughter in the bathroom. "Zoe, if you get dressed in two minutes, I'll put your hair in a new braid I learned on Youtube."

The sound of small feet thundering toward her room was immediate.

"How did you do that?" I asked, already feeling calmer.

He handed me the coffee. "I'm absolutely not above bribery."

I took a sip and nearly moaned. Perfect. Exactly what I needed.

"I think your badge is hanging up on the hook behind your coat." he added. "I remember seeing it the other night when I grabbed my coat to head back to my apartment."

"Seriously, who are you?"

"Guy who pays attention." He tapped his temple, "Also—I'm psychic." He was already unwrapping breakfast sandwiches, cutting Zoe's into smaller pieces. "You nervous about today?"

"Terrified." I grabbed my badge, clipping it on. "Excited. Ready. The usual emotional cocktail."

"You're going to be great." He said it simply, like it was fact. "You've been missed. I'm positive."

"Mom, I can't find my other shoe!" Lucas appeared, hopping on one foot.

"Kitchen table," Reed and I said in unison, then looked at each other, surprised.

Lucas grabbed his shoe from under the table. "Are you coming to school drop-off too, Reed?"

"Just helping your mom get you guys ready." Reed handed him a wrapped sandwich. "Eat in the car?"

"Okay." Lucas studied him for a moment. "You're good at mornings."

"Thanks, buddy."

Zoe emerged in purple leggings and a dinosaur shirt—not what I'd laid out. Not a stitch of pink either, but she was dressed nonetheless. "Braid time!"

Reed looked at me. "Okay if I...?"

I nodded, my mouth slightly open as Reed lifted Zoe onto a kitchen stool. He gathered her cloud of curls with practiced hands, sectioning them with the confidence of someone who'd done this before. My daughter's coils—so different from his own straight hair—yielded to his touch as he misted them with detangler and worked the comb through without a single "ouch" from Zoe. Within minutes, an intricate pattern emerged, her hair transforming into a neat, inverted French braid that usually took me twice as long to accomplish.

"Where'd you learn that?"

"I've been watching YouTube. And Gloria has three nieces, all with different hair textures—she gave me lessons."

"You learned to braid hair for us?"

He focused on securing the elastic. "Seemed useful."

My chest went tight. *Well, damn.*

"Done!" Zoe admired herself in the microwave reflection. "Pretty!"

"Very pretty. Now grab your sandwich. Time to go."

The next few minutes were controlled chaos—backpacks, lunchboxes, jackets, shoes. Reed moved through it all like he'd been doing this dance for years, knowing exactly where to help without taking over. At the car, he loaded backpacks while I buckled Zoe in. Lucas climbed into his side, already taking bites of his sandwich.

"Thank you," I said, turning to face Reed in the parking lot. "For all of this."

"Anytime." He reached out, straightening my badge. "You've got this, Maliyah."

Something in his voice, in the way he looked at me—pride and affection and certainty—made me bold.

I grabbed his jacket lapels and pulled him down, pressing my lips to his in a kiss that screamed intent and promise. And yes.

He made a surprised sound against my lips, then his hands found my waist, fingers pressing into the fabric of my blazer. His breath caught, released in a rush as he pulled me closer, the space between us vanishing. The kiss deepened, his mouth moving from hesitant to hungry in the span of a heartbeat, like a dam giving way against hurricane force winds.

"Mom!" Lucas called. "We're gonna be late!"

I pulled back, breathless. Reed's eyes were dark, a little stunned.

Through the car window, I caught Lucas's wide-eyed expression and Zoe's delighted clapping.

"Have a good day at work," I said, trying for casual and failing completely.

"Yeah. You too." His voice was rough. "I'll—uh—yeah."

I laughed, backing toward the driver's door. "Smooth talker."

"Yeah. Brain—broke."

"Good."

Harbor House felt exactly the same and completely different. The smell of coffee and industrial cleaning supplies, the sound of phones ringing and children playing in the distance—all familiar. But I was different. Walking through the door, I felt like I was stepping into a skin that was mine but with a new fit.

Sharon waved from the reception desk, Keisha called out "Welcome back, boss!" from the counseling offices, and Martin gave me a mock salute as he headed to the security station. Normal morning chaos, except for how their smiles lingered longer, their greetings carried extra warmth. It was amazing to be back. I glanced at the stack of files waiting on my desk, my outlook calendar already bleeding red with back-to-back meetings. The honeymoon period would obviously be brief.

The week flew by, days beginning and ending with Reed and my kids. By Thursday evening, I'd settled into the rhythm of work again, but my nerves were still at attention. Reed and I had seen each other every night that week—drop-offs, quick dinners, bedtime routines—but we'd yet to have any time alone to talk about the kiss.

I stood in my kitchen. The smell of garlic and basil permeated every corner of the apartment. Felicity had brought salad and dessert, the kids were setting the table with only minimal bickering, and Reed was due any minute.

"Use the good plates," I told Lucas. "The ones from the upper cabinet."

"Why?" He was already climbing onto the counter to reach them.

"Because we're having a nice dinner."

"Is it a special occasion?" Zoe asked, carefully folding napkins the way Felicity had taught her.

"No, but it feels like a good day, which calls for the good stuff," I said, my heart racing for some reason.

The knock came right at six. Reed stood on my doorstep holding flowers—not boring roses, but bright gerbera daisies in bright blues and purples.

"You didn't have to—"

"I wanted to." He stepped inside, daisies extended in one hand—his free arm wrapping around my waist. His lips brushed my cheek, then paused there, his stubble grazing my skin as he inhaled against the curve where my neck met my shoulder. His eyes closed briefly before he pulled back. "Something with garlic and—mmmm, you made Italian?"

Dinner was loud and perfect. Zoe regaled everyone with a dramatic retelling of the cafeteria's "farting incident," before I shut her down on her dinner conversation etiquette. Lucas explained a story he was writing for his class project, with Reed asking all the right questions. Macy jumped in to talk about an upcoming class trip to the Children's Museum.

Felicity kept shooting me knowing looks over her seltzer water—third dinner in a row she'd skipped wine—an unusual choice for my sister who normally loved her chardonnay.

"Can we watch a movie?" Zoe asked as we cleared plates.

"Not tonight," I said. "School tomorrow and baths are on tonight's agenda of fun."

"I'll handle dishes," Reed offered, already stacking plates while Zoe deployed her puppy dog eyes.

Felicity stepped in, "Nice try, kiddo. I'm with mom on bath time!" She turned my way, already herding the kids toward the bathroom as she winked at me. "I'll help with baths. You two finish cleaning up...together. Alone"

So subtle, my sister. We worked in comfortable silence, me washing while Reed dried. The domesticity of it made my chest ache in the best way.

"I've been thinking," he said, putting away the last plate.

"Dangerous."

He laughed, then grew serious. "I want to take you out. On a real date. Just us."

"Oh—"

"But I'm going to wait." He turned to face me fully. "Until you ask me."

"What?"

He stepped closer, not touching but close enough that I could smell his soap. "You need to be ready. Really ready. Because Maliyah..." His voice dropped. "Once you ask me out, when we do this, I need you to know—we're talking the long haul here. This isn't casual for me. I intend for it to be the last first date for either of us."

My breath caught. "That's a lot of pressure for a first date."

"No pressure. That's why I'm waiting for you to ask." He reached out, tucked a strand of hair behind my ear. "I'll wait as long as you need."

"What if I never ask?"

"Then I'll keep showing up for family dinners and birthday parties and random Tuesdays until you realize I'm not going anywhere." His hand ran through my hair at the temple, pulling my face close with the lightest of pressure. His smile was soft but certain; his voice was quiet and deep. "I'm patient. And you're worth waiting for."

Before I could respond, Zoe ran in wearing dinosaur pajamas, hair wet from her bath. "Reed! Story time!"

He looked at me, question in his eyes. I nodded.

"How about we do one story," he said. "Then bed." If routine was anything to go by, it wouldn't be just one story.

As he followed Zoe to the living room, Felicity appeared beside me. "That man is gone for you."

"I know."

"And you?"

I watched Reed settle on the couch, Zoe immediately climbing into his lap with her favorite book. "Yeah. Hey! Let's talk more about you. What's going on?"

"I don't know what you mean! Nothing is going on."

"Nope. Don't give me that. You have news and I want to hear it. I can see it in you. I'm picking up signs, woman!"

"I don't know what you mean," she said, backing toward the door with a grin that said otherwise. "And if I did have news—which I'm not saying I do—I'd probably wait a couple weeks before making it a thing. Night, sis!"

"This isn't over, woman!"

"Got to get home to Caden! Macy, let's hit the road."

Within moments, both Macy and Felicity had rushed out the door, a cloud of dust in their wakes.

I laughed, already feeling a joy for my sister even if she didn't want to share. The shadows Bryce had cast over my life were receding now, giving way to unexpected moments of brightness I hadn't thought possible again. Every day I felt a little stronger, and with that strength came ideas I hadn't dared imagine before. Not just supporting survivors after the fact, but challenging the laws that failed us long before we ever reached the shelter doors.

By Saturday morning, I was excited to see how Reed's DV program was killing it. I pulled into the community center parking lot where they were holding their final day of volunteer training. He'd texted me the night before: Want you to see this. If you've got the time, swing by around 10 in the morning?

The gymnasium buzzed with controlled energy. Twenty-two volunteers in BPD T-shirts worked through defensive positions while Gloria and two other female officers demonstrated techniques. Reed stood off to the side with his laptop and a clipboard, coordinating like a conductor with an orchestra.

I slipped in quietly, but he spotted me immediately. The smile that lit up his face made my stomach flip.

"Don't stop for me," I called when several volunteers looked over.

Gloria winked and continued her demonstration. "Remember, you're not just teaching these women how to win in an unfair fight. You're trying to help them create space to escape in the event winning isn't an option."

I watched Reed work—directing a volunteer who was setting up refreshments, answering questions from two officers, taking photos for documentation. He was in his element, competent and sure, but what struck me most was his investment. This wasn't just a project. His face said it all—focus, determination, and fun. He was having fun with this.

"Maliyah!" One of the volunteers, who I recognized as a counselor from another local shelter, jogged over during a water break. "This is incredible. Looks like the program will start at Harbor House next week?"

"Tuesday," Reed said, joining us. "Eighteen women already signed up."

"With childcare provided," the counselor added. "That's huge. Most of our clients can't leave their kids."

They chatted logistics while I watched Reed—the animation in his face, the pride in his voice. He'd built something that would help women for years to come.

When training wrapped up, volunteers chattering excitedly as they packed up, I waited while Reed finished his notes.

"So?" he asked. "What do you think?"

"I think you're amazing." The words came out more honest than I'd intended.

Pink touched his cheeks. "The team did all the real work."

"Don't do that. Don't minimize what you've built here." I stepped closer. "You saw a need, you filled it, and you did an incredible job. You're going to change lives."

"That's the plan." He closed his laptop. "You have some time to hang out? Or do you have to run already?"

This was it. The moment. My heart hammered against my ribs.

"Actually—" I took a breath. "What are you doing next Friday night?"

His whole body stilled. "Nothing specific."

"Felicity can watch the kids." The words tumbled out faster. "There's this Italian place in the North End I've been wanting to try. If you're interested. In going. With me. On a date."

The smile that spread across his face was worth every butterfly in my stomach. "Maliyah Davenport, are you asking me out?"

The word "yes" caught in my throat before I pushed it out, lifting my chin with a confidence I wasn't entirely sure I felt. My heart hammered against my ribs as I met his gaze directly. "I'm asking you out," I said, my voice steadier than my pulse. "On a real date. Just us. No kids, no work stuff, no distractions—just two adults figuring out what this could be."

He set his laptop on the bleachers, then stepped into my space, hands framing my face. "I would love to go on a date with you."

"Even with everything that comes with me? All the baggage, the complications, the kids, the history?"

"Especially with all that," he said, thumb stroking my cheek. "I want all of it. All of you."

"Okay. Friday then."

"Friday." He leaned down, pressed his forehead to mine. "Thank you for asking."

"Thank you for waiting."

We stood there in the empty gymnasium, surrounded by the echoes of strength, laughter, and appreciation, and I felt something click into place. Not perfect, not without complications, but right. This was real. I was ready.

Chapter 52:

When You Can Hear Me

REED

It had been months of dating Maliyah Davenport, and I still couldn't believe my luck.

Countless stolen moments between her demanding schedule at Harbor House and my rotating shifts. Fancy Saturday night dinners with cloth napkins and candles. Family brunches where Lucas and Zoe tagged along, Lucas insisting last weekend that my homemade pancakes beat the Uncle Caden's by a mile—not sure if it was true, but the pride in his eyes made me stand taller. Wednesday nights meant movies on her couch, Zoe inevitably conking out against my shoulder, a small puddle of drool darkening my shirt by the halfway mark.

I'd finally had the chance to relearn what it felt like to have the weight of Maliyah's hand in mine, to experience the sound of her laugh uninhibited, and to be on the receiving end of soft looks and sweet kisses. And in that time, I found myself falling deeper and deeper—knowing without an ounce of doubt that I was hopelessly in love with her.

Tonight's date—our twentieth? Thirtieth? I'd lost count, but it had been perfect. A hole-in-the-wall Vietnamese place in Dorchester that she'd heard about from one of the women at the shelter. We'd talked about everything and nothing—her plans to expand Harbor House's programming and my latest testimony in a case involving armed robbery. We talked about the kids, their highs and lows, plans for the coming summer, all the things—and then some.

"Thank you for tonight," she'd said when I walked her to her door, keys already in hand. "I had fun—as usual."

"Thank you for finding the place, and for getting Macy to babysit so I could take you out."

She'd kissed me then, soft and slow, her body pressing against mine in the hallway, until we were both breathless.

"Come inside?" The question was quiet, uncertain. "Kids will be passed out and I'm not ready for you to leave."

My heart had stuttered. "Why don't I run Macy home? You pick out a movie and we can plan to chill?"

"That's perfect." Her fingers had tightened on my jacket.

After dropping a very sleepy Macy back at home and giving her a little extra cash for staying later than we planned. I drove back to Maliyah's faster than I should have, barely making a yellow light and taking the corner onto her street sharp enough that my tires protested.

When I opened the door, I found she'd decked out the living room—popcorn, a couple of beers, pillows and blankets. My gut clenched—nerves and excitement mingling.

She'd picked out a movie. I had no idea what one, though, since I was more focused on her. Fuck, she was beautiful. And amazing. And so fucking out of my league. But she was mine. My woman. My heart. My life.

Sitting on the couch, I pulled her against me, her back to my chest, my arms wrapped around her waist. The opening credits rolled, something with explosions and dramatic music that neither of us was watching. Her head rested in the crook of my shoulder, her coconut-scented hair tickling my chin.

"Comfortable?" I asked, pressing a kiss to her temple.

"Mmm." She tilted her head back to look at me, a soft smile playing on her lips. "Very."

We stayed like that, pretending to watch whatever was on screen while my thumb traced lazy circles on her hip. Her chest rose and fell steadily, and I sensed her drifting off.

The words sat heavy in my chest, pressing against my ribs with every breath. I wasn't sure if it had been long enough to say them. Too soon. Probably. Too much pressure for her. I didn't want her to say them just because I said them. The last thing she needed was me dumping my feelings on her before she was ready.

But God, I loved her. Loved the way she commanded respect at work while still making time to be an amazing mom. Loved how she'd stopped touching her scars, like she was finally believing they didn't define her. Loved watching her light up when she talked about work and life and us.

I loved her strength and her softness and the way she'd chosen to trust me with both. I loved how smart she was—smarter than me—and how she was always open to new experiences. I loved that she included me in things with her and the kids, and that we'd seamlessly blended our lives and loved ones. I loved every single fucking thing about her.

I pressed another kiss to her hair, taking my sleeping beauty in and holding her close.

"I love you," I whispered into the darkness, my voice barely audible even to my own ears. "I wish I could tell you that when you were awake to hear it. When you could know how much you mean to me." My thumb continued its path along her hip. "But I'm terrified of putting more pressure on you. Of making you feel like you have to say it back before you're ready."

Her breathing pattern didn't change. Still that slow, steady rhythm of sleep.

"You've been through so much," I continued, the words flowing easier now that I knew she couldn't hear. "And you're doing so well—healing, moving forward, being incredible. I don't want to mess that up by dumping all this on you too soon." I swallowed hard, whispering even more quietly. "But I need you to know, even if you can't hear me right now, that you're my everything. You are my forever kind of love."

"Reed."

I froze. My heart slammed against my ribs, heat flooding my face. Her voice was quiet, sleep-rough, but definitely awake.

"Maliyah—I thought you were—"

She shifted, turning in my arms to face me. Her eyes were clear, focused, no trace of sleep in them. "How long have you been awake?"

"The whole time." A small smile played at her lips. "I was comfortable. Didn't want to move. And then you started talking and I really didn't want to interrupt."

Heat flooded my face. "So you heard—"

"All of it." She sat up slightly, her hand coming up to cup my cheek, thumb stroking along my jaw. "Every word."

"Maliyah, I didn't mean to—I shouldn't have—"

"I love you too."

The words hung in the air between us, simple and devastating and perfect.

"What?"

"I love you." She said it again, stronger this time, her eyes never leaving mine. "I love how you learned all the little things about my kids, that you're always there for them—without exception. I love how you show up for family dinners and help with morning chaos and never complain about the mess or the noise."

Her voice dropped lower. "I love how patient you've been with me. How you waited for me to be ready. How you've proven over and over that you're not going anywhere." She leaned closer, her forehead nearly touching mine. "I love you, Reed Morrison. And I'm not afraid to say it when you can hear me."

I couldn't breathe. Couldn't think. Could only stare at this incredible woman who'd just given me everything.

"Say something," she whispered, a hint of nervousness creeping into her voice.

Instead of words, I closed the distance between us, my hands framing her face as I kissed her with everything I had. She made a small sound of surprise that turned into a sigh, her arms wrapping around my neck as she kissed me back.

"I love you," I said against her lips. "I love you so much."

She kissed me again, deeper this time, her fingers tangling in my hair. We stayed like that for long minutes, trading kisses and whispered declarations, until she finally settled back against my chest with a contented sigh.

"Stay," she murmured, already drifting toward real sleep this time. "Don't wake me up early."

"I'll stay as long as you want me to." I pulled the blanket over both of us, adjusting so we were more comfortable on the couch.

"Forever then." Her words were barely a whisper as sleep began to claim her.

"Forever works for me." I kissed the top of her head, feeling her breathing even out.

I held her close, listening to the rhythm of her heartbeat against mine, and felt something settle deep in my chest. This was it. This was everything.

Down the hall, I could hear Lucas's soft snoring and the occasional rustle of Zoe turning over in her bed, and moments when she sang to herself in her dream-filled sleep. This whole family, this whole beautiful, messy, perfect life—it was mine now. Ours. And I was never letting go.

My eyes grew heavy as the movie continued playing, forgotten. Maliyah was warm and solid in my arms, her trust a gift I'd spend the rest of my life earning.

"I love you," I whispered one more time before sleep pulled me under.

This time, I knew she'd heard me.

Epilogue:

Gathering The Fragments

MALIYAH

The cool wind off Boston Harbor whipped my hair across my face as we made our way around Pleasure Bay. Lucas ran ahead, stopping every few feet to examine something—a shell, a rock, a piece of something questionable that I made him toss back.

"Mom, look!" He pointed at a far-away sailboat cutting through the choppy water. "Think I could learn to sail?"

"Maybe," I called back, tucking my hair behind my ears for the hundredth time. "Ask Reed because I'm much happier on solid ground."

Reed walked beside me, hands in his jacket pockets, looking relaxed despite the wind. Seven months of this—of us—and I still found myself stealing glances at him, still felt that flutter when he smiled at me.

In the months since he'd whispered "I love you" that night, we'd been building something real and lasting. Together. He had proven over and over that he wasn't going anywhere.

"Mama, I'm cold!" Zoe announced, materializing at my side and grabbing my hand.

"We're almost there, honey." I promised. The walk around Pleasure Bay brought us full circle—back to our starting point.

Ahead of us, on the beach, Felicity sat on a blanket with Caden. While she'd insisted on coming, she'd wanted to stay put, claiming she needed to rest.

Fair enough—I expected her to be exhausted by now. Macy was lying out alongside them on her own blanket—at thirteen, she was starting to assert a bit of independence.

"Reed, can we get ice cream after?" Zoe tugged on his jacket.

"You just said you were cold, Zo! You sure you want ice cream?"

"Ice cream won't make me any colder—it will just make it even!"

He laughed, ruffling her hair. "Well, that makes perfect sense. Guess I can't argue with your logic."

The water stretched out before us, gray-blue under gathering clouds. Something about this place—the permanence of it. The way it had weathered storms and time. It felt right for today, though I couldn't say why.

"Lucas, stay in sight!" I called as he scrambled up a rocky outcropping.

"Okay, Mom!"

Reed's hand found mine, warm from his coat pockets. I squeezed back, leaning into him slightly as we walked.

Harbor House was thriving. We'd expanded our programming, added two new counselors, and the DV self-defense classes Reed had started were now running at five different shelters across the city on a continual basis. Last month, one of our residents had used what she'd learned to escape a dangerous situation. She'd come back to thank Reed personally, and I'd watched him fight tears as she'd hugged him.

Reed kissed my temple as Zoe tugged at his other hand. "You ready for next week?" he asked.

"The hearing?" I breathed out a laugh. "Not even a little."
But I was. We both were.

We were meeting with legislators to share our experience—not just mine, but the systemic failures Reed had seen for years. It felt strange, stepping into that kind of spotlight. But if telling our story meant one woman got help faster, or one violent man lost his loophole—then it was worth it.

And Reed, as always, would be right beside me.

As we came around the bend, the wind whipped my hair into a frenzy. As we approached where Felicity and her family were waiting on the beach, I began to pull my hair into a ponytail, trying to get it off my face. I started talking about my ideas for the shelter's program expansion. "I was thinking about if I should do a run through in front of a few people first, or not. What do you think?" I finished putting my hair up and glanced over at Reed, expecting a response.

He wasn't there. I turned, words dying on my lips. Reed was on one knee behind me on the path, a small box in his hands. Lucas and Zoe had stopped running ahead and were standing beside him, wide-eyed. My heart stopped.

"Reed—"

"Maliyah Davenport," he said, his voice carrying over the wind. "You are the strongest, most incredible woman I've ever known. You've shown me what real courage looks like. What it means to heal and grow and choose love even when it's scary." His eyes were bright, focused entirely on my face. "I want to spend the rest of my life proving I'm worthy of the trust you've given me. I want to be here for every high and low, every victory and challenge. I want to be your partner, your best friend, your forever."

He opened the first box, revealing a ring that caught the light—simple, elegant, perfect.

"Will you marry me?"

I couldn't breathe. Couldn't speak. Could only stare at this man kneeling before me, offering everything.

"Yes," I finally managed, the word coming out rough. "Yes, of course yes."

He stood, sliding the ring onto my finger with shaking hands, then pulled me into a kiss that tasted like salt air and promises and home.

"Hey!" Zoe's voice broke through. "Us too!"

Reed pulled back, laughing and crying at the same time as Zoe tried to smoosh in between us to get in on the hug. "I actually have something for you both." He turned to Lucas first, getting down on his haunches. He pulled out two boxes from his jacket pocket.

"Lucas, I know things haven't always been perfect. But I hope in time you'll come to see me as someone important in your life. I hope you'll let me teach you things and support you and be there when you need me." He pulled out a wrist watch. "Remember when I taught you to tell time on a real clock?"

Lucas nodded, eyes wide.

"I've been saving this for the right moment. This watch is special." He flipped it over, revealing the polished silver back where an inscription caught the sunlight. Lucas leaned in, his dark eyes widening as he traced his finger over the engraved words I couldn't quite make out from where I stood. His bottom lip trembled for just a moment before he launched himself forward, throwing his skinny arms around Reed's neck with such force that Reed had to steady himself with one hand against the sandy path.

Lucas pulled back, his eyes glistening with unshed tears. He cradled the watch in his palms like it was made of spun glass, turning it over to read the inscription again. The silver gleamed against his brown skin as he traced the second hand's journey around the face with his index finger. "Can you put it on me?" he asked, voice barely above a whisper. Reed nodded, taking the watch with steady hands and fastening the leather band around Lucas's slender wrist, adjusting it carefully until it sat just right.

Lucas looked at Reed, his small fingers still tracing the watch face. He shifted his weight from one sneaker to the other, the worn rubber soles grinding against the sandy path. "Since you and mom are getting married," he started, voice cracking slightly, "would it be okay if I called you Rad?" His question hung in the salt-tinged air between them, fragile as sea foam. Lucas's shoulders hunched forward as he dropped his gaze to his shoes, the frayed laces trailing in the sand. "Is that dumb?" he added in a whisper so faint it nearly dissolved in the wind coming off the harbor.

"Why Rad, kid?"

Lucas scuffed his sneaker against the sand, eyes darting between the watch and Reed's face. "I don't know if I'm ready to call you dad yet," he said, voice cracking slightly as his fingers twisted the leather watchband. "But I was thinking... Reed plus Dad equals Rad." A tentative smile flickered across his face, hopeful and vulnerable. "You know?"

Reed's face crumpled. "I would be honored."

They hugged, hard and tight, and I had to press my hand to my mouth to keep from sobbing.

Reed turned to Zoe, who was practically vibrating with anticipation. "And you, my little butterfly."

He opened the last box, revealing a delicate charm bracelet with three charms attached to it. "This bracelet has three charms to start. A butterfly, because you taught me that beautiful things can fly. This little police shield has my badge number engraved in tiny little numbers, it's here so you'll always know I'm protecting you. And the last charm has birthstones—one for you, one for Lucas, one for your mom, and one for me. Because we're a family now."

Zoe's eyes were huge. "Really?"

"Really. And I promise, for every important moment in your life, we'll add a new charm—all of them. Because I'm going to be there for all of it, if you'll have me."

She launched herself at him, nearly knocking him over, and Lucas joined in, and then I was there too, all of us wrapped together on the windy trail while the harbor waves crashed below.

"We should probably head back," I said eventually, wiping my eyes. "I'm sure Felicity is exhausted and ready to head home."

We made our way over to their blankets. Lucas was examining his watch while Zoe was holding her bracelet up to catch the light. As we walked, Reed's arm was around my shoulders, and I kept staring down at my ring as it glinted in the sun that had finally broken through the clouds.

As we approached, I could see Felicity standing now, Caden beside her, both looking toward us with odd expressions.

"Felicity!" I called, waving my left hand. "Look! We're engaged!"

She smiled, but there was something strained about it. "That's wonderful! Really, I'm so happy for you."

"Are you okay?" I asked as we got closer. "You look—"

"My water broke." She said it calmly, like she was commenting on the weather. "About five minutes ago. We should probably get to the hospital."

The world tilted. "Your water—oh my God, why didn't you come get me?!"

"You were having a moment." She winced slightly. "I wasn't going to interrupt Reed proposing. Besides, contractions are still pretty far apart."

"How far apart?"

"About eight minutes." Another contraction hit, and Felicity gripped Caden's arm. "Okay, maybe seven. We really should go."

"Right. Hospital. Now." I looked at Reed, who was already pulling out his phone.

"I'll drive you," he said. "My car's closest."

We rushed to the parking lot in a chaotic blur—Lucas and Zoe asking a hundred questions, Felicity breathing through contractions, Caden gathering their things, Macy hovering anxiously nearby.

As we loaded everyone into vehicles, Felicity caught my hand. "I'm really happy for you," she said quietly. "You deserve all the happiness in the world."

"You better have that baby today! I want to share this day with my nephew for all time," I managed, and she laughed through a contraction.

"I'll make sure he knows to come quickly—after we get to the hospital first though."

Reed appeared at my elbow. "Ready?"

For a split second, I thought back to the morning Felicity told me she was pregnant...not only pregnant, but with a boy! Her hands had shaken, both of us laughing and crying as our worlds tilted and filled with light. That spark of hope she'd given me then felt a lot like this moment now.

I looked at Reed—my fiancé! A fiancé who was now calmly organizing a rush to the hospital for my sister, who'd somehow become the center of our chaotic, beautiful life.

"Ready," I said, and meant it.

For whatever came next, we were ready. Together.

If you, or someone you know...

A Note from me to you

Thank you for reading Shadowed Scars.

I don't take lightly that you chose to spend your time with Maliyah and Reed—or that you trusted me to take you through some dark places to get to the light.

This story asked a lot of you. To be honest, it asked a lot of me in the writing. There were moments that may have been difficult to read, scenes that might have hit closer to home than you expected. I can't tell you how many nights I wrote with tears running down my face. Tears of pain, suffering, joy, and elation—depended on the night and the chapter!

If any part of this book stirred something painful in you—whether it brought up your own memories, reminded you of someone you love, or simply left you feeling heavy—I want you to know: whatever your response, it is valid. It's not being dramatic. Not "too sensitive." It's human... because you're human.

So I'm asking, gently: Are you okay? Not the polite "How's it going," we offer in passing with a coworker or a neighbor. I mean really. If this story surfaced something you've been carrying, I hope and pray you have it in you to be as brave as Maliyah and reach out—to a friend, a counselor, a hotline, anyone who can hold space for you.

The idea behind Maliyah grew out of a woman I knew once, many years ago—almost 20 years ago now. She did not have the happy ending that Maliyah did, and writing this was the answer to the dream I had for her back then, even though it wasn't fulfilled. We all have a story, and we all have someone we know who has a story. If only every story could end with the joy Maliyah's did.

Because here's what I believe with my whole heart: every person deserves safety. They deserve someone who fights for them when it's hard. They deserve a love that doesn't leave bruises—on their body or their spirit. They deserve grace and joy and everything in between.

If you recognized yourself anywhere in these pages, please know that the resources listed after this note are real, free, and confidential. They exist because people like Maliyah exist in real life—professionals who've dedicated their lives to helping others find their way back to themselves.

This story is fiction, but the experiences of survivors are not. Every day, people find the courage to reach out, to leave, to heal, to love again. If that's a journey you're on, I'm rooting for you. And if you picked up this book simply wanting a love story with heart and heat and a hard-won happy ending? Thank you for that, too. Romance matters. Hope matters. Stories where broken people find their way back to each other—they matter.

With gratitude and love,

Mireille

<u>VIOLENCE & ABUSE PREVENTION RESOURCES</u>:

I tried to capture as many resources as I could, but admittedly I am not an expert—I likely left off many that could be included here. If you know of a resource that should be listed, I'd love to hear from you. And if even one person is able to make use of what's here, then everything—from the book to the research—will be well worth every moment and every tear.

If you or someone you love is experiencing domestic violence, intimate partner abuse, or coercive control, you are not alone. Support exists. There are people and organizations ready to help—confidentially, without judgment, and at any hour.

If you are in immediate danger, please call 911 (in the US).

<u>UNITED STATES RESOURCES</u>

National Domestic Violence Hotline (24/7) *Services are confidential and available in more than 200 languages.* Phone: 1-800-799-SAFE (7233) TTY: 1-800-787-3224 Text: Text "START" to 88788 Webchat: thehotline.org

Love Is Respect (Dating Abuse Support for Teens & Young Adults) Phone: 1-866-331-9474 Text: Text "LOVEIS" to 22522 Chat: loveisrespect.org

RAINN - National Sexual Assault Hotline Phone: 1-800-656-HOPE (4673) Chat: hotline.rainn.org

National Coalition Against Domestic Violence (NCADV) Resources, education, safety planning, and access to local shelters. ncadv.org

Safe Horizon Hotline: *The largest victim services agency in the United States.* 1-800-621-HOPE (4673) safehorizon.org

StrongHearts Native Helpline *Culturally grounded support for American Indian & Alaska Native communities.* Phone: 1-844-7NA-TIVE (762-8483) Chat: strongheartshelpline.org

BOSTON & MASSACHUSETTS RESOURCES

Passageway – Brigham and Women's Hospital Phone: (617) 732-8753 (Mon–Fri, 8:30am–5pm) After Hours: (617) 732-6660, beeper #31808 Email: passageway@mgb.org https://www.brighamandwomens.org/passageway *Free and confidential advocacy, safety planning, counseling, support groups, and legal advocacy. A person does not need to leave a relationship to use their services.*

HAVEN at Mass General Hospital *(Helping Abuse and Violence End Now)* Phone: (617) 724-0054 https://www.massgeneral.org/social-service/haven *Comprehensive hospital-based support services for survivors of intimate partner abuse, including advocacy, safety planning, and community resources.*

Domestic Violence SafeLink (Massachusetts 24-Hour Hotline) Phone: 1-877-785-2020 *Statewide hotline for immediate support and shelter referrals.*

Jane Doe Inc. – The Massachusetts Coalition Against Sexual Assault and Domestic Violence https://www.janedoe.org

Safety planning—whether you're staying, preparing to leave, or have already left—can significantly reduce risk. *Personalized digital safety planning and tips for protecting your devices, location privacy, and communication.* thehotline.org/plan-for-safety

If you believe your device is being monitored, try using a safe computer at a library or trusted friend's home.

Support for LGBTQ+ Survivors

The Network/La Red *Survivor-led organization providing support for LGBTQ+ individuals experiencing partner abuse.* Hotline: 617-742-4911 tnlr.org

The Trevor Project (Youth & Young Adult Crisis Support) Phone: 1-866-488-7386 thetrevorproject.org

LGBTQ National Hotline Phone: 1-888-843-4564 glbthotline.org

Support for Children & Adolescents

Childhelp National Child Abuse Hotline Phone: 1-800-4-A-CHILD (1-800-422-4453) Text & Chat: childhelphotline.org

Teen Line Text "TEEN" to 839863 teenlineonline.org

Support for Immigrant & Refugee Survivors

ASISTA (Legal Aid for Immigrant Survivors) asistahelp.org

National Immigrant Women's Advocacy Project niwaplibrary.wcl.a merican.edu

Digital Abuse & Stalking Support

Cyber Civil Rights Initiative (CCRI) *Support for tech-enabled abuse, harassment, or image-based abuse.* cybercivilrights.org

Stalking Prevention, Awareness, and Resource Center (SPARC) st alkingawareness.org

Legal Help & Shelter Resources

WomensLaw.org *State-by-state legal information on restraining orders and custody.* womenslaw.org

DomesticShelters.org *Searchable shelter and advocacy directory.* domes ticshelters.org

Legal Aid Finder (USA) lsc.gov/what-legal-aid/find-legal-aid

VictimConnect Resource Center Phone: 1-855-484-2846 victimconn ect.org

Mental Health Resources *Domestic violence often intersects with trauma, depression, and anxiety. If you're struggling, these resources can help.*

988 Suicide & Crisis Lifeline (US) Call or text 988 988lifeline.org

Crisis Text Line Text HOME to 741741 crisistextline.org

INTERNATIONAL RESOURCES

Canada Sheltersafe.ca: sheltersafe.ca (find shelters by province)

United Kingdom National Domestic Abuse Helpline (Refuge): 0808 2000 247 nationaldahelpline.org.uk

Australia 1800RESPECT: 1800 737 732 1800respect.org.au

New Zealand Shine Helpline: 0508 744 633

Women's Refuge: 0800 REFUGE (733 843)

UN Women - *Provides region-by-region hotline listings worldwide.* Global Resource List: unwomen.org

HotPeachPages https://www.hotpeachpages.net *Comprehensive international directory of domestic violence hotlines, shelters, and resources in 110+ languages, searchable by country.*

South Africa Gender-Based Violence Command Centre: 0800 428 428 (24 hours) National GBV Helpline: 0800 150 150 People Opposing Women Abuse (POWA): 011 642 4345 https://www.powa.co.za *Counseling, legal aid, and shelter referrals.*

Childline South Africa: 116 (toll-free, 24 hours) https://www.childline-sa.org.za

Kenya GBV Helpline: 1195 (24 hours, multilingual including Swahili, English, Kikuyu, Luhya, Kalenjin) *Operated by Healthcare Assistance Kenya in partnership with UN Women. Provides crisis support, referrals to shelters, medical care, and legal services.*

Coalition on Violence Against Women (COVAW) https://covaw.or.ke

Nigeria Child Helpline: 0800 800 0800, Women's Safehouse https://www.womensafehouse.org/

China All-China Women's Federation Hotline: 12338 Women and Children Psychological Counseling Hotline: 400-601-2338 *Support for survivors of domestic violence, available in Mandarin.*

India Women's Helpline: 181

Japan DV Consultation Navi: #8008 (connects to nearest support center) Domestic Violence Hotline Plus: 0120-279-889 (24 hours) Web chat available in English, Chinese, Korean, Tagalog, Thai, Vietnamese, Spanish, Portuguese https://soudanplus.jp

South Korea Women's Emergency Hotline: 1366 (24 hours) Sunflower Crisis Centers (nationwide)

Taiwan Domestic Violence Hotline: 113 (24 hours, multilingual including English, Vietnamese, Thai, Indonesian, Cambodian)

Philippines Emergency Hotline: 911 (now responds to GBV and VAW cases) Bantay Bata (Child Protection): 163

A FINAL NOTE

If you are reading this and recognizing signs of abuse in your own life, please know:

You are not alone. What happened to you is not your fault. Help is available, and your safety matters.

This story is fictional, but the experiences of survivors around the world are real.

Reaching out for support is a brave and powerful step toward reclaiming your life.

www.ingramcontent.com/pod-product-compliance
Lightning Source LLC
Chambersburg PA
CBHW050511110726
47899CB00005B/1410